A CHANCE
AT FOREVER

Books by Melissa Jagears

A Bride for Keeps
A Bride in Store
A Bride at Last

TEAVILLE MORAL SOCIETY

A Heart Most Certain
A Love So True
A Chance at Forever

Love by the Letter: An UNEXPECTED BRIDES *Novella*
from *With All My Heart Romance Collection*

Engaging the Competition: A TEAVILLE MORAL
SOCIETY *Novella* from *With This Ring? A Novella*
Collection of Proposals Gone Awry

Tied and True: A TEAVILLE MORAL SOCIETY *Novella* from
Hearts Entwined: A Historical Romance Novella Collection

A Chance at Forever

Melissa Jagears

BETHANYHOUSE
a division of Baker Publishing Group
Minneapolis, Minnesota

Published by Bethany House Publishers
11400 Hampshire Avenue South
Bloomington, Minnesota 55438
www.bethanyhouse.com

Bethany House Publishers is a division of
Baker Publishing Group, Grand Rapids, Michigan

Printed in the United States of America

Library of Congress Cataloging-in-Publication Data
Names: Jagears, Melissa, author.
Title: A chance at forever / Melissa Jagears.
Description: Minneapolis, Minnesota : Bethany House, a division of Baker
    Publishing Group, [2018] | Series: Teaville Moral Society
Identifiers: LCCN 2017038829 | ISBN 9780764217531 (trade paper) | ISBN
    9780764231414 (hardcover)
Subjects: | GSAFD: Love stories. | Christian fiction.
Classification: LCC PS3610.A368 C48 2018 | DDC 813/.6—dc23
LC record available at https://lccn.loc.gov/2017038829

Scripture quotations are from the King James Version of the Bible.

This is a work of fiction. Names, characters, incidents, and dialogues are products of the author's imagination and are not to be construed as real. Any resemblance to actual events or persons, living or dead, is entirely coincidental.

Cover design by Koechel Peterson & Associates / Minneapolis, Minnesota / Jon Godfredson
Cover mansion photo by Moments of Grace Photography

Author represented by Natasha Kern Literary Agency

18 19 20 21 22 23 24   7 6 5 4 3 2 1

To Chesley,
for wanting to be involved in my writing though
it steals time from you. Thank you for naming
my hero. I'll love you always and forever.

1

"I wish you luck, George."

"It's Aaron now. Don't forget." Aaron Firebrook tried not to let Mr. Gray's slip of the tongue make him even more nervous. Having his former teacher forget to call him by his new name was understandable, but oh how he wished no one would ever call him by his given name again.

If only every day he'd spent as George could be washed away and forgotten.

"Forgive me. It'll take me time to remember to call you that." Harrison Gray's footsteps echoed on the granite flooring of Aaron's old high school as they walked toward the conference room.

The cold rock walls surrounding them stole the warmth from the sunlight streaming through the narrow windows, and the thick scent of lemon cleaner overpowered the powdery smell of the chalk dust they disturbed as they walked through sunbeams.

This place hadn't changed at all in the past six years. Yet he'd changed so much, it was as if he were passing through this hallway for the first time.

Mr. Gray stopped in front of the conference room door and readjusted his glasses, his blue eyes small and squinty behind his lenses. "It'll also take me a while to get used to you sporting that big bushy beard."

Aaron forced himself not to reach up and tug on his whiskers. "I wanted my appearance to better reflect the new me."

Mr. Gray frowned as he took in the thick, dark beard obscuring Aaron's face. "It's certainly . . . different. Very different."

"Exactly." Aaron wiped his palms against his trousers. Hopefully shaking hands with the entire school board wouldn't prove too embarrassing. If only his hands weren't such big, sweaty meat cleavers. "I know I've already told you a hundred times, but thank you for recommending me for this position. I realize how much faith that required."

Mr. Gray clamped his hand onto Aaron's shoulder. "I saw your potential when I had you in class. I figure you can't have lost it."

"Thank you, sir." He'd forever be grateful for Mr. Gray, the only teacher who had seen past his anger when he was nothing but a fifteen-year-old bully and had focused on the hurting boy locked up inside instead.

Mr. Gray opened the door, and Aaron followed his former English teacher into a large room, where the air was thick with the smell of mildew and disuse.

"Good afternoon." Mr. Gray stopped a few feet inside and addressed the board members sitting at even intervals behind three long tables. "I'm pleased to introduce you to Aaron Firebrook, the man I'm recommending for the high school math position."

There was a chorus of welcomes, and Mr. Gray gave Aaron a light clap on his back before leaving.

Keeping his hands clenched tightly at his sides so he'd not tug on his collar, Aaron walked forward.

"Please be seated." The man in the middle of the tables pointed to the solitary chair in front of them. He was dark headed, in his forties, and didn't look familiar.

Good.

Aaron sat and took his time looking each board member in the eye. Thankfully, the tension in his body lessened with each man he didn't recognize and with each polite smile that didn't turn into a frown.

Maybe things would be all right.

Except the last member was not a man, but a woman. A blonde whose smile wasn't nearly as welcoming as the others, but then, his big size was often disquieting.

He gave her the best smile he could, considering how nervous he was. Pretty women were always a bit intimidating—especially when they held a man's future in their hands. He tore his gaze off her and faced the group.

The man in the middle consulted the paper in his hand. "Harrison says you attended school here but moved to California. What brought you back?"

Aaron quickly scanned the board members, trying once more to determine if he knew any of them. He forced himself not to pull at his tie. "Well, Mr. Gray was a good influence on me as a student. I figured if I were to teach anywhere, I would prefer to do so as his colleague. I'd love to have his advice during my first year so I might have the same impact on Teaville's children as he had on me."

He'd not mention he'd also come in hopes of righting as many of his wrongs as possible.

The men ducked their heads, consulting the copies of his application, but the woman did not. She sat still, staring directly at him, her eyebrows slightly scrunched.

He gave her a smile, but she didn't smile back.

Blond hair swept up simply, green eyes, curvy with plump cheeks. Early twenties?

He let loose a long, slow exhale and pulled his gaze away. If only he'd asked their names. But now was not the time to think through every child he'd ever known, hoping she wasn't as familiar as she seemed. If he had any hope of procuring this job, he needed to focus on giving good answers.

"So you have no teaching experience?" This from the balding man on the left. Much too old to have been in school with him.

"Correct. This would be my first year, but we all have to start somewhere."

"Why math?"

"I wasn't the best student, to be honest." In more ways than one. "But math was one of the few things I enjoyed. It had structure, and in a time of chaos in my life, I could count on it to function as expected." He'd needed what little stability he could find back then. "Though Mr. Gray was my favorite teacher, trying to interpret what some dead author wanted me to learn about life through the story of a man hunting a whale was nebulous in comparison to solving for *n*."

The man in the middle looked up from the papers in front of him. "So if you weren't the best student . . . ?"

"It's an advantage. I can understand those who struggle better than most. I think it must be hard for teachers who excelled in school to explain over and over what they found to be easy, but that certainly isn't true of me. I'm hoping my learning background makes me more patient, perhaps more understanding."

"It's not always understanding they need. Sometimes it's discipline." The white-haired gentleman who had to be in his eighties peered down his spectacles at him.

"Of course, sir." He'd not bother to explain how punishment for failing to comprehend his lessons would've made things far worse during that period of his life.

"And how exactly would you discipline them?" The woman's voice rang out with an undertone of suspicion. Had she realized he'd held his tongue to keep from elaborating on that last answer?

"I assume there's a policy I'd adhere to."

She only stared at him, her head cocked to the side.

The other board members started a list of rapid-fire questions he tried his best to answer as honestly and tactfully as possible, all the while feeling the woman's gaze boring into him. Since she wasn't asking questions, he forced himself not to look at her. It wouldn't matter if he figured out whether he knew her or not. If she knew him, he was as good as sunk. But if she didn't, this interview was his best chance to get the job he needed.

"I thank you for your time, Mr. Firebrook." The board president tapped his papers together, signaling the interview's end.

"The same to you." He rose, went to the right side table, and shook the first man's hand. Thankfully his hands weren't too sweaty. "I hope to work with you in the future."

The man nodded. "Dr. Freedman. Nice to meet you."

Each board member stood, gave him a quick handshake, and introduced himself. He worked his way to the woman at the other end, but when he got to her, she stayed seated, her chin tilted, her jaw tight.

Did she not think it appropriate for a man and woman to shake hands, despite her being on an all-male school board?

Or worse, had she realized who he was, though he still hadn't recognized her?

He held out his hand and she stared at it, her mouth scrunched to one side, but then she brought up her left hand to shake his right, giving him the most awkward handshake he'd ever received.

"Nice to meet you . . . ?"

"Miss McClain."

He blinked. That name . . . so familiar.

McClain . . . *Oh.*

"Mercy," he breathed, and his gut sank into the abyss.

She gave him a slight nod, and he looked down behind the table at the right hand she'd not used to shake his. Her sleeve ended a few inches past her elbow. No hand.

He'd need to start looking for a teaching position elsewhere— unless she chose to live up to the name her parents had given her.

"Mercy." He swallowed hard while keeping his gaze connected to hers. "Please."

She didn't say anything, so he backed away and excused himself from the room before he made a fool of himself.

11

Once in the hallway, he leaned against the wall, tilted his head back to look at the ceiling, and let out a noisy exhale. If Mercy told the others how he'd treated her years ago, he might as well wait for the meeting to adjourn. It wouldn't take more than thirty seconds of discussion before they decided against him.

2

Please?

Mercy watched George—now going by Aaron, apparently—leave the boardroom.

How did he have the gall to return to Teaville and seek to work with children? Did he think changing his name would fool the people he'd tormented? She looked back down at his signature.

Aaron Firebrook.

Upon seeing his application, she'd figured he was likely related to the worst bully she'd ever known, but to actually be him?

Ah, there. His signature started with a barely discernible *G* before the giant *A* that figured most prominently.

The man she'd known as a child as George had walked in with confidence, his wide shoulders and height filling the room as the legendary lumberjack Paul Bunyan might have.

But something hadn't felt right. With his beard and the way he spouted all the right answers, she'd not recognized him. But then one seemingly innocuous glance in her direction had thrown her back to her fifth-grade year. The last year she'd lived in Teaville.

The worst year of her life.

It hadn't mattered that he wasn't even in her class. He'd tormented her, calling her Stumpy every day without fail, making her his target in every game of tag, intimidating her friends into abandoning her, blaming her for things she'd never done, taking whatever he wanted from her lunch box.

Her fifth-grade year had been hard enough—she hadn't needed his escalating taunts to deal with as well.

And now he had the audacity to say *please* before he left the room? As if he wanted this job so desperately he'd beg?

How often had she begged him to leave her alone and he'd only laughed?

"So I'm not opposed." Mr. Hicks, the school board president, tapped his neat little stack of papers and leaned back in his chair. "He had plenty of good answers, and his size will surely command respect from the students."

"It's not as if we have more applicants," said Mr. Carter.

Mr. Lafferty, the oldest board member, squirmed in his seat, his leg likely making him uncomfortable. "We haven't had the position advertised for long. There could be more."

"Yes." She piped up. "Let's wait for more."

Mr. Hicks turned to her. "Was there something you didn't like about Mr. Firebrook?"

Please.

She closed her eyes against the image of George's—Aaron's— dark brown eyes practically dripping with desperation. Why would a man big enough to tackle and subdue any person he disliked beg her for mercy?

Mercy.

How her name plagued her sometimes. How could a woman named Mercy refuse to offer leniency without feeling as if she'd betrayed herself?

Please.

But giving Teaville's biggest bully power over innumerable children would not be merciful to them.

Discipline per the policy, he'd said.

Unlikely.

Please.

14

She scrunched her eyes tight, as if that would stop his plea from echoing in her brain.

Well, she could show him mercy by not outright exposing him, but she'd not let him have whatever he wanted. "As Mr. Lafferty said, we haven't had the advertisement up for long. There's bound to be more than one applicant, and though Mr. Firebrook has Mr. Gray's recommendation, he has yet to teach. Wouldn't we regret hiring him if an experienced teacher came along? We have two months before we have to stamp our approval on anyone."

"Is the lack of teaching experience your only hesitation?" Mr. Hicks inquired. "You agreed to Miss Jenkins for the fourth-grade position, and she didn't have teaching experience."

The young woman was a sweetheart—she posed no danger. "She teaches Sunday school." Mercy shrugged as nonchalantly as she could. "But I'm afraid it's more that I didn't exactly believe everything he said. His answers were too perfect and practiced."

"So you'd rather hire someone who answers poorly?" Mr. Hicks raised an eyebrow and crossed his arms over his chest.

She looked to Dr. Freedman, who'd grown up in Teaville. He was leaning back in his chair, fiddling with his pencil, seemingly bored and ready to be done. Had he not recognized Aaron? He was a few years older than they were, but Aaron had been big enough to terrorize quite a few children older than him. Plus Dr. Freedman had several younger siblings.

Please.

Surely God would not want George Aaron Firebrook working alone with children all day, every day. Another teacher would apply soon and be the obvious choice. "Let's just say I have an uneasy feeling about him. I'd like to wait."

"A woman's intuition." Mr. Carter let out a condescending huff.

It was no secret Mr. Carter found having a woman on the board to be a great inconvenience. But it was the first thing in her life she'd ever fought to attain, so she wouldn't let him make her feel bad about being elected.

"Yes, perhaps intuition has something to do with it." Oh, why

15

couldn't she be as mean as George—er, Aaron—and rip him to shreds in front of everyone? "We'll lose nothing by waiting. As of right now, I'm not willing to vote for him."

"He could accept another job in the meantime," said Mr. Carter.

Hopefully a job that didn't involve children. "Then our next applicants will find themselves lucky." Though since Aaron had a teaching license . . . Her stomach churned. She could keep him from this position, but what if he sought another where no one knew who he really was?

Mr. Carter scooted his chair back. "I need to get to the bank. We can decide this just as easily at another meeting. I have no reservations about hiring Mr. Firebrook."

"Then let's adjourn, and you, Miss McClain"—Mr. Hicks pointed at her—"will be the one to tell him we'll decide at a later date."

Her heart thumped in her throat at the thought, but at least she'd convinced them to wait for more applicants. "I will."

"All right—meeting adjourned."

Despite Mr. Carter's declaration of needing to get to the bank, he turned toward Mr. Lafferty and started talking stocks while she gathered her things. The others chatted as well, but she wouldn't bother trying to join them. They were wealthier and far more important than a young woman who did nothing more than help her brother and his wife run the orphanage. Just getting voted onto the board had been quite the feat.

Tucking her folder into the crook of her short arm's elbow, she sidled out from behind the table and headed for the door. Should she go to Mr. Gray's classroom in hopes of finding Aaron with him, or go later this week to the Grays' ranch, where Aaron said he'd be staying?

She put her weight against the heavy door, but it swung open easier than expected. She stumbled forward, and a huge bear paw of a hand caught her short arm under the elbow. She lost her grip on her papers, and they flew across the floor.

"I'm so sorry. I just meant to help."

"Help?" She stepped out of Aaron's hold.

"Yes, though I certainly failed to do so." He stooped to pick up her papers.

She crossed the hallway to grab the pages that had slid the farthest, with the added bonus that she'd be out of his reach. "I didn't imagine helping others would ever be an ambition of yours."

"Neither did I." He grabbed one last paper and held them out to her. "So I reckon I didn't get the job?"

"Not if I can help it."

He raised his eyebrows. "So it's not a straight *no*?" A smile split his nearly black beard.

Hmmm, she should have expected this. Caving to his pitiful *please* only guaranteed he'd dog her every step until she gave him what he wanted. Once a bully, always a bully. "You're lucky I didn't tell them why I'll not vote for you. Did you think a simple name change would keep people from recognizing you?"

"No." He fidgeted for some reason. "I didn't change my name to hide."

Then why had he changed it? The desire to ask made her fidgety, but small talk with George Aaron Firebrook was not on her list of things to do in this life. All he needed to know were the facts. "Well, we plan on interviewing other applicants, and to be clear, I will vote for one of them and encourage the board members to do likewise. Don't bother attempting to change my mind, for I am no longer a child you can intimidate."

"I'm sure you're not."

She snatched her papers back from him, stuffing them into her disorganized folder. "Besides, it's only a matter of time until Dr. Freedman remembers you, and his opinion usually sways the board."

She turned and marched toward the doors at the far end of the hall, where the afternoon light beckoned to her through the windows, promising warmth and the opportunity to get far away from Aaron.

But he followed right behind her, taking big strides to catch up.

She should've known he'd not leave her alone. Her nerves shook at his nearness, belying her assertion that he couldn't intimidate her anymore.

"Freedman?" Aaron scratched his chin through his thick beard as he kept pace beside her. "I can't remember any Freedmans. Of course, first names are more helpful to me, considering how many people I pestered."

Pestered? She nearly laughed at the understatement. Of course he couldn't remember the names of everyone he harassed. Not only were there too many to count, he probably hadn't bothered to learn their names to begin with.

"But I tell you this, Mercy—"

"Miss McClain to you." She clenched her fist.

"Of course, Miss McClain, I apologize—for that and the past anguish I caused you. But that's partly why I want to teach in Teaville. I think it'd be a good way for me to make up for my past. At least some would think so."

She stiffened and increased her pace. How did he have the nerve to imply anyone would want him in charge of children?

Her boss, Nicholas Lowe, and his wife, Lydia, ministered to the women who populated the red-light district, believing they could reform and hold better jobs, yet they wouldn't consider placing a reformed prostitute in a brothel as cook or chambermaid.

Aaron ran the brim of his felt hat through his hands. "What can I do to convince you I've changed?"

"Nothing." She continued toward the front doors. But what if he followed her off school property?

"But—"

"Trying to badger me into trusting you isn't going to get you anywhere." She stopped at the door and faced him. "There is no possible way you'll convince me you've changed in time for you to get this job. I'd suggest seeking employment elsewhere. Good day."

"I-I'm sorry. Thank you for your time, Miss McClain." He stepped back and turned away, freeing her to breathe.

His huge figure seemed slumped as he walked down the hall.

But it was likely just an act. Had to be.

He would have to change tactics to get what he wanted now, considering tripping grown women and taunting them all the way home would not be tolerated by his grown-up peers. His manipulations would have to become more underhanded or he'd end up in jail.

If Mr. Gray hadn't fallen under his spell and recommended him for the job, she'd never have seen him again.

But he'd actually acquired a teaching license. . . .

She pushed out into the cool spring afternoon before Aaron could change his mind and return to badger her.

She could save the children of her own district from his influence, but what of others? She couldn't spend her days following him around the United States telling each school about his past. She'd just have to pray that God would put him where he belonged—which was not in a classroom.

The brisk walk toward the south of town where the mansion-turned-orphanage sat perched above the railroad tracks was not as enjoyable as usual. She couldn't keep herself from looking over her shoulder to make certain Aaron wasn't following her.

Perhaps she needed to talk to Mr. Gray and convince him to withdraw his recommendation before Aaron used it to get a teaching job elsewhere. And why had Mr. Gray recommended him anyway? He'd taught Aaron in the ninth grade, and from what she'd heard, he'd not become a model citizen that year or any of his remaining high school years in Teaville, not by a long shot.

She climbed the driveway that meandered up a small hill to the three-story white mansion at the top, its red-shingled roof a shot of color amid the new spring greenery surrounding the town's fanciest residence. When she'd moved back to Teaville last year, she'd been amazed that such a grand building would be erected in this out-of-the-way prairie town. And even more amazed when she learned the owner had given up living in it to use it as an orphanage for the cast-off children of the red-light district.

And when Mr. Lowe had hired her and her brother and sister-in-law at the beginning of this year to run it for just a handful of children, she'd almost had to shake her head at the expense of it all. But Mr. Lowe and his wife had stressed that money wasn't nearly as hard to part with as children who needed help.

Slightly out of breath, Mercy slowed as she crested the hill. Worrying about her old nemesis seemed to have put speed into her steps. However, she needed to be calm before she forged into the chaos that would likely meet her.

She strolled up under the mansion's magnificent two-story portico. Its half-moon ceiling supported by four grand white columns always made her feel as if she were entering a castle instead of an orphanage.

Her sister-in-law's shrill shriek broke the spell. The only person who could elicit that sound from Patricia was Jimmy.

Mercy let herself in and followed the sound of her sister-in-law berating the thirteen-year-old for back-talking. His retorts were filled with more taunt than remorse.

Near the library, she scrunched her nose at the pungent aroma of pipe tobacco wafting from the room.

Patricia was attempting to wrestle a pipe from Jimmy's hand as he sat on the large leather couch, an amused, malicious gleam in his eye peeking out from under blond bangs in desperate need of a trim.

"Stop." Mercy rushed over and grabbed her sister-in-law's shoulders. "Please."

Patricia let go and huffed, tendrils of her nearly black hair hanging loose about her face. "I told him he can't smoke in here, and all he said was, 'Watch me.'"

The young man's smirk indicated the truth of it—and he'd probably done so just to set Patricia off.

Though he'd yet to hit puberty and was skinny despite his wide shoulders, Jimmy was already too much for either of them to handle alone, especially when one had a weak will and the other was missing a hand. Every time they lost a battle, his attitude and shenanigans worsened. Mercy moved past Patricia and swiped the bag of cherry-scented tobacco off the side table. Where had he gotten it? "Enjoy your last puffs, for my brother will deal with you when he gets home."

Please, God, let Timothy get home before dinner so he can take care of this.

Her brother had an hour before he was due home from his bank job. With only four orphans right now, three of school age, two women should easily have been able to handle the children. But they hadn't accounted for an orphan like Jimmy. He'd only been a resident for four months, and yet he'd made this job more trying than any of them had anticipated.

And now that Timothy rarely came straight home from work, Jimmy grew even more defiant.

From under his shaggy blond bangs, his squinty eyes glared at the tobacco in her hand. Then he shrugged and hiked a leg over the chair's arm. "Who cares?" He leaned back, took a puff from his pipe, and blew a slow stream of smoke in their direction.

"You see? You see what I mean?" Patricia gestured wildly at the boy, whose freckled cheeks made him look more innocent than he was.

Mercy put her good arm around Patricia's slight shoulders and whispered, "Calm yourself. He feeds off you getting hysterical."

Once they exited the library, Patricia shrugged out of her hold. "It's your turn to deal with him." She stomped forward, gesticulating wildly. "I can't take it anymore. Not only is he still smoking, but I found him rifling through my drawer of unmentionables after lunch. I didn't find anything missing, but I wouldn't be surprised to find one of my chemises fluttering from the flagpole someday, and I shall die of mortification. On top of that, he spit on my shoes. Spit! And then, as if Jimmy wasn't bad enough, Owen insisted on racing around the hallways hooting and hollering until he broke a lamp, just as I always said would happen." Patricia pulled at her hair.

Probably not the time to remind her sister-in-law that five-year-old boys tended to be loud and clumsy.

"Even Max rolled his eyes at me today." Her hands dropped

to her sides, and she closed her eyes. "I'm done. I'm going to my room."

Mercy nodded, though Patricia didn't open her eyes before turning and marching for the stairs.

She'd known she'd be better at managing the orphanage than Patricia, but she hadn't expected to be the only one doing the work or having to deal with an orphan as hard as Jimmy.

A crash sounded down the hall.

"Owen!" Cook hollered at the top of her lungs. Evidently she was ready for the day to be over as well. "Get back in here!"

Mercy sighed and headed toward the kitchen. If her brother didn't start coming home earlier, she and Patricia might both end up in the asylum.

3

Aaron swallowed his last swig of campfire-strong coffee while his former teacher frantically searched the kitchen for his class notes. Aaron looked at the clock and frowned. Should he tell Mr. Gray it was already half past the hour?

Mr. Gray's wife, Charlotte—or Charlie, as she preferred to be called—bustled back and forth with a tiny infant attached to her in a cocoon of sorts as she prepared a large pot of oatmeal and fried bacon for her ranch hands. She'd told Aaron that Indians carried their children in a similar fashion so they could get work done.

Still, there was something strange about a woman not only wearing trousers but wearing an infant as if she were a bauble.

The tiny girl didn't seem to mind though. She stayed as still as a pin, her big, dark eyes fixed on the ever-changing scenery her mother's harried movements provided.

And she was much, much quieter than she'd been all night last night.

Aaron yawned and picked up his empty coffee cup. Could his stomach handle more? He didn't know what job interviews he might get today, but he ought to be awake for them.

"You know what?" Charlie lifted a wooden spoon coated with

oatmeal clumps and pointed it at her husband. "I think they're by the bassinet."

"That's right." Mr. Gray stifled a yawn. "I worked on them while putting Alice back to sleep." He disappeared into their room off the kitchen.

His teacher had put the baby back to sleep? Aaron yawned again and scratched the back of his head. When had his own father done anything with him besides mete out punishment his mother said he'd deserved?

Of course, Charlie was no ordinary woman either. They were the oddest couple he'd ever met. Who'd ever heard of a woman rancher with a husband who didn't know how many head of cattle they owned?

He vaguely remembered Charlie from a few weeks of his ninth-grade year. Mr. Gray had broken his glasses, and she'd come to help teach. She'd made the students do strange things like stand and walk around while reading. But how had she gotten his teacher romantically interested in her? Mr. Gray's manners were refined, certainly not the rough-and-tumble sort.

"Found them, darling." He gave his wife a peck on the cheek and then planted one atop his daughter's fuzzy head. He turned to Aaron. "I hope you're ready. I'm late."

"Yes." He grabbed his jacket and thanked Charlie for breakfast before running after Mr. Gray and climbing onto the wagon seat.

Mr. Gray drove quickly toward the ranch's wide gate. He looked at his watch, then encouraged his horse to go faster. "I'm sorry about rushing you. But with Alice, we're barely getting anything done. Charlie usually has breakfast ready before the sun rises, but we didn't sleep much last night."

He'd not bother to tell him their infant had stolen his sleep as well. "That's all right. The food was nice and hot. Can't start your day off much better than with a hot breakfast." Tasty would've been good, but one out of two had kept it from being a complete failure.

"What are you planning to do today?"

Aaron stared at the brush-covered ridge in front of them, still dark with early-morning shadows. "Look for work."

"Do you really think your interview went that poorly?" Mr. Gray pushed up his glasses, as if seeing Aaron better might change his answer.

Last night, he'd told the Grays he didn't have a good feeling about getting the job, though he'd not mentioned why. "As I said, they plan to interview others, and you know what my reputation was." Though he hadn't quit his bullying ways until after high school, he'd curbed his mistreatment of others whenever his English teacher was around. For some reason, the man had actually thought him worth something and had even helped him learn to read better instead of making fun of him.

He'd ended up in Mr. Gray's class after being kicked out of Mrs. Beach's. He'd thrown his book at her after she'd laughed at him for mispronouncing *Voilà!* while reading aloud.

How was he supposed to have known that was a French word? They weren't reading a French story.

He forced his hands to unclench and his jaw to relax.

"I think you'll get the position. You've got my recommendation, and there aren't many unemployed teachers around here."

"Thanks, but I don't think it'll hurt to see what's available. Besides, I need a job for the summer if I don't plan to be a burden."

"Charlie said you're welcome to help with the ranch."

"Yes, thank you." But she had plenty of hands and didn't need to spend her time teaching him what to do. Besides, he had forgiveness to seek and couldn't do that at a ranch outside of town. "But I'm hoping to do something along the lines of teaching, even if not with the school."

Fred Hopper had answered his letter asking for forgiveness over a year ago. Aaron hadn't expected a reply since he'd treated him worse than most. Fred's manner of walking and talking indicated his brain wasn't working properly and had made him an easy target whenever Aaron had gone to school feeling his worst.

But Fred had forgiven him, and he was the one to suggest Aaron teach children who struggled to learn, to see how difficult it was for them.

He'd thought Fred's suggestion was as ludicrous as Mercy had—initially. But if he wanted to make up for his past, was that not the best way to do it?

Where he'd once tormented children, he could now protect them. Where he'd once been so angry he wanted everyone to be unhappy, he could now sympathize. Who better to turn a bully around than someone who'd spent years believing no one could ever care for him? He could be a Mr. Gray for a child who desperately needed a Mr. Gray.

Aaron pulled the list he carried from his pocket. As they bumped along at high speed, he read through the names he'd not been able to attach a surname to and descriptions of the children he'd hurt but couldn't remember anything else about. "Do you know Dr. Freedman's siblings' names or what they look like?" Mercy had said it was only a matter of time before Dr. Freedman remembered who he was. Probably would be best to figure out who they were before he ran into them.

"Quentin has two sisters and two brothers, I believe. I don't know the girls' names, but I had his brother Thomas in class. He died the following year, thrown from a horse."

"Was he in my class?"

"Oh no, he was a year ahead of Quentin. The younger boy was Jack, I think." Mr. Gray flicked his reins, calling for his horse to go even faster. "They all look alike, have the same dark hair."

Aaron read the list again in an effort not to panic at the rapid speed of the landscape passing by. He paused on Fred's name and his request.

Would he have to hold off on getting a teaching job? He didn't want to leave Teaville until he'd figured out whether the people on his list still lived here or not.

Mercy certainly did. But since she'd told him yesterday he could do nothing to make up for how he'd once treated her, he would let her cool down before asking for her forgiveness.

Iris Baymont lived here as well, last he knew. She'd been the only other person who'd answered the letters he'd sent and was the reason he'd decided to ask Mr. Gray about a job. She'd not answered his second letter, and considering the content of her first, he couldn't stay in California and do nothing to help her. Thankfully his parents had moved away from Teaville after the death of his uncle; otherwise he might not have been willing to return. "Do you know of any teaching-type jobs that aren't a part of the school district?"

"I know of something short-term. Do you remember Lydia King? Dark-haired girl with light blue eyes, always reading?"

"Yes." He hadn't pestered her much since she spent most of her time reading near teachers and was older. He'd made fun of her hand-me-down clothes several times, but he hadn't put her on his list, for if he had to beg forgiveness of everyone he'd mildly harassed, he'd be busy until the end of time.

They bumped hard over several ruts before Mr. Gray continued. "She married one of the richest men in town, Nicholas Lowe."

His brows shot up at that. "I'm surprised. I thought she was of humble means."

"She was, but opposites attract, you know." Mr. Gray's smile warmed as he stared into space, making Aaron want to shake him for taking his eyes off the road at the speed they were going.

Hitting a rut brought the man's attention back to where it belonged. "Anyway, she told Charlie last week that her husband was looking for a math tutor for an orphan at the mansion." Mr. Gray swerved around a pothole and almost hit a dog.

Aaron gripped his seat tighter.

"I meant to tell one of my colleagues who has tutored in the past, but my mind's been fuzzy lately. I'm sure my recommendation would get you that job. It's just one kid though. You'd not make enough to sustain you."

"That might work." Surely teaching math to a struggling child would be good experience. "Maybe I could find another job to go with it."

27

"Lydia's husband owns several mills and factories. You might ask him about a job with flexible hours if he wants you to tutor." They entered the outskirts of town, but Mr. Gray hardly slowed. "Want me to drop you off at one of Nicholas's properties? I'm not sure where he'll be, but someone could point you in the right direction."

Aaron looked at his timepiece, though it was hard to read as the wagon wove through traffic. "But if you're already late—"

"The lumberyard is on the way."

"If you can, that's great—though I can walk, if necessary."

"Not a problem. Tell Nicholas I'll vouch for you, and I'm sure he'll find you something."

Aaron nodded, a lump in his throat keeping him from responding—and not just because the wagon's right wheels had just traveled a few feet on the sidewalk instead of the road.

Mr. Gray's unwavering support was as humbling as Reverend MacDonald's. Though Mr. Gray had played a part in turning his life around, it was the reverend's untiring confidence that God could and would heal the wounds of his past that had finally convinced Aaron to choose the right path.

What if that silly old preacher hadn't taken such an interest in him? He'd gone to California mean enough to scare a snake into tying itself into a knot, yet the reverend had courage enough to sit with him on their lunch breaks at the mine they both worked, despite the verbal barbs Aaron spat his way. Making fun of Reverend MacDonald and his puny little church of ten people had only made the reverend pray for him all the more.

And for some reason, the longer he stuck around, acting as if Aaron was worth more than spit, the more Aaron hoped Reverend MacDonald's God was as forgiving as the reverend claimed He was.

For though the power to grind others down had given him a devilish sort of exhilaration, in the quiet of night, he'd feared the day a cosmic hand would drop from the sky and smash him into the dirt.

Because he deserved it.

The sawmill's whine preceded his first glimpse of the lumber-yard. The air was thick with sawdust and spring dew, a far cry lighter than the dank, coal dust–laden air that had filled his lungs the day he'd finally humbled himself before God and asked Him to hold back His just punishment and free him from the evil that drove Aaron to hate himself as much as he hated others.

"I still think you'll be teaching alongside me come fall, but I hope you find something for the summer." Mr. Gray pulled his horse to a stop.

The second Aaron hopped off the wagon, he jumped out of the way, his toe barely escaping the back wheel as the wagon surged forward. He waved farewell, though Mr. Gray was already racing down the street.

Aaron checked his timepiece and cringed. 8:02. Mr. Gray was late. Hopefully his unsupervised students wouldn't cause him problems.

Turning, Aaron headed for a door with *Lowe's Lumber* stenciled on the front. Inside was a normal-looking office covered with a fine layer of sawdust, except near the open window, where the breeze did the dusting.

A man with an unfortunate whopper of a big nose looked up from his desk and raised an eyebrow. "May I help you?"

It was obvious the secretary hadn't been a classmate of his, because he would've unmercifully made fun of that nose. He glanced at the placard on the man's desk. "Mr. Black, I presume?"

"Yes."

"I'm here in hopes of finding Mr. Lowe. Mr. Gray heard he was in need of a math tutor, and I would like to inquire about the job."

"You're a teacher?"

"I have the license, and I'd like to be. Just applied at the school, but work there wouldn't start until next term."

Mr. Black rose from the desk. "Let me see if he's got time."

Aaron's heart started thumping. "He's here?"

"Yes, just a second." Mr. Black crossed over to a door with a frosted window, knocked, and slipped inside.

Aaron looked around for somewhere to sit, but every seat was covered in stacks of papers or sawdust. Considering his hands had turned sweaty, he shouldn't touch anything or his palms would be caked in seconds.

Mr. Black came back out of the office, holding the door wide open. "Come this way, Mr. . . . ?"

"Firebrook."

He turned his head toward the interior of the office. "Mr. Firebrook to see you."

Aaron's heart rate ratcheted up. Thankfully he was already prepared for an interview. It couldn't be too much different from yesterday's, and he couldn't recall a single person by the name of Nicholas from his years in school. Though his being married to Lydia King could be trouble if she remembered how nasty he'd been to others.

He passed in front of Mr. Black and into the room.

A man who was probably ten years his senior, with a serious brow beneath dark, wavy hair, stood behind a plain desk. His business suit was too nice for an office such as this, but it was the only thing indicating he was as rich as Mr. Gray said.

"Come in, Mr. Firebrook. Please be seated." He pointed to another out-of-place item in the room, a green upholstered chair with brass buttons.

Aaron refrained from brushing off the seat before lowering himself.

"Mr. Black tells me Harrison sent you here about the tutoring position." Mr. Lowe settled in behind his desk.

"Yes, he recommended me to the school board for the math position as well. I'm a former pupil of his."

Mr. Lowe's smile softened his face. "That man has a way of making pupils into loyal friends."

"He certainly did of me."

Mr. Lowe's quick nod seemed to indicate Mr. Gray's recommendation really was all he needed.

If only the same had worked on Mercy.

"I have two young men in need of tutoring. How good are you at math?"

Had he not told him he had applied for the school's math position? "It was my best subject, what I hope to teach."

"I mean, would higher mathematics be out of your skill set?"

Well, it wasn't like he was a specialist. He forced himself not to squirm. "I took some higher mathematics, since that's the subject I enjoy. I can't say I'm familiar with every branch, but if I have a good textbook, I can usually figure out anything I've forgotten or haven't come across." He could certainly handle any high school textbook.

"And when could you tutor?"

"Anytime at the moment. I'm in search of a full-time job as well. I'm not looking for anything more than manual labor, so if you have a position at one of your factories I could take, I could work around those hours."

"Won't a second job hinder you from teaching come fall?"

"I might not get the position." Or rather, definitely wouldn't, but Mr. Lowe didn't need to know that. "But I'd like to stay in Teaville either way. So there's a possibility I'd keep the job. I know that situation isn't ideal for an employer, but I want to be honest. I'm willing to do anything."

Mr. Lowe sat back in his chair and tapped his chin. "What about gardening?"

Aaron tried not to wince too hard at that. Tending flowers? "Um, as I said, I'd be willing to do anything, but I can't promise I'll be good at gardening. I've not grown a thing in my life. I was thinking more like hauling crates or running a saw."

"My gardener retired on me without notice. It's the time of year our grounds will start getting out of hand. I haven't yet had anyone respond to my advertisement. If you get the teaching position, by fall, the yard won't be in such dire need of attention, and I'll have more time to find someone else."

"The timing does sound ideal, but is this position just grounds keeping, or would I be planting flowers too?" He tried not to cringe at the thought of taking care of flowers—if he'd have beaten up a man for possessing a sissified job, gardening would certainly qualify.

"Both." Mr. Lowe sported a slight grin. "But don't worry, the gardener left his collection of horticultural books in the cabin. Which, unless you desire to live somewhere else, would be yours to use. My wife can order more books, if you desire."

A house too? Reading about plants sounded boring, but the likelihood of finding a better setup was practically nil. "Would I only tutor during the school year or throughout the summer as well?"

"Oh, you'll be too busy with the grounds come summer. I do hire four boys to help when it's overwhelming. But I only need a tutor until the end of the school year. It's Max's last year, and Robert will be leaving with his brother. Though there's always a possibility I might need a tutor again, depending on the children. Could you tutor for more than just math?"

He nodded. But gardening? Hopefully he could at least keep things alive until the end of the school year. "The timing sounds ideal, so I'm willing."

Mr. Lowe's face grew serious.

Aaron rubbed his hands against his slacks. Had he said something wrong?

Mr. Lowe leaned forward. "This position is at the orphanage, and there's a boy there who's a handful—to the point I could see him causing you problems. He's only been with us for four months, but the staff has been having a difficult time . . . getting through to him. His rough past has made him quite rough himself. The ones you'd be tutoring are two of the better-behaved children who've come through, but Jimmy is . . . the opposite."

He couldn't imagine many children having a rougher childhood than he'd had. Maybe he wouldn't get the chance to teach in Teaville, but helping a hurting orphan would be just as worthy. "I was not a good child myself, so his antics shouldn't be anything I can't handle. Are there stipulations for the use of the gardener's house? If I do well enough to stay hired past the summer and don't get the teaching position, are there rules I have to follow to continue living there?"

"As long as you're the gardener, it's yours. It's a two-bedroom cabin, so if you got married it could only handle a small family."

Got married? That wouldn't happen.

"The children we help at this orphanage have come from a background of immorality, so I don't want anything of the kind on my property. I ask that you don't drink, smoke, or provide the children with such. And the only woman allowed in your cottage is your wife."

Well, that was direct. "I understand, and I have no problem with those stipulations. I'll take the job, if you'll have me."

Mr. Lowe stood and extended his arm. "Since I trust Mr. Gray's recommendations, the job is yours—and we'll see how it goes."

With free evenings come summer, he could visit the people on his list and hopefully make restitution. If it looked as if he could stay on at the orphanage, he might even withdraw his application for math teacher. Did he dare hope that doing so might make Mercy willing to forgive him?

4

Bending over to pick up a shoe in the middle of the hallway, Mercy frowned at the other one lodged under the entryway table. How many times must she tell Jimmy to put things back where they belonged? He was being willfully disobedient now, knowing he'd not get in trouble since she'd started reserving her strength for battling him over smoking, throwing things, attacking people, and cursing.

She hadn't realized how badly her desire to avoid confrontations would affect her ability to work at the orphanage.

She got on her knees to fish out the other shoe. If only she could throw this pair away and force him to go without, but his schoolteacher would likely not be thrilled with that sort of discipline.

"What are you doing?" Owen appeared next to her. The five-year-old gave her a crazy look as he stared at her, halfway stuck under the table's lower shelf.

"Cleaning, as you should be." She hauled out the shoe and swiped off cobwebs.

"But Jimmy isn't helping." His whine grated. "I don't want to clean by myself."

It was all she could do to keep from growling. Did she have to stand over Jimmy all day? "Your mess wasn't that much. You should've been done already."

Owen's big dimples showed even though he was frowning. Those dimples made it hard to get upset with him—not that she was upset with him often.

"Go upstairs and do your chores, all right? I'll see what I can do about Jimmy." Why wasn't Patricia taking care of this? Hadn't she been watching them? "Where's Mrs. McClain?"

Owen shrugged. "She tried to get Jimmy to help, but he ain't going to do what she says, so she stomped off."

Jimmy was going to drive them all out of the mansion if they couldn't figure out how to make him behave.

A knock at the front door sounded, and Mercy shooed Owen upstairs. Another insistent knock made Mercy sigh as she pushed herself off the floor.

Through the tiny beveled panes of Tiffany glass, she could make out the distorted face of Henri Beauchamp.

Likely here to try to see Caroline again. Poor chap. Mercy shook her head and reached for the door handle. When would he finally take the hint that their housekeeper, Caroline O'Conner, wanted nothing to do with him?

She had no idea why though, since Caroline was a servant and this man owned a very successful flour mill—not the usual suitor for one of her station. Surely she hadn't decided against him because he wasn't the most handsome man in the world. He was portly, yes, but his auburn stubble and slight accent held some charm.

She opened the door, but her welcoming smile grew stiff.

He stood there, holding tight to a small bundle that could only be a well-wrapped infant. "Miss McClain," he muttered as he swiftly crossed the threshold.

An infant orphan? She held her breath to keep from sighing. It wasn't this baby's fault she was already at her wits' end.

She held out her arms for the child, pushing away the sad thought of how someone so small would never know his or her mother. "Boy or girl?"

"Girl." Henri kept a tight hold on the babe, as if afraid she might steal her. "Is Miss O'Conner around?"

She raised an eyebrow. "Somewhere, yes. But she doesn't care for the orphans. I do."

He scanned her from head to toe before walking farther into the room, keeping the baby tucked in one arm. "I need Caroline."

Had he just looked at her arm and thought her incapable of holding a baby? Or was this his newest ploy at trying for the housekeeper's attention? Either way, not exactly endearing. "I'm sorry, but as I said, Caroline doesn't take the orphans."

The door to the basement stairway opened and Caroline walked in, frowning the second she caught sight of Henri. "I see the front door's been answered." She slipped back into the stairwell and started to pull the door closed behind her.

"Stop." Henri's shout was more panic than command.

Thankfully Caroline did stop.

"I found Moira."

Mercy turned as rigid as the housekeeper. He'd found Caroline's sister? Moira had been missing since winter. Having a prostitute sister had to be hard enough on Caroline's nerves, but when a woman disappeared from the red-light district, likely nothing good had happened.

Caroline turned slowly, her eyes round with hope, yet her body tense with fear. "Where is she?" She left the basement door ajar, her hands clenched in front of her.

Henri tensed. He raised his clenched fist a little, then brought it back down under the baby as if he were jabbing a knife into his gut. "I don't know."

"What do you mean, you don't know?" Caroline fisted her hands beside her. "You found her and let her go?"

"Actually, no. She found me." Henri's gaze fixed on the baby's sleeping face. "She . . . she handed me this."

36

Caroline glanced at the baby, who couldn't have been more than a week or two old. "I don't understand."

"Moira said she kept telling you to start a family you could be proud of and leave her be. She hopes you will now, if only to keep your niece from becoming like her mother."

"What?" Caroline's face scrunched up.

"The baby. She's your niece. And she needs you." Henri held out the infant to Caroline as if the child were an alien being.

She reluctantly took her and blinked with exaggeration while staring at the little wrinkled face. "I can't take care of a baby."

Mercy walked forward, putting her hand on Caroline and turning to Henri. "Where's Moira now? Did she return to the Hawk and Eagle?"

Henri's face paled as if he'd witnessed a ghost. "I think she left town."

Caroline's face grew hard. "How could you lose her?"

Henri shook his head and laid a hand on the swaddled infant Caroline held away from herself. "When she handed me this baby, I . . . Well, I was in shock. I didn't think to run after her until it was too late. The madam at the Hawk and Eagle had no knowledge of her return. I asked around, but no one has seen her."

Mercy pressed the baby closer to Caroline, encouraging her to cradle the now wriggling infant before she dropped her. "Maybe she's gone off in search of a better life, as you've always wanted her to do."

Caroline's face contorted as if she believed Mercy a fool. "No, she wouldn't . . . not without my help. . . . She couldn't." She stared at the baby, who'd started fussing. "Didn't even want to . . ."

The baby squalled, and neither Caroline nor Henri did anything to soothe her, both of them staring at the infant as if dumbfounded. Mercy wedged in and took the baby, turning the little girl onto her shoulder and patting her with her one hand.

Caroline stared at the child, as if mesmerized by Mercy's ministrations. "How am I going to care for her?"

"I don't know." Mercy shushed the infant, though she'd already stopped crying and was back to sniffling. "Perhaps it's a good thing you work at an orphanage. We can get her into a good home."

"No," Henri barked. "I mean . . ." He pulled at his tie. "It's her niece."

"But I haven't the resources to care for a child." Caroline worried her apron in her hands. "I can't work, raise her, and continue helping women in the red-light district. Where is she going to live—in the basement with me? I can't burden the staff with her just because I work here. Besides, the Lowes are always saying these children should be placed under the care of two parents."

"But the orphans had no stable family members to go to, if they had any at all." Henri rubbed his brow as if his head ached. "You're her family. She belongs with you."

"He's right." Mercy looked at the little face on her shoulder, the babe's chubby cheeks now slack with sleep. "Mr. Lowe allowed Florence to go with her grandmother even though she was a widow."

Henri took Caroline's hands. After a few moments, she took her wide, stunned eyes off the baby and turned to him.

"You never gave up on Moira. Don't give up your niece." Henri let go of her hands and paced. "I plan to help. I pledged to support that women's home you and Miss Wisely wanted to start last year, but after the idea folded, you never asked anything else of me."

Caroline stared at him as if he'd said something stupid.

The front door jiggled.

Was her brother coming home early for once? Maybe he could be of help. Mercy started for the front door, but her boss, Nicholas Lowe, entered before she got there.

The tension tightening her back and shoulders melted. He'd be far better at helping Caroline and Henri think through things than Timothy would be. Nicholas had known them far longer than anyone in this mansion. Though he and Henri no longer seemed to be friends—something concerning Caroline and her sister had caused a rift—Nicholas had never treated Henri poorly whenever he'd come around.

Her boss glanced between Henri and Caroline and then her, his brow furrowing at seeing the baby. "Who's this?"

"Moira's child."

His eyebrows rose.

Henri turned toward him and pointed. "Tell Caroline she can keep the baby and remain housekeeper."

Mercy held her breath. She'd never seen anyone have the audacity to give Nicholas a command. They might have been good friends once, but Nicholas wouldn't like being told what to do. And yet, what would Caroline do if he said no?

"Of course," Nicholas said softly, but there was a strange, probing look in his eyes as he took in Henri.

Why had he obeyed the shorter man's command without even looking affronted?

"Good." Henri nodded emphatically and then turned to look at the baby again. "Seems first thing I can do is find a wet nurse." He blew past Nicholas without a word and strode out the front door.

She'd never thought she'd see the day her boss would seem at a loss for words. And yet there he stood, his baffled look mirroring Caroline's. Maybe he was confused about what Henri had to do with the situation.

"Henri said Moira found him, gave him the baby, and left." Mercy patted the baby's back. "He wants to help since he promised to support the women's home you and Evelyn had planned last year."

Evelyn and her parents had run the orphanage before Mercy's family had taken over the job. Evelyn had also campaigned for a home to be built in the red-light district to help women have a safe place to abandon their vocation, learn a trade, and perhaps be reunited with their children, if any were in the orphanage. But the project hadn't gotten anywhere before Evelyn married and moved to Kansas City.

Nicholas shrugged. "I have no problem with him helping."

Caroline shook her head. "But you don't know what it's like trying to work while caring for an infant."

Nicholas raised his eyebrows again, a bemused expression on his face. "I don't?" He had two children under the age of four.

"Well, I mean, of course you do. But not as a single woman." She wilted. "Oh, how am I going to do it?"

"I'm sure Mercy and Patricia will help. And they'll have more free time now that I've hired a tutor for Max and Robert." He gestured toward a man Mercy hadn't noticed standing outside the front door.

She swallowed. It couldn't be.

Aaron slid into the entryway. The way he scrunched his face and pulled his mouth to the side indicated he knew exactly how unwelcome a sight he was to her.

Nicholas walked back a pace to stand beside him. "This is Aaron Firebrook. He'll be tutoring and tending the garden until the start of next school year at minimum. Aaron, this is the mansion's housekeeper, Caroline O'Conner, and one of the orphanage directors, Mercy McClain. Though I imagine you met Miss McClain when you interviewed at the school."

He swept off his hat. "I did. And I promise"—he looked straight at Mercy—"I didn't know you worked here."

"Excuse me." She handed the baby to Caroline, afraid her own trembling now exceeded the housekeeper's. "May I have a word with you, Mr. Lowe?"

He shrugged. "Of course." But he didn't move.

"In your office, if you would." She turned to Caroline, refusing to look at Aaron. "Excuse us." She then headed for the office.

Nicholas's long stride helped him catch up to her halfway down the hallway. He passed in front of her to open the door. "What's the problem?"

"Aaron—or George, rather . . ." She stopped in the middle of his office, turned, and crossed her arms over her chest. "Mr. Firebrook must have failed to tell you—as he also failed to tell the board—that he was the worst school bully that ever lived. He has no business overseeing children."

40

Nicholas leaned on the front of his desk and rubbed his jaw. "He actually did tell me he wasn't the best kid. We talked about Jimmy, and he thought his childhood might help him relate to the boy."

What? Aaron thought his ability to harass people was an asset? She kept herself rooted in place instead of rushing back to the entryway to tell him exactly how helpful his overbearing ways were not. "He was beyond not being the best kid. He exploited everyone's weaknesses for laughs."

"When did this happen?"

"All throughout his school years, as far as I know. Last time he bullied me was in 1896—when my family left town."

Nicholas shrugged. Shrugged! "Harrison vouches for him. He must have changed after that."

She paced the floor. "If Geor—Aaron couldn't keep his thoughts to himself about my arm, Camille's splotchy skin, Fred's mental faculties, and every other student's foibles and flaws, do you think he can handle the children here with any sort of empathy?"

Nicholas crossed his arms and cocked his head to the side, studying her as if she'd been the bully rather than the victim. "I don't know him well enough to say one way or the other."

Surely he could see that the time it took to interview Aaron was wholly inadequate for deciding—though she couldn't blame him for wanting to give Aaron a chance. She'd heard how perfect and practiced Aaron's answers could be. "Well, then take it from me. He shouldn't be in charge of children."

"But as you said, that was years ago." He resituated himself on his desk and frowned. "I'm afraid you wouldn't have considered me qualified to run this orphanage or help those in the red-light district eleven years ago. I myself wouldn't have liked or trusted me. It's possible for people to experience real change, especially when God gets ahold of them."

"Or Aaron has just chosen a more subtle way to manipulate people than outright bullying, like masquerading as a changed man you can trust—which I don't."

Nicholas looked at her for a few moments, then held up a hand.

"Give me a minute." He turned his head to the side and closed his eyes.

She crossed over to the sofa and sat. This wasn't the first time Nicholas had randomly shut down a conversation to think or pray or whatever he did, so she had learned to wait.

But really, what was his dilemma?

Considering the sensitive nature of the orphans' backgrounds, Nicholas was fastidious in hiring staff. Not just anyone could be trusted to treat the offspring of prostitutes well, to help them when they spit in a person's face, to enforce rules when they retaliated, and to do what was best for the children instead of themselves.

Though her own sister-in-law and brother were proving themselves to be terrible at half of those things—in fact, she wasn't doing that well herself—that didn't mean they should hire someone who'd only make matters worse.

"I want to give him a chance." Nicholas looked up and scanned the room to find where she'd taken a seat. "Consider him like John Mark."

"Who's John Mark?" And why did that matter anyway? It was what Aaron had done and what he would do that mattered.

"He's in the Bible."

"Oh." It definitely sounded like a Bible name, but . . . "Who's he again?"

"A man Paul didn't trust after he'd failed him on one of his missionary journeys. Barnabas thought Paul should allow John Mark to accompany him again—figured he needed another chance to prove himself." Nicholas walked to the chair next to the couch and sat beside her. "I know you won't like it, but I'm willing to be Aaron's Barnabas and let him have a chance. On the way over, he told me how Harrison and a reverend friend of his in California affected his life. Though he didn't go into his entire life story, I certainly sense he wants to start anew."

Words? Words were enough to erase the years of agony he'd put countless children through? "You only think he deserves a second chance because you aren't well acquainted with what he did."

"And you don't think he deserves one because you are too well acquainted." He sighed and rubbed his forehead. "Do you believe you'll be in physical danger?"

Aaron had picked up her papers yesterday, left when she'd asked him to . . . One day's worth of actions wasn't enough to base anything on, but even at his boyhood worst, he hadn't physically accosted any girls. "I don't think so, but that doesn't mean I won't be. But if you were asking me if anyone was in danger of being made to feel absolutely awful, that's a different story."

"Look. I understand why it would be difficult to be on good terms with Aaron, but I'm not asking you to befriend him." He put a hand on her shoulder. "My staff won't look the other way if they see him treat a child unkindly. And Max and Robert are old enough and self-assured enough to come tell me if something's wrong."

"And what about the other boys?" She twisted the folds of her skirt. "Did you not say he's to be the gardener?"

"Yes, he'll work the grounds while the children are in school, but they needn't go near him if they don't want to. I wouldn't mind letting him help with Jimmy though, considering the trouble you've been having with the boy. Once school's out, Jimmy will be here for far more hours, and with your brother's bank job, perhaps Aaron is exactly what we need."

Right, because what a bully needs is a grown-up bully to guide him.

"But, Mercy, if he does something worth being fired for, I won't hesitate to fire him. A bad past can certainly be indicative of a less-than-stellar future, but it's not proof of it."

She gritted her teeth and forced herself not to narrow her eyes at him, like Jimmy did when he didn't get his way.

"Are you all right?"

No, but it seemed her feelings didn't matter. "I don't think my brother will be keen on your hiring my old tormentor."

He nodded as if he understood. "I'll talk to Timothy, then."

Good. Maybe Timothy would convince him this wasn't a good

idea. Though her brother was much older, he'd been home from work a handful of times when she'd returned from school crying on days when Aaron had been especially mean.

And yet, Timothy didn't get along with Jimmy and might be thrilled that Nicholas wanted Aaron to take him in hand.

"Is there something more you'd like to discuss?"

She glanced up. Nicholas's eyes were soft with concern, and yet the rest of his face was stiff and no-nonsense, so she shook her head.

"Good." Nicholas gave her a tentative smile. "I hope you know I wouldn't do anything to put the orphans, you, or the rest of the staff in danger. But there are plenty of people here to watch Mr. Firebrook. When I introduce him to Max and Robert, I'll pay attention to how they respond to him." He patted her shoulder, then rose and left.

Mercy closed her eyes. *How am I supposed to live with Aaron across the yard? I know I've told people I'm a stronger person for having been bullied, but that doesn't mean I welcome the trial back!*

She got up and followed Nicholas out, though instead of heading to the music room, where she heard young male voices, she turned up the stairs. She'd make sure Owen had returned to his room and see if she could get Jimmy to help clean. Hopefully he wouldn't blow up at her, because right now, she'd probably blow up right back.

Aaron had been in town less than a week and already he was causing strife.

She let her hand drag on the railing as she forced her way upstairs.

The silver lining—where was the silver lining?

School.

She'd been unsure of how to inform any other districts Aaron applied to about his past, but now she'd have no such need. Once he showed his true colors, Nicholas would become his reference, and a bad reference from one of the county's richest men would hold more sway than her word—as evidenced by Nicholas ignoring her concerns just now.

She'd have to keep a constant eye on Aaron so he'd not hurt anyone more than what it took to get him fired.

But if Nicholas was right and Aaron had changed?

She'd believe it when she saw it.

5

"Mr. Firebrook?"

Aaron looked up from his efforts to re-explain a multi-step word problem to Robert. Max's dark, serious brow would have made Aaron think he was kin to Mr. Lowe if he didn't already know the boy was an orphan.

The seventeen-year-old frowned, put his paper on the desk in front of Aaron, and pointed at the second problem. "I think you marked this wrong." He ran his finger down columns of numbers in the margin. "I did it three times and got the same answer. I think you missed that this exponent is a negative one half."

Aaron pulled the paper toward himself. Max was the reason he'd been hired to tutor, but what had Mr. Lowe been thinking? The boy didn't need a tutor to challenge him. He was plenty good at challenging himself. He scanned Max's calculations. "I believe you're right." The young man wasn't beyond him in knowledge—he was just better than him. He'd feel more comfortable being Max's classmate than his tutor. "Did you rework the other one?"

"Yes, but I got that wrong. Careless mistake."

"Good." He looked at the clock and frowned. Forty-five minutes and Max was finished, yet his brother was still struggling with basic math processes he should've already mastered. "You've done all I've prepared for you. Why don't you see what the McClains would have you do?"

Max left, and Robert slumped over the table, pushing back his light brown hair. "I hate math."

Aaron gave the fifteen-year-old's shoulder a couple encouraging thumps with his fist. "If we can get you to understand a few properties—"

"I'd not even be doing this if it weren't for Max, you know." He groaned. "All I need to know is the basics to get a job. But Mr. Lowe won't let us stay here unless we go to school, and I can't mess this up for Max."

Though he'd only known the boys for a couple days, Aaron couldn't help but smile over how willing they were to sacrifice for each other. Would he have tried harder in school if he'd had someone depending on him? Or maybe it was a good thing he'd never had siblings—he couldn't imagine how much more guilt he'd be feeling if he'd ruined their lives. "The schools in Boston will likely have a wider variety of math classes to choose from."

Robert glanced toward the empty doorway, then back at him. "Max might love school so much he wants to attend a university that supposedly has the best math classes in the world, but I'm going to get a job instead."

Aaron nodded slightly. Who was he to tell the boy what to do after knowing him for less than a week? And Robert could get a job easily enough. Since the brothers cared a great deal for each other, surely Max would keep him from taking a terrible one.

"Though Mr. Lowe is going to fund Max's schooling, we can't take his charity forever. So I'll make money, and Max can get his degree. After he graduates, he can pay me back." Robert winked. "And I'll find me a girl too, make working all day worth it."

Aaron smiled. Thankfully the stresses of schoolwork hadn't completely depressed Robert's spirits. "Hope you do."

"You won't tell the Lowes, will you?"

"I figure you and Max can decide what's best for you when you get to Boston. But don't be afraid to change your mind.

School gives you an advantage over others, so . . ." He tapped his finger on Robert's paper. "Let's figure out when this train arrives in Atlanta."

"Stupid trains. They'll get there when they get there." Robert sighed and went back to scribbling with his stub of a pencil.

Watching Robert work and redirecting him when he got off track, Aaron stretched his arms and legs as he'd done a dozen times already, but it seemed the aches from constant mowing might plague him for weeks.

But at least he was doing something worth his salary. Though he'd been hired to challenge Max, if it wasn't for Robert and the grounds work, he'd feel like a highwayman come payday.

"Is Max finished already?" Cook came bustling in with something smelling of oven-kissed brown sugar. Her dark curls framed a round face that sat atop an even rounder body.

"I'm afraid so." He was going to have to put a lot more thought into these tutoring sessions if he was going to keep Max engaged for an entire hour.

"I'll try harder to get something baked earlier tomorrow, then." She slid the goodies in front of them. "Do you know where he went?"

Robert snatched the top cookie.

Aaron shook his head and gave Robert a glare. "Math first."

The boy sighed, tossed the cookie back on the pile, and picked up his pencil.

Aaron turned to Cook, only to find her glaring at him. "Robert just has two more questions—he won't starve. And no, I'm not sure where Max went."

Cook sized him up, then took two cookies and bustled out.

Aaron leaned back and closed his eyes, mentally counting the staff. So many people for so few children. Mr. Lowe had told him they'd had up to eighteen orphans at one time, but his boss didn't seem at all concerned he was spending so much on so few right now.

Oh for that much money.

Once Robert finished, grabbed his cookies, and left, Aaron

headed out. The mansion was grander than any building he'd ever been in. He'd not received a tour and was only inside to tutor and get his meals, so it would likely be months before a new detail or interesting piece of furniture wouldn't take him by surprise.

While trying to find his way to the conservatory he'd been told was at the back of the house, the hair on the back of his neck prickled. He slowed and looked over his shoulder but saw no one.

Likely Mercy watching from somewhere. He'd caught her studying him from afar several times the last couple days. Twice after hearing a noise outside the music room, where he tutored, she had come in shortly after, acting as if she had reason to be there but leaving with nothing more than what she'd brought in.

How many times had she been watching him when he hadn't noticed?

He would be flattered by any other woman as pretty as she was taking secret glances at him, but her glances were full of suspicion and mistrust—they'd never turn romantic.

A woman like her would never have romantic thoughts about a man like him. Not only was she beautiful, but as a child she'd always been kind, dependable, and bright—and it looked as if nothing had changed.

At the end of the high-ceilinged hallway, Owen, the youngest orphan, slid across the polished floor in his socks. The five-year-old used the wall to stop himself and laughed, but the second he saw Aaron, he scrambled back across the slick floor and disappeared into another room.

Aaron frowned. What had he done to scare him? "Wait."

He jogged after Owen and watched him slip under the desk in the study. Aaron ran his fingertips through his beard. Robert had tried to introduce them yesterday when the young boy had run into the music room, but Owen had left the second he spotted him—like he did today. Aaron wanted to do whatever he could to help these orphans, but he could hardly help a boy who wouldn't get within ten feet of him.

He slowly made his way over to the desk chair and pulled it out to sit. When his leg brushed against the boy, he pushed the chair back to look under the desk. "I'm sorry. What're you doing under there?"

The boy was a handsome little fellow with those golden-blond brows puckered above his big blue eyes. His pupils were so wide with fright, his irises were barely visible. "Miss McClain said I shouldn't talk to strangers or anyone I don't want to."

"She's right." He backed away a little farther. "But the staff aren't strangers. You don't have to talk to me, but I at least want you to know who I am. My name's Mr. Firebrook, and I'll be outside most of the time cutting grass. Do you like being outside?"

The boy only swallowed.

He'd better leave before the boy started to tremble. "Well, if you do, I saw a wagon in a pile of junk in the carriage house. Would you want me to wash it up for you?"

The boy's legs pushed him farther into the corner.

Aaron forced on a bright, cheery smile, pretending Owen hadn't looked at him as if he'd swallow him whole. Surely Mercy wasn't filling the five-year-old's head with terrible stories about him to frighten him away. "You let me know if you do, all right?" He stood and patted the desk, hoping that would somehow reassure the boy, before he headed toward the dining room. The conservatory was supposed to be to its south.

"Mr. Firebrook?"

He turned to see Mercy's much older brother, Timothy Mc-Clain, coming across the dining room, perhaps from the kitchen entrance.

The man's blond hair and the way the skin around his eyes crinkled made him look so much like Mercy that Aaron was surprised they were only half-siblings. He'd seen the other man arrive late yesterday while he'd been putting away his mowing machine for the night, but they'd yet to be introduced.

The man smiled as he approached, then held out his hand. Timothy's handshake was firm, but when he tried to twist it so his hand was on top in a dominant sort of gesture, Aaron resisted, keeping his arm rigid and immovable.

Timothy stepped back with a stiffer smile. "My sister and Mr. Lowe informed me you'd started working here."

"Yes." Which made him doubt Timothy's smile was genuine. Mercy wouldn't have kept his background a secret from her brother, so why had Timothy waited two days to talk to him?

"Well . . ." The man eyed him, his green eyes a muddy hazel compared with Mercy's brighter ones, and a bit more . . . unbalanced? Maybe the look stemmed from the man forcing himself not to haul his sister's former tormentor out of the building. "I came home to get something and heard you were in here. Mr. Lowe mentioned you'd be willing to work with Jimmy this summer."

Seemed Timothy hadn't been thinking about tossing him out on Mercy's behalf after all. "Yes."

"Good." The man blew out a breath and smiled again. "Why don't you start taking over now? It's only a month until summer, and I've been busy, so I'm sure the women wouldn't mind if you start—" he waved his hand in front of himself as if trying to decide on a word—"taking over his discipline."

Somehow he bet Mercy would mind. "All right."

"Great." And with that, Timothy headed toward the hallway, his dress shoes rat-a-tat-tatting across the polished floor.

Aaron rubbed the back of his neck. Had Mercy not told her brother how he'd treated her?

Of course, Timothy needn't worry he'd treat her like that again, but Mercy's reaction to his reappearance made more sense than her brother's.

Regardless, it seemed he had even more work to do, but if all the flowering things started dying, he might lose this job. He had scythed and pulled around the mower every spare hour since his arrival to get the neglected lawn under control, but he'd fallen asleep before he'd read more than a few pages of a gardening book he found in his cabin.

Once inside the conservatory, he frowned at the neglected plants and crossed over to look inside a crate. Perhaps he could find tools or . . . something to give him an idea of how to tend these plants. He started looking through the shelving when a scuffling near the interior door made him freeze. He stepped back into a dark corner and the slight scuffling sound stopped. Just as he was about to reprimand himself for being suspicious of skittering mice, Mercy walked into the room and headed for the wall of windows.

She scanned the backyard, then furrowed her brow.

"Looking for something?"

She startled, and her neck turned red as she turned toward him with her hand pressed hard against her chest. "I was, I guess. But I can't seem to think of what now."

Somehow he didn't quite believe her.

She turned away, suddenly fascinated with something outside. "I'm sure it had something to do with the children however." She cleared her throat, still not looking at him. "Have you seen Jimmy?"

"Haven't met him yet." He took a step toward her, hoping she'd turn to look at him. "I know you're worried about how I'll treat the children, but I want to assure you, I will not treat Jimmy or the others as I did you."

Her throat worked overtime as she continued to stare outside at whatever was fascinating her—though perhaps she wasn't looking at anything at all. The silence grew longer, but he forced himself not to disturb it.

"Do you remember when you tripped me and I fell into that mud puddle and everyone laughed at me?" Mercy's voice was whisper soft, yet it cut like a knife.

He nodded. He'd not only tripped her but had called her several of the new names he'd come up with the night before, along with throwing mud at her while she was down.

Her family had moved away from Teaville soon afterward. He'd actually felt a twinge of remorse back then about that.

Mercy wrapped her arms around herself, still staring out the window. "The night before, the doctor had told us my mother wouldn't survive unless we moved to a big city and spent money we didn't have on specialty doctors—though there was no guarantee she'd live even then."

His body turned cold despite the humid heat of the room.

He rubbed a hand down his face, slowly searching for something to say—but what? Did he even deserve her forgiveness?

No. He didn't. There was nothing he could do to take back his cruel actions. All he could offer was restitution.

Seeing her lips tremble, he could imagine the memories he'd just made her relive. "I take it the doctors couldn't help?"

She shrugged. "We'll never know. My parents died when their carriage flipped over hardly a week after we moved to Kansas City." She stepped toward him, a sudden anger dancing in her eyes. "And because of you, my brother and I decided not to return to Teaville. I missed the comfort of friends and extended family, plus the last years of my grandparents' lives, because of you. And nothing you can do will make up for that." She stormed past him and back into the mansion.

How could he promise never to hurt her again when his very presence upset her?

And she was right. There was nothing he could do to erase the pain from their childhoods.

6

Aaron stared out over the mansion's massive tiered garden, surveying the smattering of blooming flowers, some white, others in variations of red. Bushes grew in neat rows along stone walls with attractive arches and benches scattered throughout. Now that Robert had finished his lessons for the day, it was time to tackle the garden.

The big bad bully in charge of rose petals and tulips.

God certainly had a sense of humor.

At the spigot, Aaron unwound the heavy rubber hose and headed for the first row of vegetation. What were these plants anyway? Did they all flower? The illustrations in the first book he'd started reading were nothing but black woodcuts. Hopefully there was a book with better drawings on his shelf to help him identify these plants.

He stopped at a knee-high bush with flower buds so large they hung their heads in shame. The white of the petals could be seen compacted under the green leaf parts that kept the flower from bursting open, their thick, sweet scent already heavy in the air. But the plant was overrun with ants. The flowers likely wouldn't survive long enough to bloom if he didn't do something.

He headed back to the spigot, spun it a touch, and returned

to the bush. He stooped down, cupped one of the insect-infested flower buds, and started washing it off. He looked at the next bush and sighed at the number of ants. He could get them off, but could he keep them off? He stomped on the ants escaping into the deeper grass.

"What are you doing?"

He looked up to see a boy who'd only ever eyed him from a distance since he'd started working here. The boy's face was as smooth as a stone, but the rest of his body was rather awkwardly trying to achieve manhood. Had to be Jimmy.

"I said, what're you doing?" The boy's arms were crossed as he glared down at him.

Aaron stood. Seemed he needed to start this mentoring thing right away. They'd begin with a lesson on how to introduce oneself. He pulled his gloves off to shake the boy's hand. "It's nice to finally meet you, Jimmy—"

"Are you going to answer me?" The boy kept his arms crossed.

Had he once been this annoyingly belligerent?

He gestured toward the plants beside them. "Do you see the ants?"

The boy's arms stayed locked like steel cables across his chest. "Just because I'm an orphan doesn't make me blind."

"Right." Seemed this mentoring thing might be harder than he'd thought. "I only meant to point out that I'm taking the ants off."

"Oh, for the . . ." The boy rolled his eyes, then looked at Aaron as if he were stupid. "I thought the Lowes hired a gardener."

Aaron's hands fisted of their own accord, an old habit he hadn't quite quelled when anyone looked at him like that. He forced his hands to open and flex. "I *am* the gardener."

Jimmy looked him up and down, his eyebrows rising as if Aaron had claimed to be President Taft. "That's hard to believe."

Did this boy know something about gardening he didn't?

Though he didn't want to appear ignorant, he actually was. "Whose job would it be to save the plants from insects, but the gardener's?"

"A stupid gardener's, maybe?" The corner of the boy's lips turned up into a smirk. "That plant needs the ants."

It was Aaron's turn to raise his brow, as if questioning the boy's intellect. Everyone knew bugs were bad for plants. "And how do you know?"

He shrugged. "Because there's bunches of those where I used to live. No one bothered to take the ants off, and they came out just fine."

"Are you sure?" He looked down at the bush.

Jimmy only rolled his eyes. "More than you are."

The boy's drawl was so condescending Aaron had to grit his teeth to keep from loosing one of the many put-downs he'd used when he was Jimmy's age. "You don't have to be smart-mouthed about it." If only he didn't have to read hundreds of pages to find out whether the boy was right or not.

"What do you want me to be, then—*dumb-mouthed*?" Jimmy sneered, though maybe that was supposed to be a smile. "My smart mouth stopped you from ruining the flowers."

Aaron rubbed the back of his neck. As a child, if he'd felt needed, useful, or wanted, maybe he wouldn't have put so much time in being smart-mouthed himself. "If you're so smart, I could use you."

The boy threw up his chin. "How's that?"

"I could use your help figuring out what to do with—"

"You think I'm going to do your work for you?" How many haughty faces could this boy pull? "If so, you've lost your dog-gone mind."

"Fine." Aaron hefted the hose and walked off. "Guess I'll hire someone else to advise me."

"Hire?" Jimmy's voice cracked a bit.

Thankfully Aaron's back was turned, allowing him to wipe off his grin before turning around. "Well, maybe you wouldn't do. It requires a lot of reading, and I can tell you aren't the kind to read."

"What do you mean, I ain't the kind to read?" Jimmy looked him up and down, as if sizing him up.

Hopefully challenging him would work and not drive him away. "Just meant it'd probably be too hard for you. You wouldn't understand it well enough to be worth paying."

"How much?"

Money might not be the wisest way to get on this kid's good side, but it seemed it'd be a quick one. "Seventy cents a week until all the books are read and you've identified everything in the garden along with writing down instructions for all the plants. You'll need to give me something each week worth paying you for though. If it's done terribly, I'll only pay you thirty cents and then you're fired."

The boy tilted his chin. "A dollar a week."

He cringed. Seventy cents was already costly, but it would be worth it if he could avoid reading and could start off on Jimmy's good side. Plus, the boy would run out of books at some point. He shook his head as if rethinking the whole deal—which he was, sort of. *Ah, might as well.* "You better be worth the dollar. You want the books?"

Jimmy shrugged as if he didn't care—but he cared about that dollar, sure enough.

Aaron pointed toward his cabin. "Let's get them."

They started up the lawn, and on the mansion's porch, Mercy stood watching them, her soft green gown fluttering about her.

Was she no longer bothering to hide while spying on him?

He led Jimmy to his cabin, forcing himself not to look back at Mercy. Hopefully she'd watch as often as she liked and see that he'd changed—or at least realize she didn't need to stand over him like a hawk.

He opened his cabin's door and preceded Jimmy into his barebones parlor. He pulled open the curtains, in case Mercy wanted to glance in, and headed for the bookshelves. He gathered the books the gardener had left and handed them to Jimmy.

The poor boy's eyes widened at the height of the stack. His face turned a little stormy.

How could he keep Jimmy from backing out? "Maybe it's too much for someone your age? I should probably ask Max or Robert."

That barb stuffed the haughtiness right back into the boy. "No, I can do it. I'm just not sure I trust you to pay."

Aaron pulled out a piece of paper and wrote out their agreement. How might his life have turned out better if an adult had followed through with what he or she had promised him—or at least done as they ought? "Here." He pushed the paper across the table. "If you agree, I'll sign it."

Jimmy quickly read it and nodded.

"Good." Aaron signed his name and placed it atop the stack of books. "I hope your work impresses me."

Jimmy narrowed his eyes. "I don't exactly have the nicest penmanship."

He shrugged. "As long as I can read it. Start with instructions for roses."

"All right." Jimmy turned for the door.

A corner of Mercy's skirt fluttered into the doorway, the wind betraying her position.

Aaron quickly followed Jimmy out and grabbed her by the upper arm. She squeaked.

"Eavesdropping?"

Mercy pulled from his grasp. "Part of my job is to make sure you're not mistreating children."

"Of course, mama hen, but you don't have to sneak around to do so."

She narrowed her eyes.

Seemed teasing her even a little was a misstep.

Mercy shook her head. "If you knew when you were being watched, you'd act differently."

He couldn't help but smile. Seemed Jimmy might have learned his stubbornness from somewhere other than his past. "Mercy—"

Her eyes narrowed more. "Miss McClain."

"Yes, of course. Forgive me, Miss McClain." He swallowed his smile. He didn't want her to think he was belittling her feelings. Her wariness was indeed merited.

"What are you doing with Jimmy?" She peered past him into

the cabin, as if she could figure that out by seeing inside. "He's not your responsibility."

"Actually, your brother asked me to start working with him. I decided having him help in the garden might be a good way for him to learn self-control and earn some well-deserved pride."

"What?" Her green eyes lost their sparkle.

Was she questioning what he was doing or why he was doing it? "If someone had shown an interest in me, given me a job to do, and a chance to earn a little money, I would've—"

"No, I mean my brother." She shook her head and backed up as if confused. "He asked you to watch over one of the orphans?"

"Yes." He wouldn't bother to tell her it was also the only time Timothy had bothered to talk to him at all. It must feel like a betrayal to have her brother already trust him when she felt so strongly he shouldn't be alone with children. "I truly am sorry about how I treated you when we were growing up. I wouldn't have—"

"Don't bother making excuses." She held up her hand and took another step away, her face hardening. "No reason could excuse your merciless taunting."

He wouldn't tell anyone but God about the darkness of his childhood, even if it might gain him sympathy. He would've kept it from God himself, if possible. "I . . . I agree. There really isn't a satisfying reason."

He'd taken solace, though, in the fact that the reverend in California had insisted no one was entirely good, even if one had lived a better life than another. No matter how good someone was, they didn't live up to God's standard, but thankfully, everyone could be forgiven. "I know that what caused me to bully others doesn't justify my past behavior. But I promise, I don't want to hurt people anymore."

"See that you don't." Her lips trembled enough that her hard expression failed to sting.

"I won't, and I welcome you to follow me around, but there's no need to hide. If you get to know me, I think you'll trust the new me." It would take her far longer than it did her brother, but to be honest, he wouldn't mind having her beside him all day long. What man would? He closed his eyes and shook his head. What was he thinking? A working relationship where neither of them had to walk on eggshells was all he could hope for. "You don't happen to know anything about roses, do you? Jimmy's planning to help me by reading some books, but I'm—"

"I don't think"—something in her expression indicated she was having an argument with herself—"that it'd be wise for me to spend time with you."

He knew people from his past would likely want nothing to do with him, but for some reason, having Mercy refuse to give him a chance made his insides feel like lead. "Without time together, how can I earn your trust, if not your forgiveness?"

She only shook her head as she took a step back and turned away.

As she headed back to the mansion, he pulled out the worn list from his shirt pocket and rubbed his finger over her name. If there was nothing he could do to earn her forgiveness, should he scratch her name off? Was there anything he could do to come close to making up for what he'd done?

He was probably lucky anybody had answered his requests to make restitution. He pulled out Iris's letter and reread it. She'd made a request he didn't want to fulfill, shouldn't even, but how could he not attempt to do something to make up for how badly he'd belittled her?

Mercy had been a good-looking girl and had grown even more beautiful. But little about Iris as a schoolgirl had indicated she'd grow out of the gangly figure and awkward personality he'd tormented her about.

For if those days of torment were behind her, she would not have asked him for something so drastic.

7

Aaron slowed the pony cart that sagged under his weight and stopped on the side of Willow Street.

He retrieved Iris Baymont's letter and looked around. This couldn't be the right place. Nothing but soda fountains here . . . if the signs were to be believed. But true soda fountains wouldn't be this quiet around the lunch hour.

Maybe he hadn't heard the postman right.

The mailman hadn't known of an Iris Baymont on Willow, just the Baymonts on Second. But the man had suggested he check south of Eleventh.

Aaron blew out a breath and shook his head. Willow stretched from the far north side of town to the far south. He couldn't knock on every door.

He double-checked to make sure Iris hadn't written anything more about her whereabouts, then reread the last paragraph, which he could practically recite.

If you want to do something, then come take my son. I doubt you've grown up to be the sort of man who'd make a good parent, but you have to be better than me. So if you truly want to make up for what you put me through, come get him.

No mother with small children would live in this section of town. Was it possible she lived in a run-down apartment above a saloon? If she was desperate enough to contemplate handing over her child to him, then perhaps living in this part of town was only one in a long line of poor decisions. He'd reread this letter for months now. Such a bizarre request . . . but what if this child was in danger and he did nothing?

He surely wasn't the right person to help, but if she was crazy enough to think it a good idea to give him her son, the boy likely needed someone to step in. If his mother didn't want her child, why hadn't she taken him to the orphanage? Why offer the boy to him?

He couldn't help at all if he couldn't find her. He scanned the street again. It'd be easier to go to the Baymonts' old house, since that's where the mail carrier had delivered the first letter. Iris's sister, Ivy, had returned her letter unopened, a mean-spirited message scrawled across the back, so someone was living there, be it Ivy or her parents.

He flicked the reins. "Come on . . . you . . . pony." How could he call himself a man and holler "Giddap" to a creamy pony named Buttercup? It was bad enough he had to drive a pony instead of a horse.

Starting off down the street, Aaron uncurled his fists. He'd not be beating up anyone ever again—whether they made fun of him for driving a pony or not. With purposeful deep breaths, he kept his eyes glued to Buttercup's rump so he'd not see any amused glances from passersby.

He should've walked.

Off Maple, he turned onto Second. The neighborhood was full of kept lawns, window boxes, and a stillness that contrasted with his heartbeat's slow crescendo as he got closer to the little white house at the end of the street.

Was he only kidding himself to believe this quest for forgiveness was for anyone's good but his own?

Ivy had made it clear she didn't want to see him again. He'd disturbed Mercy's schedule since she was trying to keep an eye on him. Tutoring for less than a month would not be enough to make up for what he'd done to Fred. And though he'd paid Jason Montgomery a hundred dollars, as requested, it likely hadn't made Jason feel any better about the past than it did him.

And Iris's request? He could fulfill it, but it would just be . . . wrong.

Perhaps he should simply live the rest of his life drowning in all of the shame and guilt he deserved.

Aaron stopped across from the Baymonts' house. A set of wind chimes sounding from somewhere down the street felt too light and cheery to accompany him on his walk to the house.

But it was a walk he would take. For he had to chug along and do what he could—he'd feel worse if he did nothing. It might be hard, but it was right.

He wiped his sweaty hands on his trousers as he walked toward the house. If Ivy answered, hopefully she'd tell him where Iris was before she slammed the door in his face.

Please let their mother answer so I can comply with Ivy's request to never contact her again.

He knocked and stepped back.

A few moments later, a woman with a worn apron, thick glasses, and mussed hair answered. Her eyebrows lowered as if she was trying to figure out who he was, or maybe the thick glasses weren't helping much.

If she had gapped teeth, she'd look exactly like what he'd have expected a grown-up Iris would look like with glasses. But she didn't smile, just stared.

"Iris Baymont?"

She shook her head, her expression turning wary. "Who's asking?"

"Aaron Firebrook, though I went by George years ago." The first thing he'd done when he left Teaville was shuck that name forever. A cruel name in light of what he'd endured. Too bad he had to keep mentioning it.

The woman stiffened, and the broomstick in her right hand

crossed in front of her until the top was gripped firmly in her left. "Did you not get your letter back? What I wrote on that envelope should've made it clear I didn't want you showing up at my front door. Michael!" She hollered over her shoulder. "Get down here! I need you to escort someone off our property."

Aaron put his hands up, hoping he looked non-confrontational. "Ivy, then." The sisters had looked nearly identical, but Ivy'd had crossed eyes. The thick glasses must've helped uncross them.

She stood glaring at him, broomstick at the ready.

"I'm here because of your sister." He didn't deserve civil conversation—he wouldn't even flinch if the woman cussed him out—but he needed to find Iris. "I know I don't deserve your cooperation, but your sister answered my letter, and I'd like to talk to her."

Ivy's eyes got harder, if that were possible. "She's dead."

His heart plummeted. *Dead?* "I'm so sorry." He'd planned to convince Iris to give her child to a relative, but perhaps that wouldn't be necessary. "I assume you've been given custody of her son, then?"

"No. Don't want him anywhere near our young'uns, considering his origins." She looked as if she was barely containing the urge to spit.

His heart dropped further. His plan of convincing Iris to give her son to family didn't sound so smart now, but maybe everything was already taken care of. "Who has him, then?"

She shrugged. "We told the cops to drop him off at the Lowes' mansion. They take the likes of him."

The Lowes? Had the child already been adopted out? "How long ago did she die?"

"Last month sometime. Don't remember exactly when I was called in to identify her. A john roughed her up."

"Her husband beat her to death?" Hopefully the torment she'd suffered at Aaron's hands hadn't been the reason she'd stayed with a man who physically abused her.

The eyes behind Ivy's glasses grew round. "Are you stupid?"

That made him blink. He might be, but what had he said to make her think so?

"I said, '*a* john.' She was an upstairs girl."

An upstairs girl? He pulled out his letter. Had he missed something? "But she has a son."

"Yes. And your point is?" She called over her shoulder, "Michael!"

"Wait." He held out his hand.

She tightened her grip on the broomstick.

Wrong thing to do. He brought his hand back. "You said the boy was taken to the mansion a month ago? What was his name?"

Her lip curled a bit. "Owen, after our father. Iris ruined a perfectly good name on him."

Owen? His heartbeat went up. "Is he blond? Five years old?"

"Likely."

This whole time Iris's son had been right in front of him!

A dark-headed man just large enough to be intimidating came up behind Ivy. He shoved her behind him and opened the door wider. His hair was tousled, his nose red with illness, but his eyes were serious and his voice rattled out, "You wanting trouble?"

Aaron held up his hands again. "No trouble. I only came to town in hopes of apologizing to the people I once treated poorly." He looked to Ivy. She hadn't even read his letter. "Is there anything I can do to earn your forgiveness?"

"Get off my property, then follow that up with never coming back."

Michael jerked his chin in the direction of the street. "If I see you anywhere near her, I'll break your neck." The man kept his glassy eyes locked on him until Aaron stepped back. The door slammed a moment later.

Aaron winced as the impact ricocheted through the quiet neighborhood. He'd known he'd feel like scum when facing the men and women he'd hurt—even believed he ought to feel like scum. But how much more would he have to endure?

He returned to his pony cart, blinking repeatedly as he walked, since the world had grown fuzzy.

Iris had intended to give him Owen, a shy little five-year-old. He deserved to raise a hellion like Jimmy.

He'd never expected to marry, so he'd never given the idea of raising a child a thought—at least not until he'd received Iris's letter, but he'd hoped to talk her out of it.

But how could he go back to the mansion and do nothing for Owen? To let Iris's only request of him be sloughed off onto others?

The boy had already been there for a month . . . and no one had adopted him.

When making his plans to return to Teaville, working as a gardener at an orphanage was the last thing he would've considered doing. After failing to get the teaching job and with Mercy shutting him out, he'd begun to wonder whether he should've bothered coming back at all.

But it seemed God had put him here for a reason.

Oh, God, I'm so worthless. I know you've forgiven me, but I don't know why you'd choose me for something like this. I can see you've put me here, so I pray you'll help me do what you want me to do.

Somehow Buttercup got him home, though he hardly remembered the drive. Once he made it into the carriage house, he was surprised to see Mr. Lowe's driver dithering about.

"Is Mr. Lowe here?"

The old man's white-haired head popped up. "He is. Told me he'd be about an hour."

"Great." But his nerves belied his response. Should he truly ask for custody of Owen? Wouldn't whatever parents the Lowes found for the boy be better than him?

With Owen's quiet demeanor, dimples, and big blue eyes, someone good would surely adopt him.

Aaron left the carriage house and pulled Iris's letter from his pocket. If he read between the lines, she'd blamed him for how her life turned out. Did that mean he was also the reason she was dead?

He stopped walking and swallowed. What kind of pressures had Iris been under to make her want to give up her son? Had anyone offered to help her? Clearly her own sister hadn't. Would he have offered a soiled dove his support if guilt wasn't threatening to bury him and he'd not been asked outright?

He had to try to fulfill her wish. If he got to see her in heaven, he wanted to let her know he'd done his best to make up for how he'd treated her.

Once inside, he turned left down the hallway, vaguely remembering the office being next to the enclosed stairwell. The door was shut and had no placard, but since the other entrance was the pantry, this had to be it. He rapped on the beveled wood panels.

"Come in."

He opened the door but stopped short at the sight of Mercy standing beside Mr. Lowe's desk.

She likely wouldn't encourage their boss to grant this request. And with how his insides quaked at the thought, he didn't need a deterrent.

Or maybe that meant he shouldn't ask.

If he wasn't doing this to right his wrongs, he wouldn't think it a great idea either. But then, the reverend had told him he was a new creation, a new man. Didn't God ask His children to sacrifice for and love the least of these? "Am I interrupting something?"

"No." Mr. Lowe gestured toward the couch.

Aaron considered the dainty piece of furniture. It was too fragile for an oaf like him. He fingered the worn letter in his hand, but Mercy didn't seem inclined to leave.

He could ask for a private audience, but she'd find out what he was about at some point. Besides, she was more likely to listen to the entire story with Mr. Lowe present than not. "I received a letter from a Miss Baymont before I returned to Kansas." He swallowed hard. If he kept going, he'd be committing himself to this for . . . forever. He closed his eyes and drew in a breath. "I knew God forgave me my past, but that didn't help the people I'd wronged, and Miss Baymont was one of them. I'd started going down a list, writing each one, asking what I could do to earn their forgiveness. Most haven't answered, but she sent me the strangest letter, telling me if I wanted to help, I needed to come take her son."

Mercy's eyebrows went up, but she still stood beside Mr. Lowe's desk with her arms crossed over her middle.

"I, of course, thought only a woman out of her mind would ask that, but I never got an answer to the letter I sent back. Today, I found out she lived in the district and that she died last month."

Mr. Lowe sucked in air through his teeth.

"And that her boy is Owen." He stepped forward, opened the letter, and laid it in front of Mr. Lowe with a trembling hand. "Since Iris is dead, I'd like to fulfill her wish and look after the boy."

"You want to adopt him?" Mercy's tone was shrill.

He kept his face as placid as possible. This couldn't be easy for her, considering what she thought of him. It wasn't even easy for him to believe he was capable of guiding a young life. He knew how *not* to raise a child, but would that be enough?

But if God had changed Saul, a man who'd killed Christians, into the most influential saint of all, He could surely help Aaron figure out how to parent. He took in a big breath. "I do."

Mr. Lowe took the note, but Mercy started pacing, shaking her head. "You can't have him. We only give children to couples who've proven themselves, who are of good character and morals, who have experience raising children—"

"That's if there are no other claims, Mercy." Mr. Lowe's baritone interrupted her pacing. "And Owen was indeed Iris's boy. I'd not forget her name since it was so unusual."

Mercy fisted her hand and turned back toward Aaron. "You can't tell us you'd be better at raising him than an experienced mother and father."

He wanted to reach out and calm her, but touching her would likely only heighten her indignation. "I agree. A mother and father are best, but no one's banging down the door to adopt these children. I'll treat him well."

Mercy whirled toward their boss and leaned over his desk. "Didn't you hear Aaron say Iris couldn't be in her right mind to ask him such a thing? Aaron bullied Owen's mother, and I told you how he tormented me. So what would keep him from bullying Owen?"

She'd told Mr. Lowe how he'd treated her? Yet he hadn't fired him? He'd figured she'd kept his past a secret from Mr. Lowe for whatever reason she'd decided to keep it from the school board.

Mr. Lowe put up his hand. "Now, Mercy—"

"Excuse me." Aaron came up beside her. "I understand her misgivings. So, what if the boy remains under your guardianship until Miss McClain feels I've earned her trust in regard to how I will treat him?"

Mercy turned to look at him, frowning as if confused.

She might refuse to accept his apologies, but if he could get her to agree to this adoption, he would count her forgiveness as earned.

Mr. Lowe shook his head. "Her permission isn't needed. Besides, what happens if she never agrees? I can't hold on to the boy forever."

"We'll revisit that in, say, half a year?"

Mercy eyes went wide. "You'd wait six months?"

"Unless it's detrimental to Owen." If only he could take her hand and squeeze some trust into her. If only someone would take his hand and squeeze some confidence into him. "I could wait longer, if necessary, but only if you're still worried about my fitness as a guardian, not because the past is clouding your judgment. Can you be fair?"

Her face scrunched. She couldn't just announce she intended to be unfair, could she?

He turned back to Lowe. "Besides, I'd imagine it would be best for the boy to get to know me, hopefully even choose me on his own, to help him adjust." He wouldn't mind time to adjust himself.

"You have any problems with that, Mercy?" Lowe handed Aaron his letter.

"It's certainly more than I'd thought he'd . . ." She shrugged and turned her face away from both of them. "As you said, I'm not actually able to stop anything."

Lowe looked at her sympathetically. "He's got a point about letting Owen get to know his new guardian. Some of our past adoptions could've gone smoother if that had been possible."

"Right," she whispered.

Aaron put the note back in his breast pocket. "I'll do my best by him." Hopefully that would be enough, but surely he could give him better than what he'd had.

Mercy just shook her head, gave him a look, and left.

The silence was stark, but he took in a deep breath and gave his boss a nod. "Thank you, Mr. Lowe." Whatever this man saw in him, he was glad someone was giving him a chance.

"Good luck," his boss said, his eyes sparkling for some reason.

What could Lowe find entertaining about this situation?

"Excuse me." Aaron turned to follow Mercy out the door, in hopes she hadn't already disappeared.

She hadn't gotten far—only halfway to the music room.

He picked up his pace so he didn't have to yell. "I'm sorry if I messed up your meeting with Mr. Lowe. I'm finished."

She turned, her eyes piercing. "Are you going to withdraw your application from the school board?"

He scratched his head. "I figured I didn't have much chance of getting the job, but no."

"Why not?"

Why was she worried about that if she had the power to keep him from being hired? "That list of people I plan to ask for forgiveness? Well, it's quite the list. Do you remember Fred Hopper? When I asked what I could do to earn his forgiveness, he told me I should teach so I could learn to sympathize with children. I thought the idea absurd at first, but after I thought about it awhile, it didn't seem like such a bad idea. After all, I could be around to protect students from bullies like me. I might even be able to get through to bullies because I could understand them."

"And Owen?" She fidgeted as if she wanted to scream at him, but her question had been little more than a whisper.

70

"He's certainly in need of help." He stepped closer, glad she seemed willing to hear him out. "I know this will probably sound unbelievable, but when I was bullying people, I was very aware of what my victims wanted most. I just chose to use that knowledge against them. Whereas now, I want to use that knowledge for good."

She crossed her arms, looking him straight in the eyes, her throat working. "So what did I want most?"

His heart fluttered. Seemed he'd know right now whether or not he did indeed have the ability to read people. "You didn't want people defining you by your missing hand. You wanted to be thought of as Mercy first."

"And so you called me *stumpy* every day because . . . ?"

"Because I knew it would make you unhappy." What a horrible person he'd been.

Somehow she had the ability to keep looking at him. "And why was that your goal?"

Thankfully he hadn't been as readable as she was, for he'd rather no one find out the reason behind everything he'd done. "Because if I couldn't be happy, I didn't want anyone else to be."

"But you were more than unhappy. You were . . ."

"Evil?"

She cringed. "I'm not sure I'd call too many people evil, but you were definitely rotten, mean, and heartless."

He nodded and looked down. "Heartless is a good word for it, but not because I didn't have a heart, but because it was too painful to use at the time." He looked up at her. "But I want to use it now. Will you give me a chance?"

"Once again, Mr. Lowe is giving you one whether I would or not, but . . ." She licked her lips and sighed. "I'll try to be fair."

"Thank you." It wasn't forgiveness, but it was something. "I'm grateful for your mercy."

She gave him a sad smile and then turned away.

But his lungs expanded with optimism. God had made him a new creature in Christ, but he'd never held out much hope that anyone from his past would believe it—maybe he had a chance at having one person see he had indeed changed.

Please, God, don't fail me now. Not with Owen as my charge.

And if there's anything I can do to make Mercy happy, help me figure that out as well.

8

The mansion was too quiet. Or maybe it just seemed so after the lively discussions and laughter Mercy had enjoyed at this week's moral-society meeting. She hung her shawl on the entryway hall tree and listened for the sounds of children.

She headed down the hallway to look for her sister-in-law. No one was in the music room or parlor.

In the kitchen, Cook hummed as she rolled out a pastry crust.

"Do you know where everyone is?"

Smudging flour across her chubby face, Cook tucked a stray curl back into her cap. "I don't." She grabbed a towel and wiped her hands. "But I can help you look."

"Oh no, that's all right." Mercy held out her hand to stop her. "Are you sure?"

"Yes, but thank you." Not only did their new cook volunteer to help with things that weren't her responsibility, but Mercy had never eaten so well. She'd once thought Nicholas was incapable of hiring anyone but the best people in the world, but then he'd hired Aaron . . . and, well, her sister-in-law was likely not the best hiring decision he'd made either. Where was she?

Through the conservatory windows, she saw Max reading atop

one of the garden's stone walls. Down at the far end of the lawn, Robert was helping Owen climb a tree.

Jimmy was nowhere to be seen. Where would Patricia be if she wasn't with the three who tolerated her? If she were with Jimmy, their arguing would've clued Mercy in to their whereabouts by now.

She walked upstairs and found no one in the boys' room, but it was evident by the overflowing trash and nightclothes thrown about that Jimmy hadn't done his chores.

She knocked on her brother's bedroom door. "Patricia?"

"Come in."

She walked in and frowned at her sister-in-law lying in bed. "Are you all right?"

Patricia sighed and rolled over. "Just tired. Told the kids to leave me in peace."

She could understand the need for peace, but Patricia should at least be watching them rather than expecting the staff to do so. "Where's Jimmy?"

"As long as he isn't near me right now, I don't care." Patricia draped her arm over her eyes. "The names he called me this afternoon I shall not repeat!"

"I'm sorry. I know what kind of mouth he has." She'd been much more prepared for his unkindness than Patricia.

"I'd thought it'd be fun to raise these children since it seems we'll never have any of our own, but ugh!" She flopped her arm back down on the bed. "I hope we get a different batch soon."

A batch? That was how Patricia viewed the orphans? Was Timothy gone so much lately because he didn't want to be around them either?

Mercy didn't want to leave the orphanage, but if her brother and his wife treated these children as they treated her—as nothing more than a hardship to be borne—perhaps new directors would be best. "If this isn't what you'd hoped for, why not tell Timothy you'd prefer to go back to the way things were?"

"No, it's just . . ." Patricia fiddled with the pillow's ruffled edge, staring out the window. "I need to rest." She tucked the pillow under her head and closed her eyes. "I have a headache."

Mercy scanned Patricia's face, somehow doubting a woman with a headache could look that serene, then left, careful to keep the noise of the door's closing no louder than a soft click.

Downstairs in the library, Jimmy was sprawled on the leather couch, one leg hiked over the arm, as he snacked on crackers while reading.

"How many times have we told you not to eat anywhere but the dining room and kitchen?"

Jimmy only glanced at her before popping the rest of the cracker into his mouth.

Mercy crossed her arms. "You need to take the crackers back to the kitchen, then go upstairs and clean your room as you've been told."

"Can't." He turned a page of a book with a flower embossed on its cover. If he could read books for Aaron, he could certainly pick up.

Mercy gritted her teeth. Oftentimes, she tried not to push Jimmy—he was erratic, mean-spirited, and hurtful when backed into a corner—but the more she let things slide, the more likely she'd lose control. . . . Maybe she already had.

She had to regain power. "I told you to clean your room. You can return to your reading afterward."

Jimmy didn't even look at her, just turned a page.

"Jimmy." The deep voice behind Mercy startled them both.

Aaron stood in the doorway, his head nearly brushing the top of the doorframe. "Miss McClain told you to go upstairs and pick up. You will obey."

"I'm busy." Jimmy glared at Aaron as if he were stupid and waved his book in the air.

Aaron walked into the room and stopped beside her. "Robert and Max don't get hours at the glass factory unless their school-work and chores are finished. If you can't do so, you won't get paid for work either."

Jimmy's lips and jaw moved as if he were gathering up a whole bunch of words to spit, but then he just looked back down at his book.

"Jimmy," Aaron's voice growled low.

The boy gave him a side look, then tossed the book. "Fine." He stood and marched past them and out the door.

Mercy blinked as she watched him disappear. That was the quickest Jimmy had ever obeyed. Aaron had been here less than two weeks and he'd accomplished that? Was it because he was male and possessed the intimidating height and girth he'd once used to force children to bend to his will, or had she simply flattered herself into thinking she was better at disciplining these children than Patricia and her brother were?

Aaron was looking at her as if she should be . . . pitied?

She ducked her head. Pity from him felt worse than his taunts. "Excuse me. I'm going to make sure he does as he was told."

"Mercy, I'm sorry. I was only trying to—"

She held up her hand as she passed him. "Go garden. I'll attend to my own job." Which she was evidently worse at than a man who'd once been the bane of all children.

Once she got to the boys' room, she walked in and found it empty. So maybe Aaron wasn't better at this than she was. He might intimidate Jimmy enough to get him to pretend to obey, but the boy wouldn't actually follow through.

With a strange lightness in her step, she headed down the hallway to find Jimmy. The door to her room was slightly ajar, and she pushed it open to find him standing near her chest of drawers. "What are you doing in here?"

He turned slowly, holding up one of her ear baubles, his face a sea of indifference. "I found this in the mess on my floor." He dropped it into her open jewelry box.

The confident puff in her chest deflated. He'd actually gone straight to cleaning his room? She frowned at the simple pearl-drop earring she'd not worn for some time, though she'd lent them to Patricia weeks ago. "Thank you. But you know the rules. You're not allowed in our rooms."

"So you're going to carp on me for doing something good?" He slammed the jewelry box lid. "Why bother doing what you want if it isn't enough? Might as well be bad if I still get in trouble." He pushed past her.

Oh, why was this so hard? "Jimmy," she called as he stormed down the hallway. "Thank you for returning the earring."

He just shrugged and kept stomping toward the boys' room.

Once he disappeared, she went into her room and slumped onto the bed. If only she could feign a headache like Patricia or disappear for a few hours like her brother. What good was she if she couldn't get Jimmy to do a simple chore that Aaron had gotten him to do in two minutes?

Having Aaron take over seemed more promising for the children's upbringing than any of the McClains staying. Though Aaron would need a wife to do so, since Nicholas insisted a couple be in charge of the orphans.

She'd once believed no woman would ever want to marry George Aaron Firebrook. But some woman probably would, and he'd probably even make her happy.

She cradled her arm.

Seemed a little unfair God would gift Aaron with that sort of happiness and not her.

9

"You want me to cut all of this?" Aaron pulled back the thorny stem of a rosebush, his knees damp from kneeling in the moist soil.

"Yes, and this one too." Jimmy pointed to another spot at the bottom of the plant. "The entire branch."

Aaron inspected the stem he was holding. "But it still has a rose."

"It's dying."

"But it's still pretty." Maybe wilted, but still a brilliant red.

Jimmy huffed. "If you aren't going to do what I say, then why'd you hire me?"

He had indeed hired a thirteen-year-old to tell him what to do with the flowers. But the boy was suggesting he take off nearly a third of a blooming plant. "If you're wrong, it's on my head."

"Then give me the dollar you owe me, and I'll give you back your books. I don't care."

Aaron wiped his forehead with the back of his sleeve. He'd seen Jimmy reading the books, so surely he wasn't making things up. And the boy did care, no matter what he said, because no kid like him would do this unless he cared—for the money anyway.

If he shut Jimmy down, the boy would likely never listen to him again. The orphanage staff would probably prefer he get Jimmy to act more civilized than guarantee a spectacular show of flowers.

Aaron snipped right above the five-leaf node. He frowned at the cut flower for a second before tossing it in the wheelbarrow. "All right, where do I cut next?"

Jimmy rolled his eyes while shaking his head, and Aaron did his best not to let the boy's arrogance bother him. If Jimmy could make an adult angry or frustrated, he'd do so relentlessly. Exactly why the McClain women were having such a hard time with him.

Jimmy repeated his directions, and Aaron cut the branches he pointed to. When he stood and saw how much of the plant was gone, he nearly had an apoplectic fit.

"Don't worry. Cutting is supposed to give the plant energy for more flowers."

Except murdered plants couldn't produce any flowers. And yet he couldn't argue against the premise. "I hope you're right."

"I am."

He'd thought he was right about everything when he was thirteen too. Of course, if someone had told him he wasn't back then, he'd have turned a deaf ear.

This row of roses was either going to be a mass of blooms or a complete failure.

Had he earned enough of the boy's respect to give him any advice yet? "You know"—he moved to start pruning another bush—"I think I see the sense in cutting less-than-stellar branches, though it feels wrong. I mean, I was an awful person years ago and couldn't become a better man until I cut out a lot of how I thought and acted."

Jimmy blew out a dismissive breath. "Whatever. I've met awful people. You just thought you were bad."

"And are you bad?"

The boy rolled his eyes again, but considering the slight grin, he did think he was bad—and reveled in it.

"I've been watching you. You don't listen to authority, you shove Owen every time he walks by, and you know more curses than most men. Not many people like you, Jimmy."

"So? Feeling's mutual." Jimmy shrugged.

"I was like you once." Aaron clipped a dead stem. "I was lashing out all the time because a man meaner than the both of us hurt me real good." Seeing others enjoy their life used to make Aaron feel even more wretched, especially people like Mercy, whose deformity should've made her unhappy.

Why he'd thought making others miserable would make him feel better, he didn't know, but by the time he'd realized it was wrong, he'd done so many awful things it felt easier to continue than make up for it all.

"No one's hurt me."

Aaron glanced over at Jimmy. The boy's body had gone stiff, and his jaw tightened.

He turned to prune more. "Maybe not, but you have anger problems, as do I. As a boy, I just let the rage out whenever I felt it. Made me feel better somewhat. But I didn't realize until later I was mostly hurting myself."

Jimmy's gaze was fixated on the plants. "You can't cut out pain like you can cut off a flower." He shook his head. "I don't believe your story."

"You're right. You can't cut out pain like that. What I cut out were the habits I'd gotten into trying to ignore the pain. The only thing I've found that diminishes deep hurt is prayer."

"Prayer? That's what you're selling me?" Jimmy's scoff could likely be heard all the way up at the mansion.

Yes, indeed, Jimmy sounded just like him. What if their bullying ways stemmed from the same trauma? "Prayer might not work right away, but if you—"

"I think you've figured out how to prune well enough." Jimmy stood and waved a dismissive hand before storming away.

Aaron laid down his shears and blew out a breath. Telling Jimmy to pray had definitely been right, but he understood why the boy wouldn't want to—the fear that God would reject him, wasn't powerful enough to fix him, or would expect too much.

A giggle up near the mansion caught his attention, and he couldn't help but smile at Owen running away from Mercy, but not fast enough to avoid being caught and tickled again.

Was God expecting too much of him to adopt Owen?

If he was going to adopt the boy, he had to find a way to get past Owen's fear of him. He didn't want to push him, but staying away too long might convince Mercy he didn't care.

But he did.

They'd both been born into a terrible situation, and he knew how poorly things could go if the wrong adult got ahold of an innocent child.

Of course, Lowe wouldn't knowingly put a child in a bad situation, but Aaron knew how some people could hide who they really were from the world.

And yet, the red-light district was out there for all to see. He'd visited several saloons in California when he'd had money enough to try winning a round of cards, but he'd not once seen a child there. Was there anything that could be done to get children out before they were orphaned?

He watched Mercy start toward the garden hand in hand with Owen.

Aaron picked up his pruners and went back to clipping. Hopefully she'd pass quickly so Owen wouldn't notice him. If the boy shied away, like he did every time he came near, it wouldn't help her opinion of his parenting potential.

Mercy stopped beside him with Owen pressed against her legs. Seemed she was about to see how much the boy feared him firsthand.

Aaron snipped the last branch, his hands growing slick inside his gloves, and then looked up. "What can I do for you, Miss McClain?" He stood, taking a step back so Owen wouldn't feel crowded.

Mercy looked down at the boy tucked up against her. "Owen wanted to play marbles, but Max isn't interested and Robert's still working on whatever math problems you gave him. I'm not really good at marbles, so would you be willing?"

He blinked. She was inviting him to play with them?

She raised her eyebrows.

He took a glance down at Owen practically plastered against her legs, then back at her.

Both of them were as stiff as pipes, making him feel as if he were an honest-to-goodness fairy-tale ogre.

"I'm afraid I don't have any marbles." He'd once had everything from aggies to onionskins—for if bullies bothered to play a game, they did so to dominate—but he'd sold them the day his mother informed him his uncle would be returning to town. He'd needed all the money he could to get away from Teaville.

Mercy shook her head. "We don't let the children play for keeps. You can imagine how that might go." She held up a small bag. "We share Mr. Lowe's marbles."

"All right." He dropped his gloves into the wheelbarrow.

She pointed to their right. "The ring's under that tree." She patted Owen's back and started forward with him.

The five-year-old looked over his shoulder as she led him away, clearly not excited about Aaron joining them. But evidently he wanted to play badly enough that he followed Mercy without a fuss.

Aaron wiped his sweaty palms on his thighs. He'd begun to think Mercy would never give him a chance to earn her trust. He couldn't mess this up.

Under the tree, he grabbed a stick and deepened the grooves of the ring where the children had played enough times the grass had given up its will to live.

Mercy kneeled and opened the bag while Owen stood chewing on his lip.

Aaron smiled, but the boy didn't smile back. Instead, he crossed behind Mercy—to get as far away from Aaron as he could.

"We have four taws." Mercy pulled out the largest of the marbles and showed them to Owen. "Which would you like?"

The boy chose a blue-and-green cat's-eye and then looked at Aaron as if afraid he'd come close to pick his own.

Thankfully, Mercy tossed him a clay one. He crouched next to the taw line. "Let's just go youngest to oldest. We're playing Ringer, yes?"

Mercy nodded and set up the alleys in the middle of the ring. Owen did nothing but watch him intently. If Owen hadn't spoken to him the day he'd hidden under the desk, he'd have believed the boy mute.

He tried another smile and nodded toward the boy. "Go ahead."

Owen took one last glance at him before he knuckled down and shot, missing the marbles completely. Then Mercy hit a candy-striped glassy with hardly any force. She hadn't been kidding when she said she wasn't a good player.

Seemed he'd have to hold himself back. He shot his taw and simply scattered the line. He sighed as if he'd thought he'd get one. "Thank you for inviting me to play." He looked up at the rustling trees. "It's nice to get out of the sun."

Owen shrugged and took his turn, hitting a glassy out of the ring before he moved to go again.

Mercy picked at the straggly grass while she watched Owen hit another marble out.

After another round, Aaron settled himself in for perhaps the quietest game of marbles he'd ever played, but he'd not complain. He could use the time to prove he wasn't a terrible man—not anymore. He took a shot, barely hitting anything.

Mercy glanced at him but quickly looked back to Owen, who was trying to line up a shot.

Could she tell he was throwing the game? Hopefully. If she could see he'd put Owen's needs above his own ego, that would move him up in her estimation, right?

On his next turn, he took three marbles before he made sure to miss.

Robert came up behind them. "I've finished my work. Can I play?"

Aaron looked to Mercy. "You said you had four taws?"

She nodded and pulled out the steely.

While Robert took his first turn, not at all holding back his skills, Mercy seemed distracted by something in the garden.

Robert groaned when he left a dead duck.

Aaron nudged Mercy. "It's your turn."

"Skip me." She got up and brushed off her dress. "I'm going to check on Jimmy."

Jimmy? In the garden? Aaron threw his next shot so he could move to see whatever Mercy had been looking at.

Jimmy was a few feet away from the abandoned root cellar, his back to Mercy. The boy glanced around before darting inside.

Owen knocked Robert's taw from the ring and hooted with triumph. Aaron tried to keep his attention on the boys but couldn't keep himself from watching Mercy make her way down the hill. What was it about her that made it so hard to look away, especially when she wasn't watching him?

"What're you looking at?" Robert's voice startled him.

"It's your turn," Owen said.

He really needed to get his head back where it belonged. His relationship with Owen was much more important than whatever Mercy was doing. "Oh, nothing. Sorry." He moved to knuckle down from across the circle.

"You weren't looking at nothing." Robert stared at him as if he could see inside his head. "You were looking at Miss McClain."

"Well, yes. I was watching Mercy." Mesmerized by her was more like it.

"Mercy?" Robert's eyebrows dropped even more. "Don't tell me you're going to get friendly with Miss McClain. There aren't a lot of ladies who'd love kids like us. If she gets married, we'll only have Mrs. McClain." Robert's lip curled. "And though she sometimes acts like she likes us, you can tell she thinks we're dirty. Even when Jimmy's mean to Miss McClain, she doesn't—"

Aaron held up a hand to stop Robert before the boy got redder in the face. "No need to fret. I won't be marrying Miss McClain."

Robert pulled his head back. "Is it because of her missing hand? Why, she can make a bed faster and write prettier than me left-handed."

"It's not because of her arm." Aaron worked hard not to smile. In a blink, Robert had gone from not wanting him to marry Mercy to being mad he wouldn't. "I have nothing against her. She's a very nice woman who I can tell cares for you as much as you say she does. But it is she who would have nothing to do with me."

"Oh, well . . ." Robert scanned him as if trying to determine why Mercy would reject him. "Fine, then. Are you going to go?" He pointed at the three marbles left.

Though he told himself to focus on the game, he missed his shot and then couldn't help but take a quick look past the garden.

Because he was worried about Jimmy, of course.

Mercy was standing just outside the cellar in front of Jimmy, pointing up to the mansion.

Jimmy shrugged a shoulder and turned to walk up the hill with Mercy following.

The boy hadn't even protested?

What had he been doing in that cellar? "Excuse me. I'll be right back." He pushed off the ground.

"Are you quitting?" Robert's voice descended with disappointment.

"Can you get Miss McClain to come back?" Owen looked up at him, though he was still wide-eyed like a frightened rabbit.

As much as he wanted to promise Owen whatever he could to get himself into the five-year-old's good graces, breaking a promise would be worse. "I'll do my best. But if not, I'll be right back."

Owen didn't seem excited about that answer, but he didn't appear angry either.

As Mercy followed Jimmy up the hill, Aaron strode down toward the cellar. Had the boy started smoking there now after the women had taken away his pipe and tobacco?

When he entered the half-buried cellar, there was no smell of smoke. He let his eyes adjust to the interior and saw nothing but the pile of rubble he'd seen the day he surveyed the grounds. Cleaning this cellar was on his list of things to be done, but he likely wouldn't get to it until fall with how things were going.

Coming back out into the afternoon light, he caught Jimmy glaring at him before he disappeared inside the mansion. Mercy ducked her head inside for a moment but didn't go in, and she soon turned back for the marble game.

Aaron sped up to catch her. "Thank you for inviting me to play marbles with Owen. He's been leery of me, because I'm a stranger, I'm guessing. Your approval of my presence seems to have helped him warm up to me."

"Well . . ." She kept her focus on the boys. "Owen deserves a good home. Though you said you'd wait six months, I think it best we find out quickly whether or not he should live with you. I don't want him to miss an opportunity for a good home in the meantime."

It was all he could do to keep walking beside her and not just stop and hang his head.

She was only helping him get to know Owen because of practicality and doubt. He shook his head as he continued on. It shouldn't matter why she'd done it; he should just be thankful she had. "I hope you'll see what you need to see to make a good decision."

She turned to look up at him. "I certainly want to make the right one."

"As do I." Now that they were closer to the boys, he'd keep from arguing his case. The best thing he could do was show her he'd changed. Not only so she'd trust him with Owen, but so they could be on friendlier terms.

Any more than that—as he'd told Robert—was out of his reach.

10

Taking her time, Mercy started up the mansion's hill. The breeze was laden with the smell of freshly cut grass—a reminder of Aaron's presence, even if she couldn't see him.

It was almost as if he were inescapable, just like when they were children. Thankfully her fear of him being outright mean to the orphans seemed to be just that, a fear with nothing but memories behind it. But were several weeks of good behavior enough for her to believe he could be trusted?

The young lady they'd interviewed for the math position earlier today was highly unqualified, even a bit skittish. She obviously would not get the men's votes.

If Mercy voted for Miss Edison over Aaron, the men's opinion of her would go down drastically.

Thankfully there were two others to be interviewed before next month's meeting. Though if Aaron had really changed, maybe their past truly was hindering her from being impartial. The other applicants—for all she knew—could have been terrible children too, and could be terrible women now. She didn't know them. She had no idea how they behaved in public, much less behind closed doors.

When she crested the rise, the Lowes' wagon, piled with crates and trunks, was parked under the portico. Max and Robert pulled what looked like pieces of a small bed off the back and took them inside. Why would Nicholas have furniture delivered to the mansion? Nearly every week, the staff reported something of value being broken and discarded. Nicholas said he'd put all the mansion's fragile and valuable stuff in storage, yet the children still found things to destroy.

Aaron came out the front door, and his eyes went directly to her, as they always seemed to do. It was as if he looked for her at all times.

She tried to give him a smile.

He cocked his head, as if he wasn't certain she knew what she was doing.

And she wasn't certain either. But if the next applicants were as incompetent as the woman this morning, the teaching position would be his. So it would be best to work on having as little tension between them as possible. She stopped by the side of the wagon just as he reached the back. "What's all this?"

"The Lowes' things." He yanked two small trunks toward him but stopped before picking either up. "There's been a fire—"

She grabbed his upper arm. "Are they all right?"

He gave her a slight smile, which sort of looked . . . charming. "They are. The fire was at the lumber mill."

"Oh." She let go of him and looked toward the trunks. Stupid of her to think they'd have this much stuff if their house had burned down. "But if their house didn't burn, why are they moving their furniture here?" She looked toward town. A single tendril of lazy smoke wandered up to join the clouds above where the lumber mill was located—or had been anyway. She'd smelled smoke on her way in to town but had assumed a farmer was burning his pasture. The fire must've been put out early this morning.

"Mr. Lowe says the lumber mill is gone, as are four of the neighboring houses. Two men were hurt, and four families are without homes, three of which have no extended family in town, so the Lowes are letting them live at their place until they figure out what to do."

"Are the men hurt badly?"

"I believe so, but not to the point their lives are at risk. Nicholas is seeing to them. Lydia is getting the families settled in at the house."

How like Nicholas and Lydia to give up their time and beautiful home for others. But Lydia had to be disappointed. She'd moved from the orphanage to keep her young children from the stresses the orphanage could put on a young family, and if any orphan could cause the kind of tension Lydia wanted to avoid, Jimmy could. Mercy doubted Nicholas would act devastated about his business loss, but he had to be.

She'd do whatever she could to make this move easier. "How long are they going to stay?"

"I think it's too soon for them to know, but they talked as if they'll be here awhile." He hoisted the larger of the two trunks he'd pulled to the edge of the wagon bed and headed inside.

She looked at the smaller trunk he'd left behind. A cursive *I* decorated its top. Must be Isabelle's. Jake was too young to care where he lived, but poor Isabelle was having her world turned upside down. Hopefully the orphans would be on their best behavior to keep this from being any harder on her than it was.

Turning, Mercy crouched to put her right shoulder under the trunk, tested its weight, then slid it onto her shoulder, readjusted, and followed Aaron inside.

He'd walked into the entryway and had turned to hold the door open for Max and Robert on their way out. He frowned when he caught sight of her. "You needn't tax yourself. I have the boys to help."

"I wouldn't have taken it if I couldn't handle it." Her hand was missing, not her brain. Hadn't he said the other day he knew she didn't want to be defined by her missing hand? "You don't need two hands for everything." He might not call her stumpy anymore, but that didn't mean he didn't think it.

"I apologize, but I would've told any woman not to bother."

"Seems you miss out on a lot of help, then." She headed for the elevator, where several trunks were stacked.

Aaron grunted as he let down his trunk and turned for hers, but she was already beside the table she intended to put it on. She didn't need him thinking she was too weak to finish what she'd started. Kneeling, she slid it off her shoulder. Unfortunately, one corner caught and made her teeter a little. She narrowed her eyes at him, daring him to berate her for the wobble.

He did nothing but watch.

Was he not going back for more trunks? It seemed every day he looked at her more intensely. What was he looking for? She straightened, then glanced at her shoulder, where the trunk's leather band had bit into her flesh, and brushed the dirt off. "Well, let's get more."

He blinked rather hard. "Actually, I don't think you should . . ."

So he *had* been against her bringing in things because of her arm.

He held out his hand as if he'd heard the accusation. "There's something you can do that I can't. One of the Lowes' staff arrived crying. I don't know how the lumber mill's fire could have traumatized the young lady, but she's up readying the Lowes' rooms. Someone should check on her." He gestured with his hand as if measuring a lady at shoulder height. "She has dark blond, wavy hair."

"Sadie, maybe? Their housekeeper?"

He shrugged. "I don't know. Figured a strange man was not the best person to ask what was wrong."

He cared about what was wrong with a stranger? "All right. I'll see if I can find her."

"Thank you."

Thank you? He didn't even know the girl.

He headed back outside, walking around Max and Robert coming in with a rocking horse and a basket of toys.

She shuffled over to the curved staircase. Each step felt like it took an hour to climb. Without a single put-down, Aaron had made her feel awful.

No, she'd made herself feel awful—because she was being awful. She should be hoping Aaron had changed rather than waiting for him to do something cruel just so she could be . . . right?

Perhaps Aaron was wrong about her being the best choice to comfort anyone. She was the one getting testy over an imagined slight while he was seeking to settle the tensions in the house.

She checked the green room and found Sadie dutifully putting fresh linens on the bed, her back turned to the door. A sniffle sounded.

Mercy tapped softly on the doorjamb. "Are you all right, Sadie?"

Sadie stiffened, then pulled her apron up to her face for a quick swipe. "Of course, it's just . . . dust."

Hmmm. Sadie had no family in town who could've been affected by the fire. Maybe she didn't want to be sent back to tend the other families since she was loyal to Lydia? "Do you know how long the Lowes intend to stay here?"

She shook her head and went back to tucking in corners. "I'm sure they'll be here as long as it takes to find suitable homes for all who need one—even if Mr. Lowe has to build them himself."

"Are they leaving staff behind or bringing everyone with them?"

"Me, Pearl, and F-Franklin are coming." She flicked a bedsheet with a little more snap than necessary. "The rest are staying."

Was Franklin the problem? The butler had seemed sweet on Sadie. Did she not welcome the young man's advances? "Do you want to return to the other house?"

"Oh, it doesn't matter." Sadie flicked the bedsheet again, despite the fact that it had already settled down nicely.

Mercy moved closer and tried to use her soft, motherly voice. "It does if you're unhappy."

"I'll be unhappy either place."

Well, at least they'd moved past the excuse of dust causing the redness in her eyes. "Is there something I can do to make it better?"

She shook her head and fluffed the pillows.

"Maybe just talk?"

The young woman stopped overfluffing and sighed. She looked out the window for a second, then took a quick glance toward Mercy. "You the gossiping kind?"

"No." She lifted her nub of an arm. "Not exactly thrilled when people talk about me, so I'm not the type to do it myself."

Sadie thumped onto the bed and picked at the loose thread on the sheet's edge. "Franklin asked me to marry him last night."

She'd have smiled and offered congratulations, but the girl was entirely too sober.

Sadie picked at her fingernails. "I had to tell him"—she looked at Mercy for a second before going back to fiddling with her hands— "things about me he didn't know. Things I figured he wouldn't like—and he sure didn't."

"I'm sorry." She had no idea what those things might be, but she hardly knew the girl enough to be a trusted confidante. Perhaps Aaron really would've been the best person to speak to Sadie, for he'd likely fear telling a woman his past if he had feelings for her.

"I'd hoped he'd accept me. He's been so nice to me lately, and I thought . . ." A little squeak broke her obvious effort not to cry. Sadie brought up her apron again to pat at her face. "I don't know how I'm going to get through working with him every day, having him look at me as if I'm the worst thing that ever happened to him." She dissolved into tears.

Mercy sat on the bed and put her arm around the young woman. "There, there. Time will pass and it'll get easier. And the mansion's big enough that you and Franklin can avoid each other, if you wish." Though she'd certainly crossed paths with Aaron more than she'd thought they would.

"Not after we return to the house." Sadie quickly stood and bustled over to the closet, sniffling. She pulled out an armful of sheets. "But no use blubbering when I can't change anything. Got too much stuff to do."

Mercy didn't stop her. That was probably enough prying for today anyway.

With Sadie back to preparing the rooms and clearly done talking, Mercy might as well help the men unload, or at least make sure Owen was with Patricia. The boy was fascinated with the infrequently used elevator and would surely get in the way.

As she walked downstairs, she met her brother on the landing, lugging up a trunk.

He'd not come home this early since they'd first started living here. With the Lowes moving in, would her brother get home earlier? "Good afternoon, Timothy. Are you already done with work for the day?"

He resituated his hold on the trunk and leaned against the stairwell's wall. "Yes. Mr. Plotman heard of the fire and told me I could have the day off to help."

"Do we know any of the families affected?"

He shook his head.

No matter—she'd find out who they were from Lydia and organize the moral society to gather essentials for them. Surely the church would take up a collection too. "Have you seen Patricia?"

"She's playing checkers with Owen."

Good. The most useful thing Patricia could do was keep him out of the way. "I'll get more trunks, then."

Her brother blocked her by moving to the middle of the stair. "We don't expect you to be hefting trunks." His scornful chuckle made her face warm.

Aaron came up behind Timothy. "The more the merrier, I say."

He'd heard Timothy laugh at her? Her face heated even more. Aaron was likely only saying that because of how she'd snapped at him earlier.

"She'll just be in the way." Timothy gestured toward Max and Robert behind Aaron. "With those two and the butler, I figure we'll be stepping over each other already."

"I don't see why she couldn't—"

Mercy held up her hand to stop Aaron from fighting Timothy. Her brother might say something harsher if he stayed perturbed. "Thank you, Mr. Firebrook, for . . ." *What?* Thinking her valuable? Or at least acting as if she was? She stared blankly at his forehead.

"Would you mind moving, Mercy?" Timothy lifted the trunk a little. "I'd like to set this down."

"Oh yes, of course." She moved to the side. "I guess I'll see if I can get Jimmy to help. Have you seen him?"

"No." Her brother grunted as he hefted his trunk higher. "But I'm sure he's skulking around somewhere." He shrugged his free shoulder before climbing past.

Aaron didn't follow. Why was he staring at her so intently?

Surely he couldn't be feeling bad about her brother mocking her help, but then again, the look in his eye seemed almost pained on her behalf.

When Robert groaned farther down the stairs, she stepped in front of Aaron to let the young man pass.

"You know . . ." Aaron's voice was whisper soft, yet being so close, it seemed to rumble across her skin, holding her captive on the stair. "You shouldn't let the voices of your past or present define who you are. Let God do that. And He says you're precious." His eyes moved in a mesmerizing sort of back-and-forth motion, his pupils large in the dim stairwell. "So think of yourself that way, Mercy."

She didn't know whether to laugh or cry at such pie-in-the-sky thoughts from a man such as him.

He just stood there looking at her as if expecting a response. What did he want her to say? That the next time her brother treated her as less than valuable, she'd insist Timothy be more respectful because God said she mattered? "You and I both know I'm not worth much in a man's world—as my brother, and you quite a few years ago, made clear. God loves me, yes, but I have to live in a world where not everyone does."

He cocked his head, leaning back a little. "What happened?"

She blinked. "What do you mean?"

"You used to want to be seen as Mercy first, but you're letting your arm and others' opinions define you—just like you're defining me—with something we can't change about ourselves. But it's not who we are."

She dropped her gaze to the stair between them, and then he left her alone.

94

If only she could keep the malformed arm she was born with from affecting her future as easily as he could pretend he didn't have a terrible past. Did he realize how lucky he was to be able to mask what was undesirable about himself and live as a different person?

And who was she to thwart him when she'd do the same if given the chance?

She'd have to reconcile herself to judging him according to how he acted now, no matter how much her emotions would prefer to strip him of the chance to escape his past.

11

Mercy headed for the hall tree to collect the mail to save Franklin a trip to the post office.

Caroline walked in from the basement stairwell, looking more disheveled than usual. "Are you going to the meeting?"

"Yes. Do you want to come?" The housekeeper had only attended one moral-society meeting that Mercy knew of, but the Lowes encouraged any staff who wanted to go to do so.

"I can't. Katelyn took forever to go down." Caroline pressed the door shut softly, though her room was too far away for anything but a slam to disturb the baby. She shook her head. "I was right. I can't do my job while caring for a baby and still have time to do anything outside of this place."

"Infancy will pass quickly enough. Before you know it, she'll be in school," Mercy said. "Besides, Sadie's here to help."

"I'm what?" Sadie walked down the foyer steps, her arms full of linens, looking as exhausted as Caroline. With the Lowes getting settled into the mansion, she'd been working night and day to make sure everything was attended to.

"You're having to do both my job and yours—that's what." Caroline took the bedsheets from Sadie. "Katelyn should be down for a good two hours. Why don't you leave this to me and go to the meeting? You and Miss Sorenson seem to be enjoying each other's company lately."

When Sadie came to meetings, Miss Sorenson acted less hoity-toity and more like an amicable young woman—a very good thing.

"I wouldn't mind chatting with Stella, but there's plenty to do right now, and the work will lessen in a few days." Sadie shrugged and took back the sheets. "I'm all right."

Mrs. Lowe came down the stairs, putting on a necklace as she descended. "The work will still be here, Sadie. I know I'm ready for an hour away. Thankfully Jake's asleep, so I can go without any guilt." Lydia's eyelids drooped enough that she'd probably be better served staying home and napping with her son.

Mercy grabbed her shawl. How spoiled she was to be the only female in this house who'd slept well last night—besides her sister-in-law anyway. Patricia turned in early no matter what was going on.

Franklin walked around the corner and stopped, looking straight at Sadie.

Sadie stiffened, then shook her head. "As I said, I'm all right." She hugged the bedsheets and brushed past Lydia. "Waiting for me will only make you late." And with that, she ascended the stairs faster than Mercy had ever seen her go.

She and Lydia might as well hurry out before Aaron showed up to stare too. "Let's go." She smiled at Lydia, and they joined arms as they headed outside.

Up near the carriage house, Aaron was leading out the sturdy pony he used to pull the mowing machine. Seemed he had a sixth sense for being wherever she was lately. She blew out a breath. She'd determined to treat him according to who he was now . . . but how could she get rid of all her leftover emotions? How could she act as if the misery he'd forced upon her during the worst time of her life hadn't happened?

She scanned the carriage house as they walked closer. Where was the Lowes' driver? She pulled out her timepiece and cringed. They were already on the verge of being late.

Lydia walked up to Aaron and frowned. "Where is Mr. Parker?"

"He went to get a load of pavers from the quarry."

"That's clear out to the county line. When did he leave?"

"About thirty minutes ago."

Lydia turned to Mercy and sighed. "Seems we aren't going anywhere."

Aaron stepped closer. "Where are you needing to go?"

"The moral society meets today." Lydia shrugged. "If I'd known Mr. Parker had left, we could've made time to walk."

"I'm sorry." Aaron pulled off his floppy gardening hat and crushed its brim. "I'm the one who asked him to go."

"Don't worry yourself over it." Lydia took Mercy's arm and started for the mansion. "I suppose we'll—"

"No, wait." Aaron jogged around in front of them. "I can take you."

Mercy glanced over her shoulder. Though the carriage was there, the team needed to pull it wasn't. "I'm afraid you can't."

"Sure I can. The pony can pull the buggy."

"A buggy that is meant for two."

"Or three." Aaron passed back behind them. "Come on. I'll get Buttercup hitched and we'll go."

She certainly wanted to go to the meeting, but she didn't want to be squished up next to Aaron.

Lydia's eyes took on a dancing glimmer that belied the exhaustion weighting her eyelids. "Is that all right with you?"

Mercy nodded, though she couldn't imagine why Lydia seemed so happy about his offer. But then, Lydia had no idea how she felt about Aaron—or at least how she used to feel. Or felt now that he was . . . oh, she didn't know what he was. Too attentive, unsettling . . . everywhere.

He hitched the animal faster than Mr. Parker could've and held out his hand to her.

She didn't want to sit in the middle pressed up against him, so she pushed Lydia forward.

Maybe she'd pushed too hard, since both of them looked at her with narrowed eyes. Her face heated. How could she have been so rude? And to have pushed a high-class woman whose husband paid her family's salary, no less?

But thankfully Lydia turned back to smile at Aaron, and he helped her up.

How was it that lately she was the one feeling like the terribly behaved bully?

Because bullies refuse to consider others' feelings.

Feelings? Aaron Firebrook having feelings seemed as unlikely as a maskless raccoon.

Or maybe his old behavior had been the mask and this man had been behind it all along?

Aaron held out his hand to her, his face carefully blank.

She put her hand in his, and the second she was seated, he let go. She looked back, but he was already gone.

Sliding to the far edge of the seat, she stared at her hand in her lap. As a child she'd always wished he'd ignore her, but funny how his doing so now made her feel . . . bereft of something.

Aaron picked up the reins and drove toward the road. "Is this meeting at the Freewill Church?"

"Yes," Lydia answered.

"What is a moral society anyway?"

"A weekly gathering where we discuss the needs of our community and how to meet them," Lydia continued. "We do fundraising, put together food drives, give quilts to the needy, and anything else we can think of to help the less fortunate."

Mercy was thankful Lydia seemed happy to carry the conversation with Aaron. A few minutes passed while the two of them chatted about mundane things, but once they entered into traffic, they quieted. Aaron seemed lost in thought, and Lydia's eyes closed. Hopefully she wouldn't fall asleep sitting up, though with how tightly she was wedged between Mercy and Aaron, she certainly wouldn't fall over.

The silence grew longer, covered by the clip-clop of the pony's hooves and the sounds of the crowd. The steady rise and fall of

Lydia's chest confirmed she had indeed fallen asleep. Babies sure seemed to drain a woman's vivacity.

Mercy glanced at Aaron, but he kept his eyes on the road. Should she apologize for being rude earlier?

He'd asked her to be impartial as she considered whether or not he'd be good for Owen, but maybe she couldn't be objective. How could she separate her memories of how he once was and how he now seemed? If his name wasn't George Aaron Firebrook, she'd have been happy enough to let him adopt Owen if the five-year-old warmed up to him.

Not once since Aaron started working at the mansion had he lost his temper around the children. Even when they were belligerent, he never exchanged insults with them. And he seemed to care more for them than her brother ever had.

A half block from the church, Aaron looked to Mercy. "Which door?"

She pointed to the large wooden ones at the front of the church. "You can drop us off at the main entrance." She took hold of Lydia's arm and rubbed it to wake her.

He didn't pull up to the sidewalk, like Mr. Parker did, but drove to the side of the church and hopped down.

She stifled the desire to scoff at how gallantly he was behaving, because truly, she'd expect this behavior of a gentleman.

How long would her past with Aaron color how she felt about every little thing he did?

Not wanting him to hold her short arm, she got halfway down before he reached her.

And for some reason the brush of his hand against her back, the smell of his cologne mixed with fresh-cut grass, and the heat coming off him as he helped her down the rest of the way made her stop breathing.

She turned, but he didn't move and she had to look up.

"I'm sorry," he whispered. And he truly did look sorry. Only a pallbearer could have looked more somber.

Being so close, she had to crane her neck to see him. His height and shoulder span had made it easy to overpower everyone as a child, but she no longer feared that. "Sorry for what?"

He ducked his head and quieted his voice. "Everything I've ever done."

She hung her head. How many times was he going to apologize? And how many times was she going to refuse to forgive him?

He wanted something he couldn't just take, giving her a power over him she'd never had. Perhaps she'd let that go to her head.

Unforgiveness only kept their ugly past smoldering when she could let it turn to ash and blow away. Why was she holding on to the misery?

She let her shoulders relax with a long exhale and looked up. "I forgive you."

He straightened and his eyes widened.

Her chest inflated with a freeing breath, but she couldn't quite pull her gaze from his.

The wagon creaked behind them. "Thank you for driving us, Mr. Firebrook."

Lydia.

Mercy stepped away from Aaron so he could help their boss's wife down and turned so Lydia couldn't see the heat creeping into her cheeks.

Once Lydia was on the ground, Aaron hastened up the stairs to hold the door open for them. Mercy couldn't look at him as they passed, afraid he'd look . . . Well, what was she afraid she'd see?

Aaron stepped inside behind them.

She stopped and turned, her heart beating hard again. "No need to worry about us. We can see ourselves down."

"If it's no trouble, I'll make sure you get there. Besides, I'd like to get familiar with the church. It's quite the confusing maze of hallways and doors."

She gave him a slight nod and followed Lydia down the side hallway toward the basement stairwell. She couldn't very well tell him he wasn't allowed in the church.

The sound of women talking and laughing made its way up the stairwell, and Mercy picked up her pace.

Once they stepped inside the large basement room, Aaron quickly moved to help the women drag the quilting frame into the middle of the floor.

"Why, thank you." Mrs. Naples, the eldest of their members, tucked back the loose tendrils of gray hair that had fallen into her eyes. "And you are?"

Aaron pulled off his floppy gardening hat. "Aaron Firebrook."

"A relation of Matilda Firebrook's?"

He coughed as if the question made him uncomfortable. "I believe so, ma'am, a distant one."

"Believe so? You young'uns should keep up relations with your kinfolk, no matter how distant or old they are." She frowned at the quilt frame. "Matilda's not joining us today though."

"In that case—" Aaron cleared his throat—"might I work in her stead?"

The room turned as quiet as the stones in the wall.

He wanted to help? Whatever for? Couldn't he see this was a group of ladies?

He turned to look at her with wide, pleading eyes.

He wanted her to insist they let him stay? Evidently forgiveness hadn't been all he'd wanted from her.

Could she ever get comfortable with him invading so much of her life?

12

Silence hung heavy in the basement, making Aaron squirm. Asking the ladies to join in with their quilting had to be unusual, yes, but hadn't Lydia said they met to talk about how to help people in the community?

Though with the way the women all stood there blinking at him, maybe he should pretend he hadn't said a thing and leave.

He glanced at Mercy, but she looked like all the rest—as if he'd lost his mind.

And maybe he had, but wouldn't that be a good thing? The thoughts and actions his brain had produced a decade ago were not the kind she'd champion today.

He took a deep breath. Might as well plunge on. "I can darn socks and do my own mending, so surely I could help." It wasn't as if men couldn't sew—there were plenty of male tailors around. And if he could learn to tend to roses, why not just plummet all the way to the bottom of his manhood and do some fancy quilting too? Hopefully they were doing a pattern in the shape of manly log cabins instead of something like turtledoves.

"Why, that's better than what I can do, and they let me in." A familiar rough voice from the corner relaxed him a little. Charlie

Gray winked at him the moment he caught sight of her. At least someone in this room hadn't been shocked into silence. Though this was the last place he figured he'd find her. The few days he'd stayed with the Grays, she'd seemed more at ease lassoing calves than playing homemaker.

Mercy frowned. "I've never heard of a man joining a quilting circle."

He forced himself not to mangle his hat beyond recognition. "I wasn't really wanting to join a quilting circle. I thought you talked about the needs of the town at this meeting. If you don't want me ruining your quilt, I could sit against the wall, but I can sew better than some. It's what a man does if he isn't married and can't afford a tailor."

If a one-handed woman could sew quilts, surely he could too.

He looked up from where he'd taken a glance at Mercy's arm and was met with a withering glare—seemed she'd realized where his thoughts had gone.

He'd never make fun of her missing hand again—had even told her not to define herself by it—but surely being aware she had limitations wasn't rude, just logical.

"If they let me in, they can't have any objections to you. I doubt there's anyone less talented with a needle than me." Charlie grabbed the bassinet on the chair beside her, put her sleeping baby on the floor by her feet, and patted the empty chair. "You can sit by me since Mother's not here."

He ran his tongue around his dry mouth. If the others were this uncomfortable, should he stay? But he'd been wondering about what he could've done to help Iris Baymont get out of the district if he'd arrived before she died. He'd once frequented such places for the card playing and knew a bit about how things worked there, like how the women were more prisoner than employee. But back then he'd not . . . cared. It hadn't felt so personal.

He gave Charlie a nod and walked over. His ideas weren't exactly the most appropriate of subjects to discuss between the sexes, but it affected them whether they talked about it or not.

He sat on the chair, fearing it would collapse beneath him, but it held. The other women shuffled to their places in a hush.

Charlie handed him a spool of thread. "You good at threading needles? It takes me forever."

He wordlessly took what she handed him and threaded her needle while the other women murmured among themselves.

Charlie gestured to the woman across from them who'd chastised him for not visiting Matilda, a cousin to his great aunt, if he remembered correctly. "This is Mrs. Naples. She's in charge of the quilting. Beside her is Mrs. Wisely, our secretary. Then there's Mercy and Lydia, whom you know. Then Miss Sorenson and her mother . . ." With only ten women in attendance, hopefully he'd remember a few names. He handed the needle back to Charlie after she finished introductions.

"Oh, that needle was for you. But since you did it so fast, can you do mine too?" Charlie plucked another from her pincushion. "How good are you at shooting? I would've thought being a good shot would've made it easy to get thread through a bull's-eye, but I fail more times than not."

"I don't know about this." The young blonde across from him, Miss Sorenson, gave him a quick glance. She was about his age and quite wealthy, by the look of her dress and baubles. "This is a ladies' meeting."

Charlie huffed. "I'm not exactly a proper lady, and you let me in. And I can't even sew."

Miss Sorenson shook her head a little. "You're still female."

"It's not as if we have rules saying men aren't welcome." Mrs. Wisely, the woman with the white hair tied in a bun at the base of her neck, smiled at him. "We used to let my husband come in when he was pastor. He listened to our needs, helped fix the sewing machines, and so on."

"But he didn't sew with us."

He really should've left the moment they'd turned mute. He scooted back in his chair, but Charlie grabbed him by the arm. "I say he stays."

No one else spoke up, not even Mercy. She kept her head down and busily quilted, though no one else was.

Seemed her forgiveness hadn't wiped away all her negative emotions toward him—but he shouldn't expect it to. Hurt feelings took time to heal, but hopefully the ointment of forgiveness would help.

Mrs. Wisely smiled. "So what problems in Teaville motivated you to join us?"

So much for figuring out a way to bring the subject up delicately. "Well . . ." He pulled on his collar. "There was this classmate of mine I tried to locate upon my return. But her sister told me she worked in the red-light district."

Miss Sorenson's sigh sounded rather exasperated.

As pretty as she was, she wasn't making it very easy to like her. He put down his needle and crossed his arms. "Then she told me her sister passed on, murdered by a . . . client."

Mercy cringed and stopped quilting for a second. She might be purposely ignoring him, but at least she was listening.

He took a deep breath and plowed on. "There has to be a way to keep stuff like that from happening. I thought I could talk to the men who frequent such places, try to get them to see that a woman, no matter her choices, is someone's sister, daughter, or mother, and that treating her as anything less than a person worthy of care and consideration is wrong. But one man at a time will take forever. I was wondering if something could be done for the women in the meantime."

Miss Sorenson sighed again. "Mrs. Wisely's daughter tried helping those women last year, but nothing came of it, and we've determined it's not worth pursuing."

"No, we didn't determine it's not worth pursuing." Mrs. Wisely gave Miss Sorenson a scolding glance. "We've just not found anyone passionate about taking over where Evelyn left off." She turned back to him. "We've decided that those of us who feel called to a particular need should be in charge of coordinating efforts in that area."

"But that's just it. I'm pretty sure, since I'm a man, those women wouldn't trust me." He shook his head. Mercy barely trusted him, if she did at all. "Or at least I wouldn't be very effective. That's why I was hoping you all might help." Evidently he'd forced his way in here and made them uncomfortable for nothing. "Seems the idea isn't new though."

Mrs. Wisely frowned. "You're right—the idea isn't new, and it comes with plenty of problems."

He stared at the needle he was rolling between his fingers and turned to see what Charlie was sewing so he could follow her lead, but she was doing nothing but picking at a knot.

"It might be full of problems," Charlie said as she pulled at the tangled thread, "but that doesn't mean we should keep ignoring the need. Wasn't it just last week Mercy read us that terrible opinion column in the *Teaville Journal* vilifying the women without even mentioning the men? We all wish more people cared." She yanked on her needle, but her thread was still a rat's nest. "Seems as if we have someone who cares now."

"I . . ." Mercy was somehow sewing with more success than Charlie, and without lifting her head, she continued. "I did say I wish there were more people concerned, especially about the children."

He stared at the mesmerizing way she was sewing one-handed.

"I'm mostly concerned about those living with us." Mercy cleared her throat. "I know the moral society doesn't give much support to the orphanage since the Lowes take care of their needs, but with the fire and the extra people they're caring for, I figured they could use help, specifically in regard to Max and Robert Milligan, our two oldest orphans."

"Are those the boys who work at the factory?" Mrs. Albert, a slightly frazzled-looking woman, looked up from across the quilt.

"Yes, they work a few hours after school."

"My husband says they're good workers."

"Glad to hear that." Mercy smiled a motherly sort of smile. Robert had mentioned how she cared for them, and it sure showed.

107

He looked down. He'd not be jealous of the love she gave those boys—they deserved it.

"I don't know how well your husband knows them, Mrs. Albert, but the older one is exceptional at math, and come fall, he plans to attend a university in Boston to become a fancy mathematician. Mr. Firebrook can attest to his brilliance."

He looked up from the quilt, surprised to be invited into the conversation. "Uh, yes. I tutor him, or rather attempt to. He's more my peer in mathematics than anything else." He glanced at Lydia, forcing himself not to cringe over basically telling his boss's wife he was being paid for nothing. "I'm trying my hardest to challenge him though."

Mercy smiled at him for some reason. "The brothers are very attached to one another, so Robert will be going with Max to Boston, despite having two years left of school. Because of this, Max can't take advantage of the rooms provided by the university. I know the Lowes intend to finance them, but in light of their recent setbacks, I'd hoped we could provide them with a community scholarship of sorts."

Lydia nodded. "Nicholas and I promised to help, and we will, but we'd agreed to the expense of Boston before the fire. We've been in a dither this week discussing whether or not to encourage Max to go to Kansas City instead. He could board for free with Mrs. Wisely's daughter and son-in-law. Unfortunately, we'll have to make a decision before we know exactly how much this fire has affected us."

"Are the math programs in Kansas City as good as the ones in Boston?" Mrs. Wisely asked.

"The school in Boston is known for its prestigious math credentials." Aaron hoped he wouldn't get glared at for inserting himself. "Max needs that sort of academic stimulus."

"We'll do a bake sale. Simple enough." Mrs. Sorenson, a woman who was an older version of her attractive daughter with a spritz of gray hair, gave a quick regal nod, as if they'd decided. But unless she baked world-famous pies, bread, or pastries, they wouldn't sell enough to get the boys more than train tickets.

"I was hoping to raise more money than that." Mercy's voice was more diplomatic than his would've been. "I was thinking about an auction."

"That's a good idea." Lydia's expression brightened, the opposite reaction of Mrs. Sorenson's.

"But how will we get enough to sell in so short a time?" One of the older women whose name he couldn't remember looked up from the quilt.

Mercy shook her head. "I—"

"My father passed away two weeks ago and left plenty I could donate," Mrs. Sorenson interrupted. Her voice held no warble, her stitching unaffected, as if she talked about the weather instead of death. This woman was a haughty piece of work.

He shook his head at himself. He'd only observed her for a few minutes. What if her father had been like his? What if she was hurting now? Maybe she had a good reason to act pompous.

"I'm so sorry. I hadn't heard." Mercy tried to give Mrs. Sorenson a sympathetic look, but the older woman wasn't looking at her.

"That's all right, dear. We weren't close." She straightened in her seat. "And their house is filled with junk I don't intend to keep."

None of the ladies cringed at the hoity-toity way she'd said that. Impressive. Well, Charlie probably had—which was likely why she'd just leaned down to fuss with Alice's blanket.

"That's generous of you, Mrs. Sorenson. But what about the rest of us?" Mercy smiled as she scanned the others. His heart thudded dully upon realizing she'd purposely looked at everyone but him. "Anyone have things to donate that will draw a crowd?"

Charlie came back up from tending the baby. "Harrison and I can donate shares of beef."

"My mother wants to sell her piano, since her arthritis keeps her from playing," the woman across from him volunteered. "I'm sure she'd donate it."

109

When the conversation turned to fundraising for a missionary, he watched Mercy talk with such animation and goodwill, he had a hard time keeping his shoulders from sagging.

She'd never talk to him with such joy on her face.

He stabbed his needle into the quilt. He'd gotten the forgiveness he sought. He'd have to be content with that.

13

Mercy shoved the medical supplies she'd carried for Caroline back into the wagon with a sigh of relief. The Hawk and Eagle looked normal enough—a two-story brick business stuck in a line of nearly identical storefronts, their signs jutting out from above their doors. They were as innocent looking as the mercantiles and millineries on Main Street. But inside was a whole different matter—drinking, gambling, and womanizing done under the guise of a soda fountain.

Walking through the Hawk and Eagle packed with men watching her every step had caused her heart to pump so fast it still raced. But there had been a badly beaten woman inside needing attention.

Though they weren't looking at her, the men passing the wagon didn't help her heart settle. How could they be so bold as to stroll these sidewalks with families at home? Did they see nothing wrong with frequenting such places, where no one batted an eye after learning a woman they'd used for pleasure had been pummeled within an inch of her life?

Caroline exited the saloon, sidestepping a group of men wanting inside. Though she wore servant's clothing and carried a baby, one man looked at her in a way that made Mercy shiver.

Too many men had looked at her like that in the past half hour—she could do without ever being looked at like that again.

How did Caroline visit such evil places, often several times a week, and now with her niece? Thankfully Katelyn had slept through the whole ordeal. Since Mercy's stomach had turned at the sight of the poor, bruised woman, she'd been happy enough to hold the baby while Caroline tended the patient.

Though she wanted to help Caroline like the last orphanage director had, this should probably be her first and last time in the red-light district. No wonder her brother had forbidden her to help Caroline—it was just too much.

"I'm sorry." Caroline put a hand on her shoulder, her other arm cradling Katelyn as they stood next to the wagon. "I knew it'd be bad since they bothered to fetch me, but I've forgotten how traumatic my first visits here were for me."

Mercy held her arms tight against herself. Her missing hand made her vulnerable, but she'd never felt how much until the last thirty minutes. A young woman, whole and healthy, had been beaten so badly the doctor was worried she'd not survive. "I-I think it'd be best I don't come along next time."

"I understand." Caroline looked up at the late-afternoon sky for a second before sighing. "Let's get you home."

Mercy pointed to the bassinet in the back of the wagon. "Do you want to put Katelyn in there?"

Caroline stared down into the baby's sleeping face. "I think I'll hold her."

"All right." Mercy put the medical bag inside the bassinet and shoved it farther back.

Caroline hadn't moved, still frowning down at Katelyn. "I can't keep bringing her with me. But if you can't watch her, do I just refuse to come?"

Mercy held her thoughts, for what advice could she give based on anything other than an offhand opinion? She'd never been a mother, had never helped in the district, and Caroline knew Patricia would be at the mansion if she was not. If she'd already decided against her sister-in-law, Mercy would not bother to mention her. "I'm sure you'll figure out something. Do you want me to drive?"

"Yes, please."

Mercy followed Caroline to the passenger side of the wagon and stood behind her, a hand against her back in case Caroline lost her balance holding the baby.

Once they were settled, Mercy moved to untie Knight from the post, though she should've had Caroline do it before climbing up. If the horse had tightened his tether, she'd have quite the struggle undoing it one-handed. She dug her fingernails into the knot, but something olive green caught her eye and she stopped.

Nearly half a block away, a worn felt hat bobbed behind a burly redheaded man.

Of course there could be more than one olive-green hat in Teaville, but one like that?

The redheaded giant turned into a saloon, revealing her brother walking behind him with a man she didn't recognize. Their late father's hat sat jauntily atop Timothy's blond head, as usual.

Had Patricia sent him to check on her and Caroline?

Mercy left the horse and stepped onto the sidewalk to signal him, but he was deep in conversation. They disappeared below the crudely painted sign of the California.

He'd walked in calmly, not frantically.

And was he laughing?

Her heart and stomach sank.

"I need to check on something," she called to Caroline and rushed toward the tavern before the housekeeper could protest.

Timothy hadn't mentioned he'd started helping the Lowes with the district women, but maybe he had good reason to be here?

Please, God, let Timothy have a good reason to be here.

She forced herself to go in after him, though she could scarcely breathe with how her heart hammered inside her chest. The California's crowd was thankfully more subdued than the Hawk and Eagle's, and she quickly spotted her brother near the counter to the left. He pulled out a barstool as if he did so every day and gave the bartender a smile.

Her feet refused to move.

Was this where her brother was every time he supposedly worked late at the bank?

"Get me a whiskey sour," Timothy called, then laughed at something the man said beside him.

Whiskey? Since when did her brother drink? She fisted her hand. Kansas was a dry state. Though most knew the local police looked the other way as long as there was no ruckus, how could her brother disobey the law?

She pulled her feet out of their slog and forced herself to cross the room. Surely the shame of being caught would compel him to leave, to escort her and Caroline home, and keep him from ever returning.

At least she hoped shame would have its effect.

She ignored the pointed stares of the surrounding men and tapped her brother on the shoulder.

He turned, his smile dying a quick death. "What are you doing here?"

How dare he look at her as if she were the one in the wrong. "I have the same question for you. I came to help Caroline tend someone, whereas you don't look as if you're here for a good reason."

He got off his stool, grabbed her arm, and escorted her toward the front doors—never mind everyone stopping what they were doing to stare. "I told you never to come to the district."

She yanked her elbow from his grasp. "I assumed that was because you feared for my safety, not because you were afraid of being caught."

He latched back onto her arm. "It *is* for your safety, Mercy. You're missing a hand, for Pete's sake. Do you know what a man who's too far into his cups might do if he sees you around here?"

"You shouldn't be here." She tried to take her arm back, but he'd anchored himself better this time. "And drinking! Mr. Lowe hired us to be good examples for the children."

"I am when I'm there." He rushed her through the door and onto the sidewalk. "There's nothing wrong with a drink or two." He let go of her and crossed his arms.

She mirrored his defensive stance. "There is when Kansas is a dry state." And even if he was compelled to drink, why buy here? His money supported brothels, places that created the desperate situations their orphans had escaped from.

"I didn't ask your opinion." He glared at her just long enough to make her squirm, then glanced down the street and tipped his head toward Caroline, who was bottle-feeding the baby. "Go home with Miss O'Conner, and don't do anything foolish."

He felt no shame whatsoever over breaking the law? "Come with me. We'll talk—"

"There's nothing to talk about." Her brother put his hands on his hips as if he were addressing a child. "You do understand that, right?"

She swallowed and looked away from him. She had little say in what Timothy did—she wasn't his mother or his wife. She was a spinster sister, who would likely never be anything but, and would have to depend on him for the rest of her life. She had no income, no assets, no inheritance. The Lowes were paying her family to watch over the orphanage, not each of them separately.

And if the McClains weren't in charge of the orphanage, another family would be. One who'd have no obligation to provide for her. "Please come home, Timothy."

"I will, as I always do." He tilted his head toward the wagon.

She eyed him again, but he only wrinkled his brow, giving her a look that made her hate that he was eleven years older and thought of himself more as a father than a brother.

She tilted her chin and walked away without another word. Once she got to the wagon, she attacked the horse's tethered knot with a vengeance. A glance back told her Timothy hadn't yet returned to the bar—but he hadn't come after her either.

Finally the knot came undone, and she climbed onto the bench seat.

Caroline glanced toward her brother but went back to feeding Katelyn without a comment.

Had Caroline already known he frequented the district, or was she just being quiet because words wouldn't help?

Shaking her head, though she'd rather growl, Mercy backed up the wagon.

If she told Nicholas where Timothy spent his afternoons and he fired them, what was the likelihood that her brother would disown her? How could she support herself without him?

Though the Lowes would certainly do what they could for her, they did not need more charity cases at the moment.

14

"Aaron?" Mercy's voice sounded from somewhere behind him, interrupting the rhythm he'd set for cutting the weeds behind the carriage house.

She was calling him Aaron now? He stopped and turned around.

Though his lungs were already working overtime from exercise, they sped up at the sight of her. She tended to wear dresses in various shades of green, likely to highlight her eyes, but this one's square neck and the white undershirt's ruffled collar somehow made her prettier than the day before.

Though lately, she seemed to get prettier each day no matter what she wore.

He leaned upon his scythe, the muscles in his torso sighing with relief. "Can I help you, Miss McClain?"

"Have you seen Jimmy?"

He shook his head. They seriously needed to figure out how to keep an eye on that boy. When was he ever where he was supposed to be?

"What about Owen?"

Now, Owen missing was a little more worrisome. Aaron wiped away the sweat clinging to his hairline and looked around. "Haven't seen him either, but I sort of go into a stupor while mowing." It was a little too boring not to, and his stomach had been rumbling for the last twenty minutes. The half hour until dinner could not pass quickly enough.

"I thought I saw Jimmy go into the woods." She frowned and looked past his shoulder.

They needed to get themselves a bell for rounding up the children. The estate was too massive to search every time a child wasn't where he was supposed to be. "You've checked everywhere else?"

"Inside, yes. Owen mentioned they built a fort a while ago, so I thought I'd see if I could find it." She shrugged and forged into the brambles.

If the old tree with the haphazard planks nailed into its torso-sized branches was the fort, she could easily miss it. "It's by the pond," he called. Hopefully she'd heard him. Though there were two ponds and plenty of other spots to check.

Was he supposed to clear pathways to the fort, the meadow, the ponds, the wild blackberries, and take care of the mansion's yard too? His body ached at the thought. Lowe had said he would hire a few boys come summer to help mow, but that was still two weeks away.

Maybe he could convince Jimmy to cut paths to the places he liked to disappear to. Then again, giving Jimmy a long, sharp blade probably wasn't the wisest idea.

And why was Mercy the one looking for them? Hadn't her brother come home earlier?

Something didn't sit right with him in regard to Timothy McClain. He was well-mannered and intelligent, but for a man who was supposed to be in charge of the orphanage, he acted as if he wanted to be there about as much as Jimmy did. And since his wife seemed to be a basketful of nerves, why had they chosen to work at the orphanage? Was it because this was Mercy's dream?

For some reason, Mercy's brother and sister-in-law didn't strike him as the kind to sacrifice their desires for a spinster sister.

Aaron finished cutting the weeds along the west wall of the carriage house, then took his implements back to his cabin's lean-to.

At the well, he splashed cool water on his face and ran it through his hair.

The smell of garlic and onions coming from the mansion made his stomach twist. He scanned the woods and the yard, but Mercy hadn't returned.

With how Jimmy had been acting lately, he wouldn't put it past the boy to have tied her up. Or maybe Mercy had gotten lost, or one of them was hurt . . .

Ignoring his stomach's pleading, he headed for the woods and forged into a grassy pathway that thinned as the trees' branches grew thicker overhead. He took the trail to the pond.

The sound of chattering birds slowly turned into that of children arguing. No surprise to find Jimmy couldn't play nicely with Owen.

He'd been having some success with Jimmy while gardening, but what could he do to get closer to Owen? The game of marbles had done little to diminish the boy's fear of him. He'd tried inviting him to help with the flowers, play catch, take a ride on the pony, but the youngster always slunk away—or outright ran from him—whenever he got close.

He needed to discover why Owen was scared of him before he lost his chance to parent him.

Ahead about two hundred feet, Owen's blond little figure stared up into the tree-turned-fort with his hands on his hips. "I said, let me up there!" he hollered.

Something fell out of the tree, or rather was thrown, and hit Owen on the head.

"Ow!" The boy rubbed his head and stamped his foot. "I'm telling if you don't let me up there!"

Aaron shook his head as he forged through the undergrowth.

"Let me up!"

"How 'bout this," Jimmy hollered down, his head poking out below a branch several feet above the platform. "I'll let you up if you go kiss Miss McClain on the end of her nasty, stumpy arm."

"Yuck!" Owen shuddered. "You do it!"

"I wouldn't kiss her if you paid me. No one would. So go away."

Hopefully Mercy wasn't within earshot.

Aaron hurried forward. "Owen!" he called, but the boy didn't turn around.

Jimmy pelted the younger boy with whatever dead pods were hanging from the tree. "Leave, snot nose."

From the bushes to the right of the fort, where a trail broke through brambles, Mercy appeared. With her arms wrapped around her middle, she marched forward, struggling to keep her expression blank.

Seemed she had heard what they'd said.

She stopped below the fort and moved Owen behind her. "That's enough," Mercy said, her voice low and convincing. "Come down, Jimmy. It's time for dinner."

"I'm not eating ham and beans again," Jimmy called.

Aaron finally made the clearing, but Mercy's attention was locked onto Jimmy. "If you don't come down immediately, I'll have Mr. Firebrook tear down your fort."

Jimmy sneered over the rickety railing. "I'll just build another."

"I'll have him take that one down too." She growled a little. "You were acting better last week. Why are you being a rapscallion now?"

Why was she arguing with him? The more she fought, the more Jimmy would believe he had the upper hand. "Come down as Miss McClain told you."

Mercy startled and her neck turned red.

Jimmy leaned against the trunk as if settling in for the night.

With a few more steps and a leap, Aaron grabbed the bottom of the makeshift platform, caught hold of the rope, and yanked it down. He landed back on the ground and stilled the swinging rope. "Do you want me to come up there and haul you down, or are you going to keep your dignity and come on your own?"

Jimmy's gaze narrowed.

Seemed he'd have to back up his words. Aaron grabbed the rope and tested his weight, but Jimmy leaped off the platform before he had both feet on the first knot. The boy landed in a thick spot of muddy grass.

Good. He'd not been eager to wrestle the boy down. He let go of the rope. "Now, apologize to Miss McClain for not obeying upon first request and be on your way."

Jimmy muttered something as he brushed past Mercy, and she nodded as if his apology were acceptable, but judging by her lack-luster smile and her bad arm tucked under her good one, it hadn't mended her hurt feelings.

Had his own schoolyard taunts turned her pretty face that gloomy? She'd always been mad at him, of course, had cried even, but right now she looked as if she'd aged three years in a handful of minutes.

She patted Owen's back. "Go and wash up for dinner."

Owen trudged after Jimmy, who was making a show of stomping up the path.

Jimmy's apology hadn't been good enough, but at least he'd obeyed and offered one. "Why didn't you get after them for how they talked about you?"

Mercy moved past him to follow the children to the house, purposely avoiding looking at him. "You've said worse things."

"That doesn't mean the children shouldn't be corrected." He followed after her.

"You can't tell me no one ever tried to correct you."

"A few did."

"And did you obey?"

"That doesn't mean we give up trying to correct them."

She shrugged and continued up the path.

"Are you just resigned to being talked about poorly? You couldn't stop me from doing so when we were younger, but you could stop these children."

She looked over her shoulder at him. "With all the problems Jimmy has, you want me to focus on his petty name-calling and insults?"

She was trying to look brave, but he could see the pinched lines between her brows. "Yes, because it bothers you."

She turned back around and ducked under a low-hanging

branch. "After working with these children, you must realize that today was not the first time they've said something mean. I'm used to it."

Had his constant belittling made her believe she had to live with it? "Why not find another job, where you don't have to be subjected to such things?"

"Do you really think I can get away from people like you and Jimmy? They're everywhere."

He'd not said a mean thing to her since he'd returned. Would she ever see him for who he was now? "You can't tell me you've gotten used to insults if you're still upset over what I called you years ago."

She just continued up the path, shoulders taut, steps measured and fast.

"You told me you forgave me, but maybe you don't realize how very sorry I am. Even when I spouted those terrible things, I didn't actually mean . . . most of them. And now that I'm grown, I don't believe any of them."

He stopped for a second to detach the thorny vine that ensnared his pant leg. "I know you're tough enough to endure Jimmy's taunts since you endured mine, but I also know what it's like to live in an abusive situation. Where nothing you do, nothing you say, will ever make someone think better of you. As a little girl, you didn't have much choice but to endure my abuse, but you could find a different job now, where you're treated with respect."

She scoffed. "What job do you expect me to get?" She waved around her shortened arm. "It's not as if I have many choices. I can't sew fast enough to appease an employer or amass clients, unless they pity me. I have no talents in the arts. I get light-headed at the sight of my own blood, so that's a no to nursing. Teaching won't keep me from having children make fun of me. And marriage isn't going to happen either—as the boys just pointed out—so I go wherever my brother goes, and for now, that's the orphanage."

Years ago, her grit had driven him to try to break her, but now it only made him want to hold her. "So you actually believe what

Jimmy said, that you'll never get married because no man wants to kiss you?"

She didn't answer, though her neck turned red again. She kept trudging through the underbrush, the edge of the woods just coming into sight.

He sped up and grabbed her arm. If she made it to the lawn, he'd lose his chance to talk to her.

She wouldn't look at him, so he stepped in front of her. She kept her gaze pinned to his collarbone, but that didn't keep him from seeing her throat working hard to hide how near she was to tears.

He wanted to tip up her chin, but he knew how hard it was to look at someone while trying not to cry. "Mercy, if you believe what boys of five and thirteen say about you, you can't claim it doesn't hurt."

"You can't tell me there's no truth in what they say." Her voice came out in a rough whisper.

"The part about no one ever wanting to kiss you?"

She nodded just once.

He did lift her chin then. The sheen in her green eyes only made them look brighter.

Jimmy and Owen were wrong. Very wrong.

He leaned down, and the second his lips hit hers, he lost his breath. Though his lungs had seized, he kept his mouth against the surprising softness of her lips.

When her mouth moved against his, his body warmed in a way it never had before. He cupped the sides of her face, a perfect fit for his big hands. Her mouth broke away for a second, but he stepped closer, the feel of her making his heart—

The warmth in his body disappeared with the loud slap that echoed through the woods and the stinging pain that pulsed in his cheek. He forced his eyes to open despite the side of his face smarting.

Her green eyes bore into his, her tense muscles belying how soft she actually was. "How could you?" Her question was an angry, whispered growl.

Very easily, apparently. He closed his eyes and swallowed that answer. He stepped back, refusing to put a hand to the painful heat she'd left on his cheek.

"I don't know what's worse"—she took a step toward him as if she were a mountain lioness ready to pounce—"the names you used to call me or your manhandling me now."

Manhandling? He'd responded to the soft loveliness of her lips with a tenderness he'd never felt for . . . anyone. How could he apologize for something that had felt so . . . wonderful?

She stared at him, her body shaking with anger.

Over the past two years, he'd apologized for things he actually regretted, though hardly anyone believed him, so why would she believe he was sorry for this?

Considering the fire dancing in her eyes, she clearly thought he should apologize, if not hang from the gallows, for proving she was indeed desirable enough to kiss. "I . . . I apologize. I didn't mean to."

He certainly hadn't set out to anyway.

"Oh, I see. It was an accident." Her face got harder. She spun on her heel and stormed toward the mansion without looking back.

He took a few harried steps, intent on catching her, but slowed. What good would it do to talk to her now?

Spotting a fallen tree off the path, he waded into the grasses and sat, looking up at the fluffy clouds visible between the trees' crisscrossing branches. Dull gray clouds would've been more fitting for this moment.

He should've known kissing her wouldn't go well—not that he'd really thought that much before he'd kissed her.

And though it had ended with a slap, it hadn't felt wrong at all. She'd kissed him back at the beginning, hadn't she?

Considering she'd called him Aaron earlier, he'd somehow gone up in her estimation, but the kiss and the following slap had surely sent him back to the beginning of his quest to gain her trust.

How dare he kiss her?

Swiping at her eyes, Mercy smeared away the tears, trying her hardest to stop them from coming. The longer they flowed, the more likely someone would notice she'd been crying and would ask what was wrong.

Which was everything. Everything was wrong.

She barreled up the grassy pathway, watching her feet so she'd not trip. Not an easy task, considering the tears swimming in her eyes.

That no man would want to kiss her was not something she believed because Jimmy had said so, but because the fact was self-evident.

No man would be interested in a one-handed wife. Never had her girlhood friends asked her about the husband she dreamed of when they talked of boys, because even as little girls they'd all known she'd never marry. She'd overheard Patricia whine several times about how they'd be stuck with her forever, and Timothy had never contradicted her, just told her life was what it was.

That's why Mercy had determined to work her family out of this job instead of tattling on her brother for his drinking. Because she was stuck. No businessman who cared about his bottom line would pay her the wages she needed to live alone for the rest of her life. No man would marry a woman with a stunted arm. She'd resigned herself to that, refused to allow herself to dream of a husband and children.

But now?

How dare her body react to Aaron's kiss! He hadn't kissed her because he wanted to. He'd only kissed her to prove some point. Or worse, kissed her because he pitied her.

Her first—and likely only—kiss was with George Aaron Firebrook!

She blinked and looked at the edge of the woods only a few feet away. At some point, she'd stopped walking. She wrapped her arms around herself and forged forward again.

Aaron didn't deserve the reaction he'd just created in her. He deserved slap upon slap. And she'd . . . she'd—

"Why'd you hit him?" Owen's voice rang out like a bullet in a cavern.

Mercy pulled up short, and every part of her body flushed.

The five-year-old was standing at the edge of the lawn, peeling a long piece of dead grass.

"Didn't I tell you to go in and wash for dinner?"

Owen shrugged. "I was waiting for you."

"Well, I'm here now. Let's go." She charged toward the house. Maybe Owen would forget—

"I thought you said no matter how angry someone makes us, we aren't supposed to hit them." He caught up to walk beside her.

She didn't bother to look at him, just continued marching through the grass. At least Owen's sudden appearance had dried up her tears. "Well, yes. You shouldn't hit people." Of all the things for him to have seen. "But a gentleman is supposed to ask before kissing a woman. . . . At least the first time." Surely there were rules like that. Whenever her friends had started talking about men and future families, she'd always found a reason to excuse herself. It had been easier to walk away from such talk than sit through it. But now she didn't have the first clue what was proper for courting.

"Did the kiss hurt?" Owen's face contorted with confusion.

"Well, no." About the opposite, actually.

Which was a bad, bad thing. Oh, it would've been so much better if it had hurt . . . or been revolting. "But just because kissing doesn't hurt, doesn't mean a man should force one upon a woman."

"Well, that time Jimmy yanked my hair out, he deserved to get kicked, but you punished me for that. And that actually hurt."

She shook her head—these children and their logic were going to make her rip her own hair out. "That's different. Jimmy wasn't trying to kiss you."

"Ew." Owen stuck out his tongue. "I'd kick him for that too!"

She couldn't help but chuckle at the conversation's silly turn. "Well, I mean, if Jimmy were trying to kiss a girl—"

"He'd have slapped her back!"

126

The image of Jimmy kissing a girl and ending up in a slapping fight made her laugh outright.

Owen didn't laugh with her. He looked over his shoulder toward the woods. "Good thing Mr. Firebrook likes you, then. Otherwise he'd have beat you up."

Wait. "What do you mean, he likes me?"

Owen screwed up his face. "He told you sorry and didn't slap you back." He shrugged. "Means he likes you."

Mercy turned Owen around and pushed him up the stairs but didn't follow. She looked over her shoulder, but Aaron hadn't left the woods yet, or maybe he'd already disappeared into his cabin.

He couldn't like her—not like that. He'd only been trying to prove some point about how she shouldn't let anyone call her names anymore.

But his tentative lips on hers, and his large, rough hands sliding across her cheeks in such a gentle manner, had made her heart beat uncontrollably—right before it scared her witless.

She could not fall for her tormentor—she just couldn't. She tried to march up the stairs, but her feet felt as if they slogged through molasses.

If it wasn't for the hatred she'd felt for him for so many years, what would have kept her from going back and apologizing?

She wouldn't have slapped any other man who'd made her feel as if the world had stopped in awe of her.

15

"My brain hurts." Robert rubbed his temples as he stared at his last row of math problems. "Can I stop now? It's not as if I'm going to use ratios in real life."

Aaron smothered his smile, keeping the list of ways one could use ratios in real life to himself. "You've only got five left."

Groaning, Robert picked up his pencil again, and Aaron ran his finger down a page of *American Gardener's Assistant*. Where had he left off?

Owen's laughter drifted through the open window, and Aaron couldn't help but look up. Max tossed the ball over Mercy's head as she pretended to be unable to catch it. Owen dove for the ball and ran when Mercy chased after him.

They'd been playing in the flower garden for nearly half an hour, while Patricia watched from a bench.

Robert was staring out the window too and sighed heavily. Max had finished his work in thirty minutes, though the material was supposed to have kept him busy for an hour.

Aaron cleared his throat, and Robert gave him a side look before getting back to work. He couldn't exactly be miffed at Robert's inattention, since he himself had read the same paragraph three times already.

"Excuse me." Mrs. Lowe's musical voice sounded from the doorway.

He turned with a smile but lost it at the sight of Jimmy's angry mug as he walked into the room in front of Lydia, who was carrying Isabelle on her hip. The little girl's face was pressed against her mother's neck. Her dark little ringlets obscured her expression from view, but they didn't muffle her sniffles.

"What can I do for you?" Though he was asking Lydia, he pinned Jimmy with a warning glare.

"Jimmy was sent inside because he mouthed off to Mrs. McClain and was overly rough with Owen. But instead of going to his room, I found him snooping in mine, so I took him to the nursery. Frankly, I don't know what to do with a boy who pinches a toddler hard enough to bruise her because she wouldn't stop handing him toys." She lifted her hand but let it fall limply. "I don't want to disturb Robert's instruction, but Jimmy can't stay with me."

It seemed a shame to take Mercy away from Owen because of Jimmy's behavior. "I'll take him." He tilted his head toward the captain's chair, and Jimmy obeyed the silent command by throwing himself onto the seat, turning his back to the room.

"Thank you." Lydia sighed and turned to leave.

Isabelle peeped over her mother's shoulder just enough to look at Aaron, her big brown eyes glistening with leftover tears.

He swallowed against the anger welling up in him over a thirteen-year-old causing physical pain to someone so young. If he couldn't help the desire to tear into Jimmy over this, why had the adults in his life allowed him to get away with hurting Mercy and Fred and all the others he'd once targeted? They might not have been as young as Isabelle, but they'd been just as vulnerable.

Robert huffed and shook his head at Jimmy. "Hurting little girls makes you *so* scary."

Jimmy pinned a glare on him.

Aaron poked Robert in the arm. "Worry about yourself, please."

Jimmy closed his eyes as if settling in for a nap.

He really couldn't just let the boy get by without a reprimand after hurting Isabelle—he didn't deserve the luxury of a snooze. Aaron got up and tapped him on the shoulder.

Jimmy opened an eye.

"What are you getting out of behaving this way?"

"It's because he's mean and spiteful."

"That's enough, Robert." Seemed no matter where Jimmy went, he caused problems, even sitting here in self-important silence.

Jimmy's shrug was unconcerned. "She was annoying me, and it shut her up."

"Making her cry is hardly making her quiet." He pushed Jimmy's legs off the arm of the captain's chair. "Sit on the expensive furniture properly."

Aaron pulled over his desk chair and sat in front of the boy, who'd at least left his feet on the floor, though he wasn't exactly sitting properly. "You can't go pushing people around if respect is what you want. Fear's a type of respect, sure. It's the kind I went after at your age too. It's easier to get, but it doesn't satisfy. What do you really want?" Maybe Jimmy wanted to be kicked out of the orphanage. Nicholas had mentioned he was looking for somewhere else for Jimmy to live after catching him frightening Isabelle into handing over her piggy bank. Once Lydia told Nicholas about the pinching, he'd likely double his efforts to find Jimmy a new home.

Jimmy only closed his eyes and settled back into his chair.

Would anything he'd say get through that boy's thick skull?

Robert's chair creaked. "All you have to do to earn my respect is finish my math work." He eyed Jimmy as if trying to convince him to do it.

Aaron shook his head but couldn't help the chuckle. "Not going to happen. Finish."

Robert sighed. "I don't know why you're making me do so much work when school's almost out."

"Because it'll help you be prepared for next year."

"I already told you I'm not going back to school."

"Then it'll help prepare you for life."

Robert gave him a look he saw more often on Jimmy's face

than either of the Milligan brothers', but Aaron kept his mouth shut and raised his brows.

Robert sighed and turned back to the desk, but a shout from outside drew Robert's attention instead.

Maybe he should shut the window. If the room was quiet, Robert would finish sooner and leave him to lecture Jimmy without an audience to bicker with. That's all Jimmy seemed to do lately—pick fights until everyone stayed clear of him.

Aaron crossed over to the window and pushed the sash down.

Owen dodged Max, then threw the ball at Mercy's back. She jumped when it hit her and turned around to chase him with a huge smile on her face.

His heart clenched. He'd never seen her smile like that before.

Of course, he'd done nothing to make her smile, and after getting slapped yesterday, he likely never would.

He leaned against the window frame as he studied her. He'd been a fool to have ever messed with a girl so pretty. Of course, he'd not realized how pretty Mercy would grow up to be—not that that should've affected how he treated her. Even if she hadn't been pretty, her heart for these children was beautiful in and of itself.

And all he'd done yesterday was darken his name on her list of men she'd never consider marrying.

Why hadn't Nicholas called him into his office to fire him for misconduct—or at least reprimand him? Had Mercy not told their boss, or had Nicholas figured his getting slapped was enough to keep him from kissing her again?

She'd said she forgave him, and yet she still brought up their past in almost every conversation. If only he could make things better by letting her slap him for every insult he'd ever directed at her, every time he'd ever tripped her, every joke he'd told behind her back.

"I thought you told me you weren't going to marry Miss Mc-Clain." Robert's voice broke the silence.

Aaron frowned and turned to look at the boy. He surely couldn't have been reading his mind. "What are you talking about?"

"The day we played marbles you told me you wouldn't be marrying her."

Wouldn't and *didn't want to* were far different things. "Why aren't you doing your math instead of asking me silly questions?"

Jimmy snorted. "Because you look like a love-sick mooncalf staring out that window."

He stiffened. "No, I don't."

Robert shook his head. "We're not blind."

"Yeah, and it's making me nauseous." Jimmy faked a dry heave. "So why don't you kiss her already and be done with it?"

Aaron shook his head and looked away. Thankfully his beard covered most of his face, since it turned hot all of a sudden. "That would be *nauseated*, and you can't just go grab a woman and kiss her." He'd certainly learned that yesterday.

If Jimmy and Robert could see such thoughts on his face, he needed to be more careful about how he looked at Mercy from now on or she'd slap him again for merely looking at her.

"Why not, if you want to?" Jimmy asked.

Robert looked at Aaron with narrowed eyes. "So you don't deny liking her?"

Aaron scratched his nose. He wasn't obligated to answer pesky questions. He left the window. "You need to finish your ratios, Robert."

He shrugged. "Already have."

Good—checking his math would move them away from this conversation. Aaron scanned his work. "You can go."

Robert needed no more encouragement and was out the door.

But what to do with Jimmy?

Dinner would be in half an hour. Too late to start gardening, but with Owen acting so happy, he'd rather spend this sliver of time with him over Jimmy—though he still hadn't figured out what he'd done to make Owen so leery of him. Between tutoring, reading gardening books, and work, he hadn't had much time to come up with what he could try to do to alleviate the boy's mistrust.

"Come with me." He gathered his books and headed down the hallway, Jimmy following with leaden feet.

At the back door, he pointed outside. "I want you to run around the backyard." He drew a big circle in the air indicating the path he wanted Jimmy to follow. "Twenty minutes should be enough, but if you need longer to burn off all the energy you're spending on being a pain to everyone within arm's reach, keep running. While you run, I'd suggest you think about why it's best to treat others the way you want to be treated. I'd like to hear your thoughts on that when you're done."

The boy just eyed him.

Aaron crossed his arms and glowered. If he lost this battle, he was pretty much done. "Or if you prefer, I'll spend the rest of the day scouring your room, every inch of the grounds, and the mansion from top to bottom to find where you've stashed your pipe and tobacco."

The boy's jaw grew hard, but he walked off the porch in a huff and started around the yard. He was jogging more than running, but Aaron wouldn't quibble.

Hopefully he could make headway with Owen while Jimmy tired himself out.

He turned to see Owen digging in the dirt while the women watched him from a bench. Not exactly a good place for a ditch, but if he scolded the boy, he'd run off.

Going back into the conservatory, he laid down his books, took two trowels from the workbench, and headed outside, skirting the women. As much as he hadn't been able to keep his eyes off Mercy from inside the music room, he couldn't look at her now. Mercy might see whatever Jimmy and Robert had seen. And she wouldn't like that at all.

"Hello, buddy."

Owen quit stabbing his stick in the dirt and froze.

Aaron stooped a few feet away and flipped a trowel in his hand. "If you want to dig, I have the perfect job for you. There's a bush by the back shed that needs to be relocated." Of course, he was just going to relocate it to the burn pile, but at least that hole wouldn't be in the middle of a path.

The boy only stared at him with wide eyes, like always.

Aaron fidgeted. He'd been sure this would work. Owen had been nothing but smiles the entire hour Robert had spent struggling through his math problems.

If he couldn't figure out why Owen didn't like him, why would Mercy—or Nicholas even—trust him with the boy? Aaron rubbed his chin, letting his long whiskers slip across his knuckles. "You want to play marbles instead?"

The boy shook his head slightly, still crouched and stiff, like a gargoyle, seemingly entranced by his beard.

Aaron stopped his hand, then smoothed his whiskers down. Maybe . . .

He got up and headed toward the women.

Mercy wouldn't even look at him, but Patricia did.

"How does Owen act with Mr. Parker?"

Patricia scrunched her lips to the side. "The driver? I don't know. How should a boy act with a driver?" She looked at Mercy, who continued to stare at her lap. "He's quiet, I suppose."

"Quieter than normal?"

Patricia shrugged, yet nodded at the same time. "I guess."

"Thanks." He stalked off toward his cabin. Mr. Parker was the only other man with a beard around the orphanage. Anyone who'd ever resembled Aaron's uncle had automatically made him wary. Perhaps that was Owen's problem. He was five, after all.

He didn't know much about Owen's past except that his mother had been beaten by a return customer. But even if that man had no beard, someone else Owen feared might have one.

Which meant shaving was worth a shot.

Jimmy was now walking around the yard, but even from a distance, it was clear the boy was breathing heavily. Seemed he might need to have him do this running thing every day.

Aaron stepped into his cabin and quickly dispensed with his whiskers. As he ran the razor over his face a second time, he had to stop himself from shaking his head. He looked twelve. A baby face atop huge shoulders. His whiskers had at least covered his boyish dimples. He sighed and washed out his brush. Too late to do anything about it now.

Wiping the foamy soap off his ears, he sighed one last time at his bare skin. It had been two years since he'd shaved, and considering he'd spent most of the last few weeks in the sun, half of his face didn't match the other. If this didn't help with Owen, hopefully his beard would grow back quickly.

At least the boy might get a good laugh out of it.

He straightened his shoulders and went back to the garden.

Once again he avoided the women, for an entirely different reason this time, and grimaced at what Owen was doing now. He shouldn't have left him the trowels. Owen had done a lot more damage with them than with the sticks. He stopped beside Owen and waited for the boy to look up.

When he finally did, Owen tilted his head and furrowed his brows.

He certainly would look like an entirely different man, though nothing could disguise his bulky size. "Would you like to dig up that bush with me now?"

The boy tilted his head farther, poking out his lower lip a bit. He scanned Aaron's face twice, but then shook his head.

Aaron stooped down beside him again. "Are you looking for some sort of treasure?"

"No."

"Well, why don't we refill this trench and go to the pond, where there's mud and rocks. That way we could make rivers with our trenches." Hopefully having Jimmy tag along wouldn't ruin everything. He caught sight of Jimmy at the far edge of the lawn, kicking rocks in his path.

Owen glanced at the women, then back at him. "I can't get muddy. It's almost dinnertime, and . . ." He looked down shyly and shrugged.

"Right." Too soon to trust him that much. But the boy had actually thought about going with him, so . . .

Aaron pushed dirt back into the little ditches. "What about marbles, then?"

Owen looked at him for a second but didn't move or answer.

Aaron put a hand on his shoulder. "It's all righ—"

Without a word, Owen hopped up and went over to sit with Mercy, who'd evidently been watching them intently.

No use chasing the boy. But he'd made progress, right? Hopefully getting rid of the beard had helped. Either that or the boy had finally figured out he'd shaved and had tricked him and would never talk to him again.

He gathered the trowels and smiled at Owen as he made his way back to the conservatory. "You just tell me if you want to play marbles sometime, all right? I've been working so much I wouldn't mind doing something fun."

The boy only looked at him, but his face was more curious than frightened.

Patricia's face was bright with amusement though as she stared at him with a hand over her mouth. He couldn't bear to look at Mercy. She didn't find anything about him attractive, so his shaving certainly wouldn't have helped in that regard.

Up on the porch, the Lowes' young butler was trying to push a table out the back door, but he was hung up on the trim.

Aaron jogged up to take hold of the table's front edge.

"Thanks," Franklin huffed as he got a better grip on the back, but then he stopped and stared.

"Come on." Aaron gestured with his head. "It's heavy."

Franklin's face split into a grin right before he erupted into laughter. "Why, you look ten years old!"

Aaron scowled. "It's just because no sun's hit the lower part of my face for two years."

"No, that's not why you look twenty years younger."

Twenty? "If I looked twenty years younger, I'd be four," he growled. Whippersnapper.

Franklin just laughed again. "I figured you were in your thirties."

He narrowed his eyes at Franklin, who couldn't be more than

five years younger than him. "I'm more your brother's age than your father's."

Franklin grinned. "And here I thought you and I were too far apart in age to be friends."

Friends? He'd wanted to be friends? Aaron tripped over his feet as Franklin lifted the table and pushed him farther onto the porch. When had he ever had a friend his own age?

Mr. Gray was much older than Aaron, and he really didn't count as a friend. He'd always been his teacher. He couldn't even make himself call the man Harrison.

Franklin flipped the table over so they could set it down. "Want to help me with the chairs? Mrs. Lowe wants to have dinner out here."

"Sure."

Franklin looked back over his shoulder as they headed in. "So why'd you shave?"

"I had a hunch Owen wasn't responding to me well because of my beard. Figured it was worth shaving to see if that could help win him over."

Franklin gave him a funny look. "Win him over?"

"I'm hoping to adopt him." He followed Franklin into the mansion. "Mr. Lowe has agreed, but I want to make sure the boy's comfortable with me first."

Franklin stopped midstride and turned. "Why would you do that? Aren't you bothered by these children's background?"

"My background is similar to theirs, I'd bet. I might not have had a mother who worked in the red-light district or lost her to abuse, but I sure had a rough time of it."

"I'm sorry, but you really can't know what it's like."

"No, but I don't think his past makes that much of a difference. He still needs a home."

Franklin started again for the kitchen, shaking his head. "It's best not to attach yourself to anyone from that background. I mean, I came from the district. I should know."

Oh? And yet, Franklin seemed to have turned out fine. "It's not where you're from that matters—it's the quality of your character." Aaron grabbed two kitchen chairs. "I was from a well-off family, but I endured things no child—or adult, for that matter—should. I was quite the troublemaker because of it, but I finally realized I didn't have to be an awful person just because others were awful to me."

"But that doesn't happen often." Franklin shoved himself backward through the door while holding his chairs. "I mean, good for you for deciding to better yourself, but you can't tell me you think Jimmy is going to become a model citizen, that once a person leaves the district they won't go back to what they know, where they feel they belong."

"Seems you've been able to resist." Aaron looked into the backyard, thankful to see Jimmy jogging again. He must have a really good stash of tobacco he didn't want found. "Besides, if we don't believe these children can become decent adults and prod them to do so, then we're doing them a disservice."

Franklin slid his chairs under the table but didn't head back for more. He looked at Aaron for a moment and then ran a hand through his hair. "But don't you think if you associate with the kind of people who let you down in your childhood, you'll just be let down again?"

"I can't imagine God would be happy with me reveling in my own freedom while turning my back on those who need help as badly as I once did." Though he might never have a chance at becoming anything more than a bad memory for Mercy, he could speak truth into these children's lives.

16

"What are you doing?" Aaron's voice echoed through the carriage house.

Mercy froze with one of the horse's tethers in her hand. She turned toward Aaron but couldn't quite look him in the eye.

What was she doing? Anything and everything to avoid talking to him. To avoid seeing if he looked at her after their disaster of a kiss with regret or longing—or some other emotion that would make her even more uncomfortable.

And she was definitely not thinking about whether or not it would've been nicer if he'd kissed her after he'd shaved his beard.

"Are you going somewhere?"

"Yes," she breathed. "Caroline wanted to check on a sick family in the district, and I told her I'd go with her." Though this time, she'd not be going inside.

She'd hoped Mr. Parker would ready the wagon, but he'd taken Lydia and her children to the library.

"You could've asked me to get the wagon ready for you."

"I didn't want to disturb you." Or turn red-faced and stammer in his presence. Oh, why had he kissed her? He'd made her feel more vulnerable than when he used to taunt her until she cried.

She was done being vulnerable with this man!

"Here." He took the tether from her, his skin brushing against hers, making her jump.

He looked at her as if such a reaction was absurd—and it was.

She stepped back to give him room so they'd not touch again. Why hadn't she waited for Caroline to hitch the horse?

"Mercy!" Nicholas came striding toward the stables.

Thankfully she now had a good reason to walk far, far away from Aaron. "Yes?" She hurried out the carriage house doors but slowed upon seeing Nicholas's serious expression. Her hand grew clammy at the thought of any and all questions Nicholas might ask her about her brother. She'd decided not to outright tattle on him, but she wasn't going to lie either. Because if it were her words that got them kicked out of the mansion, her future was as uncertain as the orphans'.

"Caroline told me you were going into the district, and I have a favor to ask."

Her heartbeat fluttered back to its normal pace.

He stopped beside her, hung his hands on his hips, and blew out a breath. "A while ago, you mentioned I should consider placing Jimmy in an all-male household, and as much as I've dug my heels in about these children only going to families, I've decided to try it with Jimmy. I've talked with a few men, but, well, none were interested. But one recently changed his mind."

"Jimmy's getting adopted?"

"Not exactly," Nicholas said. "Considering our past attempts to adopt him out, I thought a trial by fire might be better than taking it slow and giving him time to chase the prospective guardian away. Besides, Mr. Ragsdale could use his help now."

"Mr. Ragsdale?" The widower had lost his son just months ago and was still wrestling with his grief. "Are you sure that's a good idea?"

"We talked it over yesterday, and I think it could work. He needs help on his farm, and the effort it will take to mold Jimmy into a decent young man will help keep Ragsdale from dwelling on things. If he agrees to take Jimmy full time, even better."

She bit the inside of her lip. This was what she'd wanted, right? To place these boys into good families before her brother ruined her chance to see it happen? "All right. When?"

"Right now, if possible. You're going right past Mr. Ragsdale's, so I thought you could take him."

"Right now?" She frowned. "That doesn't seem to be an adequate amount of time for Jimmy to adjust to the idea."

Nicholas sighed. "I know. But with the way he's been acting lately, I figured the less time he had to throw a fit the better. Franklin is helping him pack his trunk. I was going to take him, but it might be better for you to escort him since he knows you better."

Or maybe that would be worse. She pinched the bridge of her nose. Would it really matter if they gave Jimmy time to adjust? He'd always gone berserk the moment anyone talked of adopting him. But with little children in residence he could now push around . . . "All right."

"Good. We'll pray this works out as well as I hope."

She nodded, Nicholas left, and she felt Aaron come closer, his massive body warming the air behind her.

"What do you think?" she whispered without meeting his eyes. Aaron had spent more productive time with Jimmy than the rest of them. He'd somehow gotten him to work in the garden, and if any of them had had success in making Jimmy obey, it had been Aaron—though likely due more to his size than any real persuasive power.

He remained silent, and she turned to look up at him. He was looking at her as if happy she'd asked his opinion but sad about the question at the same time.

He sighed and looked away toward the front of the mansion, where Franklin was setting a trunk out by the entrance. "I don't know this Mr. Ragsdale."

"He's a good man who attends our church and has had tremendous loss this past year. His youngest daughter married and moved away last spring, then his wife died. His son recently died in

141

a tragic accident as well, so he's living alone now. But his children turned out decent."

"Were any of them difficult?"

"One girl had a forceful personality, but she ended up marrying well and seemed to have matured into a good woman. She was older than us. Do you remember a Dorothy Ragsdale?"

He shook his head.

She hadn't known her well, but she was a lot like the snooty Miss Sorenson—though Stella did seem to be softening the more time she spent with Sadie at the meetings. "What do you think about giving Jimmy no warning though?" Surely he'd think that was a bad idea and could talk Nicholas out of it easier than she could.

Aaron shrugged. "Could be terrible, could be what he needs." He shook his head and looked down at her. "He's been mean to Isabelle lately. I can understand Mr. Lowe's desire to get him out as quickly as possible."

"But surely we could protect her for a few days."

"If I'd been your father, I would've done whatever I could to keep ten-year-old me from hurting you any more than I did." His expression softened with regret. "I don't blame Lowe for worrying about that."

She closed her eyes. How was it possible to feel such a mix of feelings toward the man beside her? Anger at what he'd once done to her, yet sort of cherished knowing he wished to go back in time to protect her from himself.

"Well." He clicked his tongue. "Why don't you drive the wagon up, and I'll load his trunk. We can't overrule Lowe, but we can pray it goes well." He headed toward the mansion.

She slowly climbed into the wagon and started toward the portico. Why was she feeling so hesitant about this? Aaron was right. They couldn't question Nicholas without a good reason, and simply saying she felt uneasy wasn't enough to stop his plans.

When she pulled to a stop, Caroline was waiting with a fussy Katelyn. "Did you hear we're taking Jimmy?"

She nodded and took the baby so Caroline could climb onto the bench seat.

The boy in question walked out and glared at Aaron as he loaded his trunk.

Aaron swiped his hands on his trousers and gave the boy a nod. "Best of luck."

Jimmy made no move to climb into the wagon. Instead he fidgeted in a way that appeared more fearful than angry.

He'd always acted as if the orphanage were the last place on earth he wanted to be . . . but perhaps it truly had been an act. She turned to see him better. "Mr. Ragsdale is a good man, Jimmy. I know you don't want to go, but you must give it a try."

The baby let out a wail. Seemed Katelyn wasn't happy about leaving the mansion either.

Aaron tried to put a hand on the boy's shoulder, but Jimmy shrugged it off. Aaron stepped back and looked at Jimmy as if he could feel his pain. "You'll have a room to yourself, I bet. That's something."

Jimmy looked out over the hill toward town, standing in place as if he'd try to wait them out.

If he didn't learn to get along with others soon, the second he graduated from school—if he graduated at all—he'd likely head to the red-light district and cause problems, hurt others, and die young. Since the day Jimmy had arrived, she'd prayed he'd soften enough to become a decent man, but it seemed nothing they'd done had helped. He was still as hard as the day he'd arrived five months ago with nothing but his clothes, driven to them by a grizzled old man who'd found him shivering in the alley between two brothels.

Jimmy had told them nothing about his past.

Caroline started bouncing Katelyn in an attempt to shush her as they waited to see if Jimmy would throw a fit or capitulate.

His arms were wrapped around himself as tightly as barbed wire around a fence post. "You can't adopt me out."

"We're not." She forced herself not to tell him she had half a mind to ask Nicholas to give him some more time. "We're just seeing how this goes."

"Get in, Jimmy." Aaron's command was loud enough to be heard above Katelyn's cries, yet soft with sympathy.

"Fine." Jimmy stomped to the wagon and flopped into the bed. "But I'm not going to stay."

Mercy squeezed the reins. If that was true, were they making things worse? If Jimmy ran away, they could lose their chance to help him entirely.

Oh, she could second-guess this all day, but Aaron was right—it was Nicholas's call.

As they left the mansion property, the baby quieted with the swaying of the wagon, and Mercy glanced back to see Jimmy slumped in the corner of the wagon bed, ripping apart leftover straw.

What did this boy actually want? Maybe if he felt this was being done less to get rid of him and more because he was needed, he'd perk up. "We'd love to keep you at the mansion, but Mr. Ragsdale needs you. He lost his wife a year ago and his son just a few months back. He'll be grateful for your help."

"How'd they die?"

At least he was listening. "His wife's heart failed, and his son was in an accident. The horse he was tending trampled him in a stall. I don't know more than that."

"So you're sending me off to be a slave to this farmer who'll make me do the same chores that killed his son?" Jimmy's voice shook.

Mercy's stomach tightened as if she'd just been punched in the gut. Even Caroline winced at how she'd stumbled upon the worst thing to say. "It was an accident. Mr. Ragsdale wouldn't have asked his son to do anything he wouldn't do himself."

"You're sending me to my death." Jimmy threw the straw in his hand as hard as he could, though it only ended up littering his pant legs.

Caroline turned in her seat to glare back at him. "You're just as likely to die at the mansion with the way you disobey. Remember the time Mr. Parker almost ran you over—"

"The old man should've looked where he was going."

Caroline shook her head. "If you'd been inside doing your chores instead of sleeping on the horse blankets in the carriage house, you wouldn't have been in danger. Perhaps fear will be a good thing if it'll make you obey."

Mercy pressed her lips together to keep from smiling at Caroline's vehemence. Katelyn was either going to be a perfectly behaved angel or she would drive her aunt crazy for the rest of her life.

"If Mr. Ragsdale's son's death was an accident"—Jimmy's voice was cutting—"it wouldn't matter whether he was obeying or not."

Mercy fought the desire to sigh in frustration as they came upon Mr. Ragsdale's property. If Jimmy did run, hopefully he'd return to the mansion since it was nearby.

She looked back as they passed through the gate. Jimmy's face appeared hard, but he was curled up tight with his arms around his middle. Would anything they decided in regard to Jimmy ever feel right? "You might like it here and want to stay."

"You don't understand." His voice cracked. "Take me back."

She steeled herself against the sound of his voice breaking. He was only afraid someone would make him do as he ought. But being taught to obey would be the best thing for him, whether he believed it or not. "Give it time, Jimmy."

Mr. Ragsdale exited the barn, pulled a bandanna from his overalls' back pocket, and wiped his hands as he approached. He was in his early fifties with a head of frosty blond hair and lines around his mouth that weren't hidden by his thin mustache and beard. The man was approachable yet world-worn. Hopefully that combination of soft and hard would help Jimmy.

"Ho there!" he called.

She stopped the wagon. *God, please keep Jimmy's mouth from spilling out anything that'll make Mr. Ragsdale turn him away. But if this is a bad idea, please make it clear with something other than Jimmy's whining.*

Mr. Ragsdale came to her side to help her down, but she shook her head. "Thank you for giving this a try, Mr. Ragsdale, but I think it best we not prolong the good-bye. I'll return next week to check on him." Jimmy would likely only try to argue with her the longer they stayed. Better Mr. Ragsdale see a pouting, sulking boy than hear whatever foolish things Jimmy might say to her.

"All right." Mr. Ragsdale went to the back of the wagon, where Jimmy sat like a knot in the wood. "Nice to meet you, Jimmy. I'm hoping we can make a go of this. I can use your help."

Jimmy's backside didn't budge an inch. "I'd rather go back to the orphanage."

"They told me you aren't fond of work, but at least feeding animals and digging ditches is men's work. Much better than polishing silverware at that mansion. You'll get strong and lean and feel like you can take on the world."

Mercy cringed. A Jimmy who felt like he could take on the world would probably be even harder to handle.

The boy only glared at the man. "And if I don't want to?"

Mr. Ragsdale shoved his bandanna into his pocket and stared right back. "I'm afraid you don't have a choice, son."

Mercy closed her eyes. *Lord, don't make him have to wrestle the boy out. I'm not sure I could sleep this week if that's how I last see him.*

Jimmy's jaw wriggled, but then he huffed and slid off the wagon. "You got food?"

Hurrah for a boy's empty stomach.

"I've got ham and a sweet potato pie the neighbor lady gave me. Good enough?"

Jimmy nodded and shuffled off toward the little white farmhouse.

She turned to give Mr. Ragsdale a nod. "I hope you're able to handle him."

He gave Mercy a halfhearted smile. "Nothing I haven't dealt with before. My daughter Dorothy gave us a lot of stubborn lip around his age."

146

"Good luck, then. Feel free to call on the mansion or Mr. Lowe if you have problems." Though she couldn't guarantee they could come up with anything to help Jimmy behave any better.

Mr. Ragsdale tipped his hat and followed the boy toward the house, his steps dragging almost as much as Jimmy's. Was it wrong to ask him to deal with a hard child after he'd had such a terrible year?

Then again, he'd agreed, and something had to change before Jimmy was completely lost. Since this wasn't an official adoption, nothing would keep her from checking on him whenever she liked. Or maybe Aaron should check on him.

She huffed a silent chuckle. Just weeks ago she'd worried about Aaron having any contact with the children, and now she was thinking it best he look after one instead of her.

Turning the wagon, she rolled the tension from her shoulders and loosened her grip on the reins. Aaron had told her they could pray that the plan went well, and so she would.

A cute squeak of a noise escaped Katelyn. The infant was fast asleep, but her slack chubby cheeks made her little lips pucker as if whistling. Caroline readjusted Katelyn in her arms and sighed. "Mr. Ragsdale was right about there not being much to do at the mansion but polish silverware now that everyone's settled. I've been thinking I need to find myself somewhere else to go."

All the tension in Mercy's shoulders came rushing back. "Don't be ridiculous, Caroline. When the Lowes return to their old house, they'll need you to stay at the mansion."

"Problem is, I'm not so sure they'll move back to the other house." Caroline readjusted the baby in her arms. "I overheard them talking about contracts lost and the cost of rebuilding, wondering if it'd be better to absorb the loss and move on. And if Mr. Lowe is uncertain . . . Well, if they stay at the mansion, I'm not needed. Sadie's highly capable, younger, and without dependents."

Mercy stared at the horse as they drove through the industrial part of town. If the Lowes stayed at the mansion, her family

147

wouldn't be needed either, even if Timothy straightened out enough to be worthy of the orphanage director position.

With only four orphans under their care, it did seem lavish to pay for the upkeep of an entire mansion with double the staff. More children could show up on their doorstep any day, but if the Lowes didn't move back home . . .

"I think I've decided."

Mercy shook the gloomy thoughts from her head and turned to Caroline. "Decided what?"

"Even if the Lowes leave at some point, they've always planned to return to the mansion once their children were older. They won't need us all eventually."

True, but that time felt so far away.

"Before you take me to see Lily White, can we stop by the flour mill?"

"Beauchamp Mill?"

"Yes. If we go now we might get there before it closes. Henri said he'd support Katelyn, so I'd like to see if he'd give me a job. I've spent my inheritance helping district women, and all it got me was . . ." She stared down at Katelyn. "Well, it's got me into a predicament."

Mercy shook her head. Caroline wasn't thinking this through. "Who'd watch the baby while you worked?"

Caroline shrugged. "I'll pay someone to watch her."

Turning at the intersection, Mercy kept her mouth shut. Henri likely didn't have a job Caroline could do that would pay enough for a nanny and living expenses.

She pulled to a stop in front of Henri's mill. The smokestacks billowed, and the roar of active machinery was muffled by brick-and-concrete walls. "Let me take the baby for you."

Caroline transferred Katelyn into her arms, and the babe's soft little face pressed against Mercy's chest. How could Caroline hand this child over to someone to work in a factory all day?

The door to the mill opened, and Henri came out. His hand went up to put on his hat, but he stopped with it an inch above his head upon spotting them. He tucked the cap under his arm and headed toward the wagon. "To what do I owe this pleasure?"

Caroline fidgeted for a second before turning to climb down from the wagon.

Henri jogged straight for her, taking Caroline's arm as she stepped down onto the rutted road.

She backed away a space and brushed herself off. She looked up at the baby for a second, then back at Henri. "I guess I should've asked if you had time to talk before I got down."

He lifted a shoulder. "I'm on my way to a meeting, but I left with plenty of time to spare. Did you need something?"

"I won't keep you long, but I was wondering if your offer to support Katelyn might include giving me a job."

His expression turned incredulous. "Did something happen with the Lowes?"

"No, but you know they've moved to the mansion after the lumber mill fire, yes?" At his nod, she continued. "Well, I figure the Lowes need to trim their staff. Wondered if I might get a job at your mill or another business of yours."

He fidgeted, putting on his hat, then taking it right back off. "How do you plan to care for the baby? You can't have her with you in the mill like you can at the orphanage."

"I don't think it's fair for the Lowes to pay me to watch a child when my job is housekeeping. I could ask Mercy to care for her, but . . ." She shrugged. "Katelyn's not exactly a charity case like the others, so that's unfair too. Anyhow, the Lowes should be helping people needier than I am."

The look in Henri's eye as he shook his head only confirmed that Caroline hadn't thought her request through. "But my giving you a job wouldn't solve that problem. The jobs you could do here aren't going to pay enough for you to pay someone to watch Katelyn."

Caroline's shoulders slumped, and she looked away from him. "I didn't take the job at the orphanage to become a charity case. No one in my circumstance would demand a full salary from their employer to do a modicum of work while they cared for their own kin."

Henri shuffled his feet, turning to look toward town, then down at his watch. "Infants get easier to care for as they get older, right?"

"Easier, yes, but not so easy I can work as well as I did before." She shook her head, looking back in the direction of the mansion. "I could ask the Lowes to cut my salary, but that doesn't change the fact that I'm not needed."

Henri glanced at his timepiece again and let out a rough exhale. He looked at Caroline, though she wasn't looking at him. His expression turned wistful, and he seemed to be memorizing every aspect of her profile. "I have to go, but please, go back to the mansion and allow me time to think about what we can do that's best for Katelyn."

She nodded almost imperceptibly. "I know I've been unfairly mad at you in regard to my sister, and—"

"No you haven't. I deserved your wrath."

She looked at him then, and they stood in silence for a moment.

The moment turned a bit too intimate as they stared at each other, so Mercy busied herself with rearranging the baby's blanket. She'd never pried into Caroline's life. The housekeeper was one of the most guarded women she knew, so being witness to this somehow felt wrong.

She'd heard that Henri had had a falling-out with Nicholas and Caroline over how he viewed their charity work in the district, but she'd never heard the details.

"I'll return to the mansion and think about what else I can do too."

"Until then, Miss O'Conner."

A moment later, Henri crossed in front of their horse, his hat pulled down far enough that Mercy couldn't see his eyes, but his jaw was tense. His steps were quick as he made his way to the other side of the street and started walking in the direction they'd come.

Caroline hefted herself back into the wagon, and Mercy lifted the baby toward her.

"No." Caroline held out her hand and grabbed the reins instead. "You keep her." And then she called for the horse to go.

Mercy squirmed a bit, but keeping her thoughts to herself just wouldn't do. "I know you didn't mean for me to overhear, but I hope you don't let your inability to do things as well as you once did drive you from the orphanage. Though you're right that Katelyn is your kin and responsibility, she is the abandoned child of a prostitute, and that clearly is the type of children the Lowes are trying to help. Whether she's your niece or not, I'm sure they're happy to support you. Patricia and I could—"

"It's more than that." Caroline sighed and fiddled with the reins. "For years I pushed my sister and other prostitutes to leave the district, get a good job, and keep their family together. Yet none of them could plop themselves on a rich man's doorstep and demand to be paid to take care of their own children."

Caroline turned the horse and slowed to a walk. "I've been so adamant that these women could have a better life if they just wanted it badly enough, but I didn't stop to really consider how nearly impossible that task was. Henri once told me I was wasting my time with my sister, that she wasn't worth the effort, and I vehemently disagreed, despite how every choice she made backed him up. I kept insisting that she turn her life around, but how can I continue to advise these women to do so if I can't do it myself? And I don't even have the social stigma they have to contend with."

Mercy stared into Katelyn's sweet sleeping face.

Caroline, the Lowes, and even the previous orphanage directors had all tried to help children and women out of the district, but they'd run up against seemingly insurmountable resistance. Perhaps the only hope for these women was what Aaron had suggested—convincing the men who made the district profitable that what they were doing was wrong, one man at a time.

The whole problem was sinful hearts, plain and simple. From the men who took advantage of the pleasures of the district, to the disdain and apathy of those who never stepped in to minister to those ensnared within it.

But what could she do to persuade anyone to change their conduct when Aaron, who'd been known for his awful behavior, had done more to soften Jimmy than she had? How could she change the hearts of strangers when her own brother wouldn't listen to her about how his clandestine trips into the district could ruin their family's livelihood and reputation?

The only tool she had was prayer, and if that was so, why didn't she use it more often?

17

With his rake, Aaron dug the last of the old leaves from under the hedges running along the mansion's back porch. The birds in a bush near the conservatory flew off in a tizzy when Mercy came out the back door. He froze so as not to draw attention to himself. Not only because he still felt silly without his beard but because she'd clearly been uncomfortable around him since he'd kissed her. He didn't want to make things worse, so he'd tried to stay out of her way.

She scanned the garden, and when the dust he'd stirred up made him sniff, she headed straight for him, stopping just on the other side of the railing.

She'd been looking for him? "Good afternoon, Miss McClain."

She didn't return the greeting, but given the way she wriggled her lips, she wanted to say something.

He looked away, hoping she hadn't noticed him staring at her mouth and wouldn't assume he wanted to kiss her again. Which he did, but, well, she didn't need to know.

"When we moved back to Teaville . . ." She looked off into the distance. "I'm sure it will come as no surprise I was happy to find you'd left town, but . . . well, I was just wondering, what took you to California?"

He stopped and leaned against his rake. She'd been thinking about him? In ways other than how to avoid him?

She looked back at him. "It's rather far."

"Yes, that was my intent. The west coast was farther than the east, so I went that way."

"Why?"

He went back to raking so he didn't have to look at her. He still struggled with the guilt he harbored for how he'd once treated her, but that, mixed with the pull of attraction and the desire to be worthy of her now, made it difficult to know how to talk to her. "Remember the day you told me you and your brother decided against returning to Teaville because I'd be here? Well, I know how that feels. I had my own tormentor I never wanted to see again."

"I see." She looked down at the ground again, fiddling with the sleeve that was pinned back on her arm, seemingly in no hurry to go anywhere.

Was it possible that kissing her hadn't ruined his chance with her? If it didn't, he'd have to go slow. Like with Jimmy, pushing for everything to change at once only made him more resistant. . . . Except Jimmy wasn't there anymore. He sighed. Had taking him to Mr. Ragsdale's been the right thing to do? It'd been four days since the boy had left, and as far as he knew, Mercy had yet to check on him.

He'd been uneasy about the decision, but what business did a lowly gardener have telling the richest man in Teaville what to do with his charity cases?

Maybe Mercy could show him where Mr. Ragsdale lived and they could take turns visiting. Hopefully he'd see Jimmy at church so he could let the boy know he cared about what was happening to him.

Though Mercy still stood quietly by the railing, he forced himself back to work. What could he say to figure out if he had a chance with her without scaring her off? Telling her she looked beautiful bathed in the afternoon sunlight would be too forward; telling her he waited for glimpses of her all day long would be as well.

He glanced up and found her watching him. "Uh . . ." He cleared his throat. The hair framing her face made her look as soft and dreamy as the Monet painting in the Lowes' parlor. "I like what you've done with your hair."

Her eyebrows rose. "I do this to my hair every day. It's the only thing I can do with it."

"Well, it's nice." Perhaps that compliment had been too subtle, considering her reaction was a rebuttal and not a smile. "Shows you're practical."

"Practical? Well, I guess it's that." She rolled her eyes.

"If you don't like it, why don't you do something fancier?"

"Can't." She lifted her bad arm a fraction, and he closed his eyes and groaned. How did he always bring up her missing hand in one way or another? She probably thought that was all he paid attention to.

She sighed. "My mother used to do my hair up fancy on Sundays, but that was years ago."

He almost suggested having Patricia do it, but she'd likely complain that Mercy had the audacity to ask.

He certainly wouldn't pass up the opportunity to run his fingers through Mercy's wispy blond hair, pile it atop her head, kiss her exposed neck . . .

He blew out a breath and set down his rake. Time to head toward the well and splash himself with cold water. "Excuse me, I . . ."

Mercy was no longer looking at him but off into the distance, her cheeks drained of color, her body rigid.

He'd never actually seen someone go pale before. "Are you all right?" He turned to look where she was looking. Nothing unusual except for the plume of smoke he'd noted earlier, about a half mile away at the southern edge of town.

"That fire." Her voice came out raspy. "It's coming from Mr. Ragsdale's place." She picked up her skirts and ran down the steps. "We've got to get the firefighters."

"Now, wait a minute." He jogged to catch up as she headed toward the carriage house. "There's plenty of people burning leaves right now. I've seen smoke from fires scattered all over for the past few weeks."

She slowed but didn't stop. "After how we forced Jimmy to go, who knows what he might do." She picked up her pace as she hurried past his cabin.

"Mr. Parker's not here. He drove Mr. Lowe to Caney." He came up beside her, matching her frenzied pace. "What do you want to do?"

"Check on Jimmy. If the fire's serious, get the firefighters."

"Then I'll go with you." She was likely worrying over nothing, but he hitched Buttercup to the buggy, and Mercy hopped in immediately and perched on the edge of her seat. Minutes later he urged the pony into a run down the driveway—or at least as fast of a run as Buttercup could manage with her stocky legs.

As they got closer to Mr. Ragsdale's property, they saw that the smoke's origin was clearly coming from a haystack aflame in the pasture. He urged Buttercup to go faster, for the fire was creeping straight for the barn through the dead grasses. Jimmy was rubbing out the small flames struggling upwind with his boots, but the fire crawling to the east was an inferno. Two men were throwing buckets of water, one at the wall of flames, the other dousing the barn walls.

He handed Mercy the reins. "Get the firefighters in case we can't stop this." When the pony slowed, Aaron hopped down and ran to the men. "Do you have brooms?"

The older man he assumed to be Mr. Ragsdale stopped, his breath coming in gasps. "I didn't expect it to get away from us so quickly. There are brooms in the house."

The farmer could find them more quickly than he could. "Bring us as many as you have."

Mr. Ragsdale handed him his empty bucket and ran off. The other man continued to lob water at the barn.

Aaron filled the pail from one of the troughs, then searched for another bucket they could use. He'd helped burn fields a few times as a young man—why anyone had let a headstrong boy like him help, he didn't know, but he supposed it was for cases such as this.

Though he'd dealt with one fire gone wild, this one was further out of control. He rushed inside the barn, his heart already beating up into his throat. After dumping the contents of a small feeding bin, he ran back outside to fill it with water. He walked behind the wall of fire as quickly as he could without sloshing too much.

Mr. Ragsdale came back with two brooms and handed one to Aaron. They both dipped the ends in the water, forged closer to the heat, and swatted the fire down—one from each side, working toward the middle. The heat made Aaron's skin tighten, and a few times he had to back off since he felt hot enough to combust.

Aaron's broom started to smolder, so he wet it again, then dragged the feeder forward and dunked his head in the water. He returned to swatting out the fire, ignoring the tightness in his lungs. They only had maybe thirty yards until the fire hit the barn.

The minutes passed like hours as they beat upon the grass-eating fire. Finally, only a few feet shy of the barn, the last of the flames were tall but few. The man on the other side of the fire stopped lobbing buckets of water onto the barn and targeted the fire itself. Aaron smacked the largest of the flames with his broom, thankful the water from the bucket dampened the fire enough for him to get in and bat at the flames without burning off his eyebrows.

A few minutes later, Mr. Ragsdale smacked the last of the flames and Aaron rubbed out the smoldering grasses with his boot.

Mr. Ragsdale leaned heavily on his broom and let out a long exhale. His face was a mess of sweat and blackened ash.

Holding on to his sides as he worked to catch his breath, Aaron turned to see how Jimmy was faring. The boy had stamped out the fire spreading upwind but just stood staring at the haystack blazing away.

The man with the bucket came over and clapped a hand onto Mr. Ragsdale's shoulder. "Glad that's over."

"Yes, thanks for helping, Wyatt."

Wyatt blew out a breath and with his hands on his hips looked out over the blackened field to the burning haystack. "Since it's under control, I better get back to my farm. I don't think I shut the gate before I left." He took in a deep breath, still struggling to talk. "Might have to search for some cows."

Once the younger man started off across the field, Mr. Ragsdale turned to Aaron. "I don't know who you are, but I thank you. Name's Bill Ragsdale." He dropped his broom and walked over to shake Aaron's hand. His handshake was less than robust, but the man was clearly winded.

Not that Aaron wasn't out of breath himself. "Aaron Firebrook. I work at the orphanage." He wiped his forehead with the back of his sleeve. "Miss McClain saw the fire and wanted to check on you. She was afraid Jimmy might've had something to do with it."

Bill's face grew hard. "That's about it exactly."

Really? He'd thought she'd been paranoid. "What did he do?"

"I don't know, but he certainly wasn't doing anything to stop the fire until I came out to see what was burning." The man threw out his hand forcefully. "He was just sitting there watching the fire head toward the barn. Didn't alert me, didn't go for a bucket, nothing." Mr. Ragsdale shook his head, his expression growing harder under his ash-streaked face. "He started stamping out the fire after I showed him what to do. But even then he didn't seem too eager."

"Maybe he panicked." He was once a lot like Jimmy—irresponsible, haughty, ignorant. But to intentionally set fire to someone's property?

Would he have torched his uncle's place if he'd thought of it? His uncle certainly would've deserved that and much more.

He shook his head. No. He might have threatened it, but he'd never have done it.

"Considering the other things Jimmy's done the last four days, I don't think it's him being too stupid to know what to do. He's failed to feed and water the animals after being reminded plenty, he's let the chickens out of their coop more often than not, he's broken implements, he's left the good ones out to rust in the rain, and now he's set a fire." Bill gestured toward the haystack still ablaze. "Intentional or not, I can't keep him. I could work with him if he was simply undisciplined, but if the boy's going to try to destroy my livelihood . . ." The man's voice died off and he sniffed. "It's all I got left."

"I understand." Plenty of people had given up on him when he'd hit Jimmy's age. At least Jimmy had somewhere to go, and since Mr. Ragsdale wasn't his kin, it likely wouldn't hurt too much to be kicked out—though Jimmy would surely act as if it didn't hurt whatsoever.

If he'd set this fire intentionally though, maybe the Lowes wouldn't want him back. "I'll tell Jimmy to pack his things."

"No." Mr. Ragsdale held up his hand. "I'll get his things. I don't trust him inside unless I'm hovering over his shoulder. Caught him swiping half dollars from my coin box."

"All right." Though things were far from all right. Once Mr. Ragsdale started for his house, Aaron marched over to Jimmy, who was still scowling at the haystack.

The boy caught a glimpse of him coming and quickly looked the other way. His jaw was tight and his shoulders tense, yet the closer Aaron got, the more apparent it was that Jimmy was shaking. Was he still feeling the rush of staring down danger and subduing it, or was he afraid of how he'd be punished?

Aaron's boot snapped a stick, and Jimmy turned toward him, shaking his head. "I didn't do it."

His stomach sank. He most likely did, then. If Jimmy was worse than he'd been as a child, was he kidding himself to think he could help the boy? "I'm not sure anyone will believe you. You realize Mr. Ragsdale has the right to press charges?"

Jimmy stared blankly at the fire, one arm across his chest, clamped onto his shoulder. "I tried to stop it."

If there was any truth in what the boy said, calling him a liar would not win the boy's trust. "Regardless, you've been enough trouble that Mr. Ragsdale isn't willing to keep you."

"Where am I going now?" His bloodshot eyes blinked rapidly. From irritants, or was he on the verge of tears?

Aaron took a moment to suck some oxygen into his starving lungs. "The orphanage, as far as I know."

The boy nodded rapidly as if happy with that answer.

But Jimmy had never seemed happy there. Aaron's fists clenched and his heartbeat swelled again. Had Bill Ragsdale been treating him so poorly Jimmy wanted to get away that badly?

Aaron closed his eyes and focused on breathing again. He shouldn't react to the assumption he'd just leapt to—though it was easy to do after knowing "upstanding citizens" who'd been monsters behind closed doors. "Why would you want to leave here so badly you'd attempt to burn down a man's property?"

"I said, I didn't do it." Jimmy stomped and then hissed as if he'd hurt himself.

With such an adamant foot stamp, perhaps he hadn't set the fire. And yet, something was off.

"Mr. Ragsdale might be all right." Jimmy shrugged, his cheek twitching. "But I can't stay."

Well, at least Jimmy wasn't setting fires because Mr. Ragsdale had treated him poorly. He blew out a breath. "Why couldn't you have at least tried to get along?"

"Because I don't want to, all right?" The boy's uncharacteristic anxiety transformed back into his usual hardness.

"Why'd you light the fire?"

"I didn't! He . . . uh . . ." He scanned the ground around him as if looking for an excuse. "Well, I . . . I was smoking. Mr. Ragsdale told me I couldn't, and it just happened. Nothing I could do about it."

"You were smoking by the haystack?"

His lip twitched on one side. "Yeah."

Smoking was certainly one of Jimmy's vices, but unless he'd dozed off, he could've kept a smoldering fire from getting out of hand. "That's it?"

The boy's gaze stayed riveted to the ground where the fire's flickering flames danced as spectral shadows.

Aaron rubbed at his eyes. "I'm not sure I believe you."

"Well, it's what happened." Jimmy's jaw moved as if something were stuck in his craw.

The boy's words weren't matching how he was holding himself. Jimmy was the kind of hooligan who'd think nothing of spitting in a person's face, and yet he couldn't even look up. "Lies will only catch up with you."

He shrugged. "You'll believe what you want to believe."

It was one thing to try to force him to obey, but another to coerce a confession. He sighed. "We might as well get cleaned up while Mr. Ragsdale packs your things." He grabbed the boy's shoulder.

Jimmy winced and jerked out of his clasp.

His shoulder didn't look dirty or scorched. "What's wrong?"

"Your shirt rubbed me." The boy twisted his arm up to look at the skin above his wrist, revealing a reddened, blistering patch.

Aaron shook his head. "Why didn't you tell me you got burned?"

The boy let his arm drop. "Figured you'd say I got what I deserved."

"If it was an accident, why would I say that?"

Jimmy remained silent, his facial expression hard.

Intentional fire or not, nothing could be done to undo the repercussions. All they could do was move forward. He turned Jimmy toward the barn. "Let's soak your arm in some cool water, and I'll see if Mr. Ragsdale has any ointment." Hopefully Mr. Ragsdale's neighbor had left some water in the trough.

A horse-drawn fire truck pulled in, followed by Mercy. She pulled the pony up short as the firemen headed for the smoldering haystack.

She ran straight for them. "Oh, I'm so glad you stopped the fire. They took forever to get here!"

Aaron smiled at her running toward them. If only she were racing over because she was worried about him.

She stopped in front of Jimmy and squished his face between her hand and arm. "Are you all right?"

Once he nodded, the worry on her face transformed into a tense scowl. "What did you do?"

Jimmy wrenched out of her grip. "I didn't do anything."

Aaron rubbed the back of his neck and pushed Jimmy gently

toward the trough. "He won't admit to anything, but whatever happened, he's already living through some of the consequences. He's got a burn we need to tend to." He pointed toward the water. "Put your arm in there. It'll feel better until I can get you some salve."

The boy surprisingly obeyed without protest.

Mercy scanned the field, her eyes narrowing as she took in the firefighters' activity. "Where's Mr. Ragsdale?"

"Inside, packing Jimmy's things."

Mercy jerked her head toward him, and he could only shake his head as she slumped.

"I'll go apologize to him." She turned for the house. "It was our fault since we forced Jimmy here."

He grabbed her shoulder. "No it wasn't."

Even if they somehow deserved some of the blame, letting Jimmy believe so would only make him less likely to own up to his misdeeds.

She stepped from his grasp but didn't head toward the farmhouse, just stared at Jimmy as he held his arm in the water. She sighed. "Perhaps I need to fetch the police?"

Jimmy's eyes went wide.

"Uh, no." Though there was a possibility doing so might scare Jimmy into rethinking his life, Mercy was one of the few people who might have a chance at earning this boy's trust. "He says it was an accident. One that most likely could've been prevented if he'd behaved correctly, but an accident."

She frowned. "You believe that?"

He wanted to. He sighed and blew out a breath, keeping his eyes on Jimmy. "Mr. Ragsdale might not, but I . . . choose to." Maybe if he gave Jimmy the benefit of the doubt, the boy would start acting correctly to earn it. He turned to Mercy, who looked so uneasy he nearly reached out to pull her close. "Why don't you ask Mr. Ragsdale if he's got burn ointment?"

She nodded and headed off.

Once Mercy disappeared into the house, Jimmy looked at him. "Why are you sticking up for me?" His voice cracked, and his expression fought to stay hard despite how his throat worked overtime.

Perhaps Jimmy really hadn't done anything malicious. "Because I believe you."

"You do?" The boy's voice was so incredulous, Aaron nearly laughed.

But instead he maintained his no-nonsense expression. "I do." Someone had to or Jimmy was lost.

Jimmy's arms shook. From the cold water or from someone believing him?

Squatting beside him, Aaron waited for Jimmy to look at him again. "You might not like Mercy or anybody else at the mansion, but it's not because of anything they've done to you. I know. I once hated everyone because I couldn't stand myself. But let me tell you, if you scare off all the people remotely interested in helping you, you'll be miserable your whole life—just as miserable as you are right now."

Aaron swished his hand in the water, wishing it could wipe away the guilt that still plagued him. "I know how it feels to believe nothing but misery awaits you in this life, but that's a lie from the devil. And hurting others will never make up for the hurt someone caused you."

Jimmy tilted his chin. "Who said anyone ever hurt me?"

They stared at each other for a while, and the boy's gaze never faltered.

There were probably plenty of people born into this world who were mean for no reason, but even if Jimmy was one of them, that didn't mean no one should try to talk him out of it. "Doesn't matter. You'll still be miserable if you hurt the people who care for you, because you'll be alone in your hatred."

The boy stared at his arm in the water.

What had it been about Mr. Gray that had made Aaron reconsider how he'd behaved? It had been so long ago, he couldn't exactly remember. Maybe Mr. Gray had just been the right person at the right time. Or maybe there'd been a supernatural hand at work. "You might feel like you'll lose who you are or end up failing more if you try to be better, but real change can happen. God helped me change. He can help you."

Jimmy refused to look at him.

Aaron held his sigh as he put his hand on the back of the boy's neck and squeezed gently, hoping at least the reassuring touch, even if shrugged off, might help him realize someone understood and wouldn't give up on him.

God, please help me get this boy to see your light before he lands himself in jail.

18

"No, no, no, no, no—"

Splat.

Mercy grimaced as the Lowes' infant son threw another handful of mashed potatoes on the dining room floor with a giggle.

Patricia sniffed and resituated her napkin on her lap. "And that is why babies should be fed in the kitchen." Though she was muttering under her breath to Timothy, who sat beside her, no one at the table could've missed hearing.

Lydia turned to Patricia with a sigh. "As I said, the nursemaid is sick."

"Gah!" Jimmy jumped from his chair and wiped at a glop of potato now decorating the side of his face. "That went in my ear, you varmint." He turned to glare at Jake, who had no misgivings about slathering his own head with potato.

Robert burst out laughing.

Lydia took Jake out of his high chair. "I'm sorry, everyone. Please tell Nicholas I won't be eating with you tonight."

Patricia huffed and took a sip of tea as Lydia left with her children. "What was she thinking?"

Mercy grabbed a roll. "She was only trying to accommodate her husband's desire to eat with his wife."

Lydia did most of her own parenting, but Miss Rivers, the nursemaid, usually fed the children in the kitchen while Lydia ate with the adults.

Jimmy snarled as he dug the potato out of his ear with a napkin.

Timothy eyed the boy from across the table. "If you're going to act like an animal, you'll be asked to leave."

Mercy shook her head. Prior to the Lowes' moving in, Timothy rarely took dinners with them, but now he was there every night, playing table-manners dictator.

Nicholas walked in with a frown. He pulled out his chair but stopped before sitting while a maid placed a plate in front of him. "Where's Lydia?"

"Miss Rivers is sick, so she's with Isabelle and Jake in the kitchen," Timothy answered.

Nicholas's face fell, but Mercy's heart couldn't help but warm a touch. Not since the death of her parents had she seen how special a love between a man and a woman could be. Timothy and Patricia's lovebird days had been over for some time.

"I wish she didn't take Jake away." Owen let out a giggle and looked at Nicholas. "He's got good aim. You should've seen the potato fly into Jimmy's ear."

"Couldn't have happened to a better person." Robert sneered.

"Shut up, you—"

"Enough, Jimmy." Timothy hit the table, clattering his and Patricia's silverware. "If you can't keep your mouth shut while we eat like civilized people, you will eat in your room."

Jimmy opened his mouth wide, showing off the food he was chewing.

"Now, Jimmy." Mercy held back her sigh. Could they not have one conflict-free dinner? Jimmy had been doing so well after he'd returned from Mr. Ragsdale's, but her brother's attempts to appear as if he'd always been in control were rubbing Jimmy the wrong way. "We want you to stay—"

"No, we do not want children who act like animals at the table. Go to your room." Timothy stood and dropped his napkin. "Just because the women let you get away with this kind of behavior doesn't mean I'll tolerate it." He pointed toward the doorway.

Jimmy eyed him for a second but then shrugged and left the table. Timothy followed.

Oh dear.

Nicholas watched them walk out the door before taking a deep breath.

He'd been watching her brother closely the past few days, but Timothy hadn't seemed to notice. Did Nicholas know about her brother's trips to the district? Surely not, for wouldn't he have fired him? Maybe he was just realizing the lot of them had no parenting skills whatsoever.

Nicholas scooted closer to the table. "Have we said grace?"

"Yes, sir," Max said, then looked down at the book he had open beside his plate.

"No reading at the table." Patricia glared at Max.

Patricia had never complained about his reading before. Mercy rubbed her forehead. Must everything with her brother and sister-in-law be some sort of show for Nicholas?

Max looked at Patricia, then Mercy.

She nodded slightly. No use provoking her sister-in-law.

Thankfully, Max didn't complain or point out Patricia's inconsistency and closed his book.

Patricia grabbed her fork and knife and beamed a smile toward Nicholas. "And how was your day, Mr. Lowe?"

He looked up from the prayer she'd likely interrupted, heaved a sigh, and pulled his napkin off the table. "Long."

"I can sympathize. Today has been quite taxing."

Mercy covered her snort with a cough. Turning her head to cough again, she composed herself. She supposed it had been quite the day for Patricia, considering she'd watched the youngest children while the other ladies in the house attended the moral-society meeting before taking a trip to the library. The poor woman had to watch three children all on her own for two whole hours!

"I wanted to tell you I am enjoying your gardens immensely." Patricia ladled out some gravy for herself. "They're a little . . . wild, but lovely nonetheless."

Mercy turned to look out the windows at those wild gardens Jimmy had started helping tend again. The flowers certainly weren't growing wild from Aaron's lack of trying. Most days, the whirring of the mower's rotary blades didn't stop until it was too dark to see.

If Patricia or Timothy had one ounce of Aaron's dedication, well . . . Jimmy might've learned how to behave already. Everything good about Jimmy's progress stemmed from Aaron working with the boy, not them. Timothy would've been better off sending Jimmy outside to Aaron than to his room.

She looked at Owen, who was quietly shifting around his mound of green beans. If Aaron was going to get to know Owen well enough for the boy to feel comfortable living with him—which might be soon with how her brother was behaving—he needed more time with the boy, but the grounds were his master. Surely Aaron wouldn't agree with Patricia about how children should be seen and not heard at table.

She looked to Nicholas. "What would you say to Mr. Firebrook joining us for dinners?" She tilted her head toward Owen to let Nicholas know what she was thinking.

Patricia pshawed, then blotted her lips with her napkin. "Why would we invite staff to the table?"

Mercy looked at Nicholas, but he'd shoveled a mouthful of food into his mouth instead of reminding Patricia she was staff, just like Aaron.

Owen didn't know Aaron wanted to adopt him, so she couldn't remind Patricia of that now. "Mr. Firebrook seems to be having some success with getting Jimmy to obey—"

"Timothy's in charge of the boys' discipline, is he not?" Patricia's voice was practically dripping with condescension. "He doesn't need the gardener's help."

"I have no reservations about Aaron joining us." Nicholas gave Mercy a tilted grin that slowly grew bigger. "Why don't you invite him in?"

"Well, I . . ." *Now?* She squirmed in her seat.

"I think I hear Mr. Firebrook in the kitchen." Robert spoke around a mouthful of food, unaware that Patricia glared at him for doing so.

"Feel free to ask him to join us, Miss McClain." Nicholas's eyes sparkled as if something about the idea gave him pleasure.

"Right now?" They'd already begun eating.

Max wiped his lips. "I wouldn't mind asking him about tomorrow's work. He's been having me graph functions, but I'd rather practice matrices."

Nicholas looked at her with eyebrows raised.

She scooted back from the table. "All right, I'll see if he'll come." It would be more embarrassing not to at this point.

In the kitchen, Lydia was having no more success in keeping Jake's food off the floor than she'd had in the dining room.

Aaron was making himself a plate, his shirtsleeves rolled up, his arms still wet after washing up.

She cleared her throat, and he turned around. The smile he gave her was so wide it crinkled his eyes, but his grin quickly shrank, as if he'd realized he'd smiled too big.

"I, uh, came to invite you to the table, Mr. Firebrook, if you'd like. I . . . we figured you and Owen could use time together, plus Max has a math question." Which she couldn't reiterate since she had no idea what he'd been talking about.

Aaron frowned at his clothing. His shirt was damp, wrinkled, and dirty, along with being slightly askew under his suspenders. "I don't have anything suitable to wear, and even if I did, I'm heading right back to work."

"Oh, well . . . perhaps we could have Owen eat with you instead?" If he adopted Owen, the boy would no longer be eating in a fancy dining room.

He shook his head. "I don't think forcing him to spend time

with me would be a good idea. He's barely talking to me at this point."

Which was what she was trying to remedy. "What if we ate on the porch?"

"We?"

"Yes. If I ate with you, he'd be all right." She looked out the windows since Aaron's gaze was a touch too intense.

"That's nice of you, but I don't expect you to deal with the wind and insects for me."

"But I'd rather eat with you." Oh dear, that sounded like she wanted to eat *with him* . . . though she sort of did, just not like that . . . exactly.

He made no answer, and she turned to see his head cocked to the side as if studying a fascinating creature.

She shrugged. "I'm sure Max and Robert would rather eat out there too, but since we're doing this for Owen's sake, I wouldn't give them the option. Max can ask his math question later."

Why did Aaron look sad all of a sudden?

"Unless you wanted Robert and Max to eat with you?"

He shook his head and took in a deep breath as he stared down at the plateful of food he held. "No, as you said, this is just for Owen." He passed her, shoulders slumped, and exited through the servants' door to the porch.

She ran a hand over her hair and exhaled. She'd expected at least a small smile for wanting to help him with Owen, but he'd walked out as if she'd hurt him.

Had he hoped she wanted to eat with him for another reason?

Knowing what kind of man he was now—maybe the man he'd always been deep down—he'd not have kissed her unless he liked her, just as Owen had said. But surely he'd changed his mind now after how she'd reacted.

"Eat outside?" Little Isabelle's voice made her jump.

She turned to find the dark-eyed chubby girl looking up at her from her mother's lap. Mercy forced herself to look at Lydia, hoping her cheeks didn't look as warm as they felt.

"This might seem as if it's coming out of nowhere," Lydia started, "and perhaps it's strangely personal, but my husband, at one time in his life, was terrible to his late wife. He says he treated her in ways I cannot fathom, knowing the man that I know now. I . . ." She turned to look down at the floor, as if looking for words. "I, of course, questioned if I could be with someone with such a history, but by the time he'd told me, I'd gotten to know him well enough to realize those mistakes and the turmoil that followed had formed the man I *knew*."

Lydia looked back up and met her gaze squarely. "I barely remember Aaron from school—I was older and wrapped up in my own world—but Nicholas told me how Aaron once treated you." She put her arms around Isabelle and pulled her closer. "I can't imagine how much more difficult it would've been to believe Nicholas had changed if I'd been the one he'd hurt."

It certainly was difficult to believe the George she knew was the Aaron getting ready to eat with the five-year-old he wanted to adopt in order to make up for how he'd once treated the boy's mother. Mercy pursed her lips and had to look away from Lydia's intense gaze.

Jake swayed in his seat, his heavy eyelids fluttering as he slowly stuffed more potatoes in his mouth. Mercy couldn't help but smile at the little boy who was the spitting image of his father. Nicholas was a man she'd trusted the day she met him. Was her boss's past really as bad as Lydia claimed?

"In case you're wondering if your ability to judge Aaron is off, I thought I'd let you know Nicholas and I both think he's a good man." Lydia grabbed her hand and squeezed. "My husband trusts Aaron far more than . . . some others. But if you weren't wondering . . ." She shrugged and smiled. "Well, I'm glad you're helping Owen get to know him."

Mercy squeezed Lydia's hand back, then turned toward the dining room to fetch Owen before Lydia decided to ask her what she was thinking.

She looked out the window before disappearing down the

hallway and saw Aaron sitting in a chair, his food in front of him untouched, his head bowed in prayer.

What if Aaron still liked her?

What if she liked him back?

Would that lead to more heartache than she'd suffered at his hand years ago?

19

Aaron stopped mowing the last section of the front lawn, grabbed the towel he'd stuffed in his back pocket, and wiped at his face and neck. The further they left spring behind, the more he believed he'd melt away with this job. Thankfully the sun was going down, and the moon shone brightly in the deepening blue sky. He'd sleep well tonight since the nights were still cool, but it wouldn't be so easy in the muggy heat of August.

He walked to where he'd left his water in the shade, took a drink, and looked out over the small hill toward the pond where he'd staked four goats to munch down the meadow. He waved at one of the young men Nicholas had hired to help mow now that school was out. "James!"

The boy stopped pushing the reel mower to look at him.

"Can you put up the goats?" He pointed toward the pond, and James nodded, heading to the lean-to to put away his mower.

After draining his water, Aaron mowed his way to the pump to refill his glass, the rotary blades skimming right over the new dandelion heads.

When he turned the corner of the mansion, he slowed. Mercy stood on the porch scanning the grounds for something. When she caught sight of him, she headed down the steps in a rush.

She was coming to talk to him? He stopped to wipe off his neck again. She'd started talking to him cordially whenever they found themselves together, and he couldn't have been happier. Well, he might've been happier if he knew she wouldn't mind another kiss, but he couldn't find that out without asking, and just the thought of doing so made his hands sweat.

As she got closer, he wiped his palms against his trousers though there was no reason to worry about kissing now. He probably smelled so awful, she'd slap him for stepping too close.

She stopped in front of him. "Do you know where Jimmy is?"

He kept his shoulders stiff though they wanted to droop, just like his heart had. Of course she hadn't come looking for him, let alone had any thoughts of kissing in that pretty head of hers. "I saw him about thirty minutes ago on the back porch, but I didn't pay much attention to where he went from there."

"I told him not to go outside." Her little foot stomp made him grin. "Which way did he go?"

"I'm not sure he went anywhere. Maybe he figured the porch wasn't technically outside?" The boy had been working hard to obey Mercy since he'd returned from Ragsdale's, but it was clearly difficult for him, especially when given too many demands. With Timothy cracking down on him lately, Jimmy exploded pretty much every other day.

Aaron looked at the sun's low position and shook his head. "It's getting late. I'll look out here, if you look inside. It's easy enough to miss someone in a house so large."

She shook her head and sighed. "I've looked everywhere, and no one's seen him. I'm going to check the carriage house and hope he's not at the fort, since it's getting dark. If you find him, send him inside immediately. He's yet to clean his room."

Aaron forced himself not to shake his head. How had she let Jimmy go an entire day without accomplishing his one chore? But he wouldn't lecture Mercy about being firmer with Jimmy. He didn't want their current, unspoken truce to disappear in a puff of smoke. If anything was going up in smoke right now, it would be in whatever pipe or cigar Jimmy had gone into hiding with. His attempts to obey the no-smoking rule likely fueled his irritability. "If I find him, I'll escort him to either you or Cook so he can't slink off again."

"Thank you." She headed toward the carriage house, and he put away his mower and scanned the grounds. Where might Jimmy be this time? Several of the sheds and outbuildings would keep him hidden. If the boy was smoking in the woods, Aaron might as well wait for him to return rather than search blindly for him.

He washed at the pump and looked around, deciding to check the half-sunken cellar on the backyard slope, where Jimmy had disappeared the day of the marble game.

He turned off the spigot and headed down the hill. Earlier that week, he'd noticed several flattened grass pathways near the cellar that had kept his mower from cutting efficiently. Might be the result of water runoff or animals, but the cellar would make a good hiding place, since nothing valuable was stored there. He'd yet to clean it out—definitely a winter project.

Once he passed the oak tree, sounds of someone talking made him look around. Had Mercy found Jimmy? Seeing no one, he kept going. Probably just the young men Nicholas had hired putting their mowers in the shed.

He took his time walking down the gentle slope, stretching his arms. He no longer ached all day long, but he still collapsed into bed every night. Did this job ever get easier?

Of course, he might not find out. Though Lowe had complimented him on his hard work before leaving on a business trip this afternoon, his ability to do manual labor wouldn't keep his boss from advertising in the fall for a bona fide gardener.

He'd heard the school board was supposed to finish hiring in a little over two weeks. Would Mercy change her mind about barring him from the teaching position before then? She'd forgiven him and seemed all right with him helping with the children now . . . but she'd yet to agree to let him adopt Owen.

As he got closer to the cellar, the muffled voices grew louder—though he still couldn't place where they were coming from.

Wouldn't Mercy have told him if another orphan had gone missing? Though if the rest had done their chores, maybe she hadn't worried about them.

A scuffling, a muffled growl, and an "Oof" proved the voices he was overhearing were more than just a conversation.

Racing down the stairs to the cellar entrance, his heightened breathing kept him from hearing much of the muffled noises.

He ducked under the nearly collapsed doorway, his body blocking the waning sunlight. He couldn't see a thing, though a cry made his heartbeat tick up a notch. He widened his eyes, hoping his vision would adjust to the dimness.

The movement of shadows was undeniably that of people wrestling about on the floor.

"Hey!" he barked. "Who's in here?"

"Get off m—" A boy's voice was cut off.

Aaron stumbled over a root that had grown up through the dirt floor. He raised his arms in case he needed to block a punch. "Who—?"

"He makes me do it. I swear!" Jimmy's voice came out like a desperate whine. "I don't want to. He makes me—"

"Shut up," said the other voice, low and menacing, cutting Jimmy off.

Aaron's stomach did an empty flip, and he tasted bile. His skin flashed hot.

No.

He'd wondered if someone had mistreated Jimmy in the same way he'd been mistreated, and yet he'd assumed the boy was safe at the orphanage.

How could he have been so dense?

Blackness crowded Aaron's vision, nearly obscuring the cellar's pervasive darkness.

A whimper was followed by some sort of sickening squelch, like a hand to a throat.

He knew far too well what would happen to Jimmy if he struggled too much. Or if he didn't struggle at all.

How many people on this earth had to endure such cruelty before God stopped it?

Aaron's whole body shook as he charged forward, but he stumbled over a junk pile he could barely see. The boy's stifled cry sent his pulse up like a rocket.

The sounds of anguish were perfect echoes of the ones he'd tried to swallow so many years ago. Memories he'd forced into the abyss swelled up over him, making his heart race, his breath cinch, and time slow as if he were being swept away in a raging sea.

He had to stop the nightmare.

He charged toward the struggling shadows and latched on to the bigger shape on top, surprised by the weight of the body. He flung the man toward the wall and scrambled after him with a shout.

The stranger put his head down and charged forward, hitting Aaron like a battering ram, sending them both into the wall. Aaron slumped forward but quickly recovered to catch the man by the shirt. They wrestled for a grip on each other, but the man twisted out of his grasp and headed straight for Jimmy's cowering figure.

This man would never touch Jimmy again, so help him God.

Aaron grabbed him from behind and flung him back, but the man recovered quickly, getting in a sucker punch to Aaron's jaw, adding stars to the darkness.

Aaron struck back blindly, hitting something soft.

Before his vision cleared, the man snaked his arm around his throat, and a new-made darkness annihilated Aaron's senses.

He was all too familiar with massive hands denying him breath, how his heart would nearly explode knowing what was coming, being powerless to stop it. Always the choice between submitting in agony or fighting, which would only enrage his uncle.

Aaron stilled and quit fighting for breath, calming the panic. He was bigger now. Stronger.

He dug his hands into the arm crushing his throat, pulling it inches away, and gained a breath. With a surge of energy backed by a primal growl, he escaped the headlock.

The second he caught his breath, he lost it when a fist crashed into his soft lower back.

The pain flashed with a light that didn't help him see in the dark. He winced and stumbled forward.

He spun around, despite the dizziness, and lumbered after the man. He couldn't let him get away—he had to answer for his wickedness. For all the hurt he'd caused.

Aaron caught his assailant just as he blocked the entrance, obliterating the faint light and darkening all the shadows.

He yanked the man back, flipping him onto the ground, and tried to pin his writhing form to the floor. "How does it feel to be the one struggling now?"

How often had he forced himself not to resist in order to shorten the humiliation he'd have to endure? Hoping submission would earn him a reprieve from his uncle's attentions because he'd been "a good boy"?

His uncle's fist hit him so hard he heard a ringing in his ears. "Get off me!"

"You think I'm going to let you go, when I finally have you under my control?" He wrenched his uncle up a little, leaning away from a wild swing. "You think I'm ever going to be 'good' for you again?"

Being "good" only added to the shame, heightening the desire to die and be free from the recurring shredding of his dignity.

Aaron pressed a knee into his uncle's gut and sent a right hook into his face, then another. And another.

"Stop!" A soft female voice behind him registered as he took another swing.

A tearful voice sounded from the corner. "Don't hurt him anymore."

And then an otherworldly dash of cold pulled back the blackness. The man pinned beneath him, looking up with total hatred marring his face, was not his uncle. Of course he wasn't. He hadn't ever been. How had he . . . ?

Aaron's labored, rage-infused breathing made it impossible to hear anything but his lungs working overly hard, making his sense of sight exquisitely acute. The young man's bruises were already coloring, his swollen face that of a man twenty years old instead of forty. A trickle of blood shone crimson amid his sparse whiskers, rage swirling in his eyes as he writhed under Aaron's weight.

Aaron's whole body shook, but he didn't let him go. Though the young man might not be able to get away from him, that didn't mean he couldn't overpower Jimmy.

"Get off him," Jimmy pleaded.

He wouldn't. He turned to the boy. "If he's making you do the unfathomable, why would you ask for his freedom?"

The young man under him stilled—probably expecting mercy he didn't deserve.

Jimmy tentatively slid forward, looking at Aaron and then at the man whose shirt was firmly embedded in Aaron's fist. Jimmy looked toward the exit as if about to flee, but he backed up and rubbed his neck, staring at the man on the ground. "He's my . . . brother."

Aaron's shaking didn't lessen. "So? Family can inflict upon you a shame so deep that blood means nothing."

"No, I mean . . ." Jimmy shrugged. "I mean he wasn't doing anything more than telling me what to do and . . . and . . . things like that. He's like Miss McClain, just pushier."

"What?" His body somehow shook even harder. "You mean he wasn't . . . ?"

What had he done? Had he just beaten up a man because Jimmy was a defiant, disobedient child, like always?

Aaron let go of the young man's shirt and lurched back, hitting the earthen wall behind him with a thud.

He couldn't stop shaking. He held up his swollen hands and watched as his victim ran out of the cellar and into the night. How had he lost control so badly? How had his brain shut down enough he'd . . . he'd . . .

His breathing grew shallow, and he fought to gulp in air.

God was supposed to help him repress his anger and shame. But in the blink of an eye, he'd become a bully again. An honest-to-goodness bully—or maybe worse.

He'd just hurt someone because he could, because it made him feel better.

A featherlight hand settled upon his right shoulder, and he turned to find Mercy's face inches from his.

The shaking stopped, and his body lost all its heat.

Mercy—the female voice that had broken through his haze of fury.

Now she'd never see him as anything other than what he once was—still was. She'd watched him tear into someone who'd done nothing more than tussle with his younger brother. How she must despise him.

"Aaron?" Her voice was soft, as if it were a million miles away.

He couldn't breathe. He was going to be fired. She'd turn him in to the police. She'd keep Owen from him. He'd never kiss her again, let alone breathe the same air.

Just one moment in time and his old ways had resurfaced, ruining his life, his entire reason for coming to Teaville, all chances of being forgiven gone.

"I . . ." He swallowed again, searching for something to say, though no words were good enough.

Her hand seared the cold flesh beneath his sleeve.

He scrambled to stand, then backed toward the exit, holding his throbbing hands up in front of him, noting a sharp pang where he'd split the skin across his knuckles.

"Aaron . . ."

The moment the cool evening air hit his neck, he turned and rushed up the stairs and toward the woods, barely running well enough to stay upright.

The Holy Spirit was supposed to check his old ways—but he'd completely lost all sanity.

He stumbled into the undergrowth, crashing through limbs and tripping over roots. The greenbriers ensnared his pants, ripping fabric and flesh. When he ran up against a thick wall of cedars, he dropped heavily to his knees.

An unmanly wail tore out of his throat, though the sound barely registered.

Rough, heaving sobs possessed him, and pain twisted his stomach. What he'd just done and what he'd once endured burned a hole in his middle. Despite the dirt and pine needles embedded in his palms, he ground his hands into his eye sockets. But no matter how hard he pressed against his eyes, he couldn't stop the memories flashing before him, the pain ripping him in two, the hopelessness that pulled him to the ground.

Tears poured out like a flood—useless tears. They couldn't cleanse him from anything.

He had worked so hard to suppress the memories so he'd never lash out again. He'd summoned up the courage to live as the man he'd always wanted to be but never felt he could be.

But his depraved self had resurfaced in all its glory.

The time he'd lived in the light made it that much harder to plunge back into the darkness.

20

Mercy moved the flickering lamp closer as she stitched her second quilt block of the day. The moral society had decided to quickly piece together another quilt top for next week's auction to benefit Max and Robert, and everyone had taken blocks home.

But instead of starting her next seam, Mercy leaned toward the darkened window, straining to hear whatever sound was coming from outside. Was it the steady whirring of a mower despite the sun having set more than an hour ago?

In the week since the fight in the cellar, if she went anywhere near Aaron, he'd find work to do elsewhere. Now that summer had arrived, she spent a lot of time with the children in the backyard, and the grass had grown higher than it should have. Surely he wasn't mowing in the dark to evade her.

The wind stirred the curtains, but no shadowy movement confirmed Aaron's presence. Then a gust of wind rattled the pampas grass. That must have been it. And yet she was a little disappointed not to see him roaming about in the dark. She'd seen so little of him in the past six days.

Though he avoided her, the hopelessness in his posture and expression couldn't be masked, even from afar.

Aaron had run from the cellar as if chased by wolves, and she'd assumed the other man had run off to report the assault. She'd braced herself for the impending chaos, but the police never came.

Had the other man started the fight and Aaron was the one not pressing charges? She'd hardly figured out what was happening before it was over.

Though she'd felt like running after Aaron, she'd stayed in the cellar to make sure Jimmy was all right.

He'd had nothing but a bruise to his right cheekbone and a serious case of evasiveness.

Upon asking why he'd never told them about his brother, Jimmy quickly denied having a real brother. He'd said all street children called each other brother and sister because they very well could be, considering hardly any of them knew who their father was.

And yet the man who'd rushed past her had been at least twenty years old, and Jimmy had said he wasn't from the Teaville district.

Of course, Jimmy had an answer for that too. The man was the older brother of a friend of his at school who lived in the district. They couldn't get smokes on their own, so Zachary, as Jimmy called him, brought them some.

At least the mystery of where he got his tobacco was solved.

But when she'd asked if they should report Zachary for whatever it was he was forcing Jimmy to do, the boy had called her a busybody and stalked off for the mansion. Since then, he'd refused to talk to her at all.

She'd asked Caroline if she knew who Zachary was, but she had no idea. None of Jimmy's teachers could guess who Jimmy's "friend" might be, considering his classmates spent as little time with him as possible.

It was as if Zachary didn't exist.

She glanced at the clock and shook her head. She'd wanted to get this block finished tonight, but it wasn't meant to be. Stuffing the material into her basket, she headed toward the kitchen for a glass of milk.

A faint sound slowed her footsteps, and she cupped her ear in an attempt to hear it again.

A *thunk* in the kitchen, and the sound of someone grumbling.

Everyone had turned in for the night, though she hadn't seen her brother return. Patricia had said he'd come home ill and went to bed immediately. Strange, because her brother rarely holed up when sick—rather he grumped about like a bear.

A short expletive confirmed her brother was indeed in the kitchen. Had he come down in search of medicine? How like Patricia to send him down himself rather than get up in the middle of the night and risk being seen in her nightcap.

Mercy turned into the kitchen and frowned at the darkness. Why hadn't Timothy lit a lamp? She felt along the wall for the knob and turned on the gas light.

Timothy was draped over the sink.

"What—?"

The sound of his retching made her stomach catch.

She wasn't much of a nurse, but she couldn't just let him stand over there alone. She grabbed a towel and headed over. "I'm so sorry you're sick." And here she'd thought Patricia had been covering for him being out late again. Ever since Nicholas had left on his business trip, Timothy had gone right back to staying out late.

Did he think Lydia wouldn't notice?

Mercy put her hand on his back and handed him the towel. "What can I get you? Some water, crackers, ginger?"

"Fried eggs."

"Fried eggs?" Surely that wouldn't sit well on a sick stomach.

"And coffee."

She felt his head to make sure he wasn't delirious. Clammy but . . .

He turned to look at her and winced. "Can you turn down the light?"

The alcohol smell was overwhelming, despite being mixed with smoke and the pungent odor of his getting sick. She pushed away and shook her head at him. "You're drunk." How had she not realized that immediately?

Had Patricia known? Surely she couldn't have known hours ago when she'd said he'd come home sick, since he hadn't been here at all. Had Patricia known he was out drinking or only hoping to distract them from noticing how often he'd been gone this week? "I cannot believe you."

Timothy grimaced. "Talk quieter, would ya?" He stumbled toward a chair and tried to sit down but almost missed. Thankfully he caught himself before he crashed on the floor. "You gonna make me eggs or not?" he slurred.

She ground her jaw. "No, because the smell will make someone wonder who's cooking this late, and they'll come find you like this. I thought you said one or two drinks didn't hurt anybody. I thought you weren't a bad role model for the boys."

"It's not as if they're awake to see me. And I don't know how—" He hiccupped and then groaned with a wince. "I don't know how I got drunk. They must've given me something different." His head swooped to the side as he stared at her through eyes narrowed in pain. "What are *you* doing up?"

How dare he use an accusatory tone with her. "I was working on a charity project."

He rolled his eyes but winced with the gesture and let his head loll with a groan.

She took a seat next to him. "You're going to get us kicked out of here."

"Don't worry." He waved his hand in front of him in a jerky motion. "I got it under control."

Right, he was completely in control. "Do you know the position you're putting me in?"

He slapped the table and winced again. "You think I want to feel like this?" He dry heaved, and she tossed a rag toward him, but thankfully his stomach didn't betray him.

"You cannot come home like this ever again!"

He winced at her shout.

Though she had little sympathy for his headache, she didn't want to alert the house to his drunken state either. She leaned forward to speak more softly. "If you can't be what the Lowes need you to be, resign. Because if they have to fire you, not only is there scandal to deal with, but they'll have to scramble for someone to replace us. They have better things to do."

He waved his hand up and down as if he could lower her volume by flapping his hand in the air. "I heard you already. Plenty loud too. Now what about that coffee?"

She pursed her lips to keep from telling him to make it himself. Considering how wobbly he was, he'd likely drop the percolator and wake the entire household. She pushed away from the table with a huff and went to make him coffee, though drinking it this late at night wouldn't help him sleep—and that, more than coffee, would likely be best.

But if coffee would convince him to go upstairs sooner, where he could moan and groan behind closed doors, she'd make him a gallon.

A sweep of lights illuminated the windows behind her. She stiffened.

A car at this time of night?

The only person who'd have a visitor in an automobile would be Nicholas, and he was still on his business trip.

She set up the percolator and pulled the coffee from the cupboard as quietly as she could, but she'd wait to start brewing until after Franklin or Caroline answered the door, lest the aroma cause them to investigate.

The front door's hinges whined—no knock. She held her breath.

"Welcome home, sir," Franklin said, his voice muffled by the distance.

Her breath hitched.

Nicholas must've had Henri drive him home in his sporty little speedster. She threw a glare at her brother to warn him to be silent. His lolling head and glazed eyes indicated he did not realize his boss had come home.

"You're a day early." Franklin's voice rumbled.

"Yes." Nicholas's voice was louder.

She froze. Had he moved into the hallway? Her fingers trembled, so she set down the cup she was holding. What if he came into the kitchen instead of heading upstairs directly?

The sound of something soft dropped on the floor. Then the shuffling of footsteps ceased. "Is my wife still up?"

Oh, please let him go check.

"The light in the music room is Miss McClain doing needle-work, I believe." Franklin grunted, likely picking something up—a suitcase, perhaps.

Oh, why had she turned up the lights so high in the kitchen? If either of them decided to check on her in the music room and found her missing . . .

"Mrs. Lowe retired with Jake early this evening. He was fussing over his teeth. Miss Rivers put Isabelle to bed."

"Thanks. Put these away, would you?" Nicholas audibly yawned, and then footsteps ebbed, followed by the familiar creak of the spiral staircase's steps.

Mercy leaned heavily against the counter to keep from melting onto the floor. Seemed she'd have time to sober up Timothy before letting him go upstairs.

If only Franklin went straight to his room and didn't come looking . . .

She went to the switch and turned down the lamp, hoping it was no brighter than the moonlight and wouldn't catch Franklin's attention, but she needed to see to make coffee.

The mansion went still again—except for the man mumbling and groaning at the table behind her.

"Hush, Timothy, or Nicholas will find you out," she whispered across the room. She'd thought about telling Nicholas about seeing Timothy in the district, but with the fire, Max and Robert leaving, and the stress between Jimmy and Aaron right now, she couldn't imagine leaving Lydia to deal with all the orphans and her own two children with only the household staff to help during the day, since Nicholas was gone so much trying to salvage his businesses and tend to his displaced workers.

But with how things were going, it wouldn't be long before her brother got himself fired without any admission from her.

She dumped the coffee grounds in, then went to the table and sat across from him to whisper. "You say you won't get drunk again, but do you not see why you can't drink at all anymore? It's only a matter of ti—"

Timothy stood up so fast he knocked over his chair and raced to the sink to empty his stomach again.

She winced with every clatter of the chair and every retch in the sink, waiting for the sound of rushing footsteps coming to expose them.

After he quieted, she unclamped her hand from the table. Seemed no one had come to check on the noise.

Oh, how was she going to get through tonight? And why wasn't this Patricia's job? She dug through the drawers for another towel and cleaner.

After wiping Timothy up and taking care of the sink, she poured him coffee and sat across from him, counting the ticks of the clock. She wasn't about to make eggs. The percolating coffee had emitted enough noises and smells.

"Mercy?" Nicholas's voice sounded from down the hallway.

She nearly jumped out of her skin, and her heart raced.

Her brother didn't even move from where he'd slumped atop the table.

Nicholas would soon discover she wasn't in the music room, and since she'd left the lights on, he'd assume she'd not gone to bed.

And then he'd notice the kitchen light.

21

Mercy rounded the table and shook her brother's shoulder. "Get up, Timothy," she whispered through clenched teeth.

Nicholas's footfalls sounded far away, but it was only a matter of time before he'd find them.

Timothy moaned and let his head slump to the other side to sort of look up at her. "No, I'm fine right here."

"You are not." She pulled back his chair, wincing at the scraping sound that would bring Nicholas faster. She glanced about the room. Where to put her brother? She could stuff him in the butler's pantry, but if he got sick again, he'd be found. Sending him off around the dining room might work . . . if he could be quiet enough to sneak around without alerting Nicholas. Unlikely.

She shook her head and pulled him to stand. She couldn't trust her brother to do anything at the moment—or at all, actually.

"Come on." She pulled him toward the back door. She didn't want Aaron to see her brother drunk either, but he was likely already asleep. "You can sit on the stairs. The fresh air might do you good."

Timothy tried to wrench himself from her grip but was too weak. "I walked all the way home in the fresh air."

"Evidently your skull's too thick for it to penetrate. Regardless, Nicholas is coming."

"Well, why didn't you say so?" He stumbled forward and unfortunately grabbed the doorknob on his way out and shut the door hard behind him.

She pressed her hand against the door's windowpane to stop its rattling and groaned. What possible excuse could she give for that slam?

"You're up late." Nicholas's voice made her whirl around.

"Why, yes. I couldn't sleep, so I . . . decided to sew on the quilt but got famished."

He stared pointedly at the table. "Coffee isn't going to help much with sleeping or hunger."

She took in a shuddery breath. "Well, no, but I figured since I wasn't sleeping . . ." She forced herself not to shake her head. What had her brother ever done for her that deserved her lying to cover for him?

He did provide for her. He'd applied for this job to supplement his bank salary precisely because of the burden she was to him. It wasn't as if he didn't do anything.

Nicholas walked to the table and sat. "Do you mind if I join you?"

Mind? It was the worst thing that could happen right now. "No, of course not." She forced herself to walk away from the door, thankful he hadn't asked why she'd been outside. "You want coffee?"

He shook his head, weary lines tracing his forehead. "No. I'm quite ready to go to sleep. I've been traveling most of the day."

"Then, why don't you head upstairs?" And yet, hadn't he already gone up?

Something rustled outside, so she cleared her throat and rushed to turn on the faucet and wash for no reason. She took her time, wondering how long she could do so without looking absurd.

Nicholas leaned back in his chair and stretched, wincing as if sore. "Lydia wasn't about to let me sleep until I talked to you."

Mercy stilled. Had Lydia taken note of Timothy's absences and informed him? But if they planned on firing them, surely Nicholas would have waited until morning. She slowly turned off the water, listening for noises outside but hearing none. She pulled another towel from the drawer.

"Lydia's concerned about you."

Me? She stopped drying her hand for a second but then continued. She'd been quiet this past week, yes, but she'd also had children to attend and an eighth of a quilt to piece together with just one hand. That should've been enough to cover for any unusual contemplativeness. "I told her she shouldn't be."

"Yes, she said she tried to talk to you several times, but you seemed lost in thought . . . and purposely avoiding Aaron."

She nodded. Mostly true, but she wasn't avoiding Aaron, he was avoiding her.

"We realize you might not feel comfortable explaining certain . . . things. But if you won't talk to Lydia about what's bothering you, she thought maybe—since I'm the one who dismisses staff—you could at least tell me if someone needs to be fired. I don't need the whole story, but if Aaron has hurt you, I'll pack him up this instant."

Oh goodness, was that what Lydia had assumed was wrong? Though with the way Aaron took pains to avoid her, along with how she'd asked Patricia to watch the children more so she could ask after this Zachary person around town, she could see the jump. "That's not it."

Nicholas sighed in relief, which turned into a yawn. "Could you tell me what's wrong, then? I'd like to set Lydia at ease so I can get some sleep."

His sleepy grin made her want to smile back. If only she didn't feel like a criminal hiding her brother on the other side of the door. "Aaron's not my problem." Timothy was a far bigger problem. "I've been trying to figure out something in regard to Jimmy." She really didn't have an obligation to tell Nicholas about the incident in the cellar—since Aaron clearly regretted it and this Zachary

191

person wasn't pressing charges—and yet Jimmy was everyone's problem. "I, um, was talking to Jimmy and got him to admit someone was bringing him tobacco. He said a young man named Zachary, whose brother is supposedly a classmate of Jimmy's, is supplying him, but no one knows who Zachary is."

Nicholas rubbed his chin. "Do you have more information than a name?"

She shook her head. She hadn't gotten a good look at him when he ran out of the cellar. She'd been more focused on stopping Aaron before he did something else that would drown him in guilt—not that he wasn't drowning in it anyway. "He's young, but not so young he's a child. His little brother supposedly lives in the district, but Jimmy's teachers say he doesn't have any friends."

And though she completely understood why no one wanted to interact with Jimmy, her heart ached a little at the thought. Would some of his bad behaviors disappear if he had a friend?

"I don't know any Zacharys who fit that description. He's not a child we've worked with in the past, but I could ask around."

She nodded, though if they found him, what good would it do?

"Have you considered Jimmy may not have told you the truth? He might have given you a false name to keep you from finding this man."

"Yes." She'd gotten nowhere with any of the information he'd given her.

"Do you think my talking to him would do any good?"

She shook her head. If only he knew how confused she was about what she should and shouldn't do right now. "I think anybody else prying into it would make Jimmy more resistant to talking." And might even get Aaron into trouble if Nicholas learned of the fight. "Please tell Lydia she has no reason to fret over me."

He stood, then yawned. "I'll try."

She breathed a sigh when he turned to leave the kitchen.

Once his footsteps grew silent, she counted slowly to one hundred before going to the back door. At least Timothy had had the wherewithal to stay silent after the initial noise.

Oh, how awful it was to be caught between her loyalty to him and their boss.

She opened the door and found him slumped halfway down the porch steps. "Timothy," she whispered, but he didn't move.

She walked down and prodded him with her foot, but all that moved was his head, lolling from one side to the other. "Timothy." She shook him harder and got no response but a light moan.

Out cold. She couldn't just leave him out here for the servants to find in the morning. And she certainly hadn't the strength to drag him upstairs.

She marched back into the kitchen, filled a glass with water, and returned to throw it in Timothy's face.

He sputtered. "What?" He waved his hands about his head as if warding off a swarm of bees.

"Shhhh!" She hoped the water cleared his head better than the coffee. "It's time for you to head to bed before anyone else comes by."

He rubbed both his hands down his face and flicked the water from his hair. "You didn't have to throw water on me."

"And you shouldn't have come home drunk."

He sighed as if annoyed, but got up. "You're being ridiculous."

She kept her lips pressed tight to keep from arguing more, lest he decide to argue all the way through the mansion. She followed him upstairs, holding her breath as they passed through the hallway, not daring to breathe freely until he was shut behind his own door.

She trudged to her room and slumped onto the bed. What chance had they of not being kicked out within the month if Timothy couldn't get ahold of himself? Even if Nicholas hadn't come home unexpectedly, they could've been caught by any number of people.

But he'd said this was his first time drunk, and he'd not do it again.

She'd given Aaron a chance; should she not give her brother one?

And yet, Timothy hadn't seemed the least bit sorry. Hopefully he'd feel remorse come morning.

Strange to find herself wishing he was more like Aaron.

Lydia was right. The Aaron she knew now wouldn't do anything to hurt anyone if he could help it, and if he did, he'd feel the guilt deeply and apologize repeatedly.

He had indeed changed, and she could no longer act as if he hadn't.

Slipping down off the edge of the bed, she kneeled to petition God to change Timothy just as significantly.

22

Aaron lugged another crate of glass vases and knickknacks from the Sorensons' wagon, hefted it onto his shoulder, and headed inside the mansion to put it with the other auction donations. He'd been carting things up to the third floor all morning, and when he finished that, there were tables and chairs to bring up and set pieces to build for the Shakespeare scenes Max and some of his friends were going to perform. He'd be busy for days. Perhaps that's why Nicholas hadn't fired him for fighting yet—they needed his help too much right now to let go of a strong back.

If they were letting him stay so he'd have time enough to get information out of Jimmy, they shouldn't bother. He'd tried a couple of times to talk to the boy, to figure out what he'd misinterpreted and what the man he'd beaten up was actually making him do, but Jimmy refused to talk. Though he still rolled his eyes and sneered plenty.

Aaron glanced at Mercy talking to her sister-in-law near the music room but made himself look away as he headed for the stairs. He'd at least expected a reprimand from Nicholas—a garnishment, something. He certainly wouldn't complain about the work, since he wanted the auction to be a success, but when would the ax fall?

He stomped up the last of the stairs, set down his crate, and followed Franklin down for more.

"Aaron?" Nicholas looked up at him from the bottom of the staircase.

Despite his heart already beating hard from all the hauling and stair climbing, his heart found a way to go faster. "Yes, sir?"

Nicholas beckoned him to follow and headed for his office.

Aaron tried hard to keep his feet from dragging down the staircase. When he stepped off the last stair, he headed across the foyer, keeping his head down so he couldn't see if Mercy was watching him. Surely she knew why Nicholas was calling him to the office. Would her eyes be filled with pity or vindication?

He didn't want to know.

Nicholas entered the office first and walked to his desk.

Aaron slid in and closed the door behind him. "Sir?"

"I want you to take this upstairs for the auction." He put a hand atop a fancy globe on a wooden stand by his desk. "I've been meaning to take it up, but I keep forgetting, and my lawyer just brought me another stack of paperwork." He picked the globe up and set it in front of him. "It's not exactly heavy, just awkward."

The globe? He exhaled loudly. "Was that all you wanted?"

Nicholas cocked an eyebrow. "Yes. Was there something else you needed to discuss?"

Need? Not exactly, but extricating the pins and needles he was on would be nice. "Has Mercy spoken to you about . . . anything unusual after you returned?"

"No." Nicholas drew up taller. "Is there something I need to know?"

Aaron shook his head. His boss probably should know, but he'd not do anything stupid before the auction. He didn't want to make things harder on the staff right now. If this auction was a success, he might feel as if he'd done something worthwhile here before being asked to leave.

"Unless you mean Mercy telling me this morning that she had no objections to me starting the paperwork for you to adopt Owen. I wouldn't call that unusual though, since I had no doubt she would agree at some point. It's clear you aren't who you once were."

He blinked. She'd decided to let him have Owen . . . this morning? Surely that wasn't right. "*When* did she tell you this?"

"Did she not tell you?" He made a tsking noise. "I guess I just ruined her surprise."

Aaron shook his head but kept his mouth shut to keep from uttering nonsense. A surprise was an understatement.

Nicholas moved back to his desk. "Of course, I'd like to know if you intend to keep him with you in the gardener's cottage or plan to move elsewhere, and when you plan to assume the boy's care—those sorts of things. But we can talk about that later."

Aaron's mouth felt numb, but he forced himself to ask again. "I'm sorry, but are you certain she told you this morning?"

"Yes." Nicholas stopped gathering up papers. "Has something recently come up that will keep you from adopting Owen?"

He'd figured beating up Jimmy's brother a week ago would've done that. But if she'd told him only this morning . . . something wasn't making sense. "Uh . . . no, sir."

"As I said, we can talk through details and paperwork later." Nicholas pointed toward the globe. "Don't forget that."

His feet moved forward, though his brain was foggy. "Can I continue on as gardener if I don't get the teaching position?" Would Mercy change her mind about keeping him from that? He'd pretty much given up the hope of teaching in Teaville, but what if . . . ?

"Figured you might want to. The transition for Owen might not be as difficult that way, and you'll have no problem keeping him well fed, since Cook will see to that." He smiled. "But yes, you're welcome to raise your son in the gardener's cottage."

His son. Though he'd set out to convince Mercy to allow him to have Owen, he'd not let himself think that far.

A son, with no wife to help him. What had Iris been thinking?

Perhaps he needed to stop asking people what they wanted him to do to earn their forgiveness. Who knew what other crazy things he might find himself obligated to do. If Iris hadn't realized how completely insane it was to ask the man who'd tormented her to raise her son, who knew what his other victims might come up with.

Nicholas was staring at him.

Aaron rubbed his hands on his trousers. "Thank you, sir. I'd like time to think that over." Though Owen would appreciate Cook's cooking over his, staying in the cottage meant he'd be living right next to Mercy. Would he feel as if she were judging his every parenting decision? And yet she'd decided last week's round of fisticuffs with Jimmy's brother wasn't a reason to keep Owen from him.

"Oh, I forgot to tell you, there are some easels in the pump room. I saw the women carrying up paintings and thought they might like to use them for display."

Aaron hefted the globe. "All right. I'll get them."

Nicholas was already back to work, so Aaron walked out the door and halfway down the hall before he realized he was going the wrong way. He turned back for the stairwell, but Mercy had just slipped inside.

He stopped. What would he say to her?

He should thank her, though he was more inclined to ask what was wrong with her. Why had she told Nicholas she agreed to Owen's adoption when her belief that he shouldn't be anywhere near children had been justified by the fight last week?

But he couldn't talk to her in a stairwell with a huge globe between them. He set it against the wall. If he got the easels, he wouldn't be following on her heels. He headed toward the basement stairs.

Today's goal of staying busy and out of Mercy's way had gone out the window.

Should he tell her she'd made a mistake?

Because she had.

But if he didn't take Owen, he'd feel as if he'd failed the boy and Iris both.

Dodging Franklin and Max carrying a settee through the entryway, Aaron slipped into the servants' stairwell and headed to the basement.

The long room behind the basement stairs was filled with all sorts of things stacked along the walls, but where were the easels? He walked the length of the room, hoping to spot them before he had to start digging around.

The door slammed above him, and a baby's fussing accompanied a shuffling set of footsteps. Caroline must be headed down to put the baby to sleep.

Thank you, God, for not giving me Owen as a baby. I'm not sure how I'll do raising him, but I'd have been lost with what to do with an infant.

Katelyn cried louder, and Caroline shushed her.

Maybe if he stayed on as gardener, he and Caroline could help each other. Being single with a child couldn't be easy. Perhaps he could offer to help her if she'd help him—though what he could possibly do to help her he didn't know.

Ah, the easels. He pulled three of them out from behind some sort of cart. He'd have to wash them before taking them to the third floor.

The servants' door above the pump room slammed again, and this time, the footsteps were louder and quicker.

"Caroline!" a man's voice called, the thick accent belonging to Henri.

"What are you doing down here?"

Aaron picked up the easels and headed for the doorway. Maybe Henri would take them up so he could get the globe.

"I've been trying to get you alone for days now so I can ask you to marry me, but you won't stand still."

Aaron froze. This was definitely not a conversation to interrupt. He took a step back into the pump room to keep from being seen.

Hopefully she'd say yes and they'd move on, never to know he'd overheard.

"What?" Caroline's incredulous tone must've surprised the baby, since she quit fussing.

"You asked me to help you figure out a way to raise Katelyn

without burdening the Lowes, and I can't think of a better way than for us—"

"No," Caroline answered.

Aaron winced and held his breath.

"I know you don't want much to do with me, but the marriage can be . . . convenient, if you so wish. That way, you can care for the baby without needing to worry about—"

"I wouldn't want you to marry someone you care nothing for just because you feel guilty about what I said to you last year. It's not your fault my sister went into prostitution in some misguided attempt to give me a chance with you."

Aaron closed his eyes. He shouldn't be privy to this conversation, but part of him couldn't help but be curious.

"But you said—"

"Please." Caroline's voice had grown misty. "I didn't tell you about how Moira saved me from the life she now leads to guilt you into caring for me. I know you don't feel anything for me—"

"I don't feel guilt in regard to you." Henri's voice lowered in intensity. "Do you really think no man would want to protect or help you? All you've done and all you've sacrificed for those no one else cares about hasn't gone unnoticed."

"That may be true, but I know men. They want attractive women. And any man who once pursued my sister could not be attracted to me."

"Look at me, Caroline." Henri's footsteps echoed in the hallway. "Am I at all attractive? Even when we were young I wasn't much to look at, and now I'm older and fatter. What I can't understand is what you saw in *me* back then."

"You were nice to me." Caroline's voice choked, and she shushed the baby, even though Katelyn's grousing had subsided, perhaps mesmerized by the insistent voices. "You didn't pay me much mind, but you were never mean when I got in the way, and you weren't unseemly like the other men who came to see my sister. And you seemed to genuinely care for her, which was admirable compared to the others."

She sniffed. "And then years later, I saw you helping Nick assist the red-light women."

"You liked me even then?"

"No. I mean . . . I was over you by then, but that doesn't mean I couldn't still admire you."

A thick silence descended for a moment, and Aaron tensed to keep from moving, in case the slightest movement would echo against the concrete walls.

"Did Nick ever . . ." Henri cleared his throat. "Did he tell you why we aren't friends anymore?"

"I'm not privy to his personal affairs, but I'd guessed it's because he's too religious."

"No. I mean . . . he is. But that's not why we're no longer friends. It's because I wasn't helping the women out of compassion, like you and Nick do. I was doing it for selfish reasons. . . ." Henri muttered something Aaron couldn't hear.

Aaron put his head against the concrete wall, wanting to pray for them to be done so he wouldn't feel like a cad for eavesdropping, but it seemed they needed this conversation too much for him to disrupt it. He just hoped he'd not sneeze or something.

"I'm afraid to say too much because . . ." Henri's voice warbled. "Well, my proposal still stands. I want to help you live as you please, to allow you to focus on the baby, to want for nothing. You came to me asking for a job, and this is the job, to be a mother and homemaker. And maybe come to care for me a little, to see if your old feelings for me could return. I'll do the earning money part."

"Why would you be willing to change your life for us?"

Aaron held his breath. *Come on, Henri, just tell her.* The man's voice was too breathy and uneven to mask his true feelings. No man talked to a woman like that if he felt nothing for her.

"If you're willing to have me, I'd be gaining quite a bit, actually—a wife I don't deserve and a family to keep the loneliness at bay. I might have to give up some things, yes, but at some time a man has to grow up, right? I've thought this through, Caroline.

I've even begun to hope for it. I could do some good, make up for the past, be worth something to somebody, and I . . ."

The basement turned quiet, and Aaron held his breath. Had they moved away, or had they heard him and realized they weren't alone?

His heart thumped loudly in his ears, and the shallow breaths he allowed himself to take sounded like a rush of wind. But at least he didn't hear footsteps coming toward him.

"I don't know, Henri. I don't know." And then soft, shuffling footsteps receded down the hallway.

"Please," Henri called after her. "Please think about it." The tone of his voice revealed his heartbreak from being turned down. It was subtle, but it was there.

"All right." Caroline's voice was far enough away that her words were almost too soft to hear. And then a door shut.

A spell of silence, and then a man's heavy footsteps started up the stairs.

Aaron allowed himself to breathe again.

It'd probably be best to wait a minute or two in case either of them saw him leave and realized he'd been close enough to overhear.

What had come between the two of them to alienate them so? Something terrible Henri did in the past, obviously. And yet he still had the courage to tell Caroline he was in love with her. Well, not in words, but if Aaron could hear it in the man's voice, then surely Caroline had to have an inkling.

If Jimmy and Robert could see he wanted to kiss Mercy, surely Mercy at least realized he didn't hate her anymore, not that he'd ever hated her. He'd only hated himself for not being able to be like her.

What if he explained his past to Mercy? She'd overheard him reliving his memories the night in the cellar, so she must have some idea. She might be horrified to learn the details, and it might not help her understand why he'd once treated her so poorly, but at least she would know why he'd gone temporarily mad that night.

And yet she hadn't told Nicholas what happened. If he'd beaten that young man up a month ago, she most certainly would have.

He had to know. If she could see him at his worst and somehow think he was still worth something . . .

He picked up the easels, and after a glance into the hallway to be sure no one would see him leave the pump room, he headed out as nonchalantly as possible.

Yet his heart tripped all over itself. He hoped his feet wouldn't follow in kind as he made his way upstairs.

He'd never told anyone his story—except for the reverend in California. But if he was going to tell someone else, it should be Mercy, the girl who'd borne the brunt of his anger in years past, the woman who evidently saw something redeemable in him when he'd thought he'd lost all hope of redemption.

23

Aaron thumped up the last of the stairs with the newly cleaned easels and forged into the busy third-floor ballroom, where the moral-society ladies were arranging things for Friday's auction.

Mercy was still working on the west side of the room, as she had been when he'd brought up the globe earlier, but now she was alone. Which meant he might be able to talk to her.

His internal temperature rocketed, and his hands turned slippery.

"Here." He held out the easels to Mrs. Sorenson. She'd been bossing everyone around all afternoon, despite the auction being Mercy's idea, so he might as well skip straight to letting her decide what to do with the easels. "Mr. Lowe thought these would help display your father's paintings."

She looked down her dainty nose as if worried he'd brought her something questionable but then waved her hand toward a corner. "Stick them over there."

He caught himself backing away as if she were royalty—though she *was* wearing an awful lot of jewelry for a workday. Dressed as she was, maybe that was how she justified barely working. He shook his head at his attitude while walking to put the easels where she'd indicated. He knew better than to judge someone based on actions alone.

After he put the easels in the corner, he looked across the room. Mercy was still by herself.

He crossed the ballroom, swallowing hard with each step.

Her white cotton shirtwaist was slightly askew as she scrubbed the top of a table seemingly stained with rust. Her navy skirt swished with the action, and he had to look up to keep from watching the movements.

He cleared his throat. "Miss McClain."

She turned to look up at him, her eyes surprisingly warm.

How could she look at him like that? He hadn't been able to look at himself in the mirror until yesterday, and then only because Robert had made fun of his hair.

His breath stuttered out. "Mr. Lowe called me to his office earlier, but not for the reason I expected. Could you . . ." His voice disappeared. He cleared his throat to encourage it to return. "Could you tell me why I'm not fired?"

She pursed her lips, her expression hesitant and . . . seemingly compassionate. "Judging by the look in your eye that night with Jimmy and Zachary, I figured you would punish yourself plenty for what happened."

Zachary? Somehow knowing the young man's name made the dark hole that had been trying to suck him under all week even bigger. "You knew him?"

She shook her head and looked toward Jimmy, who was standing by the nearby wall, polishing knickknacks. She lowered her voice. "That's the only information I've gotten out of Jimmy since then. And I'm not even sure that's his real name. Have you learned anything about what the man was doing with Jimmy?"

"No, unfortunately." He pulled at the hair at the nape of his neck. "I wish I did, but the boy won't talk to me either."

He stepped closer. "Jimmy keeping things to himself isn't new, but the way I acted the other night . . ." Had she seen less of the fight than he'd guessed? But surely she'd seen enough to know he'd been out of control. "I don't know how you could entrust me with Owen when my actions last week prove little about me has changed."

"That's not true. Years ago, you wanted to hurt people because you'd been hurt, but now you don't. That night, you thought you were protecting Jimmy from the same abuse you'd endured, but the moment you realized you weren't, you quit."

A slight bout of something like dizziness hit him. When had anyone paid that close attention to him? Not his parents—or anyone he'd ever known for that matter. He'd been careful to keep everyone ignorant of the pain that had once driven him, lest they guess the details.

He cleared his throat. "I . . ." He cleared his throat again, but he couldn't continue.

"Hey!" Franklin called from across the ballroom from the stairwell. "Can someone help me with the chair I got stuck in here?"

Robert scurried over to help.

Most everyone else was across the room, but Jimmy wasn't. And he'd stopped dusting.

Surely the boy wasn't close enough to have heard what Mercy said—but if anyone else had a guess at what his secret entailed, it would be Jimmy. If he'd paid attention to what he'd said as he beat up Zachary . . . Maybe he hadn't much of a secret left at all.

What felt like a wet blanket of heat wrapped tightly around him, and his throat closed up.

A waft of cool air blew across his neck, and he turned to see Mercy opening the door to the smokers' balcony a few feet away. She raised an eyebrow and tilted her head toward the out-of-doors.

He followed her out as quickly as he could, despite his body's desire to run far, far away.

There was no need to panic over the thought she might already know his secret. After all, he'd come up planning to tell her about his past.

Outside, Mercy leaned against the railing, her heavy navy skirt and dusty shirtwaist doing nothing for her figure. However, the wisps of blond hair framing her face, the blush of hard work, and the dirt smudge underlining her pink lips somehow made her exceptionally pleasant to look at.

He didn't know whether his breath hadn't yet returned from his earlier panic or if her beauty had stolen it anew.

Mercy's eyes grew confused, and he quickly looked away.

Even if she could see something good in him, she'd never care whether he thought her beautiful or not.

He placed his elbows upon the iron railing and looked out over the gentle roll of hills toward Oklahoma. "I know you'll probably find it hard to believe, but I've worked diligently to get a handle on my anger. I thought I'd done it . . . but now we both know I was only kidding myself."

She stayed quiet, and he slid closer to the wall so no one could see him through the glass doors behind them. What he was trying to hide, exactly, he didn't know, but staying out of everyone's way had brought him some solace lately. If he didn't interact with anyone, he couldn't cause problems.

He played with his hands, watching his fingers slip through each other. "I talked to a reverend in California two years ago who made me believe I could put on the 'new man' if I trusted Christ, that I could shuck my old ways. But it seems I can't." He pressed the heel of his hand against the warmth creeping into his eyes. He was a former bully for pity's sake; he didn't even deserve his own sympathy. "Seems the nightmare of my childhood will always be deep inside me, ready to erupt. I'll never be how I want to be."

She moved closer, and he couldn't get away unless he wanted to climb the wall.

"I'm guessing you're talking about the verse that says you're to put off the old man, which is corrupt according to deceitful lusts?"

"Yeah, that's the one."

"Do you know the verses after that?"

He shrugged. He'd surely read them, but he couldn't come up with what they were.

"The next one says, 'And be renewed in the spirit of your mind.'

That's how you prepare to put on the new man. Becoming who God wants you to be can't be accomplished through willpower alone—we all fail at that. It's letting God change you from within so your renewed mind makes you fit and able to be your new self."

"But surely God wants me to suppress the old me. He's not responsible for my failing to do so."

"God wants you to follow His commands, yes, but Aaron . . ." She put her hand on his arm. His skin suddenly turned cold, but he couldn't make himself pull away. "You alone aren't powerful enough to combat the deceitful desires mentioned in that verse. Your flesh will always be at war with the good you want to do, but hope is found in God's power. You don't become holy and righteous by mustering it up. You don't create the new man. God does. Renewing the spirit of your mind is how you put on that new man God created to be righteous and holy."

He'd not felt anything close to holy and righteous that night in the cellar. "What am I doing wrong, then?"

"It's a process, Aaron. I'm not always my best either." She huffed as if displeased with herself. "But I know some of the ways to renew your mind are spending time looking to Him, praying, reading His Word. The more you do that, the more His power changes you from the inside out, because you're filled with it."

He looked away from her and toward the bright sky.

So putting on the new man wasn't completely his responsibility to shoulder? And yet, God wasn't liable for the evil he'd done or would do. "How do you renew your mind again?"

"Prayer, study, repentance, thanking God for all He's done—daily, for all our lives."

He closed his eyes.

A renewed mind is what I want, God. I know I already asked you to save me to go to heaven, but I need the me here on earth to be fixed and saved as well. I don't have the power to fight myself every moment of every day. I've been trying to earn forgiveness, trying hard to be what I'm supposed to be, but nothing I do feels like it even scratches the surface. I can't do it. I just can't.

He'd definitely proven he couldn't, but Someone could.

If he could trust God to get him to heaven, he needed to trust that God could work miracles in him here on earth too—because if he continued to rely on himself, well, he'd only keep proving how ineffectual he was.

He looked over at Mercy. Her grin was warm, and her eyes were . . .

Had anyone ever looked at him like that—like they were proud? Like they cared?

He didn't deserve it. "I'm sorry for what I did to you as a child—"

"Aaron." She held out her hand. "You've apologized to me enough already."

"But it doesn't really mean anything unless you know why I did what I did to you. I mean, of course I can be sorry, but how do you know I wasn't plain being mean to you?"

"But you weren't, right?"

"Though I'll understand if you never want anything to do with me afterward, I want you to know . . ." His voice faded so much he wasn't sure she could hear him, but he pushed the words out anyway. "If . . . you weren't able to figure it out from my raving in the cellar, my uncle did things to me as a child . . . that I'd rather not go into. Things no man should do to another. He made me hate myself."

He turned his face away from her, staring at some nondescript point in front of him. "I couldn't stand seeing others happy since I believed I never could be, and you . . . you were happy. Without an arm, you were happy." His voice was beginning to sound desperate, but he had to spit the rest out. "For years, I was bent on destroying everyone's happiness since I couldn't have it. My uncle's abuse grew to the point I figured no woman would ever want me—and maybe no woman ever will. But at some point, I'd realized you were the kind of girl I would've wanted to marry. You were always looking out for others, quiet, and helpful. And well, I knew no girl like you would want to have anything to do with me, which made me push you away all the more." He sniffed back the tears he couldn't contain any longer.

And for some reason she was crying too.

"I wanted to hurt you so badly you'd turn on me so I could truly hate you. But you never did, and I never could. I didn't realize until years later why I treated you as I had. If I could go back and tell my twelve-year-old self how my behavior would not get me what I wanted, I'm not sure I'd have believed—"

The door opened, and he clamped his mouth shut, quickly looking down to hide his tears from whoever had come out.

Mercy's hand took hold of his upper arm and she squeezed. "I promise, Aaron, I forgive you," she said low enough he barely heard.

"Mercy?" Nicholas's voice burst through the silence. "Have you seen your brother?"

She quickly turned. "I'm afraid not, but what can I help you with?" She scurried forward and sniffed.

"Are you all right?"

"It's just the dust. I had to get some fresh air before I cleaned any more tables." Her voice grew muffled as she crossed the threshold into the ballroom. "What is it you needed my brother for? Surely I can do what needs to be done."

"He said he'd be here." Nicholas's voice was thinly veiled with agitation. "Could you tell me where he's been? The—"

And then the door shut.

Aaron breathed out a deep sigh and wiped at his eyes with his shirtsleeve.

Dust indeed.

Rather the surety of forgiveness.

For Mercy truly had forgiven him, believing he could and would become a better man. So much so, she'd entrusted Owen to his care.

He didn't need anything else to be happy. He really didn't.

24

Polishing what must've been her thirtieth vase, Mercy couldn't imagine selling them all unless the bidders were generous. Now, where was that pretty one with the irises on it? Someone would want that, and yet it seemed to have disappeared. Everything had to sell for them to have any chance of bringing in enough money for Max and Robert.

If this auction wasn't a success, not only would she have failed the Milligan brothers, but she'd have wasted the moral-society women's and Nicholas's staff's time.

Mercy let herself look about the ballroom to see if Aaron was hauling anything else up. He hadn't been upstairs for a while now, and she couldn't help but notice he was missing.

"Now, now." Mrs. Sorenson rushed over and put her hands under the black vase Mercy still held. "Be careful with this one. My father got it from Belize."

"Of course I will." Mercy attempted to look contrite despite the fact she'd been in no danger of dropping the vase. Thankfully, Stella's mother immediately left to instruct Mrs. Wisely on the best way to display her grandmother's jewelry box.

Did Mrs. Sorenson intend to visit all the auction winners and tell them what to do with her family's "junk," as she'd called it?

Mercy couldn't help but chuckle at how pretentious Mrs. Sorenson was acting, but who was she to look down on someone's foibles and misdeeds?

She'd hated Aaron her whole life, never stopping to think about the person behind the torment. Her mother had insisted she pray for Aaron whenever she came home crying, to heap blessings upon her enemy, but she'd refused.

What if she'd prayed like Momma had told her to? Would his life have turned around sooner? Would he have hurt fewer people if one victim had proven she'd cared?

A huge *whomp* from behind her made her jump. Everyone stopped talking and turned to look toward the front of the ballroom.

Franklin held up his hands as if in surrender. "Sorry. I didn't mean to drop them." At his feet was a pile of lumber he was using to build the Shakespeare set pieces.

Mrs. Sorenson walked over to him, hands on her hips. "Do be careful. You could've frightened someone into dropping something worth more than your annual salary." She tipped her chin, then headed off somewhere else before seeing Franklin screw up his face as if making ready to spit at her.

Mercy twisted the rag in her hand. Had she made a face as sour as that the day Aaron had returned to Teaville? She probably had.

She picked up the last vase to clean. She should've prayed for him when he'd returned to town instead of working against him. If she had, Owen might already be enjoying time with his new father.

"Miss Mercy?"

Mercy turned toward Sadie with a smile. She'd tried to convince the young housekeeper to call her by her first name several times. Seemed Sadie had chosen a compromise. "Yes, Sadie?"

"I've finished cleaning the phonograph and the clocks. What should I do next?"

Mercy looked around and frowned. Stella was supposed to have helped her clean the clocks. "Where's Miss Sorenson?"

"She's taking a break."

Mercy tried not to sigh at another of Stella's breaks. With her mother roaming about the room doing nothing but barking unnecessary commands, the two of them might as well have stayed home. But Stella likely hadn't wanted to pass up a chance to chat with Sadie. "I'm almost done with this table, so . . ." She looked around at what remained to be done. "Maybe you could inventory the player piano rolls?" She beckoned for Sadie to follow her to the table next to the platform Franklin was building.

Once there, she turned, but Sadie lagged behind, her gaze pinned on Franklin hammering a brace to the back of a wooden tree, her expression that of a kicked puppy's.

Mercy looked toward Franklin and frowned. Maybe she could make up for not praying for Aaron by praying for these two. Whenever she caught them looking at each other—when the other one wasn't looking, of course—they seemed miserable.

Sadie finally stopped beside her.

Franklin had started hammering again, so Mercy braved a question. "Have you two talked?"

Sadie shook her head as if clearing it of cobwebs and tore her gaze away from the young butler. "No, but don't worry about that, Miss Mercy. You just tell me what to do."

Mrs. Sorenson charged toward them from across the room. Had some of these piano rolls belonged to her late father? Even if none had, Mrs. Sorenson would likely find fault with how she planned to deal with them.

Mercy brushed dirt off one particularly grimy box. "Unless Mrs. Sorenson has another idea for us, why don't you check if the right songs are in the right boxes."

Mrs. Sorenson blew past them in an animated huff, stopping in front of Franklin, hands on her hips again. "Could you please hammer more quietly?"

Franklin looked up, confused. "I'm not sure that's possible, ma'am. Not unless you want this to take forever."

"If it takes you longer to do so, then so be it. You're giving me a headache."

Before Mercy could cover her amused smirk, Mrs. Sorenson turned toward her.

"I need to talk to you."

She swiped the smile off her lips. "All right." Mrs. Sorenson had never bothered to discuss anything with her before.

The older woman rubbed her hands together. "I've been making a mental tally of all we have and what's still to come, and I believe we shall make a splendid amount of money from this."

Mercy let her smile return. "I certainly hope so."

Mrs. Sorenson's face quickly turned serious. "So I'm wanting to discuss the cap for what we're giving the boys."

When had they ever talked about a cap? "What are you talking about?"

"A cap, as in how much of the proceeds they'll be given."

Had that ever been in question? Mercy tucked a loose strand of hair behind her ear. "All proceeds will be given to them."

Mrs. Sorenson looked down her nose at Mercy, as if she were a simpleton. "There must be a cap. The valuables I alone have donated will fetch more than boys of their nature will need."

"I'm afraid I don't know what you mean by 'their nature.'" Or rather, if she did, she hoped her tone of voice would keep Mrs. Sorenson from spouting her opinion next to Franklin, who'd once been a resident of the orphanage. "You won't find many other young men as hardworking and dependable as the Milligans."

"Yes, yes." Mrs. Sorenson nodded her head, as if placating her, but then moved closer. "But you and I both know these boys haven't been away from the red-light district long enough to forget the low morals they were instilled with. If we give them more money than they need, they'll use it ill. So I was thinking three hundred dollars would be plenty. That's a generous workingman's annual salary."

Mercy wished she had two fists to clench. "Max will be attending school for more than a year."

"Ah, yes, but at the meeting, Mrs. Lowe said Robert planned to get a job instead of continuing his education." She shrugged as if this conversation was as mundane as discussing the lunch menu.

"Anything we fetch over three hundred dollars would be better put to use for other Teaville needs."

Mercy looked at Sadie, who'd been standing quietly beside them. The younger woman's face had gone pale.

So this wasn't a dream. This discussion was actually happening.

How could she respond without offending Mrs. Sorenson? The woman had donated a lot for this auction, so her heart had to be in the right place, even if her beliefs weren't. "I'm afraid living on the East Coast is more expensive than living here—"

"Correct." The older woman smiled, putting her finger up as if Mercy were a student who'd aced an exam. "Which is why I was telling Troy last night—and he thought I had the right of it—that a Kansas City school would be plenty good enough for them. If they went there, the buying power of three hundred dollars would multiply."

Mercy blinked. Hadn't she or Lydia mentioned that Kansas City was a last resort? "If we collect enough to send them to Boston, we will. Max's intellect is worth it." Franklin's hammer had gone quiet, so she lowered her voice. "You know the moral society has chosen to give handmade quilts to the poor instead of cheap wool blankets because we decided not to give the poor what's good enough for 'their kind' but what we would give our own family members. We should do the same for Max and Robert."

"Yes, but as mentioned, Robert plans to work." Mrs. Sorenson didn't seem the least bit deterred. "The money necessary for tuition in Boston is too extravagant for a boy who hasn't the education my own daughter has. Why, Stella's tutors declared her to have an excellent mind, and if she couldn't attend such a prestigious college, why should he?" Mrs. Sorenson's face lost all hints of congeniality. "And why should my boy have to compete against one of such a background for a spot in that school, if he wishes to go?"

Sadie moved to the table and pretended to fiddle with the piano boxes as Mercy just stood there blinking.

Mrs. Sorenson sniffed. "Troy and I spent a good deal of money on private schools and tutoring so our children wouldn't be forced to socialize with those who'd lead them astray." Mrs. Sorenson leaned closer. "It's not right to be so extravagant as to send these two boys to Boston when many parents sacrifice years of wages to be sure their sons learn apart from the riffraff. The Milligans will surely be content with whatever charity they get, and we can use the rest of the money for other worthy projects."

"Um . . ." How was she supposed to respond without agreeing, yet keep Mrs. Sorenson's support?

Without her donations, would they bring in enough money? Three hundred was better than nothing. . . .

"Miss Mercy, why aren't you saying anything?" Sadie's voice behind her was rough and scratchy.

She turned to see a mask of rage marring Sadie's pretty face, a towel crumpled in her right fist.

"I was just thinking. . . ."

"Well, I've thought enough, and that's the most sanctimonious bunch of nonsense I've ever heard." Sadie nodded with enough vehemence she might as well have placed an exclamation point in the air with her head.

Mrs. Sorenson took a step back. "Why, I never."

Sadie walked straight toward Mrs. Sorenson, her hands balled on her hips. "Do you actually think it right to keep poor children from a good education because somehow rich children are worth more? Well, in case you aren't aware, a lot of the fathers of those 'high-society' boys frequent the district. Your sons don't need Max and Robert to corrupt them—their own fathers can do it, along with the mothers who refuse to acknowledge that their children have vices that need to be whipped out of them as surely as the children from the poorest homes."

Mrs. Sorenson's face was pinched. "Perhaps those high-society men who frequent such areas wouldn't do so if they'd stayed away from the influence of those beneath them."

"Hogwash." Sadie snapped her fingers. "Not one child in this orphanage—even the worst-behaving one we have—can corrupt a man who has good values. The attitudes of the rich, evil men who frequent the district have more of a corrupting influence on their sons than any poor boy in need of schooling, I assure you."

"And how are you so certain?" Mrs. Sorenson's face turned bright pink. "You're just a housekeeper—a very young lady who got a position higher than merited because of your looks."

"I know," Sadie spat, "because Mrs. Lowe rescued me from the clutches of such men." Sadie's body jerked, and she bit her lip. Her neck and face flushed bright.

Mercy's blood ran cold. Was that true? Hopefully Sadie hadn't said that loud enough the others had heard. Her words insinuated—

"You mean you . . . were . . ." Mrs. Sorenson's eyes grew wide, and she put a hand to her throat.

Sadie's nod was subtle but definitive.

Mrs. Sorenson took a step back, as if she'd stepped upon unholy ground, then glanced toward her daughter, who now sat silently near the table filled with clocks.

In fact, the whole room was silent. Most everyone was acting busy, but they'd not worked this quietly all day. When had they started listening?

Mercy looked for the oldest member of their group, Mrs. Wisely. If only Nicholas or Lydia were here, they would've stopped this conversation before it'd gotten out of hand.

Mrs. Wisely stood by the paintings, not even pretending to be making a list of donations anymore.

"Stella," Mrs. Sorenson called across the ballroom, beckoning to her daughter.

The pretty blonde cringed.

Mercy could imagine her sinking realization that she was about to have to choose between her friend and her mother. And the poor woman would have to choose her mother.

Sadie's face was stone hard, though it softened a little as Stella got closer. "I've enjoyed being your friend, Stella. I may not have made you a better person, but I sure hope you don't feel as if I've made you worse."

217

Sadie looked toward Franklin, who was no longer pretending to be working. "If people stopped worrying about where Max and I came from, what we could've done or witnessed, they might see us as a blessing. Spending your life excluding people you've decided are beneath you can rob you of a wonderful life with some of them." Sadie gave Mercy a look that was only seconds away from being ruined with tears, then turned and stormed off.

"Well." Mrs. Sorenson shook herself as if Sadie's words had landed on her like dust. "Such an outburst clearly indicates she is not of good stock. At least now Miss Price will no longer be in our group and can't affect us anymore."

Not in their group? Sadie?

Mrs. Sorenson had attended meetings since the beginning of the year. Did she not sympathize with the mission of the moral society? She hadn't participated much beyond the meetings, but surely she'd realized the thoughts lurking in her head weren't held by the rest of them.

Mercy cleared her throat in an attempt to find words. "I'm sorry?" She cleared her throat again. "Why do you think Sadie won't be returning?"

Mrs. Sorenson tucked her chin and frowned as if Mercy had spouted gibberish.

Mrs. Wisely came between them, her body and expression rigid. "We don't ban people from the moral society because of their past."

"But such a past?" Mrs. Sorenson shook her head at Mrs. Wisely as if she should have been old enough to know better. "How can we be considered a moral society with members such as her?"

"All are welcome to join us if they *truly* want to help make our community a better place. We might, however, vote out members if their present immoral or uncharitable actions make them unsuitable."

Mrs. Sorenson looked aghast. "Did you not hear what she insinuated?"

"I heard," Mercy answered, her pulse pounding as the entire room watched. What could she do to keep this woman from besmirching

Sadie's name about town? Surely the rest of them would keep it to themselves, but if this was how Mrs. Sorenson felt . . .

Mrs. Sorenson pulled Stella to her side. "Then you understand why Miss Price cannot be part of a group where you, my daughter, and other vulnerable young women spend so much of their time."

How dare she pull her and Stella into this as if they were too weak to make good decisions on their own? Her whole body trembled, and her heart raced. "Shunning Sadie, who has proven to be nothing but a sweet, shy, hardworking girl, would be wrong if we intend to help those less fortunate than ourselves. How would kicking out a member whose past is like those we're trying to reach make us more effective?"

Oh, and wasn't that a pretty speech she'd just made. And yet the truth was, Mrs. Sorenson's view of Sadie was no different than how Mercy had viewed Aaron only weeks ago. She'd judged him solely by his past, unwilling to see who he was at present. She clenched her arm across her middle. "I . . . I struggle with how I perceive people too, Mrs. Sorenson. But being moral isn't doing what's easiest or what makes you feel comfortable, but rather, it's choosing to do right even when it hurts, when it costs, when it's difficult. So if you force out the girl you were once happy enough to let your daughter befriend, I won't have anything more to do with such a moral society."

Mrs. Sorenson scoffed. "If she returns, I won't. Since I've donated far more to the moral society than you or she ever will, it's easy enough to see who'd benefit the society more."

"But, Mrs. Sorenson, it's not who—"

A heavy hand gripped her shoulder and squeezed hard.

She winced and looked up at her brother.

"Let's not argue anymore about Miss Price. It's probably best she no longer be involved." His jaw was set, and his eyes had that penetrating look indicating he'd brook no argument.

And here she'd thought Mrs. Sorenson's speech had been outlandish. Was he truly suggesting, in front of everyone, that Sadie's

219

past made her unsuitable to help, yet his current trips to the district shouldn't affect his position at the orphanage?

"But—"

"No buts. It's best to stay out of it." His gaze stayed pinned to hers. He seemed rather certain she'd not call him out on his own hypocrisy.

His behavior wasn't the business of anyone in this room, and yet the audacity!

Charlie moseyed up to her other side, her arms across her chest. "I figure God would prefer us to choose our members by their morals, not by their pocketbooks."

"What would you know, Mrs. Gray? You can't even recognize that wearing menswear is inappropriate."

"It's called a split skirt, and I don't know of no men wearing them."

Mercy held up her hand to stop Mrs. Sorenson from entering the brawl their feistiest member was likely itching for. She didn't want anyone leaving the moral society, if she could help it. Mrs. Sorenson had donated time and hours for the orphans' betterment, even if she disagreed on how they could be bettered.

She was not an enemy. There might even be hurt or pain behind her bitter assumptions.

And her brother wasn't an enemy either, though he was certainly trying his best to ruin her opportunity to do the one job she thought herself capable of—the one job she'd like to see through before returning to housekeeping with Patricia. "I appreciate the help you are to the society, Mrs. Sorenson. But this auction was planned to benefit Max and Robert, so all proceeds will go to them. We can plan another fundraiser to meet other needs."

"I agree," said Mrs. Wisely with a nod.

The other moral-society members, who'd been brave enough to step up to the battle lines, muttered agreement too. Well, all except Stella. The poor girl looked as if she'd swallowed a frog.

Timothy took a deep breath but didn't say anything.

"Fine," Mrs. Sorenson huffed. "I'll take my things back and

wait to donate them to a cause I'm more passionate about." She turned to Franklin, who was no longer kneeling with his hammer in hand but rather sitting on the floor, his legs splayed out and his body slumped as if he'd just run several miles. "Mr. Cleghorn, it seems I need your help reloading my things."

She turned and headed toward the tables filled with her late father's possessions, her heels clacking hard against the wooden floor. Before reaching the table, she turned back with a frown, since the quiet of the room had likely alerted her to the fact that Franklin hadn't followed.

He unfolded himself and stood. "I'm sorry, but I'm going to find Sadie and make sure she's all right." He laid down his hammer and headed for the stairwell.

Mrs. Sorenson turned immediately and looked past Mercy's shoulder. "Mr. Firebrook?"

Mercy turned to see him sitting at a table beside her, leaning against its top as if he'd been there quite a while.

"Sure, I'll help." He flashed Mercy a genuine smile and whispered as he passed, "It'll get her out quicker." He strolled across the room in the older woman's angry wake.

"This entire table here." Mrs. Sorenson pointed to her father's war memorabilia. "And this stack of watercolor paintings—no, first the jewelry."

Timothy went over to help, and Mercy leaned against the table. Oh, what had she done? Not only had she ruined the auction by fussing over Mrs. Sorenson's uncharitable attitude, but she'd let her brother's hypocrisy go unchallenged.

Charlie smacked her shoulder as hard as a man might smack another. "Right proud of you." Then she sauntered back to the saddle she'd been polishing.

Proud? Had Charlie not watched her forfeit all these donations because she'd chosen to take down Mrs. Sorenson's pride in front of everyone? Without the Sorensons' things, the moral society's work, advertising, and time had been wasted.

Mercy closed her eyes and slumped. Telling Max and Robert

they would have to go to Boston underfunded or choose a less prestigious school would not be one of her proudest moments.

Stella sneaked over to her side. Though she was taller than Mercy, she'd slumped to her height. "Would you tell Sadie goodbye for me?"

Mercy nodded, and Stella left to help carry away the valuable items already listed in the auction advertisements.

With all the "help" she'd been to the orphans lately, maybe her brother wasn't the only one who would be better off not working at the mansion.

25

Mercy followed her brother and Franklin down the stairs as they carried out the last of Mrs. Sorenson's donated items.

Though the other moral-society members were rearranging the remaining donations to cover the emptied tables, she couldn't stay upstairs any longer. Nor could she handle one more person telling her how proud they were that she'd stood up to Mrs. Sorenson.

If they only knew she'd chosen not to expose Timothy's hypocrisy because she was afraid of what would happen to her. . . .

Well, she'd no longer keep Timothy's secret from the one person who most needed to know.

In the music room, Patricia was reading on the couch, while Owen lay on the Persian rug, drawing what looked like a castle full of potbellied stickmen.

Mercy sat in the chair next to her sister-in-law, wrapping her hand in the folds of her skirt. How did one start a conversation that would end with exposing someone's spouse as a secret drunk?

"Owen?" She cleared her throat. "Why don't you see if Cook has any treats?"

His eyes went wide. "Like cookies?" He didn't even wait for her to answer before scrambling off the floor and out the door.

Patricia laid the book on her chest and frowned at Mercy. "Why would you spoil his appetite this close to dinner?"

Because it had been the surest way to have him disappear for a while. "I wanted to talk to you about something."

Patricia rubbed a hand across her brow. "I heard about Sadie."

She'd heard about Sadie? What about Mrs. Sorenson? "I suppose Timothy talked to you?"

"Yes." Patricia stiffened. "I'm surprised Sadie brought up . . . well, such a past."

"I certainly don't think she meant to." The poor girl hadn't been thinking clearly in the heat of the argument. "Please tell me you won't tell anyone."

Patricia shrugged. "Not my business, but I must say, a woman like that working here with so many men on staff . . ."

Did she really think that possible of Sadie? Though the Lowes' young housekeeper had only lived with them a few weeks, Patricia should've at least recognized Sadie was dependable and loyal. Of course, since Patricia hadn't bothered to do more than learn her name so Sadie would bring her clean bedding and mop up spills, perhaps she wouldn't have figured that out about her.

"I'm not worried about Sadie's behavior, Patricia." Learning of her past had been a surprise, but it was clear that Sadie had put that life behind her. Right now, her brother's future was much more concerning. Mercy sat on the edge of her seat, trying not to cringe too much as she plunged into what needed to be said. "I am, however, worried about your husband's behavior."

Patricia only stared at her.

"Not too long ago, I was in the district with Caroline to tend a woman, and I . . . I saw Timothy at a saloon." Was there any way to soften this blow? "I'm afraid his job hasn't been keeping him out late. He's been missing so often because he's out drinking. He even came home drunk a few nights ago."

Patricia didn't move.

The clock ticked, and Mercy braced herself for an outburst of some kind.

Patricia resituated herself on the sofa. "Is that all?"

Mercy blinked. "What do you mean, 'Is that all'?"

"I know he drinks." She shrugged.

"You do?" And here Mercy had been feeling guilty for keeping such information from her.

Patricia nodded, looking as if there were no problem whatsoever.

"Are you not worried?" Mercy shook her head. "Don't you think Nicholas will dismiss us if he finds out? Which won't be long if Timothy comes home drunk again."

"That was the only time he's come home drunk. It was a . . . misstep. He realizes he had too much that night, but most men drink, law or not." Patricia laid aside her book. "Mr. Lowe's a reasonable enough man. If Timothy isn't hurting anyone, there's no problem."

"Did you not hear that I found him in the district? That's not going to be looked upon kindly by the Lowes. But even more, his drinking keeps him from being here as often as he should be, which causes the children to suffer."

"How so?" Patricia threw back her shoulders, her voice pinched. "Are you implying your brother is worse than whatever mother or father these children once had? Sure he drinks—maybe a little too much that one time—but he doesn't abuse the children. They're fed, they're perfectly happy, they're fine."

Mercy clenched her fist. And here she'd thought if she told Patricia about Timothy's drinking, she'd have someone to help convince him to sober up and become the guardian he was supposed to be. "If he wasn't so busy drinking, he could've spent more time with Jimmy. If he had, perhaps the boy wouldn't be the discipline problem he is."

Patricia pshawed. "Jimmy will always be a problem."

"So that's it? You think there's nothing wrong with Timothy continuing to work here as is?" How could her sister-in-law seem so unruffled?

"You and I are here, aren't we? Max and Robert are well educated and will soon be off to a school they would've had no hope of attending without us." She gestured with her hands as if the children were in front of them. "Owen will soon be adopted, so all we've got left is Jimmy. Hopefully we can make some headway on getting him to behave before more orphans come along."

Did Patricia really think the two of them had a hand in those positive outcomes? Aaron, in less than two months' time, was more responsible for the children's promising futures than they were.

"Besides, you can't want to return to cleaning house again, enduring whatever miserable cook we can afford." Patricia indicated the room with her palm up, as if offering Mercy the finest of accommodations. "We'd miss having this house, the gardens, the driver . . ."

And all the spontaneous naps Patricia took when she pawned her duties off on the house staff. "I do enjoy the house—who wouldn't?—but it comes with obligations we're barely meeting."

"We've not been here long, Mercy," Patricia insisted. "We'll settle in soon enough."

That was all they needed to do? Settle in?

Patricia picked her book back up, and Mercy closed her eyes. And she'd thought talking to Timothy had been like talking to a brick.

Once her heartbeat returned to normal, she rose and headed into the hallway. The children would be better off with different houseparents. Despite her own good intentions, nothing she or her family had done in half a year had had any significant impact on the children.

But did she want to return to the life she'd once had with Patricia and Timothy, knowing how very differently they saw the world?

She wandered toward the open front door just in time to see Mrs. Sorenson and Stella drive away, the wagon behind them piled high with donations.

Henri's speedster turned onto the driveway, kicking up a cloud of dust as he gave the horses a wide berth.

Caroline came out to stand beside her, Katelyn tied to her chest with the wide strip of cloth Charlie had brought to show her how to work with a baby while keeping both hands free. "I'm proud of you, Mercy."

Mercy shook her head. Seemed leaving the ballroom hadn't saved her from the praises she didn't deserve. "Standing up to Mrs. Sorenson only hurt Max and Robert. And you know just as well as I do that I let Timothy get away with condemning Sadie for her past when his current secrets are inexcusable."

Caroline turned from watching Henri's car speeding toward them. "I wasn't actually talking about how you handled those two, but rather how you barely blinked an eye at Sadie's story. She was sure she'd lose friends if anyone found out—just as she lost Franklin—but you stuck by her."

"So that was the problem between them?" Hopefully Franklin would get past his disappointment and see Sadie for the sweet, loving girl she was now. Just like she'd learned to see the good in Aaron. "But I thought Franklin came from the red-light district."

"Yes, but he didn't know about Sadie's past until she told him. He'd wanted to leave everything about the district behind him forever."

"And Henri?" Mercy nodded toward the automobile seconds away from driving up under the portico. She raised her voice to be heard above the rumble of the engine. "What keeps you apart?"

Caroline didn't respond, the engine's roar echoing loudly off the mansion's stone columns. Katelyn startled awake, and Caroline struggled to get her niece out of the makeshift sling.

When Henri cut the engine, Caroline turned to Mercy while patting a sniffling Katelyn. "Seems I'm doing what I'm proud you didn't do. His past makes me reluctant to trust him."

Henri hoisted himself out of the driver's seat of his jaunty little vehicle, but Caroline stayed in place, not running off as she was wont to do whenever he showed up.

He pulled off his hat and approached them with hesitant steps. He looked Caroline up and down, his lips twitching, as if he wanted to say something but couldn't decide on what.

"Good afternoon, Mr. Beauchamp," Mercy said, though there wasn't much good about it thus far.

"And to you as well. Too pleasant a day to stay indoors, don't you think?" He looked back to Caroline and cleared his throat. "You wouldn't happen to want to go on a drive in the fastest car in Teaville?"

Considering he was one of four townsmen who'd purchased an automobile just to race it, Mercy couldn't help but smile at his boast.

Caroline fidgeted. "Unfortunately, I'm busy."

Henri's face stayed unaffected, though Caroline's constant rejection had to hurt. "I understand."

"I mean . . ." Caroline shuffled her feet and moved Katelyn to her other shoulder. "I could've gone, but we've had a crisis. Mrs. Sorenson left in a huff, taking all her donations for the auction with her. I expect Mercy's going to ask us to start scrounging up replacements. We've only got four days."

He looked over his shoulder, as if he could still see the Sorensons, but then turned back, his eyebrows scrunched. "Why would Mrs. Sorenson do that?"

As if having a roomful of people watch her lose half the auction's donations hadn't been bad enough, Mercy now had to recount her misstep to Henri. "I'm afraid it's my fault. I shouldn't have assumed Mrs. Sorenson knew all proceeds would go to Max and Robert. She thought her donations could be used for other projects as well."

Caroline shook her head. "Mercy's making it sound more benign than it was. Mrs. Sorenson knew very well that this auction was for the boys, but she wanted to change the rules since she thought they didn't deserve as much as we were likely to get." Caroline readjusted Katelyn, who'd started to fuss.

"But I should've found a way to stand up to her without making her mad." Mercy sighed. "What do you think, Mr. Beauchamp? You've been invited to the auction. If seventy percent of the items listed on the auction bill aren't there, wouldn't you be upset?" She turned to frown at Caroline. "I think we should call it off. The chance of us collecting enough to make this worthwhile is near nil now."

Henri rubbed his chin. "What about my car?"

Mercy waited for him to continue, for surely he didn't mean he wanted to donate his car.

Caroline sputtered. "Your car?"

"Yes, my car. I know several men who'd have a bidding war over it."

"Your car?" Caroline repeated, her expression dumbfounded.

Henri only nodded, though his lips wriggled a bit.

He truly meant to donate it? Something fluttered in Mercy's stomach. Though she wanted this auction to be a success, she couldn't imagine someone giving up something so precious on behalf of orphans he didn't know. Mercy laid her hand against his arm. "I appreciate that, Mr. Beauchamp, I really do, but maybe you should think about it more before you commit." He wouldn't be able to replace his vehicle without traveling to a big city and spending a great deal of money. And did he really want to donate that much to Max and Robert? His support was certainly encouraging, but she had no intention of asking people to pauper themselves on Max and Robert's behalf.

"I already have." Though he was responding to her, he was looking at Caroline. "I've been thinking about selling it, since I hope to need more than two seats in the future. I might as well donate it to a good cause, yes?"

Caroline's expression was half astonishment, half . . . longing?

"So . . . about that drive?" Henri's voice wavered, but he held out his arm to Caroline. "Since I'll be getting rid of my speedster sooner than expected, I'd enjoy your company."

For some reason Caroline looked to her.

Mercy leaned closer to whisper in the woman's ear. "If his past is all that's making you hesitate, why don't you try focusing on his future instead?"

When she stepped away, Caroline still looked indecisive.

Mercy nodded, as if trying to encourage a child to be brave.

Caroline took a deep breath. "All right."

Henri's face wasn't big enough to contain his smile.

"How about I take Katelyn?" Mercy said.

Henri hurried to open the passenger door while Caroline disentangled herself from the baby. After helping Caroline into the passenger seat, Henri gave Mercy a grin and a wink before heading to his own side.

Caroline looked positively stiff. Mercy almost felt the need to take in a few deep breaths on her behalf. When Henri zipped off, Caroline had to loosen up or risk getting battered, considering Henri seemed intent on showing her how fast his little car could go in the space of a heartbeat.

If there was indeed a bidding war, his sleek two-seater might bring in enough for the Milligans to live two to three years in Boston.

She'd known that standing up to Mrs. Sorenson had been the right thing to do, but she'd not even thought to ask God to save the auction—she'd just written it off as ruined.

And here He'd rescued them within the hour.

If she exposed her brother, would God somehow make that right too?

A throat cleared to her right, startling her. Thankfully she'd had a good hold on the baby.

Aaron stepped onto the porch, a sheepish look on his face. "Sorry for scaring you." He lifted up his pruners. "I didn't think you noticed me with how loud Henri's car was."

"No, I'm afraid I didn't." She smiled despite the day's troubles. Aaron hadn't spoken to her much today, not with the dragging up and down of Mrs. Sorenson's things. She hadn't realized how much she'd missed his large yet humble presence.

He wasn't quite looking her in the eye, and he fiddled with his pruners as if he couldn't decide which hand should hold them. "I don't have a fancy car, but I do have legs. Would you be willing to go on a walk with me?"

Her heart fluttered a little.

If someone had told her just weeks ago that her heart would skip a beat over George Aaron Firebrook, she'd have called them mad.

Perhaps she should stop worrying so much about what needed to happen with the orphans and her family and wait to see what crazy, wonderful things God seemed eager to orchestrate all on His own.

"I think that sounds delightful." She couldn't have wiped her smile off if she'd tried.

His expression, a mixture of pleasure and panic, made her smile all the more.

26

Aaron stood frozen under the portico. Mercy had actually agreed to take a walk with him? And with a big smile on her face, no less? His hands were so slippery, he had to hold tight to his pruners to keep from dropping them.

Mercy looked over her shoulder at the mansion's front door and frowned. "Though maybe I ought to check on Sadie before I do anything for pleasure."

Pleasure? Had she just equated a walk with him as pleasure? "Sadie and Franklin are talking in the rose garden. Their conversation didn't look as if it needed an audience, so I found somewhere else to be." Though it wouldn't have been the first time this month he'd overheard a couple's emotional turmoil.

Mercy patted Katelyn on the back, staring off into space. "Where would we walk?"

He'd not thought that far ahead, considering he'd braced himself to be turned down. But after seeing Caroline reconsider spending time with Henri, he'd thought he'd try.

Where could they go? He looked around, then pointed down to the right of the long driveway, where a pond lay hidden in the trees at the base of the hill. "The front pond?"

She grimaced. "That's quite a walk with a baby."

"I could get the carriage."

Her expression was seconds away from telling him no.

"Or maybe we could walk the driveway, if you'd rather. Give me a second." He propped his clippers against the wall and headed inside before she could say no. What was he thinking to suggest pushing a baby carriage to the pond over soggy ruts and bumps?

Owen skipped into the entryway and smiled up at him. Aaron rubbed his smooth jaw. Shaving had been worth seeing that smile, even if he did cringe at his reflection every morning. "Do you know where the baby's carriage is? Miss McClain needs it."

The boy shrugged, then looked out the open front door. "Where's she going?"

"Well, we were going to the pond, but—"

"I want to go to the pond." The little boy's lower lip curved downward in an exaggerated pout.

How could he not ask the boy to come along, especially since he'd not had much time with him this past week? Maybe he and Mercy could take turns carrying the baby. "Would you like to go with us?"

Owen bounded up on the balls of his feet. "Could I drive Katelyn in the pony cart? I'll be real slow and careful, just like Mr. Lowe always says."

He'd seen Lowe let Owen drive Buttons several times. The nag wouldn't go fast even if a tornado chased her. But Owen was only five. "I don't think so. Maybe when you're older."

"What if Robert did it?"

"Did what?" The older boy had just walked into the foyer, his face now scrunched in confusion.

"Drive me and Katelyn to the pond in the pony cart!" Owen ran up to Robert and grabbed him tightly around the waist, looking up at him with big sad eyes. "Please?"

Robert just looked down at him with a sigh. "Will you leave me alone for the rest of the afternoon if I do?"

"Yes!" Owen jumped nearly a foot, then ran straight out the door.

Aaron had to swallow his desire to chuckle at the look of long-suffering on Robert's face. "He's been that clingy, huh?"

"He almost makes me wish school wasn't out for summer." Robert drew in a deep breath as he shuffled past toward the front door. "I don't think I can take another minute of him begging me to play with his farm animals."

"You've likely made his day." Aaron disappeared into the basement and grabbed the bassinet Caroline used whenever she went into town with the wagon.

Mercy was sitting on the low wall at the edge of the portico when he returned. "The boys are going?"

"I hope that's all right." He took a step forward, fiddling with the bassinet in his hands. "The pony cart will make taking Katelyn to the pond easier, and Owen wants to go. Though with how slow Buttons clomps along, it might take all night."

Mercy smiled at him in a way that made his heart thump harder. "It's fine. I'm glad he wants to spend time with you."

Could it be she'd not only forgiven him but had lost all of her mistrust of him in regard to the children too? He rubbed his hands against his trousers as he followed her toward the carriage house. Even if she had, that didn't mean their tentative friendship would become something more.

And yet that smile . . .

In the carriage house, Jimmy, without protest, helped Robert attach Buttons to the pony cart. Seemed Mercy and Lowe's decision to give Jimmy chores in the carriage house instead of the mansion had been a good move. Though his submissive behavior might be based more on having seen Zachary run off the property with a bloody nose and a couple black eyes.

Aaron pressed his lips together to keep from apologizing for the fight again. The last time he'd tried, Jimmy had quit talking to him altogether.

"There," Robert said as he helped Owen onto the seat. "We're ready to go."

Buttons was much less ready. She sighed repeatedly as she took her time backing out of the carriage house.

Once Robert got Buttons onto the drive, Mercy settled Katelyn into the back and strapped the bassinet down. "Go no faster than a walk."

"We won't!" Owen turned to Aaron with a smile as large as the sun. "Which pond are we going to?"

Aaron pointed to the shimmer of water nestled down in the trees. "The one up front. There's a path right behind that huge hackberry on the drive."

"Let's go, then." Robert flicked the reins, and Buttons turned her head to look at Aaron as if he'd just sentenced her to purgatory. But at Owen's impatient "Giddap" and Robert's gentle flick of the reins, she picked up her hooves and begrudgingly started forward.

The farther Robert drove with Owen chattering nonstop at his side, the more Aaron's insides jittered. He put his hands in his pockets and forced himself to walk alongside Mercy. He'd invited her on this walk, so it was his duty to come up with something to talk about, but his tongue felt like sawdust.

Mercy looked back at the carriage house before they turned onto the path behind the pony cart. "Jimmy didn't complain about hitching up Buttons. The improvement in his behavior is one reason I believe Owen will do well with you. I think you've done Jimmy good."

Aaron stopped for a second. "I think his improvement has little to do with me—surely it's despite me."

"You're not giving yourself enough credit. I've seen you work with him."

"You've forgotten what happened in the root cellar. He hasn't acted like himself since then, and who could blame him? I'm very happy you've forgiven me, but I'd have thought my loss of control would've made me go down in your estimation, not up."

"You need to stop chastising yourself for that."

He nearly tripped on a tree root. Had she already pushed the incident off into the past and forgotten it—after she'd done her

235

best to convince both Nicholas and the school board not to hire him because of how he'd treated people a decade ago? "Easier said than done."

She sighed. "I understand that." She forged forward on the path, suddenly silent, and he followed her lead. The light rustling of the trees, the cool breeze, and the break from work should've made a pleasant walk, but something was obviously weighing heavily upon Mercy, if her expression was any indication.

Robert had stopped at the edge of the pond, where Buttons happily ripped up lush grass by the mouthfuls. By the time they caught up, Katelyn had fallen asleep.

Owen squirmed in his seat. "Can we go around the pond?"

Aaron nodded and Robert started off, but Mercy moved to sit on the roughhewn bench under the willow tree instead.

Squirrels nattered in the trees above, and Aaron tried to enjoy the smell of mud, cedar, and honeysuckle. Robert prodded Buttons to ignore the deep green grasses, and Owen whistled at birds, but Mercy's silence was disconcerting. Had asking her on a walk been a bad idea?

Bringing up what had happened in the cellar seemed to have been.

"Why don't you sit with me?" she called from behind him.

He swallowed and turned to look at the tiny bench. Did she not realize how big he was or that her skirt covered more than half the seat? He walked over and lowered himself onto the edge, then leaned forward, elbows on his knees.

She didn't say anything, just watched the children make their way around the pond and disappear behind a stand of trees.

The longer he couldn't think of something to say, the sweatier his palms got. What did she think of him, asking her to walk but sitting silent as a stone? "I want to thank you for giving me another chance. You could've easily gotten rid of me."

She turned to look at him, that soft smile causing his heart to trip again. "That's not my goal anymore."

He fidgeted. This bench truly was small. She was the same

distance away from him that time he'd kissed her. All it would take to touch her lips was to lean.

She ran her tongue between her lips, and he quickly turned to check on the children's progress.

"I . . ." The way his voice cracked made his neck heat. He cleared his throat. "I'm grateful you've changed your mind about getting rid of me, but I'm not so sure my taking Owen is a good idea anymore."

"I don't agree. In fact, I've been praying he quickly sees you're . nothing to be scared of, and that you two become a family sooner rather than later."

He shook his head, not knowing what he'd done to make her change her mind so drastically. "I overheard Henri talking about how a mother and a father were ideal for these children. I'm not sure I'll ever be able to provide that." He glanced over at her and was taken in by the strange look in her eyes. Worry? Sadness? Longing?

His breath caught. Longing? For him? Surely not. He wasn't worthy of her.

He looked back at her lips, and they were moving—mesmerizingly so.

"You haven't asked to kiss me," she breathed.

He tore his gaze off her mouth and looked up into her green eyes, her pupils large and less than a foot away. How had he gotten so close? He jumped off his seat as if a clinker sizzled beneath him. "Sorry." His face felt as if he'd leaned into a fire. He'd not meant to lean forward. What was wrong with him? He'd almost gotten slapped a second time. "I guess I ought to leave. . . ." And yet, he couldn't just abandon her here with the children.

She tugged on his sleeve near the elbow.

He tensed, anticipating a narrow-eyed, singeing glare when he turned, but instead she was grinning.

"Well, why don't you ask?"

He blinked. *Ask what?* His heart was racing too much to think straight.

237

She stood up beside him, her smile pulling hard to one side. "Well?"

She couldn't really be inviting him to kiss her.

His throat turned as dry as tinder, and his feet felt as heavy as lead. "Would you . . ." His heart hammered so hard he couldn't hear his own words. What had he been saying?

The wind ruffled her hair, and the noises of the woods disappeared. He didn't want to hurt her again, didn't want to send her off running like before. He didn't—

"I hope you aren't still mad at me for slapping you."

He blinked, her moving lips breaking his trance. "What? No." He blew out a long breath. "I was never mad. I deserved it."

"No you didn't." She looked down at the ground between them. "I didn't want . . . Or rather, I hadn't wanted my one and only kiss . . ."

No man had ever kissed her?

". . . to be from a man like you—or rather, from the man I thought you were. . . ." Her words petered out, but she looked up at him as if lost and expecting him to help her find the way.

His kiss had been her one and only? All vestiges of heart flutterings disappeared. "Then I definitely shouldn't kiss you again."

"You shouldn't?" Her voice squeaked.

He closed his eyes and shook his head. "No. Because your first good kiss should be with someone far better than me."

"It's too late for that." Her voice was barely more than a whisper. "No other man could give me my first good kiss."

He opened his eyes and frowned down at her. "But I thought you said—"

She put a finger against his lips. "I didn't slap you because you kissed me poorly, or whatever excuse I came up with to justify myself in the moment. I slapped you because . . . you made my heart speed up and my arms tingle and . . . I was more upset you'd created those reactions in me than anything else. Reactions I was afraid would run through my mind over and over, and they did. Because, though the kiss was short, I . . . I'd never felt like that before."

She'd enjoyed his kiss? Thoughts of their kiss had repeated in his mind as well, yet if he could replace it with one that didn't end in a slap, so much the better. Unable to help himself, he took her hand from his mouth, pulled her closer, and took one last breath before he gave in to his desire to kiss her again and hope for a better ending.

Her mouth yielded to his, as it had in his dreams.

The softness of her skin, the silkiness of her hair, and the sweetness of her breath made the world around him go dark.

She pulled back a little, and he moved with her, desperate to show her something he couldn't even begin to articulate. She pulled farther away, but he couldn't help but steal one last second of her lips, slap coming or no.

She tipped her head down, and the flat of her hand pressed atop his heart. Her gaze stayed locked on his chest. "Aaron—"

"I know." He forced himself to step back. "I should've asked."

"Uh . . ." Owen's voice startled him, and Aaron quickly jumped to put distance between them.

The boy looked mildly repelled. "Didn't you hear us? I asked if we could go around the pond again."

Mercy released a nervous-sounding giggle, her freckles disappearing under the pink color covering her cheeks. "I'm sorry we were . . . I mean, I'm sorry you saw—"

"We've seen worse." Robert shrugged.

They'd seen worse? Aaron put a hand through his hair, his own cheeks likely as red as Mercy's now.

"Well, maybe not that exactly."

That? Robert had seen a worse kiss than that? He'd thought it had gone pretty well compared with the last one.

"I mean, I never saw anybody kiss my mother like . . . like he loved her. I bet Owen didn't either." Robert's voice went soft. "What we saw . . ." He turned his head and looked out over the pond, his throat working extra hard.

Aaron turned cold. No boy should ever have seen what these two had. Aaron swallowed. Just like no boy should've ever gone through what he'd endured as a child. "I'm sorry about your mother, but she had the love you gave her, right?"

Robert nodded, though he seemed more interested in staring at the reins in his hands than continuing the conversation.

Aaron turned to Mercy, who was staring at him.

Kissed her like he loved her.

Was she waiting for him to deny or affirm Robert's assumption? He rubbed his hands against his trousers. Those feelings and emotions crept in before one voiced the words, right? It wasn't as if he *didn't* love her, but could he say it?

Katelyn began fussing, and Mercy headed over to comfort the baby. "I think it best we return so I can help upstairs."

Right. The auction.

Owen sighed and poked out his lower lip.

"We can come down another day, darling." Mercy patted the boy's leg and motioned for Robert to head up the hill in front of them.

Robert started Buttons up the slight incline, and Katelyn's cries quieted with the swaying of the pony cart.

Mercy glanced over her shoulder at him as she followed the boys up.

He made his feet move forward.

Love.

Had Robert seen something in him he'd not yet recognized himself?

27

"Miss McClain, what can I do for you?" A. K. Glass's manager and Max and Robert's boss, Mr. MacDonald, came into his office, where Mercy had been sitting for the last ten minutes.

She stood and turned to face him. "I'm sorry I came without an appointment, but Max said you weren't coming to the auction tonight." She couldn't keep from fiddling with her reticule's strings. So few townspeople could buy Henri's car, or anything expensive for that matter. But Mr. MacDonald had money enough, and an interest in the boys, so his sudden decision not to attend was concerning. Had the loss of Mrs. Sorenson's donations gotten around town? They'd collected enough in the past three days to feel good about continuing, but what if Mrs. Sorenson's reason for leaving had come to light? What would happen to Sadie?

"I'm sorry." He walked behind his desk and dropped the papers he'd been carrying. "I'd planned on coming, but the wife is sick. We've got five kids at home, three of which are down with whatever she has. She's been miserable for the last two days."

Mercy let out the breath she'd been holding. It seemed he'd not heard of Sadie's past. "I'm sorry to hear that. Is it something serious?"

"No, I don't think so—just what's going around. Head

241

congestion, pain, malaise. But I wouldn't feel right leaving for the night after she's struggled all day."

The symptoms sounded similar to what Katelyn had come down with yesterday. Mercy sighed. She was thankful he had a noble reason for not attending, but his presence would definitely be missed. "If she's still unwell after the weekend, let me know. I could come by for an hour or two to help."

"Thank you, Miss McClain, but the worst seems to be over. She's just exhausted from the lack of sleep, but I'll keep your offer in mind."

"All right, then." She forced herself not to frown. "I am sorry you won't be at the auction tonight to hear Max and Robert's speeches. They do admire you."

"They're good workers, considering their upbringing." He dug into his pocket. "Before you go . . . I was planning to drop this off once Amelia got better, but you could take it now." He pulled out a money clip. "I'd planned to find fifty dollars' worth of stuff to buy, but I'll just donate it." He pulled out several bills.

Fifty dollars? Why, that was more than a month's wages. "I-I don't know what to say, besides thank you." Evidently, she was just as bad as the children about letting a lecture go in one ear and out the other. Hadn't she reminded herself after Henri donated his car that God would get the boys what they needed, with or without her effort? And yet she'd gotten so anxious over one man's nonattendance, she'd walked across town hoping to convince him to come, worrying that if he didn't, the whole auction would end up a disaster.

Mr. MacDonald handed her the money. "My pleasure. Max will do us proud, I'm sure."

She left with a lightness in her step, yet she took her time walking down the glass factory's stairs. She'd been antsy to leave the mansion, not only because she'd heard Mr. MacDonald wasn't planning to come but because she'd also needed to get away from Aaron. Not because he was pestering her, but because she was overly aware of where he was at all times.

242

She couldn't stop thinking about what Robert had said after catching them kissing.

Was he right? Did Aaron love her?

Unfortunately, Robert's sad story about never seeing a man kiss his mother with any sort of affection had turned the happy moment into a sad one.

Nicholas preferred the children be adopted by a husband and wife, and of course she agreed, since that would be the most financially stable option. But she'd never thought about the orphans' need to observe a loving couple. If these children never saw a healthy relationship, they might believe good marriages were nothing but fairy tales and forgo waiting to marry someone who loved them, or even treated them well.

And yet she'd agreed to let Aaron have Owen, for it was the boy's mother's wish. Since Aaron had grown up with a distorted sense of family, did he too know nothing about healthy relationships?

He'd mentioned he wasn't sure he'd ever be able to provide Owen with a mother. Did he not think about her as a future wife? Did he just kiss any and every woman he felt like kissing?

And to think, he was the last man on earth she ever thought she'd be worrying about *why* he was kissing her.

She pushed open the factory's side door and stepped into the fresh air, taking a huge draught of it into her lungs.

And here she was, still thinking of Aaron. Time to think about something else. Caroline had asked her to check on Lily White while she was in town. The dove and her children had been sick for a week now, and were likely how Katelyn had caught her cold.

Taking care to make sure no one was around, Mercy slipped the fifty dollars into her boot. Having money on her person made her even more nervous about heading toward the red-light district, even if Lily lived on the edge of it, but she couldn't deny the children medicine.

Mercy walked as quickly as she could. The faster she checked on them, the faster she could get back to somewhere she felt comfortable.

At the Whites' little cabin, she knocked but got no answer. Well, besides a hacking cough.

Not wanting to stand on the street too long, she turned the knob and found the door unlocked. She opened it a crack. "Hello?" No answer. "I'm Miss McClain. I've come with medicine."

Another cough and the soft screech of someone trying to talk without a voice.

She opened the door slowly and stepped inside the mess of a cabin, quite dark despite the afternoon sun. All of the shades were pulled, and no one had lit any lamps.

The sound of a child whimpering made her heart hurt, so she searched for a lamp and lit it.

In the corner, a large bed looked to have the mother and her children huddled up under a blanket that should've been sufficient for this muggy day, but they were all shivering.

"Who are you?" a woman's voice croaked from the bed.

"Caroline's friend." She came to the bedside and reached over to feel the woman's head. Hot, but not frightfully so. The child beside her tossed and turned fitfully, but the baby in the woman's arms was quite still. With a tremor in her hand, Mercy felt the baby's head. Thankfully the infant was hot rather than cold.

"Who are you?" This time a different voice sounded behind her. A boy about Jimmy's age stood in a doorway.

"My name's Mercy, and I've come to check on your family. Are you not sick?"

"I'm the first one over it, though I still don't feel too great." The scratchiness in his throat became more noticeable as he spoke.

At least he could help her find things she needed. "Would you get some water for me?"

He shrugged but went off without a fuss. Seemed he was better at obeying than Jimmy.

Taking the infant from the mother's arms, she changed the babe's diaper. The fact that the cloth was dry was quite worrisome.

Mercy swaddled the little girl back up, coaxed her into swal-

244

lowing a spoonful of medicine, then attempted to encourage the mother to nurse her.

Neither of them seemed to have the strength or desire to do so.

The boy returned with a full pitcher, and she helped the mother and little girl in the bed take a dose of medicine and a glassful of water. Before either of them finished drinking, they sank back down under the covers.

The baby had yet to wake enough to nurse, and with the way the woman lay there, hardly aware of her surroundings, would she smother the infant?

Mercy picked the baby back up and tried to coax water into her mouth with a spoon.

The boy sat slumped in the chair beside her, watching.

"I want you to give them water every fifteen minutes, all right?" She handed him the baby and towel she'd used to catch the water dribbling from her slack mouth. "Use this spoon unless you have clean bottles. Make sure you see her throat moving—that means she's swallowing. Why don't you try to get her to drink while I look for something?"

The boy sighed and coughed, but he seemed confident enough with the baby she could leave him.

In the other room, she found a small trunk. After emptying its contents, she took a woolen blanket and folded it to fit the bottom before dragging the chest into the front room. She pushed it against the bed and the nightstand, then took the babe from her older brother and set her in the makeshift bassinet. She pulled the lamp closer to be sure the infant didn't sink too far into the improvised mattress when something shiny caught her eye by the wall between the bed and table.

A golden circle with a blue center. Her breath stilled. It couldn't be.

She reached past the trunk to pick it up.

In her hand lay a blue-enameled, double cuff link identical to the ones Patricia had given Timothy for their anniversary last year.

Had she seen Timothy wearing them lately? She hadn't, but

she didn't pay attention to what he wore every day. What were the chances another man would have this exact same set with this particular swirl pattern? Patricia had bought the costly pair in Kansas City.

But how could it be her brother's? There was no reason for him to ever have been in Lily White's cabin.

Could it have been stolen? She looked around but didn't see the other, and who kept things they'd stolen lying about on the floor?

Of course, maybe they'd stolen both and lost one, but with Timothy's drinking, the hours of unaccountable absence, the way he'd been at odds with his wife for a while now . . .

Mercy sank to her knees beside the trunk, staring at the cufflink.

And here she'd thought the stresses of the orphanage had caused her brother's marital discord and driven him to drink. Perhaps it wasn't the orphanage's fault at all.

The woman beside her groaned, and Mercy closed her eyes. This woman had likely played a huge part in her family's unraveling.

But as Aaron and Sadie had said, these women wouldn't be here if not for the men. If the men would choose to be upright, honest, faithful . . . She wrapped her hand tightly around the cuff link, until it bit into her skin. She pressed the blunted end of her other arm against her temple, wanting to banish the sudden jolt of a headache.

What was Timothy thinking? Drinking was bad enough. How could he possibly justify this?

Now wasn't the time to mentally interrogate her brother. Nothing she could do in this cabin would fix her family.

Besides, she could be leaping to the wrong conclusion.

Oh please, God. Let me be assuming things that just aren't true.

She pushed herself off her knees, dropped the cuff link into her pocket, and stuffed a handful of rags into the water left in the pitcher. She looked to the boy, who stared at her listlessly. "I know you don't feel well, but you need to make sure your family's fevers stay down, especially your baby sister's. Put these rags on them like this." Mercy showed the boy how to care for his sick family with orders to fetch the doctor if his baby sister stayed lethargic much longer.

Once he sat next to his mother and took over, Mercy exited the cabin, only to lean against the door, fingering the cuff link in her pocket.

What was she going to do? How could confronting her brother with such an accusation turn out any better than when she'd confronted him about his drinking?

She closed her eyes against the sun and shook her head. Whatever she decided to do, she couldn't do it tonight.

Her world might be crumbling, but she'd not let Robert and Max suffer because of it. She had an auction to run.

28

"I'm sorry to interrupt."

Mercy stopped arranging last-minute donations on the ballroom table and looked over her shoulder at Mrs. Wisely. "No problem. Is the auctioneer here?" With the number of people slowly trickling into the ballroom, she'd hoped to have seen him earlier.

"Yes, Mr. Hollingford arrived about twenty minutes ago. He's downstairs asking Henri about the car's details."

Good. Mercy handed Owen a fistful of scrap paper. If he was going to be underfoot all night, he might as well help. "Take this to the trash chute, darling."

Owen skipped off, and Mercy took a second glance at the clock on the table. "Is it half past six already?" Surely the clock was wrong. There should be far more people here if this auction was going to go well.

Mrs. Wisely chuckled and tapped the donated timepiece. "No, it's five forty-five. This one needs to be wound. What I came to ask you was, have you seen my grandmother's tortoiseshell combs? I figured Mrs. Naples might like them, but I can't find them."

Mercy looked around the ballroom packed with tables piled high with more things than Mrs. Sorenson had left with. Last-minute donations had poured in so fast half of the items were still a jumble. "I'm afraid I haven't."

Mrs. Wisely moved to Mercy's other side to flip through a stack of canvases leaning against the table. "Do you remember if that water lily painting belonged to Mrs. Sorenson? I wanted to bid on it but haven't seen it either."

Mercy puffed out a breath. "I don't think it was hers, but with all the paintings she had, I wouldn't be surprised if someone accidentally sent her home with it."

Mrs. Wisely frowned at the last painting, then leaned them back against the table. "Well, I hope it's somewhere, because I have the perfect place for it." She turned back to Mercy. "Is there anything I can get you before I check on Mr. Hollingford again?"

She shook her head. She'd given Mrs. Wisely the job of dealing with the auctioneer because she wasn't sure she could handle much tonight. She put her hand in her pocket and fingered the cuff link. "Have you seen my brother? He promised to help."

"I haven't. But when I do, I'll tell him you're looking for him."

"I . . ."

Mrs. Wisely must not have heard her and walked off, weaving through the auction goers clumped in front of tables. Hopefully the older woman would be too busy to find Timothy, because Mercy wasn't particularly interested in talking to her brother at the moment. She'd only been hoping he was here, as he should be.

Owen skipped back. "Now what?"

She shook her head. The boy wanted to help, but her patience was on edge. "Have you seen the painting of a pond with water lilies on it?"

He nodded his head.

"Where is it?"

He shook his head.

So much for that lead. But what could she expect from a five-year-old? She beckoned him to follow. "Help me look through these stacks for it, would you?"

They flipped through the paintings, but looking at the tops, she was fairly certain they'd not find it. Lately, all sorts of things had gone missing, only to show up in the strangest places.

They'd yet to find Patricia's opal ring, the prism that had hung in the music room's window, and a crystal ashtray Owen swore he'd not taken outside to play with in the mud.

What if her brother was pawning mansion property to pay for his carousing? Wouldn't Patricia have noticed him spending more lately? Even if she could overlook her husband's bar tabs, surely she wouldn't tolerate his spending money on being unfaithful.

Mercy glanced across the room at Patricia, who was once again sitting and fanning herself as the rest of the women unpacked last-minute items and straightened chairs.

Mercy put her hand into her pocket to confirm that Mr. Mac-Donald's money was still there.

Since God had orchestrated all of these last-minute donations, she shouldn't worry about a few missing pieces.

If only she had peace about what she needed to do after the auction. She squeezed the money in her hand. She didn't know for certain that her brother had visited Miss Lily White, and the thought of confronting him with such an accusation made her stomach tie itself in knots.

"Be careful, Jimmy, or you'll drop them." Cook's voice, more frustrated than normal, traveled across the room.

"I made it all the way up the stairs with them, didn't I?" The boy sneered at her back while carrying a tray of hors d'oeuvres.

Cook skirted a group of women admiring jewelry, shooting a glare over her shoulder. "You need to drop the attitude."

"Oh, like this?" He stopped beside her and dropped his platter onto the table. A couple sandwiches flopped onto the tablecloth.

Cook set down her own platter and gathered up the ruined snacks. "Why they ever let you help, I don't know." She turned to glare at Mercy for a second before dumping the little sandwiches into a nearby trash bin.

Mercy rubbed a hand down her face. Why had Jimmy's churlish attitude returned this week? He'd been doing so well.

Mercy sighed and reached for Owen. "Come on. Seems I need to go have a talk with Jimmy."

Owen stuck his little hand in hers and jumped and skipped beside her as if she were going to ask Jimmy to play rather than lecture the boy.

Jimmy watched her advance with a smirk on his face. He probably expected her to banish him to his room. He'd been complaining about working since he rolled out of bed, so that was likely what he wanted.

Of course, torturing the staff with a belligerent child today might be worse than caving to him. "What's the matter, Jimmy?"

"Nothing." His smirk widened. "I got the snacks up here safe and sound, didn't I?"

Cook shook her head and bustled off.

Didn't he understand how important this night could be, even for him? Any number of auction goers could be potential adoptive parents, and Robert and Max's speeches could move them to want to help an orphan. If Jimmy had any chance of being adopted after the fire at Mr. Ragsdale's, he couldn't make such a bad impression in front of so many. "You need to work harder at being kind and respectful. No one wants to adopt a boy who fights with them over everything."

"Well, maybe I don't want to be adopted. You ever think about that?"

She frowned down at Owen. Thankfully he seemed to be more interested in something happening across the room than in listening to Jimmy. She lowered her voice, hoping Owen's attention remained elsewhere. "Have you considered that this orphanage might not be here forever? If it closes and everyone in town thinks you're a troublemaker, no one's going to take you in. Would you rather be sent off to some orphanage across the state or settled into a nice home here?"

"I don't need anybody. I can live on my own."

At thirteen? If he did so, what hope was there that he'd not end up in jail? "That's what I'm afraid of, Jimmy."

He turned to storm off, but she snatched his arm.

"Please try harder to be lovable. Make it easier on all of us, all right? I promise, if you act better, your life will get better."

He yanked his arm from her hand and opened his mouth to retort, but something behind her squelched his response. He shut his mouth and glared past her shoulder before spinning and stomping away.

She turned to find Aaron walking toward her and couldn't help but smile at how his mere presence had made Jimmy straighten up a little. At least someone was affecting the boy for the better.

Aaron glanced down to her mouth for a second, and she held her breath as he neared.

Had he had as much trouble as she had these last few days, trying to think of anything other than their kiss?

Well, until her brother and his cuff link filled her head with far worse ruminations.

"Are you ready?" He stopped in front of her.

"I suppose I have to be, since people are already crowding in." Some things could've been better arranged, but if items got sold in a crate, so be it.

Aaron stood looking at her as if they weren't in a room filled with people and Owen wasn't looking up at both of them.

Could people tell they'd kissed just by looking at them?

She had to do something other than stare back. The money in her pocket crinkled under her hand, and she latched onto that. "I went into town today and got a monetary donation from Mr. MacDonald. A providential way to start off the evening, I think."

Of course, discovering where her brother wiled away his hours when he wasn't at the mansion had immediately squashed all the happy feelings the fifty-dollar donation had given her.

"I'm glad." Aaron's smile remained lazy and settled.

Sadie and Franklin passed by, his hand at the small of her back. If they could work through their issues, perhaps she and Aaron had a chance. Was it possible she might not need her brother's protection forever?

"What's that look for?"

She blinked up at him. "What look?"

"You dropped the furrowed brow and looked utterly content for a second."

She put her hand to her cheek. Oh, she had to be careful. Though she'd learned not to judge Aaron by how he once acted, that didn't mean she should hope he'd marry her.

Though if she wanted to tell anyone about what she'd found out today, it would be him. Along with all her hopes, her worries, the funny things she noticed throughout the day.

And if he just happened to want to kiss her again—

"How much did you get?" His eyes twinkled.

"What?" Her body flushed. If she wasn't careful, everyone in the room would know how she was feeling about him before the auction was over. "Oh, the donation. Fifty dollars."

Aaron's eyebrows shot up. "That's great. You're well on your way to getting Max and Robert what they need."

She hoped so. But what about the rest of the orphans? What about—?

"Don't fret." Aaron pulled her hand away from where she was worrying her lace collar. "You've done a superb job with the boys, and their speeches will persuade many into being generous."

A superb job with the boys? Timothy and Patricia certainly hadn't done much for the orphans, and what she'd done had little to do with how well they'd turned out.

Owen tugged on her skirt. "Can I have something to drink?"

She put a hand to the back of her neck and looked down at him. "Oh, honey, this isn't a good time for me to leave."

"But I'm thirsty."

"I can take him," Aaron offered.

Owen pressed against her legs as if he'd gone back to being wary of Aaron.

She stooped down beside the boy. He had to get more comfortable with his soon-to-be guardian quickly, for once she confronted her brother, if her suspicions turned out to be true, Owen would likely be under Aaron's care sooner than expected. "Go with Mr. Firebrook and get yourself a drink."

Owen didn't say anything, just stared into her eyes, his body tense.

She rubbed his arms. "On your way down, ask him all those questions you were asking me earlier: why some birds sing pretty and some don't, what happens to your food when you eat it, and all the others I haven't had time to answer. Aaron's pretty special. He wants to help all the children he can. I bet he'll be happy to answer anything you ask him."

Owen gave a little roll of his shoulders but dragged his feet forward.

Aaron looked at her for a second, his Adam's apple bobbing with a big swallow, but then nodded at Owen. "I'm not sure I know the answer to the bird question, but—"

"Are you just going to tell me it's because God made it so, like Mrs. McClain does?" Owen sighed.

Aaron chuckled. "Well, that's the easy answer. But this world has reason and thought behind it—since God designed it—and science helps us figure that out. I bet since we're both smart fellows, we can come up with a good guess, or what we call a hypothesis."

"You sound like a teacher."

Despite Owen spitting that out as if it were an insult, Aaron smiled even bigger. "I'm afraid that's because I . . . am one."

And her heart melted, right then and there, as the realization spread over his face. Yes, he'd become a teacher. A good one. Even if he wasn't going to school every day or getting paid a teacher's salary, he was making a difference. He might not be able to make up for his past entirely, but she couldn't fault his attempts.

Aaron put his hand on the back of Owen's neck, herding him off toward the exit. "Come, let's get you water."

Across the room, her brother's laughter stole her attention.

So he'd finally arrived.

She let out a sigh, yet it didn't make her feel much better. Though she didn't have to worry now about what he might be doing, that didn't change the fact that she would have to figure out if what he did when he wasn't here was bad enough to tell Nicholas.

Timothy looked relaxed conversing with a wealthy-looking couple while Patricia hung on his arm. For all the world, they looked as if they were happy together.

Butterflies fluttered in Mercy's stomach. But they weren't happy butterflies.

If she told Nicholas about what she'd found at Lily White's, what would happen? Timothy should definitely not be in charge of these children if he dallied with prostitutes, but he'd likely blame her if Nicholas fired him. What if her brother refused to provide for her in any way?

She couldn't count on Aaron to save her, for even if they became romantically involved, he'd not propose tomorrow—maybe not even a year from now, if he ever would.

"Mercy?"

She turned, and her mouth fell open. "Evelyn?" She rushed over to her friend, standing in a navy blue gown that bespoke her new wealth. She pulled her into a huge hug, despite the woman being a good six inches taller than her. "Whatever are you doing here? I haven't seen you in months."

Evelyn backed away a little, looking her up and down, as if Mercy's work dress, loose hair, and dirt smudges were worth noticing.

Evelyn no longer looked like she used to when she had run this orphanage. She was a fine city lady now. The eyelet work around her shirtwaist's collar, neckline, sleeves, and wrists was exquisitely fine. And that didn't even take into account her fancy hairstyle and jewelry.

"I'm so glad to see you again." Evelyn looked around her, nodding at someone in the crowd. "You've been busy, I see."

"Yes." She smiled at how easy it felt to be standing beside Evelyn again. Though they hadn't known each other long before she'd married and moved away, Evelyn was one of the nicest women she'd ever known.

Owen skidded in between them, grabbed Mercy's sleeve, and tugged for attention. "I'm hungry."

She glanced around for Aaron. "Where's Mr. Firebrook? Weren't you supposed to—?"

"He told me I had to ask you."

"Do you ever stop eating?" Feeding him lately had become an all-day project.

"You know," Evelyn said as she knelt beside him, "my girl isn't much older than you, and she's always hungry. I'm in the habit of having something in my bag at all times. Do you like oatmeal cookies?"

He stiffened, his eyes wide. "With raisins?"

Evelyn grimaced. "I'm afraid so."

"Good!" He rubbed his tummy and made an exaggerated slurp noise. "Those are so yummy."

Evelyn's laugh was high and bright. "And here I thought you'd turn your nose up at them. My husband picks out the raisins." She glanced up at Mercy and frowned. "Sorry. I should've asked first."

How could she say no when Owen's smile was so big the dimple above his lip was on display? "It's fine."

Owen did a little fidgety dance as he waited for Evelyn to unwrap the brown paper encasing the cookies.

Once he had a treat in each hand, Mercy turned him around. "Why don't you go sit on the balcony so the birds can clean up your crumbs?"

"All right. I'll even share my raisins with them."

"You don't need—" But it was of no use telling him not to, since he was already halfway across the room.

"Is he one of the orphans?"

She turned back to Evelyn with a smile. "He is. Adorable, huh?"

"Yes . . ." Her friend's gaze seemed glued to Owen's retreating form, a longing look in her eye. She'd adopted two of the mansion's orphans months ago and had hoped to adopt Max and Robert as well. But Max had decided to continue his schooling in Teaville, and Robert had wanted to stay with his brother.

"Our gardener has started the process of adopting him."

"Oh?" Evelyn's features quickly schooled themselves. "I hope they do well together."

"I believe they will." She was grateful she didn't have to explain to Evelyn how long it had taken her to see the truth of that. "What's brought you here?"

Evelyn took her eyes off Owen, who was now sitting with legs splayed on the balcony. "Why, the auction, of course."

Mercy shook her head. "You can't tell me you came all the way down from Kansas City for this auction."

"No, I came here for Max and Robert, and"—she turned in a wide circle, scanning the room—"Lydia wrote that they were selling the Hopkins landscape painting that used to hang in my room. I think they purposely put it in the auction to entice me down." She rubbed her hands together and winked. "Since David said I could spend however much I wish, I intend to bid extravagantly—for the sake of the boys, of course."

"Of course." She swallowed against the thickness in her throat. As Aaron had said, she needn't worry, for God would take care of these boys.

She blinked against the warmth of unexpected tears. Confronting Mrs. Sorenson hadn't been fun, but it had been right, and God had taken care of the aftermath.

And God would take care of her. Her brother wasn't ultimately responsible for seeing to her needs. God was.

29

Aaron sat in the back of the ballroom, his foot tapping as the bidding on the diamond-and-sapphire ring Mercy had oohed and aahed over exceeded his savings. Not that he should've spent all his pennies on such a thing, but he'd hoped he could've gotten it for a steal.

He took a deep breath and moved to the back window. At least Max and Robert would benefit from the bidding war. With nothing to bid on and Owen sitting with the other children, he figured he might as well find somewhere else to be or he'd end up staring at Mercy all night.

She sat near the front with Charlie and Harrison Gray, laughing at something someone had said or done.

It would be easy enough to go sit beside Mr. Gray, but if his teacher's wife figured out how he felt about Mercy . . . Well, Charlie Gray's brand of matchmaking was likely the kind that would make everyone squirm.

He looked out the window, the shadows just starting to darken the manicured lawn and neatly trimmed bushes. He'd worked hard this past week to make sure the grounds made his employer look good, but now he didn't have anything to do. With the auction nearly over, he'd soon be needed to help load wagons, but other than that, he had the night off. Maybe he should read one of his gardening books. Before he could turn from the window, he noticed a person dart across the lawn and duck behind one of the garden's short walls.

Jimmy?

Earlier, the boy's attitude had gotten the better of him, and Nicholas had sent him to his room, so the boy shouldn't be outside. But when did Jimmy ever obey? He'd done well after returning from Mr. Ragsdale's, but that hadn't lasted long.

Aaron scanned the garden, waiting for him to reappear, but he saw no one. Was the person lying down behind the wall, or had he missed him leaving? Aaron sighed and made his way to the stairs. Who else but Jimmy could it be?

Of course the boy would take advantage of everyone being distracted to do as he pleased. And with the terrible way he'd acted earlier, what if he was in the mood to destroy things? He'd believed Jimmy hadn't set the fire at Mr. Ragsdale's, but that didn't mean he'd never burn something down.

Picking up his pace, but not enough to alarm people, Aaron made his way down two flights of stairs and out the back door. He walked through the garden, hoping to find Jimmy smoking, slumped behind the wall. But he wasn't there.

Aaron sighed and hopped atop the low stone wall to see if he could spot the boy, or at least a tendril of smoke coming from his pipe.

A nearly imperceptible sound turned his head to the east. Was Jimmy in the cellar again?

Aaron jumped off the wall and approached the cellar slowly, his fingers stretched apart to keep them from forming fists. He would not lose control again and spring into an unnecessary fight. Taking deep, slow breaths he walked at a normal pace toward the cellar. Scraping noises sounded from the half-buried outbuilding, but no voices.

Aaron descended the stairwell quietly.

Please let me be about to disturb nothing more than a coon or a stray cat.

259

Dim light seeped into the cellar from behind him, and he could just make out Jimmy dragging a shabby mattress toward the trash pile, which, strangely, now contained paintings, polished vases, and intact dishware.

He cleared his throat, and Jimmy jumped a few inches, throwing the mattress halfway onto the pile.

"What are you doing?" Aaron took the last step down into the crumbling cellar.

"Smoking."

Aaron stood there with his hands on his hips. "Don't lie."

"I'm not." Jimmy grabbed something off the ground and held it up—a woman's silver cigarette case. "See?"

Where would he have gotten that? Though with the number of people in attendance tonight, he could've swiped it off half a dozen ladies. "Why don't you tell me the truth?"

Jimmy stood stone-faced.

Aaron walked the last two steps toward him, then flung the mattress back. He stared at a pile of silverware, a set of crystal bowls, a clock, the gardening shears he'd thought he'd lost, plus a couple dozen other shiny things. He pointed to a picture tucked behind a mirror. "That's the water lily painting Mrs. Wisely wanted to bid on tonight. Did you think we'd not notice it missing?"

Jimmy shrugged and then, quick as a wink, darted for the door.

Aaron rushed forward and caught him by the arm at the last second. The boy yanked against him and kicked his shin, but Aaron refused to loosen his grip. After taking a few more wild blows, he wrapped Jimmy in a hard embrace, keeping as calm as he could while the boy kicked his legs, clawed at his face, and cursed nonstop.

After a couple long minutes, the boy finally slumped.

Aaron loosened his hold, but only enough to keep from hurting Jimmy. "Tell me, why are you stealing from people who are bending over backward to help you when everyone else would've kicked you out for how you behave?"

"You've got it all wrong." Jimmy's voice was winded yet still defiant.

"I'm not stupid. All right, maybe I was stupid the last time I caught you in here and let my anger get the best of me. . . . But wait . . . does Zachary have something to do with your stealing?" He forced himself not to tighten his grip on Jimmy's arm, though the familiar heat of anger and regret welled inside him. "He wasn't doing anything to you at all, was he? Or if he was, you likely started it."

Jimmy stayed as stiff as a board. "It doesn't matter," he said through clenched teeth.

"Yes it does." Shaking the boy wouldn't do him any good. Instead, Aaron took three long, steady breaths. "Everything you or I do matters, for good or for ill. The more terrible things you do, the more likely you'll find yourself alone in this world."

"I'm already alone."

"It certainly is hard to have friends when you act as you do."

"You don't understand." Jimmy tried to wiggle free again but quickly gave up. "Friends just mess everything up."

"How so?"

The boy stilled. It was almost as if Aaron could hear the boy's jaw wiring shut.

"Come on, tell me." Should he chance losing his grip by releasing him enough to look him in the eye? "I know what it's like not to have friends. I'd like to be yours if you let me. But you have to tell me what you're up to so I can help."

"You don't want to be my friend. You just want me to talk," he spat.

"No, I want to help. But if you're unwilling, I could haul you to the police station."

"Don't."

Was that desperation in his voice?

Did jail actually frighten him? "And why shouldn't I? The evidence to lock you up is all right here."

"I'm not the one stealing."

"Right, and I'm heir to the throne of England."

Jimmy shrugged against him. "I mean, I'm not doing it because I want to. My mother's making me."

Mother? "But only orphans live in an orphanage."

"I'm orphan enough, since she cares nothing for me. If I don't steal, she . . . she . . ."

"She what?" His temperature shot up again, but he forced himself to work on breathing calmly. He'd not go after someone in a fit of rage based on this boy's insinuations again.

Jimmy did nothing more than shake his head.

"Fine, if she's the one making you steal, we'll make a police report and put her behind bars."

Jimmy's heart beat hard against the arm Aaron had clamped across his chest. "Oh no. Once she got out, I'd be doomed."

"How doomed?" The fact that Jimmy's heart had noticeably kicked up convinced him Jimmy's mother was a real threat.

"Let me go." The boy suddenly dropped and almost escaped his hold.

"No." Aaron struggled to get a better grip as he went down with him to the ground.

"If you don't let me go, I can't show you."

Aaron stilled, trying to catch his breath. Should he trust him? He could drag Jimmy to the police, but it wouldn't do any good unless he talked. Turning so he was between Jimmy and the door, he released him, holding out his arms, poised to catch him again.

Jimmy started rolling up his sleeve.

Did the boy intend to fight him? Had he not seen what he'd done to his brother? "Jim—"

"There." Jimmy thrust out his arm.

Aaron narrowed his eyes, trying to see whatever it was he was showing him. "The burn you got after you set fire to Mr. Ragsdale's haystack?" Surely Jimmy didn't think he was stupid enough to forget where that scar had come from.

"I didn't start the fire. One of my mother's lovers did. Nothing I stole from the farmer was half as good as what I swiped from here, so Zachary told me to get back to the mansion. I tried to behave bad enough Mr. Ragsdale would send me back, but she sent Joe to speed things up."

"And the burn?"

Jimmy rolled his sleeve back down and slumped against the wall. "Mr. Ragsdale wasn't so bad he deserved having his stuff burned down, so I tried to stop Joe. He burned me with his Magic Pocket Lamp for trying. After I begged him to let me go, he threw a burning, oil-soaked rag into the haystack."

The boy's face grew hard. "Don't mess with my mother, Mr. Firebrook. Even if you decided you could hit a woman, you can't hit all the goons she works with. They're greedy and mean, every last one of them. One's even a copper who covers for her."

Quite the tale for a thirteen-year-old to pull together out of thin air. Aaron relaxed a little. "I don't know about the police, but I'm sure Mr. Lowe and I can keep you safe until we figure out what to do. But first we have to take this stuff back. The Lowes are having a hard enough time financing their charities and businesses right now without you stealing things."

"But we can't take this stuff back. If she finds out I returned it, she'll send someone to get me."

"How's she going to know?"

"Because I don't choose what I steal. Zachary tells me what to get and where to find it. Someone hides it—a maid, maybe, I don't know—and if no one notices long enough, it's my job to bring it here so Zachary can take it to my mother. He's never been in the mansion though, so sometimes he doesn't give me good directions."

Aaron pointed to the paintings. "And the stuff from the auction?"

He shrugged. "I decided to pick up a few things. It's not like anyone will miss them with all they've got up there. And if Max and Robert get charity, why can't I? Zachary says my mother's already mad at me since I haven't been able to smuggle much out this past week." He huffed and folded his hands over his chest. "It's not my fault the house is so full of people getting ready for this stupid auction I can't sneak things out."

"And you say you don't know who in the house is working for your mother?"

Jimmy wilted, shaking his head. "They won't tell me. Said I'm too stupid not to get caught if I do it myself."

Since the boy's explanation made him look weak, it was probably true. Aaron ran a hand through his hair. If Jimmy's mother was fine with a man burning her son and destroying a random man's property, she was heartless and dangerous. They needed a plan, but there wasn't enough time to think one through.

A slight uptick of noise drew his attention. Backing out of the cellar but keeping his eye on Jimmy, he walked up just enough to hear chairs screeching and excited conversations floating out of the open ballroom windows.

The auction was over. No chance to return these items onto the block. And within minutes, the staff would notice he wasn't helping load wagons.

He scanned the stuff in the pile. "When's Zachary coming to get this?"

"Tonight. Says with all the people leaving with stuff, no one will notice him."

The pocket watches, hair combs, jewelry, silverware, and all the rest were simply too much to let disappear. Aaron leaned over, picked up a vase, and tucked it under his arm. "Grab as much as you can carry and help me take everything to my cabin."

Jimmy only stood there.

Apparently coming clean about his illegal activity didn't make him any more inclined to obey.

Aaron stuffed a watch and a couple of forks into his pocket. He picked up a golden horse statue and thrust it toward Jimmy. "We don't have much time before people notice I'm missing, and if Zachary's waiting until the crowds are milling around outside, we've only got a handful of minutes to get this stuff out of here."

"Didn't you hear me?" Jimmy shook his head. "I'll be in trouble if Zachary finds nothing here. Do you think he'll just shrug his shoulders and leave without trying to get me?"

"He won't be able to, because you'll be helping me load wagons. Stay within my sight at all times." He piled more into Jimmy's arms, then turned him around and gave him a light shove. "Let's go."

Jimmy's steps were sluggish, but at least he started forward. "You might as well just turn me in. If there's not a cellar full of stuff tonight, they'll know something's wrong. If they find out I've snitched on them . . ."

"That's why you're to stay with me at all times."

"You mean . . . you believe me?" Jimmy's voice shook as he looked back, his mouth near trembling.

"I believe you're in danger, yes." If he'd had the guts years ago to tell someone what his uncle was doing to him, he'd have feared for his life too. If his uncle had gotten wind of his tattling, Aaron might not have survived his next encounter with his namesake. "Don't worry—we'll figure out what to do to keep you safe."

Even if the boy turned out to be lying, Aaron would do what he could to help him until his story was disproven. "Come on." Aaron prodded him up the cellar steps.

Jimmy huffed and trudged up onto the lawn.

Illuminated in the dying sunset's light, the silhouettes of several wagons pulled into position in the drive. How long until someone realized he wasn't up there helping? Night seemed to be in a hurry, thankfully. Though the sky was not fully dark, the stars were out and the deepening shadows should keep people from noticing what they were doing.

Quietly, they made their way among the shadows, carting armfuls of goods from cellar to cabin as Aaron kept a lookout for Zachary or anyone else who might be watching. If the men who were coming to collect this stuff showed up before they finished, would he find himself in a fight once again?

On their third and final trip, a small, dark form bustled out of the mansion's shadow.

Aaron grabbed Jimmy and pulled him close. "Get to the cabin—stay quiet."

The shadow kept coming.

Aaron gave the boy a slight push and then put himself between Jimmy and the shadowy figure, his body tense, his fists ready. But the figure transformed into the round, petite form of Cook, and his muscles unwound.

"Mr. Firebrook?" Cook dipped her head in such a way she was probably squinting in an effort to see him.

"Yes?" His heart started to pound. He set the painting he had behind him in hopes she'd not notice it. Who could he trust? The Lowes and Mercy, of course, but who was hiding these things for Jimmy? He thought well of all the staff, but someone was pretending to be more loyal than they were.

"The men are looking for you up at the wagons. They need—" She stopped short and cocked her head to the side. "What are you doing with those things?"

If she was Jimmy's mother's accomplice, hopefully all he had now were things the boy had tried to swipe on his own. "Taking care of them. Tell everyone I'll be up soon. I'm almost done." Picking the painting off the ground, he turned for the cabin.

The canvas under his arm didn't move with him.

"Now, wait a minute." Cook's grip on the painting held fast. "I didn't see you bid on anything, and this is—"

"I'll explain later." When he could think of something he *could* tell her without fear of alerting Jimmy's mother's plant that the ruse had been discovered.

The little woman snapped upright. "Or you can tell me now."

"I don't have—"

"Mr. Firebrook." Her tone warmed with warning.

"I'm putting them somewhere until I have time to get them to their rightful owner." He gently tugged at the painting. Thankfully she loosened her grasp. "Because as you said, I need to get to the wagons."

He walked as nonchalantly as he could toward the cabin, only allowing himself one look over his shoulder to see what Cook was doing.

She'd disappeared.

His chest puffed with a huge inhale, and he sped up to check on Jimmy.

They'd not lit any lamps, and the shadows of night had overtaken his cabin. "Jimmy?" He set down the painting and the last vase full of silverware he'd taken from the cellar.

The sound of the wind and horses' neighing and stomping in the distance were all that answered.

Sweeping his gaze back and forth, Aaron squinted but saw no one. He made his way to his bedroom. "Jimmy?"

With nothing but silence in his ears, his heartbeat filled up the noiseless void. "Jimmy," he called louder this time. With a quick turn of the switch, he started the lights.

The boy was nowhere to be seen.

He scrambled outside and jogged to the wagons. Had Jimmy started loading?

The only people he recognized in the crowd were Max and Franklin.

He tried to breathe evenly so his brain would work.

Which way would Jimmy go? Had the people his mother sent already found him? Had he gone back inside the mansion? Had he played Aaron for a fool and was now warning his accomplice that their plans had been foiled?

Aaron shook the doubt from his mind. He could worry about that later. If Jimmy's story was true, he had little time to save him if the worst had happened.

30

With a big smile on her face, Lydia finished counting the money the auction had generated and closed the cashbox. "We did so well, Mercy. This was a great idea."

Mercy carried a full dustpan to the trash chute in the wall that went all the way down to the basement. "Did we get enough to send them to Boston?" If Max and Robert were completely taken care of, would that alleviate her guilt over what she'd said to Jimmy earlier? How could she have told him he was unlovable and unwanted?

When she'd heard Nicholas had sent Jimmy to his room after he'd cursed at a guest, she had wondered if what she'd said was responsible for his escalating belligerence. Just when she was ready-ing to confront her brother, she'd caused problems elsewhere.

Lydia stood and stretched. "Enough that I feel certain they can make it on their own if Robert brings in a modest income."

She sighed. "I'd hoped we'd get enough he wouldn't have to work and would change his mind and finish school."

Lydia shook her head. "Though their every need is met here, Robert's always begging for more hours at the glass factory, and he's asked several times to quit school to work full time. I believe they'll do just fine, so I'm going to count them a success." She slipped her arm around Mercy's shoulders. "And you've been a big part of that. Not only because of tonight, but because of the work you've put into them as well. You should have a smile on your face."

"But they were easy." She squeezed the handle of the dustpan. "It's the harder children I'm not sure I've helped any."

"Like Jimmy?" Lydia backed up to look at her.

"I feel like we're failing him." Though he'd responded to Aaron for a while, he'd reverted right back to his old self. And any hope of her brother getting through to him was now gone.

"Sometimes we come to the point where all we can do is pray. God knows what each child needs, and maybe it's nothing we have."

But watching Jimmy flounder was agony. She crossed over to the portico balcony. A wagon full of auction winnings was leaving mansion property, the light of its lanterns barely visible at the end of the drive. Had her brother helped at all with the loading? She'd not seen him since before the auction started.

And Jimmy had gotten out of work entirely with a few choice words.

Was he in fact unlovable? Hard to love, yes, but how had telling him that done him any good? She rubbed her arm below her elbow and headed back to help finish the sweeping. How would she have felt to have had some trusted adult tell her she'd been unlovable? Aaron and a few other classmates had told her she was worthless—and she'd had a hard time not believing them—but she'd had parents who'd loved her deeply and many men and women in her church who'd treated her no differently than the other children. Their love and acceptance made up for how her peers constantly pointed out her flaws.

A quick thumping echoed up the nearby stairwell, and Aaron charged into the ballroom.

She was about to smile, but the way his eyes darted about made her call out to him instead. "What's the matter?"

His wide-eyed gaze took in each person helping them clean up before looking at her. "Uh, is Jimmy up here?"

"If he is, he's avoiding me."

Aaron turned back around and rushed downstairs.

"I wonder what Jimmy did this time." Franklin shook his head as he and Mr. Parker walked past her with a table, the last bit of furniture that had sold at auction.

She sighed. Evidently the first thing Jimmy did was escape his room. Who knew what he'd done after that? But if anyone could handle him, it'd be Aaron—though he had seemed a bit frantic. "Could you check on them, Mr. Cleghorn?"

Franklin gave her a nod and backed into the elevator with his end of the table.

Lydia walked up to her with the cashbox tucked under her arm. "I'm going to put this in the safe and make sure Nicholas has gotten our two into bed." Her expression turned amused. "Knowing Isabelle, though, he's probably reading her favorite fairy tale three times over and hasn't even started in with the water requests."

If only her brother's care of the orphans gave her the joy Lydia always had when talking about Nicholas's care of their children.

After helping the maids finish the floors, Mercy headed downstairs, her feet heavy with the knowledge that her family might be packing up a wagon and heading off the property themselves within the week.

As she entered the second-floor hallway, her brother passed by without a glance toward her. She took another step forward, her heart thundering and her palms clammy. She'd thought she'd not see him until tomorrow. "Timothy?"

He stopped and turned, a newspaper in hand.

As a little girl she'd thought he was the greatest, strongest, wisest big brother a girl could ever have. She wouldn't sleep tonight unless she knew whether or not that childhood image of him was completely tarnished.

Though she should probably ask about Jimmy first, in case her next question didn't go so well. "Have you checked on Jimmy?"

"Why?"

"Mr. Firebrook is looking for him."

Her brother shook his head. "Figures he'd not stay put." He blew out an indifferent huff. "Let the gardener take care of him. If I don't have to deal with Jimmy until morning, I'll count myself lucky."

"How can you say that? An orphanage director shouldn't talk of his charges that way. Perhaps . . ." Mercy swallowed and forced herself to continue. "Perhaps this isn't the best job for . . . us. I think it might be best if you go back to concentrating on banking, especially considering what I learned in the district earlier today." Her voice trembled, but she kept her gaze fixed on him so she wouldn't miss any tell or tic that would confirm the truth.

"You know I'm against you going there." His expression grew strained.

Oh, God, is there any hope he's only worried for my safety instead of his anonymity?

She swallowed twice so she could continue. "I know, but I had to help Caroline. She's been tending a woman named Lily White." She watched his face, but he showed no recognition. "I gave her medicine, took care of her sick children, and found this." She pulled his blue double cuff link from her pocket.

He looked at the item in her hand, his jaw hard. After a moment of silence, he took it and slipped it into his breast pocket.

She left her empty palm out between them. "Are you not going to say anything?"

He shrugged, his face carefully blank. "Thanks for finding it for me."

"That's all you're going to say?" She dropped her hand. "You're not even going to have the decency to redden over where I found it?"

He rolled up his newspaper. "I see no reason to discuss it with you."

A thumping behind her on the stairwell grew louder and faster.

So he'd not outright deny it? He wasn't even going to make up a lame excuse? "So it's true? You're not just drinking in the saloons, you're . . ." Oh she just couldn't say it.

Timothy heaved a sigh. "As I said, I don't think this is an appropriate conversation to be having with my sister."

If she'd had two hands, she might have been tempted to strangle him. "I think we should discuss it, considering it affects our work—"

"Are you saying I'm not good enough to watch a few kids?" He cocked his head and looked at her with narrowed eyes.

Not these kids anyway. "What I'm saying is there's no shame in stepping down from a job that's not right for you."

"I didn't ask for your opinions, Mercy. Nothing I choose to do with my free time will keep us from the job we've been hired to do. I suggest you keep your thoughts about my personal business to yourself."

But his partaking in what the red-light district offered meant he wasn't worthy of this job. He was too often absent. He wasn't the role model the boys needed.

And once someone with a big mouth discovered what Timothy was up to, the scandal would darken the orphanage's reputation.

His personal business was not private enough to keep it from affecting others, no matter what he said.

But there was no time to discuss it right now with someone coming down the stairs. "At least check on Jimmy."

He sighed. "I'll take care of Jimmy. Don't worry."

"Hey, Miss McClain!" Max appeared at the bottom of the stairwell.

Though usually not a demonstrative young man, he came up behind her and gave her a giant hug. "Thank you for getting us enough money to go to Boston."

She patted the hand he left on her shoulder and mustered up a smile, though it was quite stiff. "I won't say it was nothing, but I would've worked ten times harder if I'd had to."

Timothy started off for his room. Did he really think their conversation was over?

Of course he would, considering he'd told her to keep her opinions to herself. She rooted her feet to the floor to keep from charging after him.

At least he hadn't been gallivanting about in the district tonight

. . . or had he? She'd seen him at the beginning of the auction, but he'd not been there during the bidding.

She scrunched her eyes tight.

"Are you all right, Miss McClain?"

She nodded but couldn't muster a smile again. "Just tired."

"Would you like me to tuck Owen in for you?"

"I'd be grateful if you would, Max." The smile slowly returned, and she took in a big gulp of air.

He frowned at her. "Why don't you go get yourself some chamomile tea or something? You look as if you're coming down with something."

The churning in her gut definitely was making her feel ill, but it wasn't because she was sick. "I might just do that." Otherwise she'd never get to sleep.

She looked down the hall toward the Lowes' room as Max headed to Owen's. Telling Nicholas about her brother's moral failings tonight wasn't worth interrupting Nicholas's family routine. Holding the information a few more hours wouldn't hurt any sleeping boys.

And no need to barge in on Patricia. She'd let her sister-in-law hear about her husband's infidelity from his own mouth. After Nicholas was informed and fired them, Timothy would have to confess to her soon enough.

Mercy trudged down the stairs and toward the kitchen. Nothing that could calm what ailed her would be found there, but she might as well try something in hopes of not tossing and turning all night, imagining how her conversation with Nicholas would go come morning, how she could have any sort of good relationship with her brother once they were fired, or what would happen to her once her family was dismissed from the mansion.

In the kitchen with only a solitary candle alight on the table, Caroline sat alone with her head in her hands.

"I'm sorry if I'm intruding." Mercy turned up a lamp and headed toward the icebox. Had Caroline come down with whatever Katelyn had? "Do you need me to get you something?"

Caroline didn't move. Her teacup sat beside her, full and ignored.

After pouring herself a glass of buttermilk, Mercy sat beside Caroline and waited for her to look up, but she didn't. "Are you all right?" she whispered. Though Caroline was quite reserved, she wasn't one for ignoring people. Had she fallen asleep propped up like that?

Mercy put her hand on the housekeeper's shoulder.

Caroline shook her head, sat back, and wiped at her eyes.

Caroline was crying? She'd never seen the woman in tears before. "Have you come down with what Katelyn has? Do I need to get you medicine?"

The sound that came from the head housekeeper was a cross between a hiccup and laugh. Caroline hung her head in her hands again. "As if medicine could fix it."

"What needs to be fixed?" She lightly rubbed the woman's back, not knowing what to do to comfort someone usually so stalwart.

Caroline took her teacup into her hands, but instead of drinking it, she stared at the brown liquid. "I went to check on Lily White's family, to make sure she got the medicine I gave you."

"I'm sorry I didn't tell you I delivered it, what with the auction and all. . . ." She'd been so blindsided by her brother's involvement with Lily, she'd not thought to tell Caroline she'd taken care of the Whites. Did Caroline know about her brother and Lily? Mercy's stomach churned enough she could've made her own buttermilk.

"It's not that." Caroline played with her spoon. "Katelyn's croup was getting bad, and Mrs. Lowe said evening air helps. I was pacing the porch with her, but figured I could do something more useful while I was out. So I went to check on them. But . . ."

Had she found them dead? With all the worrying Mercy had done over her brother, she'd not thought about the Whites after she'd left. "Are they all right?"

She nodded but didn't say anything more.

"Well then, what did you find when you got there?"

"That I'm a gullible woman." She shoved her tea away.

Mercy flinched at the anger in Caroline's voice. What kind of answer was that? "You found out you were gullible?"

"Yes, because I believed the nice things Henri told me on that ride he took me on the other day."

What could Caroline have learned about Henri from the prostitute? Mercy pressed her eyes shut and gritted her teeth. Did she learn the same thing she'd learned about her brother earlier, that a man she loved visited Lily?

"Lily was feeling better—physically, but not in her head. She got to talking. . . ." Caroline added a spoonful of sugar to her tea but made no move to drink it. "When district women are sick and unable to work, that's the worst time for them. They aren't distracted by simply surviving, and they start to think about their lives. About how they wish it would end, or if they should end it themselves . . ." Caroline dropped her spoon and leaned back in her chair. "You probably didn't notice, but Lily's pregnant on top of being sick, and she said . . . Well, she knows my sister."

Caroline looked at the candle's flame flickering in front of her, then snuffed it out. "Lily said she's been thinking about how to get rid of her baby this time and was thinking about doing what my sister did—convince one of her johns the baby was his."

"But why would any man believe a prostitute could know who the father was unless she was more of a . . . mistress?" Sometimes Mercy could only shake her head at the topics not fit for polite society she found herself discussing.

Caroline snorted. "You're right, she wouldn't. . . . But if the man takes the baby, he at least believes it could be his."

Caroline's sister's baby . . . Henri.

But would he have truly . . . ? Oh, if her own brother would, then what would stop a single, rich man like Henri—who didn't even profess to be a Christian—from doing so? The heaviness in her gut was likely only a fraction of the sinking feeling Caroline must have had when she'd put those thoughts together.

Mercy shook her head. "We shouldn't jump to conclusions."

"I didn't. Lily mentioned Henri by name." Caroline's words came out so rough, her throat had to be hurting.

It wasn't her own heart breaking, but it felt shattered, nonetheless. "I'm sorry."

"Yes, well, I should've known a man who could stay angry for years over a slight to his ego couldn't be a truly good man. He doesn't want me. He wants a free nanny—for life. Excuse me." She pushed back in her chair, making the legs screech across the kitchen floor. "I'm going to check on Katelyn." She left without taking one sip of her tea.

Mercy stared at her buttermilk. Did Caroline have the right of it?

Prostitutes weren't known for being moral—in more ways than one. Lily or Moira could've lied.

But Henri had insisted on paying for the baby's care.

Mercy took a big gulp of buttermilk, then held her head just as Caroline had earlier. How could the men they'd counted on fail them so badly?

31

Mercy stifled a yawn as she listened to the school board members argue about funding. She'd not slept much last night, unable to stop thinking about what she was going to tell Nicholas. Timothy hadn't outright confessed to her, but he'd said enough that Nicholas could take what she knew and ferret out what happened from there.

After finally getting to sleep, she'd slept too long, not only missing her chance to talk to Nicholas but breakfast as well. She wasn't the only adult in the mansion responsible for the children, but now she'd have to apologize for her sloth as well as for her brother's debauchery once she returned home.

She picked up her pencil and underlined the names of the three candidates for the high school math position for the twentieth time. The newest and final name on the list belonged to a Miss Roundtree, a young lady with sparkly blue eyes and a contagious smile. But with the way her voice was all sugar, enthusiasm, and light, she was much better suited for working with young children. She'd talked to the board members interviewing her as if they were no taller than her kneecap and had just learned their ABCs.

Mercy could imagine how Max and Robert would react to being talked to like that—especially since Miss Roundtree had only taken the minimal amount of math required to obtain her teaching license.

"All right, all right." Mr. Hicks put up his hands, waving them as if he were telling people to sit, though no one had left their seats. "We're obviously not going to settle the funding problem in one day. We can think things through and talk again next meeting."

The board president gathered the papers in front of him and then continued. "Let's finish the hiring. We have Firebrook, Tate, and Roundtree to consider for the math position since Miss Edison pulled her application."

"I don't see how Miss Roundtree would fare well in the high school," Mr. Carter said.

Though Mr. Carter always favored men over women applicants, she had to agree with him in this case.

"And Mrs. Tate." Mr. Lafferty shook his head. "I don't think she wants to teach as much as she wants to discipline. She sounded like a dictator."

Mr. Carter crossed his arms over his chest and leaned back in his seat as if he were board president. "You can't deny some of the town children need discipline rather badly."

"But she's been fired from two school districts. That's hard to overlook."

"That leaves us with Mr. Firebrook." Mr. Hicks turned to Mercy. "You're the one who objected to him. Can you elaborate on why you think he's not fit—at least not more fit than these other two?" He looked at his papers and frowned. "We've not received any more applications. Doesn't mean we won't, but I'd like detailed reasons on why we shouldn't hire Mr. Firebrook at this point."

She took a drink of water before looking up. "I no longer have any objections. I'd give him the job."

"Now wait a second." Dr. Freedman turned to Mercy. "You had a strong aversion to him at his interview and pushed us to consider others. Surely Miss Roundtree's naïveté and Mrs. Tate's hardness can't be so off-putting you've dismissed your reservations. What was your objection?"

She took another sip of her water, hoping she'd not have to divulge too much, since Dr. Freedman might remember Aaron tormenting his younger siblings. "He's worked at the mansion with me for nearly two months. I had told Mr. Lowe I wasn't keen on his being hired, but I have no say in the hiring there, so he gave Mr. Firebrook the job. I've now watched him tutor math, both to an exceptional student and a struggling one, and I think he's done very well."

"That doesn't explain your original objection."

If only Dr. Freedman weren't so stubbornly thorough. Probably a good quality for a doctor, but not an endearing one at the moment. "I knew him as a child and didn't have fond memories of him, but I've changed my mind."

"I recognized the Firebrook name." Dr. Freedman looked at his notes, tapping his fingers on the table. "You say he attended school here?"

"Yes." Hadn't Aaron said so at his interview?

"I don't remember an Aaron Firebrook. I definitely remember a George." Dr. Freedman's brows furrowed, as if he saw something concerning.

Her lungs collapsed. There wasn't anything she could do to keep him from remembering now.

"Can I see his application again?" Dr. Freedman held out his hand for Mr. Hicks's pile of papers and flipped to the last page. "Does this G in front of his signature stand for George?"

"Yes." She kept her expression as passionless as possible.

"The boy who bullied anyone and everyone?" He looked up in the air for only a second, then shook his head. "I should've figured that out. The beard though . . ." He turned to look at her with narrowed eyes. "You knew he was George but chose not to say anything?"

"As I said, I've been around him for months now and believe him to have become a better man."

"Why didn't you completely denounce him at his interview?" Dr. Freedman frowned as he looked at the rest of the board. "He was the worst bully I've ever met. Not to me personally, but toward my younger brother." He looked back at Mercy and stared at her missing hand.

She tucked her arm behind the table.

"I'm sure George harassed you mercilessly in school, so why would you say nothing?"

"He . . ." How could she get Dr. Freedman to see what had taken her weeks to realize? "I did plan to tell you after the interview, but when he came to shake our hands, well, that obviously made him remember who I was, but then he . . . he asked that I give him a chance."

"A chance?" Dr. Freedman's brows raised. "You alone decided to give him a chance?"

She fiddled with her skirt and couldn't make herself look up. "I figured we'd find someone better soon enough. Besides, who am I to make judgments about a person I've not seen for over a decade?" Though she'd not realized that at first, she should have. "But I've been afforded the opportunity to see the type of man he's become. He truly has changed. He cares about people, about kids, about being a better man."

"And this is why women are a liability in any sort of official position; they're swayed by how they feel instead of what they know." Mr. Carter harrumphed.

"I'm sorry?" She did look up then. Mr. Carter made known his opinion on women being the inferior sex readily and repeatedly, but he was wrong. "My emotion got the best of me back at the interview, when I realized who he was. That's why I wanted to look for someone else, despite his qualifications. But emotion is not getting the best of me now. I've seen with my own eyes he's become a good man, and I believe with all my heart he'll be a good teacher."

Mr. Carter leaned forward. Though he was clear across the room, it seemed as if he were trying to get in her face. "Oh? *With all your heart?*" His smile turned patronizing. "Did he play paramour? Did he realize you were the obstacle to his goals and woo you into believing he was a swell guy?"

Her muscles tightened.

"If asking for a second chance was all it took to keep you quiet, he probably realized you were easy prey." He glanced toward her arm behind the table. "A bully can use charm just as easily as force."

As Mr. Carter would certainly know.

She kept her gaze on him but found it hard to reply. If these men found out Aaron had kissed her, would they agree with Mr. Carter?

And if that's the first thing Mr. Carter believed Aaron would do, and he'd in fact done so . . . No, it couldn't be . . . Though with what Timothy and Henri were about, maybe she really was as gullible as Mr. Carter thought her.

"Well?" Mr. Carter's smirk had grown so big she could likely have smacked it off from across the room.

Even if Aaron had charmed her to get this job, that didn't negate the fact that he'd done well tutoring Max and Robert and handled Jimmy better than any of the adults at the orphanage. "If you don't believe my assessment, ask Mr. Lowe. He's seen Aaron tutor and interact with the children, and he'd not fall victim to whatever charm you suggest Aaron might've used on me." There. If that wasn't a logical enough answer, she didn't know what was.

She turned to Dr. Freedman. "Don't judge him hastily. If a man can't change, then we're all doomed. But he has, and I believe he'll do an excellent job."

Dr. Freedman's expression didn't soften. "I can't in good conscience hire a man who's proven to be capable of hurting the vulnerable."

"It's time to vote." Mr. Carter slapped the table, looking across at her. "I say Mrs. Tate."

Mr. Lafferty smoothed his white beard with his hand in the rhythmical way he always did when contemplating his vote. "Miss Roundtree needs the job since her parents left her with nothing and she has a young brother to care for. And certainly no students would come to harm under her."

"Though they might not learn much," Mercy added, though

she was fairly certain nothing she could say now would sway them. Dr. Freedman certainly had more influence than she ever would.

"She's plenty capable of reading the textbook and forming plans." Dr. Freedman nodded. "I vote Miss Roundtree as well."

The men down the table all voted, one for Mrs. Tate and the rest for Miss Roundtree.

Perhaps she was indeed emotional and gullible, but she couldn't vote against Aaron when he'd proven himself—to her at least. "I vote for Mr. Firebrook."

Mr. Carter rolled his eyes, and Mr. Hicks called an end to the meeting.

The others stood up around her, their chairs scraping against the plank flooring, but she couldn't make herself leave her seat. She had no one to blame but herself for bringing in these other applicants and causing Aaron to lose the job he'd hoped for—that he was right for.

She couldn't help the tears brimming in her eyes as she stared at her malformed arm. It had taken her a long time to forgive Aaron.

How long would she have to wait to be forgiven by him?

32

Mercy walked slowly toward the mansion, looking for Aaron but not seeing him. He'd become so much a part of the landscape, she expected to see him every time she was out-of-doors. But how could she face him now, knowing she was responsible for killing his dream?

She couldn't make up for what she'd done, but she'd ask his forgiveness anyway, just as he'd asked for hers. And he'd likely forgive her far faster than she had him, which would make her feel even worse.

Would he stay at the mansion and garden, or look to teach elsewhere?

Earning the forgiveness of a previous classmate was tied up in his promise to teach, so he'd likely leave. Her heart flipped at the thought.

But what if Mr. Carter was right? What if Aaron left immediately, acting as if he had no romantic attachment to her whatsoever? What if he'd only kissed her in an attempt to get her to sway the school board on his behalf?

If Caroline could be snookered into believing a man's feelings were genuine, could Mercy be failing to see who Aaron really was? Had his kisses clouded her ability to be level-headed?

No, she believed Aaron's story—a man wouldn't bring up details like that about himself unless they were heartbreakingly true.

But if he had only led her along, oh, it would hurt.

He'd become far more than her past nemesis. He'd become the person she thought of in the quiet, the man she admired for trying to reconcile himself to those he'd hurt, a sinner courageous enough to allow God to break and remold him, the man who'd helped her believe that misfits could change with God's grace and men's long-suffering.

Oh, which uncomfortable task should she do first? Tell Nicholas about her brother or tell Aaron she'd cost him the job he was perfect for?

She'd find Nicholas. Finding out if Aaron had actual feelings for her or had only charmed her could wait a little longer. Surely no one would blame a woman in love for doing that.

She stopped midstep. In love? She blew out a shaky breath and stared at the ground, swallowing against uncertainty. Could she truly be in love? But how could she not love a man who owned up to his mistakes and tried his hardest to be better every day? Oh, how scary it was to be in love after his motives had been called into question.

Granted, Mr. Carter didn't know Aaron, but she'd known Timothy her whole life and somehow didn't know him at all. The same could be true of Aaron.

But Aaron couldn't be that great of an actor. She'd watched him with each of the boys, seen his raw emotions in the cellar, and heard the warble in his voice when he'd feared he'd never become the man God wanted him to be.

He just had to be the Aaron she'd come to know.

Oh, how she hoped Mr. Carter was wrong. For if Aaron hadn't changed, what hope was there for Timothy?

She forged inside the mansion and took off her lightweight shawl. She listened for the sound of Franklin's dress shoes clipping along the polished floor but heard nothing.

The young man was hardly ever remiss in welcoming people to the mansion.

She'd expected to ask him where Nicholas was rather than wander around the property. She needed to tell him about Timothy before her courage and conviction waned.

In the library, instead of Nicholas, she found Timothy reading. She wavered on the threshold.

Shouldn't she give Timothy the chance to keep some of his dignity and resign instead of being fired?

Thankful he was alone, she forced herself to step inside the room, which smelled of leather and pages.

Owen's hoot drew her gaze to the window. Patricia was sitting atop a garden wall, her body hunched, her foot swinging in a bored rhythm as she watched Owen kick a ball to Robert. Jimmy was nowhere to be seen, but that wasn't a surprise. "May I speak with you?"

Timothy looked up and sighed, then lowered his book.

She supposed that was a yes. "In regard to what I learned about you and Lily White, I think—"

A knock sounded on the doorframe, and Franklin stepped into the library. "Pardon me, but Cook doesn't want to dish up a plate for Jimmy again unless he's here. Has Jimmy been found?"

Jimmy hadn't come to breakfast?

Timothy tossed his book onto the table. "No, and if he doesn't return by dinnertime, he'll go without that meal as well."

She glared at her brother. "Don't tell me you didn't actually check up on him last night. You promised."

Timothy huffed. "I told you I'd take care of him. Jimmy only wants attention, and we've been giving it to him. Hours of wandering around looking for him, hours of lectures he disregards. Well, maybe a night curled up in the barn or wherever he decided to pout will do him good. Once he realizes we aren't going to let him lead us on a merry chase any longer, he'll come out of hiding."

She clenched her teeth hard to keep from railing at her brother. "Did Aaron or Mr. Lowe agree to this plan?"

"I haven't a need to talk to either of them. This is *my* job." Her brother's eyes pierced into hers. "Not theirs."

Patricia stomped into the room past Franklin and let out a frustrated groan that turned into a cough. "All right, it's your turn to watch the boys." Patricia's voice was high-pitched and congested. She snuffled and pulled out a handkerchief. "My head feels worse every minute, and I can't take them anymore. When I told Robert to stop ripping up grass, he told me I shouldn't put so much starch in my tatted pantalets!" Her expression was so infused with shock and horror Mercy barely kept her smile hidden.

The amused sparkle in Franklin's eyes as he turned to leave made it impossible for Mercy to hold in her chuckle, but Patricia was too incensed and congested to notice the laughter or the fact that she'd repeated the insult in Franklin's presence. "I'm going to burrow myself into bed now. Tell Cook to send up broth for me when she sends some up for Max."

"What's wrong with Max?" Had they all caught what Katelyn had?

Patricia wiped her nose. "He started with fever chills early this morning and has been sleeping most of the day. We should've never allowed Caroline to help Cook this week while tending to that sick—" She stopped and shook her head, covering what she'd almost said with a sorry excuse for a sneeze. "Baby."

That certainly hadn't been what she'd almost said.

"My brain is so clogged." Patricia continued wiping her nose. "I can't be held accountable for anything I say." She took a quick glance at Mercy, then wilted against the wall as if she were a melodramatic actress about to swoon. "I'm going to bed now." She glanced at Timothy, but he did nothing but nod.

She left in a huff.

Timothy pushed himself out of his chair. "Seems I have children to attend." He stopped in the doorway, tapping his fingers against the wood frame before turning back to look at her. "If you haven't noticed, not every man is as lucky as Lowe, blessed with a wife he can respect. If you fault me for needing to get away from the mess of a woman she is sometimes . . . you know as well as I do that Lowe won't keep me on staff if you tell him where I find my solace. He's too holier-than-thou when it comes to those tramps."

Oh, how she wished he'd chosen to stay silent, for then she might have hoped he felt remorse.

"If you snitch, we'll be homeless—perhaps even jobless, considering the bank president tends to think as Lowe does."

She shook her head at him. "You can always get a different job. They're replaceable—marriages aren't."

"I could, but as for your remaining under my roof, if you take this away from me . . ." He gave her a long look, then took his leave.

Mercy stood with her eyes closed for a good long while, her heart beating sluggishly. So there was no hope he'd resign peacefully.

But she had to do what was right—for Timothy's good, for everyone's.

She stood looking out the window until she saw her brother throw a ball to Owen, an action that would've made her smile only weeks ago. His refusal to do what was best for these children and even his own family was his fault, not hers.

Mercy left the library and walked through the mansion in search of Nicholas. She should've asked Franklin where he was before he'd left.

In the kitchen, Cook was busy stirring pots, her dark curls plastered to her neck, damp with sweat.

"Have you seen Franklin?"

Her spoon clattered on the stove, but Cook picked it back up and put a hand to her heart. "He's looking for Jimmy." She wiped her glistening, pale forehead. Was the whole mansion coming down with sickness?

"What about Mr. Lowe?"

"In the nursery, as far as I know." She turned her back and started whipping whatever it was she had in a pot.

Mercy watched for a second, but since Cook was energetic enough to whisk like that, perhaps she wasn't sick.

Mercy headed for the second floor, praying she wouldn't come across anybody on her way there. She didn't have the energy to engage in small talk.

In the nursery, Nicholas was flat on his back in the middle of the large rug. His son wiggled above him, cradled in his hands as he dipped the little boy back and forth. "Here comes Jake the bumblebee. Swoooooping down to—"

"Excuse me."

Nicholas looked over at her as if he'd been caught raiding the cookie jar, but he left Jake giggling high above him.

She cleared her throat but hesitated. Her next words would irrevocably affect her own life and many others'. But keeping the truth to herself wouldn't fix the problem. "Can I talk to you?"

Nicholas rocked up into a sitting position, depositing Jake in his lap. "Of course."

She came in and slumped against the wall. "My brother . . ." Oh, there just wasn't an easy way to say this. She moved to sit in the rocker. "I saw him heading into a saloon about a month ago when I was helping Caroline."

Nicholas stilled, and his eyes dulled.

"He claimed he only drank occasionally, that it didn't affect him. But then he came home drunk the same night you returned from your business trip. Told me it was his first and last time. I'm sorry. I shouldn't have kept that from you, but I really wanted to believe he wouldn't do it again." She fidgeted in hopes of finding a comfy spot on the seat, but perhaps there was no possibility of getting comfortable now. "But there's more." She took a deep breath. "Since Katelyn's sick, Caroline asked me to take medicine to Lily White's family yesterday. When I did, I found my brother's cuff link beside the bed."

Nicholas's expression turned pensive. "Let's not jump to conclusions. Any number of men could have similar cuff links."

"Unfortunately, no." If only she had that hope to cling to. "Not only is the cuff link a rather unique one, but I returned it to my brother last night, telling him where I found it. He simply thanked me for returning it. He didn't deny he'd lost it there. And just now, he told me to keep my mouth shut about him visiting her."

After about half a minute of looking off into space, Nicholas gently set Jake down beside him and swept a pile of blocks up against his son's chubby legs. "I suppose you know what this means?"

"Yes." Her voice came out whisper thin. "My brother is not fit to be in charge of these children."

Nicholas got up and put a hand on her shoulder, giving her a gentle squeeze. "I'm sorry for you and Patricia, but yes, if Timothy doesn't deny it, and you said Caroline saw him at the saloon as well . . ."

She nodded.

"Then yes, I can't keep him in my employ, not when these kids need to know that not all men are like those they encounter in the red-light district. I'd had some concerns about him, but I'd been so busy with paperwork and dealing with the people the fire displaced that I've been preoccupied."

"Excuse me." Cook poked her head into the room with a frown. She stepped across the threshold, put a platter of cookies on the bureau, and wrung her hands. "I'm sorry to overhear, but I feel I should apologize for keeping some things to myself."

Mercy's heart plummeted. How many people already knew about how her brother was disgracing his family?

Nicholas took his hand from Mercy's shoulder. "Go on."

"It's just that . . ." Cook bit her lip. "I've seen some suspicious things, but I've kept them to myself since you and your wife seem to be such good judges of character. I've never worked with such an upstanding staff, and . . ." She glanced at Mercy for a second before dropping her gaze to the ground. "Since Mr. McClain is Mercy's kin, well, I didn't want to say anything unless I knew for certain. Wanted to give him the benefit of the doubt. I'd suspected Mr. McClain might be drinking, but I didn't know about the rest. But in regard to Mr. Firebrook—"

Nicholas's brows furrowed. "Aaron?"

Cook nodded, and Mercy's heart sank even deeper.

No.

She fisted her hand in her lap.

Please, don't let her have anything bad to say about Aaron.

Cook closed her eyes as if gathering her thoughts. "I just went to check on Mr. Firebrook, since he hadn't come to breakfast. There's a lot of sick people today." She pushed back the curls lying damp on her forehead.

"Are you ill as well, Miss Jamison?" Nicholas must have noticed how shaky and pale Cook looked.

"I'm not coming down with anything, no. Just worrying about my great aunt. She's not much longer for this world. I was hoping you'd allow me a few days off to see her one last time."

"I could have someone cover for you for a few days, Miss Jamison." Cook let out a stuttered sigh. "Thank you."

He gave her a short nod, but he screwed up his lips. "But what's this about Mr. Firebrook?"

Mercy held her breath and clamped onto the rocker's arm. Surely he wasn't acting in a way that would make Cook think he was doing something amiss like her brother was.

Cook looked down at her hands. "I hadn't seen him all day. And last night, well, he was acting suspicious. When I went out to his cabin, I . . ." She scrunched her face up tight, then gave a little nod and a rush of words flew out. "I found a lot of missing things in his parlor."

"Missing things?" Nicholas looked away just long enough to grab the lint Jake was about to stuff in his mouth.

"Yes. The fancy copper kettle I thought I'd misplaced is in his cabin, along with the painting Mrs. Wisely wanted last night, and a jumble of other stuff all piled up."

Mercy's hand had somehow found her throat. Why would Aaron have those things? "What are you saying?"

"I'm saying, me and some of the staff have noticed things disappearing, and I can't deny what I've seen with my own eyes." She shook her head. "Mr. Firebrook is stealing from the orphanage."

"I don't believe it," Mercy whispered. Aaron would have no reason to steal things. He wanted to teach. He wanted to make up for past wrongs. He wanted to become a better man.

Nicholas shook his head and picked up Jake. "I'll need to see this for myself." He marched out of the room.

Mercy somehow made her feet follow him into the hallway, though each step felt as if her soles were made of lead.

Aaron could not be two-faced, not after she'd just stood up for him at the board meeting.

But why would there be stolen property in his cabin?

Somehow little Jake seemed to sense something was amiss and stopped chattering, popped his thumb into his mouth, and laid his head on his father's shoulder.

"I'm sorry, Miss McClain." Cook came up beside her, her pale lips twitching, her brow creased with tension. "I know how you'd come to like him."

Like him? She loved him.

Cook veered off for the basement as Mercy followed Nicholas out through the front door he held open for her. Their silent walk to Aaron's cottage seemed to take forever, yet they got there all too quickly.

Nicholas knocked on the door and turned the knob. "Aaron?" The cabin was dark, but light spilled in with them, illuminating table, chairs, and a loveseat stacked with items as if the parlor were a storeroom. The water lily painting Mrs. Wisely had asked about last night lay against the loveseat's arm.

A wave of cold, not unlike the first shivers of a fever, swept through her, except she wasn't sick.

When she had asked Aaron about the painting last night, he'd said he'd look for it, but here it was.

She stepped in behind Nicholas and took in the silverware and knickknacks scattered about.

And Mrs. Wisely's grandmother's tortoiseshell combs.

Why did Aaron have all this stuff out here? And where was he?

Nicholas picked up a candlestick she'd seen many times in the

291

mansion's foyer. She'd noticed it had disappeared a few days ago, but she'd assumed Caroline or Sadie had moved it. She'd not given its disappearance a thought past that.

Nicholas put the candlestick down and forged into the bedroom, turning on the lamp.

But she couldn't follow. No matter what he found there, it didn't change the evidence piled up in front of her.

But why?

Just an hour ago, she'd refused to believe Mr. Carter when he'd insinuated Aaron was duping her to win the math position, though doing so could've helped him get the job. But stealing wouldn't help him become a teacher or help any children.

But what if teaching hadn't ever been his true goal?

Surely it had been, considering all the work he'd put into Jimmy. Except Jimmy was missing too.

She sniffed. Once Aaron returned, he'd have a good explanation for this—he had to.

Nicholas came out of the bedroom, shaking his head. "We need to find Aaron so he can explain."

She nodded, rubbing her arm in a lonely hug.

Oh please, God, don't let my judgment be off so badly. I mean, I know I had no idea what my brother was up to, but he's never been that good to me. But Aaron . . .

Nicholas gestured for her to walk out in front of him, and he shut the door behind them, producing a soft click. But it felt more like a final thud.

What if Aaron didn't have a good reason for that stuff to be in his cabin? Or what if he never returned? Never before had he left his job unfinished without letting someone know where he was going.

Up ahead, a rider had stopped at the mansion's door and dismounted.

Hopefully the man wouldn't stick around wanting to talk. She wasn't sure her voice would work well enough to acknowledge anyone right now.

Cook answered his knock. The man dipped his head and handed her something before turning to mount his horse and ride off.

Nicholas gave a small wave to the rider as he passed, but the man only tipped his hat and continued on. Nicholas watched him head down the hill. "Do you know who that was?"

She shook her head.

Cook was just about to back into the mansion when Nicholas called out, "Is that message for me?"

She froze, pressing a folded piece of paper against her chest, her eyes wide and her face nearly as white as cream.

Nicholas put speed into his step and reached out to steady the woman. "Are you certain you're feeling all right?"

"No. I'm not." She folded up the paper into a tiny square, her hands trembling. "It's a message . . . from my cousin. Aunt Freda asked for me by name, but . . . she likely won't survive long enough to see me."

"You don't know until you try." Nicholas gave her arm a slight shake. "Go as soon as you can pack."

"Thank you." Cook rushed back into the mansion.

Mercy hung back as Nicholas followed Cook inside.

How soon until she'd be packing up herself? Even if Timothy and Patricia would allow her to come with them after being fired, she just couldn't.

She could ask to stay on until the Lowes hired new directors, but if Aaron wasn't who she believed him to be, if she didn't need to wait around for him to declare himself . . .

No, he'd be back. Within the day. With a good explanation. Surely. Surely he would.

33

Stumbling forward in the morning light, Aaron approached the run-down house where he hoped to find Zachary, or at least someone who'd actually seen Jimmy. He was done with wild-goose chases.

He stopped walking to yawn, thankful to be back in Teaville. Yesterday and the night before he'd run from one vague clue to another, one town to the next. He'd barely let himself sleep last night, but he'd needed it since he'd not slept the night before.

His borrowed horse's gait had been lazy and slow this morning, and he'd almost fallen asleep several times. He should've had another cup of coffee before leaving the hotel, but the place was dank and smelled of mildew, and he'd been eager to return to see if Nicholas had found out anything, especially after a lodger he'd eaten breakfast with yesterday had said he'd purchased something from a man in Teaville who matched Zachary's description two weeks ago, and he'd mentioned the young man had sported a black eye.

Hopefully he'd find Jimmy's alleged brother here. Once he'd figured out Jimmy had no brother, he'd started to get somewhere.

Though after two nights and a day of running around like a decapitated chicken, time was now his foe. If Zachary wasn't here, he was out of ideas. Hopefully Nicholas had already pieced together Zachary or Jimmy's whereabouts using the information he'd sent with a man he'd met who had agreed to stop at the mansion on his way home.

Was it too much to hope Jimmy had disappeared on his own, being the disobedient boy he always was, and had returned to the mansion unharmed?

A dog barked as he approached the half-painted, two-story house, and the porch's slats creaked below him. He winced when one cracked beneath his full weight, and he gingerly made his way to the dog-scratched white door and knocked.

They might be upset with him coming so early, but he was not in the mood to wait a few hours to be sure everyone was awake. He needed a new set of clothes, a nap, a—

"What do you want?" A woman's groggy voice called from behind the door.

To know that Jimmy was all right. But after two nights, he was only hoping to find him. "I'm looking for Zachary."

"What do you want with him?"

His heart leapt, the jolt of hope as good as stout coffee. "I'm trying to locate a mutual acquaintance."

A woman with a rough face and a terrifying scowl opened the door, though the chain kept them separated. "Who?"

"Jimmy."

She blinked her sleep-filled eyes. "What've they done?"

Plenty probably, but their crimes could be dealt with later. "I don't know that they've done anything, but I think Jimmy's in trouble, and I need to find him."

"You the police?" Her eyes narrowed, and a boy of about seven squished in front of her flannel wrapper to get a look at the stranger. His hair was a mess, but he looked as if he could be kin to the young man Aaron had punched in the cellar.

"I'm not the police."

The door shut.

Had she actually wanted the police?

295

"Zach!" Her rusty holler leaked through the house as if it were a sieve. "Wake up! Someone wants you!"

An answering shout filled with curses made Aaron cringe and glance at the houses stacked down the block. Hopefully they weren't waking the entire street.

There was a door slam, and then things went quiet.

Several minutes later after much thumping, the front door opened again, this time wide. Zachary's scowl was made less menacing by the wrinkle indentations across his cheek. "What do you want?"

The woman he assumed was Zachary's mother came up behind the young man, her hand clasping her wrapper closed. "Ask your question and be done with it."

"Do you know where Jimmy's mother lives?"

Zachary shrugged. "Don't know a Jimmy."

"Then we're done here." The woman came forward to shut the door. "He doesn't know him."

Aaron put his foot forward to keep the door from closing. "Not so fast. I've seen him with Jimmy."

The young man's acne-scarred face hardened.

"He's thirteen, blond hair, squinty eyes, freckles, a thin face, and wide shoulders."

Zachary moved back. "Could be lots of people."

All right—he'd not come this far and lost this much sleep for this hoodlum to lie. "Are you going to pretend I didn't give you a shiner when I found you wrestling with Jimmy?"

The woman's scowl deepened. "You're the one who beat up my boy?"

He looked away from her to keep from saying yes. "If you help me find Jimmy, that'll make you look a little better when you're hauled in later for stealing. Lying isn't going to save you."

"I haven't been stealing anything."

Zachary's mother moved in front of him, puffing up her shoulders. "Get off my property."

"I will, once I know where to find Jimmy. That's all I want. Tell me and I'll leave."

"Glenn." The woman pushed her younger son out the door. "Get the cops."

The boy zipped out beneath Aaron's arm and through the overgrown yard.

Aaron sighed. He'd probably get in trouble for harassing them or something. Could he connect Zachary to burglarizing the mansion without Jimmy? Charges based on simple accusation wouldn't stick. "All I want is an idea of where Jimmy could be—an address, a person to talk to. Just let me know how you'd find him, and I'll leave."

"Told you I don't know him."

"Yes, you do. I'm not an idiot, and neither are you."

"That's right. I'm not." Zachary's ruddy face was half stubbornness and half amusement at having the upper hand.

"Listen, I don't care what you've done, though I'm sure you've done plenty. All I want is Jimmy."

Zachary's lips only curved up more.

The woman pushed against the door, pinching Aaron's foot against the doorjamb. "Look, mister, he says he doesn't know him, so leave."

He should, but might his bullying experience be worth something—as long as he kept it under control? He pushed back against the door and leaned closer to the young man. "Maybe you know Jimmy's mother, then? Sharp-Eyed Jane?"

Zachary's mother frowned. Did she know Jane?

"Since I don't know Jimmy, how would I know his mother?"

A man's deep voice boomed from somewhere in the house with a curse. "Just tell the man what he wants and let me get back to sleep."

The mother scowled at Aaron. "The witch you're looking for is usually playing cards at the Wet Whistle. She's about as crooked as they come. I wouldn't step within three feet of her, and if she has a son, heaven help him. Now leave us alone."

She pushed on the door again, and he slipped his foot out. The door's slam shot air into his face, ruffling his hair.

"Thank you," he said to the door.

But he'd already been to the Wet Whistle on a previous lead, and everyone there claimed to know nothing. He rubbed his eyes. The weight of sleeplessness and starting all over again made his head hurt. The mansion was only a mile across town, but he should probably wait and follow Zachary. Surely he'd feel compelled to go off and tell Jimmy someone was looking for him.

Aaron turned to make his way back across the dilapidated porch. He'd have to appear as if he'd left and then find a good hiding place to—

"Excuse us, sir."

Aaron turned to see two policemen striding toward him, and Zachary's little brother, Glenn, running to catch up.

He turned onto the main sidewalk and headed for them. Hopefully they'd be willing to help him search. Of course, if he ended up talking to the copper Jimmy claimed worked with his mother, they might not be any help at all. "Good morning, officers."

The dark-haired policeman came closer. "This boy says you and his mother are having a row."

He eyed Glenn, who was the same size as Owen. He supposed he shouldn't be surprised that a family who knew where Sharp-Eyed Jane gambled would be trouble. "We weren't. I was simply asking after a boy who's gone missing. He normally resides at the Lowes' orphanage and is about this tall, thirteen, blond with freckles, and green squinty eyes. The son of a woman named Sharp-Eyed Jane."

The lighter-haired cop took a step around the taller one, his eyes narrowing as he took Aaron in from head to toe. "Who are you?"

"Aaron Firebrook, the Lowes' gardener." He turned back to talk to the one who'd appeared to be listening instead of scowling. "His name is—"

"You're under arrest."

Aaron looked back to the shorter officer, then glanced over his shoulder to see if someone was behind him. But there was no one. He frowned. "Me?"

"Yes." The man's eyes gleamed, and he licked his lips.

Aaron's hands started sweating, and he blinked several times over. What had he done? "I wasn't arguing with the boy's mother, but even if I were, surely you don't arrest people over spats."

"No, but for theft we do." The man unhooked a pair of handcuffs from his belt and twirled them around his index finger.

A cool breeze blew across Aaron's now-sweaty neck, and he shivered. "What did I steal?"

The darker-headed one took a step closer, his expression grim. "We ask that you cooperate, sir."

The short one with the handcuffs pointed to Aaron's hands and smirked. "Put those behind your back."

Despite the urge to pummel them both—considering they were smaller than he was—he did as he was told. Did he know the younger one from school, or did the man just find arresting people exciting?

If the officer had recognized him, Aaron had likely beaten him up in the past. "I'll cooperate. Just tell me what I stole."

The cold, metal bracelets slipped around his wrists.

"A lot, as you know." The man behind him tightened the handcuffs until they bit into his flesh. "Paintings, jewelry, trinkets. I'll read you the list once we get you locked up, if you'd like to refresh your memory."

He shook his head. Had the man he'd entrusted to deliver his message to the mansion yesterday neglected to do so? "I know what you're talking about, but that's why I'm out here trying to find . . ." Should he implicate Jimmy? He wasn't exactly responsible for the stealing, though if he were behind bars he'd at least be safe.

His mother likely deserved the cell, but if she heard someone was after her, she might hurt Jimmy. "I'm trying to find the boy who can tell us who's stealing those things."

"Right. Someone else decided your cabin was a good place to store his loot, and you had no idea what was happening."

"No, that's not it, though I can see how my disappearance looks bad." He flinched as the man behind him shoved him forward on the sidewalk. "I assume Mr. Lowe reported me? Let me talk to him, and I can clear this up."

"You'll have plenty of time to talk through your excuses with a lawyer."

"We don't have to go through all of that—just let me talk to Nicholas Lowe."

"Sure, buddy." The man behind him jabbed a baton between his shoulder blades, causing him to trip. When the officer came around to walk beside him, he looked him up and down several times, narrowing in on his face. "You're not Aaron, are you? You're George?"

Aaron sighed. The officer would not believe anything he said now. "My name's George Aaron Firebrook." He turned to look at Zachary's younger brother, who was following behind them, looking far too enthralled with watching a man being arrested. "I know your brother claims he doesn't know Jimmy, but he does." Aaron hoped Glenn would listen. "Jimmy's in trouble and needs help. Please go tell Mr. Nicholas Lowe at the mansion that—"

He got jabbed in the back again, rougher this time. "That's enough out of you."

He swallowed the curse he would've spat so easily years ago and forced himself to march forward.

The little boy stopped walking but hadn't turned toward the mansion.

If only Glenn would go find Nicholas, he'd be exonerated soon enough. If not, all he could do was cooperate so he'd be released quickly once things were cleared up.

Please, Lord, keep Jimmy safe until I can get out and find him.

34

"How could you?"

The high-pitched feminine hiss startled Mercy, and she dropped her lotion. She turned to see Patricia, who'd swung open her door and was sending her an eyeful of daggers—an expression she'd hoped to avoid seeing from her brother.

Nicholas hadn't fired Timothy yesterday, likely praying about it while he searched for Jimmy and Aaron—neither of whom had been found.

But she'd expected Nicholas would fire her brother soon, so she'd kept out of the way. She didn't regret telling Nicholas about Timothy, but she figured it'd be best to avoid seeing her brother until he was out of the house, so he didn't blow up at her in front of the children.

Patricia barged into Mercy's room and jabbed her in the arm.

Mercy tensed. Surely Nicholas wouldn't have told Patricia she was the reason they were fired.

"Just an hour ago, Mr. Lowe claimed that with so few orphans he no longer needed us, though more could come any day. If he was cutting back on his financial obligations, fine. But when I asked to adopt Owen, he said no, though the gardener isn't going to get him now." She crossed her arms and glared. "When I asked Timothy why Lowe would deny us a child, he said it was your fault."

What? Though she could understand he didn't want to own up to the real reason, how could he dump the blame on her? He could've simply told Patricia they had to accept Nicholas's decision, since Nicholas seemed to be giving him that out.

Patricia leaned closer, her clove-scented breath blowing against Mercy's cheek. "I don't know how you found out about your brother's indulgences, but what right did you have to tell anybody?"

Mercy backed away to look at Patricia. She'd known?

"It's not as if he'll change because of this, but at least I had children to occupy myself with. What made you think it was a good idea to bring up *your* brother's moral failings to that holier-than-thou Lowe, knowing he'd kick us out? You didn't think about me at all, did you?"

Mercy reached for Patricia's shoulder, but the other woman jerked away.

"I'm sorry, but I *was* thinking about you. I thought being at the mansion was making things worse, since it gave Timothy too much idle time. I hoped that if he went back to—"

"You should've asked me what I wanted." Patricia sniffed. "At least here I had servants and distractions, books and gardens."

Tears built up behind Mercy's eyes. Had she done the wrong thing? Surely she hadn't, not if these orphans needed a healthy marriage to model their own future relationships after. No, Nicholas had the right to know.

Oh, there was no winning. "I'm sorry, Patricia. I really am."

"Well, that won't do us any good. But at least Timothy promised me you won't be coming with us." And with that she turned and stomped out.

Mercy sank onto the bed and stared at herself in the mirror. Would she ever see them again? She blinked against the warmth in her eyes. She'd not meant to lose the few family members she had left, but she'd wanted what was right for them. That had to count for something, didn't it?

And what if Aaron never turned up? Two nights and almost two days had gone by without a word from him. Nicholas had made a report to the police, and he and Franklin had searched for him and Jimmy without success.

The hope that Aaron had a good explanation for his disappearance and the things in his cabin lessened with every passing hour.

"Excuse me." Sadie popped her head into the room. "I'm sorry to disturb you, but Mr. Beauchamp is asking to see you."

"Me?" What could Henri want from her?

Sadie disappeared back into the hallway, and Mercy picked up her lotion and put it back on the dressing table before heading downstairs. Hopefully Henri wouldn't ask her for advice on how to fix his crumbling relationship with Caroline. She was obviously not the right person to get involved in anyone's relationships, considering how her own family members wanted nothing to do with her.

From the top of the staircase, she could see Henri a floor below, pacing the foyer, his hat going from one hand to the other in quick succession. The second she stepped onto the landing, he raced to the bottom of the staircase and gripped the baluster. "Please help me, Miss McClain."

From the way he strangled the staircase newel and the desperate look in his eye, one might think he was begging to be released from jail.

"I must see Caroline, but she has refused to see me." He held a piece of paper that shook in his hand.

She slowed as she came down the stairs, shaking her head. She'd muddied up enough things already. Her help would likely get him the opposite of what he wanted, or at least make it harder somehow.

"I know she found out about Katelyn, and that you know too since she said so in this letter." He waved the piece of paper in front of him. "I've been here for two hours and have knocked on her door, but she refuses to come out. I've sent the butler down with a note, but she's refused to take it. And I can't holler what needs to be said through a door."

He left the bottom of the stairwell and started pacing again.

"I need to talk to her, at least once!" The desperation in his voice sounded exactly like Aaron's the day he'd interviewed for the teaching position and then realized gaining her approval was his only hope of getting the job.

She'd let his pleas stop her from doing what she'd believed right at the time, and though she'd changed her mind later, it seemed she had been right from the beginning. She couldn't trust her instincts or her compassion.

But who was she to make decisions for Caroline? "I'll try."

He latched onto her hand. "Thank you."

"But I can't—I won't—force her."

He nodded solemnly, but his eyes lit with hope.

How many people was she going to disappoint today? She blew out a breath and headed downstairs. At Caroline's door, she knocked lightly, in case Katelyn was sleeping.

"Oh for goodness' sake, why won't you leave me alone?"

Though it wasn't funny, she chuckled a little at the woman's exasperation. "It's me. Mercy."

Caroline's door opened a crack, and she peeped out as if afraid a monster would barge in. She sighed and opened the door. "At least I know you aren't going to try and prod me into seeing Henri."

"Prod? Well . . . no."

"Don't tell me he's still here and begged you to come down?" She huffed and rolled her eyes. Caroline was rarely this expressive. But at least she didn't ask her to leave.

Mercy moved to sit next to Katelyn, who was jerking her feet around on the thin mattress as if trying to get somewhere sideways. Mercy captured her little fist, and the babe grasped her finger.

Caroline stood staring out the tiny window at the top of her basement room.

"Can you tell me why you won't talk to him?" She couldn't help but pick the baby up and nestle her in her lap. "It might be hard to do, but you could get your questions answered."

"I can't think of anything he could say that would make things better, and I can't . . ." She swallowed hard and looked away.

"He says he only wants to talk once. If you don't want to talk again—"

Caroline sniffed, and was that other sound a muffled sob?

Mercy put Katelyn down, got up, and wrapped her arms around Caroline. "What's wrong?"

"I just really wanted to believe him." Her voice cracked, and she broke away to search for a handkerchief. "I wish . . . I wish I hadn't fallen in love with him all over again."

Oh, how she could relate to that regret, though she'd only had the opportunity to regret falling in love once.

Caroline shook herself. "I couldn't help myself, I guess. And when he spoke so well of me, like he'd actually come to care for me . . ." Her voice died off and she sniffled.

"I think he really does care for you, Caroline."

"Then, what about her?" Caroline gestured toward Katelyn.

"Well, I don't know much about her. All you and I know is what Henri initially said and what a prostitute said. Perhaps you need to hear Henri out." The evidence of the crime he was accused of wasn't piled up for everyone to see, like Aaron's. Maybe there'd been a misunderstanding. "It might not be pleasurable, but I think you should talk to him rather than wonder forever. And if you choose never to speak to him again, I'm sure Nicholas will inform Henri he's no longer welcome here."

"Fine." And with a quick swipe at her eyes and a second to stuff her handkerchief in her pocket, Caroline became stoic again. She crossed over to the mattress and swaddled Katelyn. "But you're going with me to keep me from doing anything emotionally foolish."

If there was ever a woman who didn't need someone to keep her from being foolish, it was Caroline. But if that's the sort of support she wanted, Mercy would give it to her.

At the top of the stairs, the foyer was silent. Henri was nowhere to be seen.

"Well," Caroline huffed.

Sadie came around the hallway and pointed toward the front doors. "He said he'd be out there."

Caroline snatched Mercy's hand and pulled her outside.

Henri turned around at the sound of the door opening, and his body went limp for a second. Then he strode toward them, glancing down to where Caroline was constricting the blood flow to Mercy's good arm.

He stopped in front of them, and Mercy tried to tug her wrist from Caroline's grip.

"Stay." Caroline turned to her with pleading eyes.

"I will, but . . ." She disengaged herself. "Why don't I hold the baby while you talk?"

Caroline stared at her for a couple seconds before handing Katelyn to her.

Once she had the baby, Mercy pointed to the low wall at the end of the portico. "I'll just sit there." She wasn't particularly keen on standing between them.

Henri watched her until she sat down, his jaw rocking back and forth, then turned back to Caroline. He folded his hands in front of himself and hung his head, his shoulders slumping with the action. "I can't deny there's a possibility Katelyn's my child."

Caroline's face went blank.

Mercy winced. Well, that was blunt.

Henri heaved a huge sigh. "Of course I can't prove she's mine either. But it is possible, and for that I'm sorry." He continued to stare at their feet. "I've been sorry about that for a long time. Sorry I ever visited Moira, sorry I ever let my hatred build until I wanted to be . . . vindicated. I turned my back on everything I believed in."

He turned to pace. "I might not have the same convictions Nick does with all his talk of God, but I'd always thought myself a good man, just like you're a good woman, without all that religion. But then . . . then I went against my own conscience. I broke my own rules. I didn't need God to tell me I'd sinned, because what I'd done was wrong. Very wrong. I . . . I'll spare you the details, but we all do wrong, don't we?"

He gestured wildly about as if indicating the whole world. "But I've gone past what even I'd forgive." He stopped at the edge of the portico and looked out, his back to both of them. "I've been struggling with what to do with that sin for almost a year now."

After a quiet moment, he turned and looked at Caroline, his eyes puffy and red. "Do you remember the day you came to my office with David Kingsman, begging me for that women's shelter you and Miss Wisely—I mean, you and Mrs. Kingsman—wanted?"

Caroline nodded almost imperceptibly.

"I was angry."

She nodded emphatically at that.

"I was drowning in guilt, because it wasn't but a little while before that, that I . . . Well, I'd gone against my convictions and had become the kind of man Nick and you and all the others hated— the type of man who created the need for the red-light district."

He turned and walked straight back to Caroline. "I'd seen my error and thoroughly despised myself. I only saw her the once and didn't even know she'd disappeared until you told me. I didn't really want to find her, but I wanted to prove to you, and myself, that I could be good. While searching for her, I wondered why I'd been so focused on Moira my whole life, when it was you I . . ."

He cleared his throat as though covering over what he'd been about to say. He looked back at Katelyn. "I didn't actually find Moira. She sent me a letter that told me to come get my child."

Mercy fidgeted, though she knew he wasn't staring at her but rather the baby in her arms.

"Of course, knowing what Moira does for a living, I doubted the claim, and yet, it could've been true. When she handed me the baby, the slight red sheen of her hair made me think there was a possibility. Moira suggested you raise her, and I agreed. Who could be better to raise her than you? She may or may not be mine, but there's no doubt she's your kin, and I figured I'd do whatever I could to help you."

Caroline wrapped her arms about herself, the first hint of vulnerability she'd displayed since he'd started his speech. "So I'm only worthy of taking care of your mistakes?"

"No! That's not it." He reached out as if wanting to take her hands, but since she backed away, he let them fall limply to his side. "That day you came to my office with David knocked sense into me. Your story about how Moira saved you from prostitution and how you'd given up your life to help her contrasted so sharply with my own selfishness. I never really wanted to marry Moira—she'd only hurt my pride. And what was a whack to my ego compared to the evil I'd done to her? But you . . ." He let out a rush of air. "When I thought of who I would want to marry, the only person I could think of was you."

He held out his hands in front of him as if he could see his sins caked upon his palms. "But I knew my secret. I knew I didn't deserve you."

"And you don't." Caroline's voice was hard.

"You're right. I don't." Henri alternately nodded and shook his head, as if resignation and denial wrestled for dominion within him. "But I want you to know, before I had any idea Katelyn existed, I'd thought about you. That's why I had to talk to you. You're wrong to think I want to marry you only to hide what I've done. I proposed hoping you'd come to at least accept me, if not love me. And when you took that ride with me, I thought I might even have a chance at gaining the real thing."

Caroline seemed to wake up from the reverie she'd been in. "How could you think our marriage could've been the real thing if you kept the possibility of Katelyn being your daughter a secret?"

"I wasn't going to." He ran his hands through his hair. "But that sort of information isn't the kind of thing you bring up the first time the woman you admire finally agrees to take a ride with you."

"It should've at least come up when you offered marriage."

He breathed heavily. "Yes, but I'd wronged you so badly, and you hadn't yet warmed up to me, and . . . well, I figured I'd lose you if I brought that up first thing." He huffed. "I doubted you'd keep me anyway once I told you, but I was hoping to show you my feelings were genuine before you turned me down. Plus, I didn't want you to feel obligated to marry me in order to keep Katelyn."

"You don't want her?" Caroline frowned over at Katelyn, and

Mercy froze, as if not moving could keep them from realizing she was still there.

He looked up at the ceiling of the two-story portico. "It's not that I don't want her, but if she's only going to have one parent, she's better off with you than me."

Katelyn started fussing in Mercy's arms, as if she knew she was being talked about. Her cries would escalate if not soothed quickly. Mercy stood to bounce her, wondering if she shouldn't just quietly slip away and let them talk in private despite Caroline's insistence she stay.

It was clear by the look on Henri's face, the anxiety in his pacing, and the way his speech varied between tender and erratic, that he meant everything he said.

Though Mercy had found plenty of reasons to question her discernment skills lately, not trusting anyone, no matter what they said, would be a sad way to live life. Caroline might not want to do anything "emotionally foolish," but after listening to him, she'd advise Caroline to heed her emotions.

Her friend probably wouldn't care for that advice.

Henri reached into his pocket. "So here." He pulled out a key and dangled it between them.

"What's this?" Caroline made no attempt to reach for it.

"It's a key to a house, a light blue two-story clapboard on Maple and Second, number two forty-six. It's yours and Katelyn's, fully paid, no strings attached."

Caroline continued to stare at the key. "I-I can't accept a house."

Henri straightened to his full height, which was likely only a half inch taller than Caroline's. "The day after you came to ask me for a job, I started searching for a place. You asked for help, and if you were determined to work, I wanted to make sure you had somewhere to live. It's in your name. Not even I can take it away from you. You could sell it, rent it—it's yours."

He took Caroline's hand and curled her fingers around the key. "I shouldn't have kept the baby's possible origins from you the day I proposed, but I was drowning in hope that I'd be blessed with something I didn't deserve, and I was scared to lose you. But however you choose to think about what I've done, please don't hate Katelyn because of me. I'll send you money to support her. Whether she's mine or not, she's an orphan in need of support, and the Lowes shouldn't have to be the only ones in this town doing so. If you need more, just ask and I'll send it to you. I know you won't ask for more than you need because you're that good."

"I can't keep a baby who belongs to someone else," Caroline whispered while shaking her head.

"If you feel that way, I'll give up all claim to her. I'd just ask that you'd let me see her once in a while." He looked down at his hands, which he kept clasping and unclasping. "She doesn't need to know I might be her father, but . . . when we meet on the street, I'd just ask that you let me ask her how she's doing in school or what she got for her birthday without hurrying her away from me."

Caroline dropped her gaze to the key in her hand.

"If you don't want to speak to me again, I'll do my best to do nothing more than acknowledge you in situations where it would be rude not to. You can request things for Katelyn through writing without fear of needing to pay me back."

He lifted the note he'd waved at Mercy in the entryway. "You accused me of only wanting to marry you to hide my mistakes. It was a huge mistake, yes. But I didn't ask you to marry me because I wanted to cover up for Katelyn. It was because I'd finally gotten up my nerve to ask the woman I love, but don't deserve, to marry me. I love you, whether Katelyn exists or not."

He stood silently, and Mercy held her breath as Caroline just stared at the key in her hand.

After an agonizingly slow half minute, he hung his head and backed away. When Caroline didn't move, he turned and headed for a four-seater Ford Model K parked in the drive.

Caroline didn't watch him walk away. She just stood staring at the key in her hand. And then a tear fell.

Tucking the baby against her chest, Mercy stood and approached her friend, placing her hand on Caroline's shoulder. "If you wanted to run after him, I don't particularly think that would be an emotional mistake. I've never seen a man more repentant and sincere."

Caroline looked up at her, blinking repeatedly, the corners of her mouth twitching.

Mercy gave her a small nod and smiled.

"Wait," Caroline called, and then she scurried off the porch. "Henri."

He turned slowly, and a smile both hopeful and heartbreakingly fragile grew on his lips the closer she got.

Caroline nearly tripped into his arms, and he caught her face between his hands. His desperate kiss made Mercy's heart throb with both a sad and happy ache.

She turned her back on the couple who didn't need an audience any longer and rocked Katelyn, who still made noises that promised to become full-blown cries if something wasn't done soon. "Let's go get you a bottle. Seems your parents could use some time to themselves."

35

Mercy strolled listlessly through the garden, letting her fingers brush against the wilting roses.

Tomorrow would be one week since the auction.

One week since Aaron had disappeared without a word.

And one week until Robert and Max left for Boston, leaving only Owen at the orphanage until Jimmy or any new orphans showed up.

There wasn't much for her to do here while waiting on Nicholas and Lydia to find new directors, or while waiting for news of Aaron that would likely wreck her heart.

She couldn't help but frown up at the mansion as she made her way inside to avoid the rain arriving from the southwest. Though she'd had far happier memories in her childhood home, in this place, she'd gained what she needed to stand up for what was right. She'd also learned how far she still had to grow. Those lessons hadn't been particularly pleasant, but they were irreplaceable.

It had also been where she'd had her first kiss, and for some reason, the memory of it hadn't turned sour, despite what sort of man had stolen it from her.

Except her heart still refused to believe Aaron was anything short of good.

Until Aaron was found, she might as well stop trying to force herself into believing he was a criminal. Her brother was as awful as the evidence showed, but Henri, though he'd conceded he'd done wrong, had not meant to hurt anyone, cared how his failure affected others, and was doing what he could to make restitution.

Aaron had seemed exactly like that sort of man.

But whether he returned a thief, returned with a perfectly good explanation, or never returned at all, what good would it do to stay here pining and agonizing?

In all the disasters that had come from her doing what was right lately, God had come through for her in ways she hadn't expected. He would come through again—but maybe Aaron wouldn't be a part of it. A sad thought, that, but one that had to be faced.

She found Lydia in the parlor with her arm around Sadie. The young blonde was hunched over, with her hands covering her eyes. Franklin was standing in the back of the room, staring out the window toward the storm clouds rolling in.

Mercy walked in as quietly as she could. "Is Sadie all right?"

The young housekeeper looked up at her with red-rimmed eyes and shrugged.

"Sadie's trying to convince me she needs to leave for our family's sake, but that's ridiculous." Lydia huffed and jostled the younger woman a little, as if to convince her.

"Why's that?" Mercy perched on the edge of the rocker, not quite convinced she wouldn't need to leave to make broth, since the girl looked utterly drained, if not ill.

Sadie looked off to the side, avoiding Mercy's gaze. "There are whispers about me . . . in town."

"You were never a prostitute. Not really," Lydia insisted.

If there'd been enough room on the loveseat, Mercy would have moved to Sadie's other side and hugged her. Instead, she leaned forward to squeeze her knee. "I'm so sorry." Especially since there was just as much a chance her brother and Patricia were at fault for the whispers as Mrs. Sorenson. There was no doubt in Mercy's mind that everyone else who'd heard the distraught girl's confession would've kept it to themselves.

Lydia looked across at Mercy. "I've told her I don't care. If people are going to be that way, then—"

"I can only imagine what they'll say about your children being under my influence." Sadie grasped Lydia's hand and squeezed it hard enough Mercy could see her muscles tremble. "I will do nothing to hurt you, not after you rescued me."

Mercy shook her head. "Don't let crazy people decide what you can or can't do."

Sadie frowned at Mercy's arm before looking up at her. "You know as well as I do how cruel children can be. I don't think it's absurd to think people will tell their children to shun Isabelle and Jake because of me."

Mercy couldn't argue. "Then what are you going to do?"

Sadie glanced at Franklin for a second, then sat up straight and nodded, as if making an official decree. "I'm going to Kansas City to see if the Kingsmans can find me a job, just like they do for the soiled doves the Lowes have convinced to try for a better life."

"If you fear the rumors, you can't go alone." Franklin's voice was adamant.

"I could go with her," Mercy said. Seeing Evelyn again would lift her spirits a little. And though she was sure the Lowes would let her stay on until they found a couple to run the orphanage, she'd need another job at some point. If Evelyn and David could find work for reformed prostitutes, surely they could find a position for a crippled woman.

"But why let anyone shame Sadie into going anywhere?" Franklin whipped around. "If you got married right now, the rumors would stop before they gained teeth, and then you could continue working for the Lowes." Franklin marched over and got down on one knee in front of Sadie. "So why don't we?"

"Get married?" Sadie shook her head. "If you're against people shaming me into leaving, you shouldn't let people shame you into marrying."

"But they wouldn't be. I've never stopped wanting to marry you. It's just . . ." He looked down at the floor. "I was wrong. Just like whoever's spreading rumors about you over something you had no choice in."

He took a deep breath and grabbed both of her hands. "I'd already planned to try to win back your trust so I could propose again someday. But, well, I can't bear to think people will believe you're running away because you're ashamed of something you shouldn't be ashamed of. Not when I could save you. So . . . would you be willing?"

Sadie stared at her lap and sniffed a couple times. "Are you sure? The rumors might not die."

"More sure than I've ever been." Franklin rubbed his thumb across the back of her hand.

If Sadie would've just looked up at his expression, she wouldn't have had to ask.

"But what about our jobs?"

Lydia shrugged, a big smile on her face. "What about them?"

"Are you all right with married servants?" Sadie looked more sad about the possibility of Lydia turning her out than the thought of fleeing to Kansas City due to rumors.

Mercy cleared her throat. "You're in need of new orphanage directors, right? Married ones. What about that?"

Sadie's blue eyes grew wide. "What? We can't do that. We're too young."

"Age and maturity are two different things." Now it was Mercy's turn to sit up straight and nod her head regally. "There are people older than you right now trying to spoil your reputation based on little more than a hint of your past."

"But Franklin doesn't want to be connected to—"

"Now hold on." He put up his hand. "If the Lowes offered it, why shouldn't we take it? Aaron told me a while ago that he figured God would be sad if we reveled in our freedom and turned our backs on those we can understand like no one else."

Tears pricked Mercy's eyes. How could Aaron have said such things and not be the man she thought him to be?

315

Franklin inched closer to Sadie. "We both were rescued by the Lowes and understand the red-light district children better than anyone here. Why wouldn't we volunteer our lives to make sure they are given what we've got?" He looked to Lydia, who was rubbing her chin, her eyes alight.

"I can't promise anything without talking to Nicholas, but I can't imagine a more perfect couple to take over."

Franklin nodded, looking much older than his nineteen years, then turned back to Sadie. "What do you say? Will you forgive me for thinking there was anything about you that made you unsuitable for me?"

"Yes," she whispered.

And with that, both Mercy and Lydia quietly stood and slipped out of the room.

Lydia closed the door softly behind her and sighed. "I'm so glad those two have straightened things out between them."

"Me too. I hope your husband agrees to let them take over the orphanage, though they are quite young."

"I think he will. We'd be here to advise them, of course, and plenty of couples start off with children quite young. I'm glad you thought of it." She gave her a side glance. "If they do take over, what do you hope to do?"

The Lowes would likely allow her to take over Sadie's position as housekeeper if she asked, but though Lydia and Nicholas wouldn't think less of her for taking a lower position, she'd feel uncomfortable in such a role under a friend. "I think I'll try what Sadie was planning—see if Evelyn can find me work."

Though she was happy for Sadie and Franklin, her heart was so heavy with the loss of a future with Aaron that she likely would only dampen the gaiety of their wedding festivities. "I'd like to leave as soon as possible, if that's all right with you."

Lydia put a hand on Mercy's arm. "I hope you don't think I was hinting for you to leave."

"No, of course not." She started forward, not sure where she was going exactly, but figuring Sadie and Franklin didn't need to find them right outside the door when they left the parlor. "But there are so many reasons for me to go. I could ask Evelyn if she's interested in adopting Owen. She seemed rather taken with him at the auction, and it could relieve some of your financial burden."

"That's nothing to worry about." Lydia shook her head as she walked beside her.

Mercy smiled a little. "I knew you'd say that, but if I'm going to take advantage of one friend's hospitality, perhaps it shouldn't be the one trying to finance half the town's charity cases while dealing with financial setback." She slowed as they approached the French doors that opened onto the eastern porch. The view of residences amid industrial buildings and green trees spread for miles, the house she'd once lived in with her brother and sister-in-law among them. She didn't know where they were at the moment, but they'd likely find a place in that area. "Besides, I think it'd be best to find a job elsewhere so the rift between my brother and me doesn't cause people to speculate." Though she feared Patricia was right about her brother not changing his ways, if he did attempt to turn around, she didn't want speculation over what had happened between them to make it harder for him to straighten out his life.

"And Aaron?"

She avoided looking into Lydia's eyes lest her friend see how much it hurt to talk of him. "If they find him and he ends up in court, they won't need me to testify. If he's not guilty . . ." She swallowed hard, letting herself send up a quick prayer for that outcome. "If he asks, please let him know where I am."

36

Aaron leaned his forehead against the jail cell bars. Had he really been locked up five whole days? He didn't understand legal things, but keeping him from talking to anyone this long was excessive.

Surely Nicholas was fair-minded enough to come hear his story. Since Aaron had yet to be given a chance to talk to the lawyer he kept asking for, perhaps Nicholas hadn't been informed he was in custody.

If what Jimmy said was true and corrupt cops were aiding his mother, who knew how long he might be imprisoned. Officer Foster was clearly taking pleasure in taunting his former tormentor, but might he also be in cahoots with Jimmy's mother?

Aaron groaned. In his desperation to get out and search for Jimmy, he shouldn't have spilled out so much information to the lawmen detaining him.

He pushed away from the bars and paced his little cell, four steps—that was it—and back.

Had the boy been found? If he'd returned to the mansion, had he blamed Aaron for his criminal activities? Maybe that was why he was still in jail.

Mercy had finally believed he'd become a new man, right? If she hadn't, she wouldn't have asked for his kiss. So surely she would've come to hear his story—if they'd been told.

He pressed his forehead against the cold, grimy bars again.

And yet it wasn't that long ago she hadn't believed anything he'd said. Two months was a short time in light of the years he'd antagonized her. Had she gone back to believing the worst of him?

The clank of the main door echoed through the hallway of cells, but conversations, snoring, and someone's whistling continued on.

The short, brown-haired Officer Foster, who Aaron had finally remembered was named Dennis, swaggered down the aisle in front of the cells, swinging his baton in lazy circles.

Dennis had hit puberty late in life. He'd been the size of a ten-year-old up until their last year of high school, making him easy to bully.

Stopping in front of the desk across from Aaron, Dennis leaned back against it, crossed his arms, and grinned.

Smiling back probably wouldn't help any, so he'd try to apologize—again. "Did I mention I'm sorry?"

"Sorry you got caught for theft?" Dennis sneered. "Or sorry you're having to answer to 'Small Fry Foster'?"

How many times did he have to say this? "I'm not talking about the theft, because I can't be sorry for something I didn't do, but I am sorry for humiliating you as a child. Please tell me you've at least told Mr. Lowe you've taken me into custody." Considering how wide Dennis smiled every time he came in, he might actually believe Aaron was falsely accused and didn't care.

This man didn't want apologies; he wanted revenge.

A door slam somewhere down the hall dragged up the image of Owen's Aunt Ivy slamming the door in his face. He closed his eyes and sighed. Walking away from Ivy without her forgiveness hadn't been so rough after all.

The sound of steady footsteps stopped in front of him, and he opened his eyes to find Nicholas standing before him, his face blank.

Aaron closed his eyes again for a second. Finally.

Please let him believe me—not because I don't deserve

punishment for what I've done in the past, but because someone needs to find Jimmy.

Dennis walked up beside Nicholas. "You don't have to talk to him if you don't want to. We've got his statement, which you can read at your leisure."

"No, please!" Aaron reached out to grab Nicholas but stopped short to keep from wrinkling his fine wool suit. "Hear me out, for Jimmy's sake."

Nicholas dismissed Dennis with a toss of his head.

Hallelujah! If he hadn't been holding on to the bars, Aaron might have fallen at Nicholas's feet. "Has Jimmy returned to the mansion?"

Nicholas seemed to think over whether or not he should answer but then shook his head.

Aaron let loose a curse he shouldn't have. "Sorry." Jails weren't known to be filled with high-caliber men, and he'd been surrounded by foul language for days. "Did you not get my message?"

Nicholas's face scrunched. "Message?"

"A man I met in Caney said he would be traveling through Teaville. Said he was willing to stop by the mansion to tell you what I was doing."

"Not that I know of." Nicholas dragged a hand through his hair. "Wait, when would he have come by?"

"He said he was going straight home. He'd have been there on Saturday."

Nicholas's face grew strained. "Either it wasn't delivered or someone else got it first."

"Was that why you didn't come sooner?"

"I didn't know you were here until this morning."

Aaron glared at Dennis, who still stood behind Nicholas with his arms across his chest, a slight upturn to his cocky lips. How many times had he asked Dennis to ask Nicholas to come? What had Nicholas been thinking of him this whole time?

But it didn't matter what his boss thought of him if Jimmy was still missing.

"I didn't steal your stuff. It was Jimmy. I was trying to find—".

"Pshaw." Dennis rolled his eyes. "Big bad George is blaming his crimes on a kid?" He strutted forward. "What? Are you afraid? Worried there'll be men in the jury who'll remember you from our school days and make sure you get the punishment you deserve?"

Aaron shook his head. "I'm better off than I deserve. I understand that full well, but that doesn't negate who did what." He turned back to Nicholas. "The boy was stealing because his mother sent him to the mansion to do so. He said someone on staff decided what was to be stolen and after hiding it for a while to determine if anyone noticed it missing, Jimmy was informed of where to find it. Then he took it to a cellar on your property, where someone picked it up. He disappeared so often because he was smuggling things out."

Nicholas hadn't moved. Was he believing any of this?

"They're forcing him to do it, Nicholas. The burn he got at Ragsdale's was because he tried to stop one of his mother's henchmen, not because he set the fire. She'd sent someone there to make sure Ragsdale kicked Jimmy out so he could return to the mansion. I'm not in the house much, but has anyone mentioned finding things in odd places or gone altogether?"

Nicholas didn't respond, but at least he appeared to be listening.

He plunged on. "I know Jimmy's all gruff and spittle, but the boy was shaking when he told me about his abusive mother. I know Mercy didn't tell you about the time we found him fighting with a stranger in the root cellar because she was trying to save my job, but I misinterpreted what was happening and beat the man up. When it was likely he was only—"

"Mercy saw you beating someone up on my property and didn't tell me?" Nicholas's face was no longer calm.

Aaron grimaced. Hopefully he hadn't gotten Mercy into trouble. "Yes, sir. Please don't hold it against her. She . . . she saw how terrible I felt and decided my guilt was punishment enough." His chest tightened at the thought of how she likely now believed her trust had been misplaced. "Anyway, the man who hauls the loot off your property was due to pick things up on the night of the auction. I couldn't let that happen, but we had to load wagons, so Jimmy and I took the things to my cabin, but Cook detained me long enough that Jimmy got away. I don't know whether he ran on his own or was taken."

Nicholas turned toward Officer Foster and pointed at the padlock. "You can release him."

Really? In spite of how improbable his story sounded? The tightness in Aaron's chest loosened, and he drew in his first full breath since he had been jailed.

"Now, wait a minute." Dennis placed a hand atop his key ring, as if fearing Nicholas might wrestle him for it. "No need to be hasty. Let us check on what he said. Let's—"

"No, I believe him." Nicholas's chest lifted with a big breath of air, as if he was just as relieved as Aaron. "Drop the charges."

Dennis shook his head while waving a finger. "I know you're a savvy businessman . . . but I'm savvy when it comes to criminals. They know how to sound like they're not lying because it's second nature to them."

Aaron blew out a long breath and started counting to ten.

"Thank you for your concern, Officer Foster." Nicholas's voice was much cooler than Aaron's would've been. "But if I'm wrong, all I lose is the chance to regain what's been stolen from me. But if he's right, Jimmy's in trouble, and I'll need Aaron's help."

"Fine." Dennis slid the keys around the ring, looking for the right one. "Want us to press charges against this Jimmy, then?"

Nicholas stepped aside to give the officer access to the lock. "Not yet. But could you ask the officers to inform us if they see him? He's blond, has a very angular face, and his shoulders are rather broad for a thirteen-year-old. Green eyes, big attitude."

"Hmm." Dennis jiggled the key in the lock. "I'd say we already have him."

"What?" The second the bars opened, Aaron flew into the corridor and grabbed Dennis by the lapels. "I've been telling you since I got here that Jimmy was in trouble. Were you not listening?"

Dennis flicked away Aaron's hands and brushed off his shirt. "Watch it. I can arrest you again for assaulting an officer." He glared at him for a second before heading down the corridor. "You can come see if this is who you're looking for. We caught him breaking and entering. He wouldn't tell us his name."

Aaron charged after him. "I described him several times over."

Dennis shrugged. "I don't waste my time listening to inmates. Courts and lawyers are paid to do that."

"You never got around to sending me a lawyer."

"He was busy."

Sure he was. Dennis had dragged his feet in getting him a lawyer just to antagonize him. Aaron clenched his hands tight. He needed to see whether or not Jimmy was safe first, then he could deal with this arrogant lout, if need be.

Dennis stopped in front of the last cell and shook the barred door. The clanging filled the entire jail block. "Get up."

The gray wool lump on the cot didn't move. The cell was miniature, compared to the others, as if the builders had incorrectly divided the square footage.

"You've got visitors."

The lump groaned and rolled up to sit.

Aaron nearly cried. "You're safe."

Jimmy jerked his head toward them, and his gaze flew to Nicholas. "Did Mr. Firebrook tell you I didn't steal your stuff?"

"Now wait a minute." Aaron held out his hand. "You stole the stuff. Don't lie even a little. Trust him with the truth."

"Fine. My mother made me tell you I had no parents so I could swipe your things." Jimmy's voice was quiet as he stared at his lap. "If I don't do what she wants, she hurts me." He turned to face them. "So can I go now?"

Dennis laughed. "You're in here for breaking and entering. They can't free you."

"Mother made me do that too."

"These fellas might feel sorry for you being a weak momma's boy, but I don't."

Jimmy got up and charged at Dennis, who just laughed and stood out of reach.

Aaron swallowed. Watching someone taunt someone he cared about, someone so young and hurting, made his chest ache. To think, he'd done that to dozens of people over the years. He'd caused so much hurt he couldn't fix.

Nicholas reached for Jimmy, but the boy pulled his arms back inside the cell and stepped away from the bars.

Nicholas turned to Dennis with a scowl. "No need to goad him, Officer Foster."

"And you're not my boss. Take it up with the chief, if you'd like." He spun the key ring around his finger. "Criminals don't get special treatment because of their age."

Aaron had to look away from Dennis to keep from throttling him and landing himself back in a cell. "Why were you breaking and entering?"

Jimmy flopped onto the far end of his cot, nearly collapsing it. "Zachary told my mother how much I lost the night I ran away. She said I had until the morning to get her no less than twenty dollars' worth of stuff or she'd take it out of my backside." He shrugged. "I couldn't go back to the mansion, since you would've told everyone I was a thief by then."

"I hadn't told anyone. I was trying to find you to make sure you were all right."

Jimmy just gave him a side glance.

Nicholas leaned against the wall beside the cell's bars. "Why didn't you come tell us you were being forced to steal?"

Jimmy glanced at Dennis. "Like you'd believe me."

"Seems Mr. Firebrook did," Nicholas said.

Aaron leaned against the bars, as if getting closer to the boy might help Jimmy believe them. "I told you we'd help you get free of her. We can go to the courts and have her declared unfit."

"You think that'll work?" The boy's voice was sharp and loud, echoing against the stone walls. "Some of these coppers and judgers are in cahoots with her. What if they give me back to her? Do you know what she'll do to me?" His fists clenched his blanket so tightly his whole body trembled.

Aaron crouched to his level. "I understand your fear. When I was growing up, all I ever wanted was a different life. And if someone had cared for me like the Lowes care for you, I might have gotten it much sooner."

Jimmy seemed to fold even farther into himself, hunched like a homeless man in the rain. "And if it doesn't work?" His voice was barely audible.

"Aren't you in danger already?"

Jimmy just stared at him, his eyes reddening.

"She's not going to stop hurting you, no matter what, is she?"

He could've sworn Jimmy shook his head a little, but all the boy did was stare.

"The problem about staying with your mother is she's pushing you to commit crime. Though I understand why you obey her, you're responsible for your choices. Years ago, I treated my classmates poorly—one being Officer Foster, here—because of how my uncle treated me. But the hurt I caused was still hurt *I* caused—no one else. Officer Foster doesn't like me now and probably never will. I'm the one who humiliated him, not my uncle."

Jimmy seemed to be listening, but his face had grown so hard Aaron couldn't read him.

Nicholas laid a hand on Aaron's shoulder. "I think we best go."

"What!" Jimmy shot up. "You're going to leave me here?"

Nicholas crossed his arms, but it was more a patient gesture than a defensive one. "Are you going to take responsibility for what you've done and trust us to help, or are you going to go back to how things were? We don't need you back how you were. If you don't trust us to fix this situation, we can't help you."

The boy huffed and sat with a thump.

Aaron got up slowly, hoping that by the time he reached his full height Jimmy would change his mind, but the boy kept his eyes trained on the stone wall across from him.

But when he'd been thirteen, he'd not have trusted an adult

either. It had taken him an entire decade to feel kindly toward anyone, to trust anyone. He hadn't wanted anyone to get close enough to hurt him. . . .

But Mercy? Yeah, he'd risk getting hurt if Mercy was willing to become a part of his life. He wanted to have her trust more than finding a good job, getting through to Jimmy, or gaining anyone's forgiveness.

But that didn't mean he'd give up on Jimmy. "I'll pray for you."

The boy didn't respond, so Aaron followed Nicholas out of the jail and through the office.

Once they exited the building, Nicholas looked at him. "You look rough."

"I'm sure I do." Aaron ran his hands through his hair and scratched an itch behind his ear. He sure hoped he hadn't picked up any bugs while he was in there. Since he hadn't bathed for days, he stepped away from Nicholas to keep from offending his nose. "Thank you for getting me out."

Nicholas sighed. "I'm just sorry you were there so long. Officer Foster's drunk with power, but he generally does as he should. He's not the worst officer in the place, but if you bullied him in the past, he was likely enjoying his power more than usual."

Aaron took a deep breath. Dennis may have dragged his feet, but he'd finally done what he was supposed to. Aaron kicked a rock onto the street. He would have to let it go. "I hope you don't take offense at Jimmy not trusting you. I grew up in a predicament like Jimmy's, and it's hard to trust people."

"I didn't have a childhood like you two, but I had a rough couple of years in my twenties. I know how it is to have a hard time trusting." He tucked his hands into his pockets. "It's certainly not a fun way to live."

"No, it's not." Aaron rubbed his eyes and yawned. He'd had nothing to do for five days, yet his brain hadn't shut off enough to get decent sleep. "Thank you for believing me. I don't know why you did, but I'm grateful."

"You've done nothing to make me doubt your word." Nicholas

slapped him on the back and jostled his shoulder. "You're a hard worker who requires little oversight. Plus, you completely changed Mercy's mind about you, and if you could do that—"

"So she doesn't believe me a thief?" His heart lifted.

Nicholas didn't make eye contact. "I'm afraid we both couldn't reconcile the evidence and your extended disappearance with any other conclusion."

Aaron's heart plummeted back down. He trudged forward alongside Nicholas. "Well, no matter. I mean, I can see why. I'll just have to explain."

After crossing an intersection, Nicholas cleared his throat. "To do so, you'll have to write her in Kansas City."

Aaron somehow continued to walk despite his body going numb. "Kansas City?"

"Did you meet Evelyn Kingsman at the auction? She's a tall lady with dark hair, and she was wearing a dark blue felt hat. Her husband has several businesses in Kansas City, and Mercy's hoping they can help her find a job there."

"But why would Mercy need a job? What about the orphanage?"

Nicholas walked in silence for a bit. "Timothy and I came to the realization that there was no reason for them to continue on at the orphanage. Mercy and her brother had a falling out, unfortunately, so she decided to find somewhere else to live."

She hadn't bothered to wait around to see how he fared in court? To hear his side of the story? He ran a hand through his hair, and his feet quit moving.

About ten paces ahead, Nicholas turned and headed back. "Something wrong?"

"I-I just thought she'd believed in me. I know she informed you of how I treated her when we were children, but I thought I'd proven that I could be trusted, that I . . ." He swallowed.

Oh, what did it matter now?

"Well"—Nicholas put his hands back in his pockets—"you might be interested to know that Mercy told my wife if you weren't guilty she wanted you to know where she was."

His body started to tingle back to life.

"And several days ago, Dr. Freedman, a school board member, took it upon himself to come to my office and inform me I should fire you. He said he'd not realized who you were at the interview, but after Mercy recommended you for the teaching position this past Saturday, he'd figured it out. He was flabbergasted she'd vouch for you but was thankful she resigned days later. Told me a woman's emotions couldn't be trusted, and if she championed you, I should fire her too."

She'd voted to give him the job at the high school?

"Do you still want to teach?"

He started walking again. "Yes, but since the board decided against me, I'd have to look elsewhere."

"I hear there are plenty of teaching positions in Kansas City."

37

"King me!" Alex Kingsman, Evelyn's adorable seven-year-old adopted daughter, plunked her red chip onto the opposite side of the board.

Mercy tried not to giggle at the girl's lack of sympathy for having jumped two of Mercy's pieces to land in that spot.

Scott, Alex's older brother and another former Teaville orphan, just shook his head as he drew in a sketchbook. Evidently he and his father sketched together every Sunday, but today David had been called to his office for an unexpected business visit.

Evelyn snickered a bit but kept her eyes on her needlework.

Mercy sighed as she stacked Alex's pieces and then pushed one of hers forward on the board. She'd been in Kansas City a little over two weeks but had yet to find a job. She couldn't do much for the Kingsmans, since their staff took care of everything, but she could play the fun aunt on a visit.

Alex jumped three chips in a row. "You've got to start trying, Miss McClain."

"I am, actually." She hadn't meant to set the girl up for that triple jump. As happy as she was to play games with Alex—so Evelyn

329

could work on a layette for the fall baby she was expecting—she couldn't keep her mind on the game.

She looked toward the letter tray again, knowing it was as empty as it had been five minutes ago. Why hadn't Lydia sent her any mail?

Had Max and Robert gotten off to Boston all right? Had Jimmy been found safe? Was Owen adjusting to being the only orphan at the mansion, or had others arrived while she'd been away?

Surely Lydia would let her know what happened to Aaron—if he hadn't completely disappeared.

"Are you going to take your turn or not?"

"What?" She shook her head and looked at the board. Her two remaining pieces were stuck in the corner, trapped by Alex's seven.

"Love." Evelyn put down the little cotton nightgown she was covering with white work. "I think Miss McClain is preoccupied. Why don't you get your drawings and work on them? Your father should return soon and will be happy if you joined him."

Mercy took in a deep breath, hoping that it would help her focus. "I don't mind playing." It wasn't as if she was doing anything else in this house to earn her keep. She'd hoped to have a job by now, but the Kingsmans mainly had contacts with factory owners, since reformed prostitutes wanted to blend in with the masses. But millwork, sewing, and the like weren't places for a woman who'd slow production.

With each passing day, she came to a better understanding of how desperate women could do desperate things if they hadn't good friends or family.

Hopefully they'd hear about a childcare position for her soon, or else she might as well go back to Teaville and . . . what? Beg her brother to take her back?

She pushed her checker forward and immediately winced.

Alex took the piece with her king.

"Mercy?" David came into the parlor. His broad grin lit up the room.

"Yes?" If he wasn't married, she might've found herself trying to get him to smile at her more often. Her friend had certainly married a handsome man.

"Are you free?"

"If being utterly annihilated by your seven-year-old makes me free, then I certainly am."

He tsked at his daughter. "I told you not to be ruthless. You'll scare away our guest."

Alex reset the board. "She hasn't left yet."

He came over and mussed his daughter's blond hair. "You'll have to save your next trouncing for later. She has a job interview." His smile was much brighter than such news demanded.

"You mean right now? On a Sunday?" Mercy felt her hair to make sure her simple twist hadn't fallen.

"Yes. And after listening to this man's offer, I think this is the job we've been praying for." He reached for his wife's hand and squeezed it. "Someone I trust implicitly recommended him. If you want the job, I think you should take it."

Mercy blew out a breath and smoothed her skirt, her heart skittering uncontrollably despite the good news. But if David was certain this interview would end with her employment and it didn't, what hope was there she could ever get a good job?

And if she wasn't chosen, would their hospitality wear thin?

She shook her head at the thought. They wouldn't kick her out, but it would certainly make her feel better if she wasn't a complete charity case.

Evelyn smiled at her from her chair. "Good luck."

David kissed the top of his wife's head before leading Mercy to his office. He opened the door, winked, put a hand to her back, and pushed her in.

The door clicked shut behind her.

He wasn't even going to introduce them? She took a deep breath and scanned the room to find a man in the shadows staring out the window. His dark hair needed a trim and curled over his suit coat's collar, his shoulders were . . .

She frowned as she scanned the large man again. Aaron?

He turned around and confirmed her suspicion. The expression on his face was an odd mixture of worry and delight.

"Aren't you supposed to be . . . ?"

"In jail?"

She swallowed hard. He wouldn't hurt her. Somehow she believed that, no matter what he'd done. But if he'd evaded capture . . .

"No. I'm not supposed to be in jail. Though, for all the rotten things I've done, it would be a fitting place for me." He sucked in a loud breath. "Having me behind bars would no doubt make some happy."

It wouldn't make her happy. "Did Nicholas drop the charges?"

"Yes, because those things weren't in my cabin because I'd stolen them—I was keeping Jimmy and Zachary from doing so."

Jimmy? That wasn't hard to believe at all. The tension in her muscles fled, and she sat before her legs failed her. She no longer had to scold her heart for thinking about Aaron every day. "But why didn't you tell us where you were?"

"Seems Cook wasn't on the up-and-up. I sent a note, but she intercepted it and left. And then I found myself behind bars. Unfortunately, my jailer—Dennis Foster—decided to bully me as I'd done to him so long ago." He came to sit in a chair beside her. "As for Jimmy, on the night of the auction, he told me he was forced to steal and was afraid of what would happen if he didn't deliver the things he was supposed to. I told him I'd keep him safe, but he disappeared on me."

"And then you disappeared." She watched him rub his palms against his slacks repeatedly. Why was he uneasy? Her heart picked up. "Please tell me Jimmy's all right."

"He's safe. He was caught burglarizing another home in hopes of replacing the things in my cabin. He had a week to think through his future in jail, but the fear of his mother didn't go away as long as she was free. But we found her."

She frowned. "You mean he wasn't an orphan?"

Aaron shook his head. "His mother had him tell Nicholas she

was dead so he could steal from the Lowes. Whenever you tried to adopt him out, he behaved badly so he could remain at the mansion."

"So now that his mother has been caught, is he . . . better behaved?" Somehow she couldn't imagine a well-behaved Jimmy.

Aaron snickered. "He tells staff where he's going now and attempts to do his chores without a fuss, but he's still . . . hard." He sighed and looked at his hands between his knees. "I'm afraid I know all too well how difficult it is to feel safe enough to be vulnerable."

She picked at her skirt. As much as she was glad to hear Jimmy was safe, she almost wished Lydia had told her in a letter rather than having Aaron come and talk to her so . . . businesslike. She swallowed against the tightness in her chest and stared at her lap. Perhaps she still did have to tell her heart to stop thinking about him so often. "So what happens when his mother gets out of jail?"

"In hopes of getting a lighter sentence, she gave up her rights to Jimmy. I intend to adopt him."

"That's going to be . . . difficult." Would Nicholas let Aaron have both Jimmy and Owen? It would be a lot for one man.

"Correct, but difficult things need to be done by somebody, yes?" A ghost of a grin showed up on his face. "I could wait until I felt more prepared or to see if someone else might take him, but how many months or years would go by without Jimmy feeling secure or wanted?"

She could only sit and stare at the man she'd once thought the world would be better off without. What would've happened had someone chosen to love him as a child despite his behavior or showered him with the prayers she'd thought he didn't deserve?

She couldn't imagine he'd have turned out better, but he'd probably have less guilt and shame to deal with, and fewer people would've been hurt.

"I'm sure it wasn't easy for you to confront Mrs. Sorenson about her attitude toward Sadie, but it was right, so you did it anyway." He turned to look at her, his dark brown eyes filled with the same pleading look she'd caved to the day of his interview. "Nor could it have been easy to champion me for that teaching position after the board called your sanity into question after figuring out I'd once bullied you."

He'd heard about that? She stared at David's mahogany desk. "I knew what sort of man you'd become. You deserved the position."

"So I've convinced you I'm not who I used to be?" His smile trembled a bit.

"You've proven yourself to be one of the best men I've ever met, and I should've . . . waited for you to come back, to hear your explanation, but . . ." Her throat closed off with tears.

"But what?"

She rubbed her eye. "I couldn't bear the thought of seeing you again if you weren't the man you'd convinced me you were."

"Then you left because you were upset with me?"

She shrugged. It was more because she'd been gutted, believing her dreams of a future with him had been nothing more than fancy, as Mr. Carter had said. She fiddled with the pleats of her skirt. "Partially, but I also need a job and figured this would be a better place than Teaville to look."

"Yes, in light of that . . ." He moved to sit on the edge of his seat, his knees now only inches from hers. "I'll be teaching math here in Kansas City come fall."

"That's wonderful." Though what did his job have to do with hers? Wait, hadn't David said this was a job interview?

"I plan to adopt both Owen and Jimmy before moving, and, well, a new job and two children is a lot to juggle. I'm willing to sacrifice an easier life to help them, but I'm not dense. I know I'm going to need help. That's why I came to see you."

So this was the job? "Since you'll be teaching, they'll have the same hours as you. They're not young. You won't need a nursemaid."

"Well, no." He fidgeted in his chair enough she could feel the floor wiggle beneath them. "But you see, I never had a good example of parenting, but I figure yours must've been great. You were such a good kid. When I treated you poorly, you never retaliated."

334

Oh, why must he compliment her after the weeks she'd treated him unfairly? "What would you have me do?"

"Love the boys."

She shrugged. "I already do. You don't have to pay me for that. If I find a job here, I'm willing to visit them weekly, if you'd like."

"I'd rather have you around more often." He took her hand. "Although I don't doubt you'll continue to love them, what I'm hoping for is that you'll love me."

Her heart stuttered. There was no need for him to hope for that—she already did.

He played with her fingers, rubbing them between his calloused ones. "I'll be returning to Teaville to garden until the end of the summer, as I promised Lowe. So what I came to ask was, would you be willing to return to the mansion and get to know all three of us better, in hopes you'll move here with us in the fall as my wife and their mother?"

How was she supposed to answer such a question when her throat was filling with tears?

His eyes seemed even darker as he frowned at her attempts to keep from sobbing. "The Lowes said they'd be happy to have you back to help the Cleghorns adjust to their new role as directors."

She cleared her throat, hoping she could answer his question without garbling it completely, but she couldn't force out a word.

He looked down. "You don't have to promise me anything." He put a fist against his chest. "I realize I'm probably the last man you wanted to end up with. And though I have the noblest intentions with the boys, I'm afraid I might not be the greatest parent. If we were to have children, you'd have to be sure I'm the father you'd want for them." His breath came out stuttered. "And though I don't want to live up to my name—the name given to all the eldest males in the Firebrook family, including my uncle George—I'm hoping you'd be willing to live up to yours, because I will need mercy, and lots of it, because things from my past still haunt me. I definitely don't deserve the mercy you've already bestowed upon me, so if you choose to tell me no, I'll understand."

She cupped his bristly cheek with her hand and smiled through her tears. "It's me who doesn't deserve you."

He captured her cold hand with his warm one and closed his eyes.

"However, I'll only go back to Teaville with you if you promise one thing."

His eyes flew open. "What's that?"

"You must promise if someone interrupts our next kiss, it won't take so long to get around to kissing me again."

"I'll agree to that." His eyes roamed over her face, nice and slow. If ever a time came that she doubted he thought her beautiful, all she'd have to do was remember the warmth in his eyes at this moment.

He pulled her to stand, and the height and breadth of him that had once made her tremble in fear beckoned to her. He pulled her close, making her feel more secure than she had in a long time.

The gentle weight of his lips against hers made her feel just as cherished as the evening he'd stolen a kiss in the woods. And the taste of his tears proved the hard heart he'd once possessed had been softened by the omnipotent God who could lovingly use the worst days of a person's past to make their future exquisite, for He could make *all things work together for good to them that love God.*

Epilogue

"Oh no." Mercy groaned. Her two-month-old son had finally stopped squirming and fussing, and warmth now soaked into the shoulder of her dress.

"What happened?" Aaron looked back at her from the driver's seat as he slowed their Ford in front of Teaville's newest church, located on the edge of what remained of the town's red-light district.

She braced her arm against Aaron's seat back to keep from flying forward with the baby as their vehicle stopped. "Samuel spit up on me." She pulled her snuggly warm bundle off her shoulder. He'd evidently fallen asleep the minute he decorated her dress.

From where he was sitting up front, Owen handed her a rag from the bag on the floorboards, and Aaron came around to open her door and take Samuel.

She wiped at the spot, but the silk of her nicest dress was soaked. "And I'd wanted to look my best today."

Aaron smiled. "We could find some water to spill on your other shoulder to make it match."

She rolled her eyes.

"Just wear the rag, Ma." Owen leaned over to drape the cloth over her shoulder.

337

"Not exactly the accessory I was hoping to wear."

"I think this tiny person makes a rather fine ornament." Aaron placed Samuel back on her shoulder. His little eyelids didn't even flutter. "And no one's going to notice that wet spot since his toes are exposed for all the women to gush over." He helped her out of the automobile.

"Maybe I should've left him with Patricia." Her sister-in-law had yet to conceive a child and had truly seemed willing to watch Samuel, though there was still a hint of animosity in how Timothy and Patricia treated her whenever they visited. Thankfully Timothy had decided three Christmases ago to stop shunning her family, but theirs still wasn't the best relationship. "But I wanted Jimmy to see that his whole family is here for him."

"Everyone's here for Jimmy, and he won't care about your dress." Aaron put his arm around her waist and brought her close as they rounded the automobile. "You look beautiful."

"I just wish we hadn't gotten here so late." Which they were all the time now. Life with a newborn was quite . . . demanding. She looked around at the newly sodded churchyard and couldn't help but notice how small the crowd was. None of them were strangers, and she and Aaron hadn't lived in Teaville for the past five years. "I was hoping there'd be people here who hadn't come solely to support him. He'll need a congregation if he's going to preach."

She forced herself not to shake her head at that last sentence. A preacher—the last thing she'd thought Jimmy would choose as a profession when they'd first adopted him, and it still seemed odd. He was barely nineteen and still rather . . . hardheaded.

Glancing up to the front stairs of the stone church, she caught a glimpse of his slicked-back blond hair. The main building was a beautiful light-stone chapel with a belled steeple and intricate ironwork. In the back was a dormitory of sorts to act as a shelter for abused and abandoned women and children.

Jimmy was talking to Henri near the lectern, where they would address the people who'd come for the dedication ceremony for Kingsman Chapel and Evelyn House. Her boy was stiff and tense, nodding his head seriously while Henri talked to him as if giving instructions.

She cuddled Samuel a little tighter. She'd have a whole eighteen years or so with him. Hopefully that much time would make her feel more confident that she'd done all she could to prepare him for life. Letting go of Jimmy already made it difficult not to worry.

That first year of being wed had been hard enough for her and Aaron to adjust to each other, but they'd also had a rebellious fourteen-year-old to contend with. She'd been afraid they'd sabotaged their marriage by taking on two orphans so early in their relationship, but things had smoothed out around year two, and then when Jimmy dedicated himself to the Lord, year three had felt like a holiday—though he never lost his propensity to be strong-willed.

"How are you, Miss Mercy?" Sadie came over and hugged Mercy from the side. "And isn't he precious?" she cooed as she ran a finger down Samuel's wrinkled little nose, then tickled the bottom of his feet. "And look at these toes."

Mercy caught Aaron giving her the "I told you so" look as he walked away, likely headed straight for Harrison to talk teacher talk.

She turned back to Sadie. How grown-up she looked. "I didn't expect to see you here. Who's watching the orphans at the mansion?"

"No one—we brought them along." She pointed to the lone tree on the property, where Franklin was dislodging a little boy's foot from where his shoe had wedged into a forked branch. "We've decided to attend this church with the children. Some of them have been worrying about their old friends and feeling guilty about escaping this place when others can't." A little boy of about five came to stand by Sadie and looked up at Samuel with a curious eye.

Sadie put her hand on the boy's head and tucked him up against her skirt. "So we've volunteered to teach Sunday school. It might only be for our own children and the orphans to begin with, but hopefully some street kids will come."

Mercy glanced over to the tree where Evelyn had joined Franklin to rescue another little boy too afraid to climb down. "I bet Evelyn was thrilled to hear you'd be ministering to the street children."

"Yes." Sadie smiled at the woman the mission was being named after. "I think after hearing our plans, we've made her wish she could move back and take over."

"But she's needed in Kansas City." How many reformed prostitutes had the Kingsmans found new jobs for in the past five years? It wasn't as many as they'd hoped for, but for all those women, it was a new chance at life.

"I agree. She's definitely needed in Kansas City." David came up beside them, stopping to watch his wife with his arms crossed over his chest and a twinkle in his eye. "Don't you dare entice her away from me."

Mercy laughed. "Of course I wouldn't, because then she'd be moving away from me too." She and Evelyn had become close since she'd moved to Kansas City, and she doubted a more loyal wife and friend could be found.

"Attention, please." Henri thumped a gavel-looking thing on the lectern, and the handful of people gathered about the stairs.

Mercy smiled at Caroline, who was standing behind her mayor-husband with a baby about Samuel's age cradled in her arms. Five-year-old Katelyn crouched at Caroline's feet, quietly spinning a top.

"I want to thank all of you for coming today. I know we aren't much of a crowd, but on behalf of the city, I wanted to acknowledge the time, money, and dedication many of you have sacrificed for our neediest residents so they can have a safe place to go when they have nowhere else to turn."

He smiled back at his wife. "Many thanks goes to my wife and Evelyn Kingsman, since so much of their lives has been spent tirelessly pleading for the district women to be helped instead of shunned. I hope this place will be the sanctuary you two have worked so hard to provide." He gestured toward a dark-headed young man in the crowd. "To Max Milligan, who offered his architectural prowess to design such a lovely place, thank you. No church in this town can rival the beauty of this tiny chapel. Am I right?" He swung his arm back to encourage them to admire Max's work.

The crowd clapped, and Max shrugged as if it had been nothing.

But it was more than nothing. Despite his young age, his reputation for precision and efficiency had spread quickly, and the young man was never in want of a project. Not only was this stone chapel a beauty, but he and Robert had pieced together the sixteen stained-glass windows themselves.

Once the applause died, Henri gripped the lectern again. "As I pledged when I was first elected mayor, and will pledge again with reelection upon us, I will do whatever I can to keep the needy from floundering when we enforce laws that shut down disreputable employers. I'm proud to sponsor this chapel, for even if I'm successful at stamping out all corruption, there will always be a need for a place of charity and hope. And so"—he turned to gesture for Jimmy to come forward—"let us hear from the pastor of Kingsman Chapel."

The crowd applauded, but Mercy could barely do anything but keep hold of Samuel as Jimmy strode toward the lectern. He looked confident, with his shoulders back and chin up, but the hand in his right pocket was moving. He was undoubtedly rubbing the indentation he'd made into the little sandstone cross Owen had given him two years ago, on the day he'd been baptized.

Jimmy stopped at the lectern and looked straight at her.

He'd sought her out before his father?

Within a second, Aaron's arm slipped around her waist, and he pulled her close.

Jimmy shifted his gaze to his father, clearly finding it difficult to swallow. "Thank you . . ."

Aaron gave him a little nod and hugged her tighter.

Jimmy nodded back and then looked at her, his mouth twitching with emotion he so rarely displayed. "Thank you." And then he looked out over the rest of the crowd, summoning up a tight smile. "You don't know how grateful I am to be given the opportunity to pastor my first church a stone's throw from where I grew up in poverty and neglect, and to be able to work with the Lowes, who provided me my first safe place to live."

He nodded toward Nicholas and Lydia, who were sitting on a bench with their four children, plus the three siblings they were about to adopt. Now that their business was booming again, it seemed Lydia was intent on filling her town house with little ones.

He shifted his attention back to her and Aaron. "And to my parents, who loved me even when I was unlovable."

Mercy couldn't help the tears that fell at the soft sound of that word on his lips.

Unlovable. How had she ever called him that? Seeing him so grown-up and taking on such a big responsibility made her heart fill with as much pride as the day the midwife laid Samuel in her arms.

"I'm thankful to work with Queenie, who's already given me plenty of advice on how to help the people in this area and who will be running the women's portion of this ministry. And to the Cleghorns, who've volunteered to help with the children." He looked to his paper on the lectern. "With hope and faith, let us dedicate this building to be utilized as a House of the Lord, wherein will be preached the Gospel of Christ, and in which God the Father, the Son, and the Holy Spirit will be worshiped and glorified."

The crowd answered with a loud "Amen."

Jimmy gestured for Evelyn to come forward to pray, but Mercy couldn't focus on her friend's words.

Oh, Lord, please bless and use Jimmy as you've done with Aaron. May there be men and women who'll come to Jimmy years from now to let him know that his ministry influenced their lives for the better, just as Aaron's students are already coming back to tell him how his faith in them to do the good, hard things in life saved them from making poor decisions.

Aaron squeezed her shoulder, and she looked up to find everyone had moved toward the church entrance.

Owen looked at her with pleading eyes. "Can I go get cookies before they're gone?"

"Only if you promise to leave enough for others."

He nodded and caught up with the crowd. Mercy shook her head. "They'll think we don't feed him."

Aaron chuckled. "I saw the amount of baked goods these women prepared. He can't eat everything."

"Don't challenge him." Her smile died a little as she watched the crowd head in. "If only we could be sure Jimmy will have people to minister to. There isn't a single person here from the district, and Jimmy spent days inviting people. He has to be disappointed."

"You must not have noticed where Caroline went during Jimmy's speech." He tipped his head to the left while he started walking them slowly toward the church.

In the shadows of the abandoned building next door, a woman with gaunt cheeks and hollow eyes stood in a defeated slump as she nodded halfheartedly at whatever Caroline was saying to her.

The streetwalker looked over at them, and Mercy quit staring. "Hopefully she comes in," she whispered, though there was no chance she could hear them.

He rubbed her arm. "She likely won't, considering the state of her attire compared to how this group came dressed to the nines. But hopefully next week."

Mercy stared up at the intricate steeple Max had designed. "And to think, a few years ago, we worried that once Jimmy left home, we'd be visiting him in prison."

"Not sure many churches would be willing to give such a blunt, inexperienced young man a chance at pastoring. We'll need to pray he keeps his job at the railroad so he can afford to work here."

The crowd had disappeared indoors, but Aaron barely moved them forward. She looked up at him with a raised eyebrow. "Why are we walking so slowly?"

He tightened his arm around her. "Because I'm not looking forward to the hours we have to drive home with you in the back with Samuel. Keeps me from being able to put my arm around you."

She kissed his shoulder since her one arm had Samuel and the other was pinned under his grip. "You're silly. It's only another day of traveling."

"I wish we would've taken the train—then you could've sat on my lap the whole way here and back."

Her cheeks heated. "That'd be quite scandalous, don't you think?"

He laughed. "Sounds rather nice to me."

"We'd be kicked off the train."

"They wouldn't dare, not with a baby in tow." He stopped at the bottom of the stairs.

Mercy looked up at the open doorway and listened to the good-natured laughter and conversation going on inside. "It's going to be hard to go in there and not start trying to advise Jimmy on what to do, how to behave, and all I wish I could be sure he knows before we have to leave."

"As I always say, God calls us to do hard things." He wrapped his arms around both her and Samuel and pressed his lips against her forehead. "You've got to trust you did your best." His lips traveled to her temple and then down behind her ear.

A delicious shiver made her scrunch up her shoulders. "What are you doing?"

"Loving you—the one thing God called me to do that's easy." He leaned back and smiled at her, his dark brown eyes roaming her face in a way that left no doubt that he did indeed love her more than any other. "Forever isn't long enough to love you, but I'm glad I have the chance to try."

A chance to love him forever didn't seem long enough for her either, but she was perfectly happy she had it.

Acknowledgments

To turn a story into the best book it can be, it takes more than the author to make it so.

This book first went through my critique partner, Naomi Rawlings, who has the guts to tell me when she, as a reader, would lay my book down and choose another. She bears the brunt of my messy drafts.

I am forever grateful for the team at Bethany House and my agent, who read through the book looking for ways to polish the story, along with Bethany House's sales and marketing teams that work hard to get this story into readers' hands. I'm not sure the art department could have made an author happier with her covers than they have made me with this series.

I would also like to thank my team of beta readers this time around: Karen Riekeman, Andrea Strong, and Amy Parker. Even when they feel they aren't helping because "they just plain enjoyed it," they help me know the book has gotten to the point it should be.

My family, as always, pays the most for these books. I thank them for supporting my writing though I often stare off into space at dinner and they have to ask me what book I'm worrying about when I don't pass the salt.

There are days I wonder what I've gotten myself into, often

facedown on the floor beseeching God to get me out of the writing mess I've created. Thank You for listening to this mess of a woman.

To my readers, I'm thankful for your loyalty, the notes you send me, and the reviews that let me know my stories have had a higher purpose than entertainment. It pushes me to keep going when I'm that mess on the floor.

Much to her introverted self's delight, ACFW Carol Award winner and double INSPY finalist **Melissa Jagears** hardly needs to leave home to be a homeschooling mother and novelist. She lives in Kansas with her husband and three children and can be found online at Facebook, Pinterest, Goodreads, and www.melissa jagears.com. Feel free to drop her a note at mjagears@gmail.com, or you can find her current mailing address and a list of her books on her website.